THOSE IN I

NIGEL KNOWLES

This book is dedicated to my wife Jennifer,
our daughter Natasha and son Keiran.

STAR 18 WELCH GATE
AND BEWDLEY
GARTER WORCS. DY12 2AT
PUBLISHERS Tel: 0299 402343

Printed by Stargold Ltd. Kidderminster

British Library
Cataloguing-in-Publication
Data. A Catalogue record
for this book is available
from the British Library.

1st August 1992.

ISBN 0 9519130 0 X

STAR AND GARTER BOOKS
Those in Favour © 1992

Nigel Knowles was born in Worcester in 1946. His first School was knocked down to make way for the Kidderminster Ring Road, his Grammar School was closed and the carpet factory where he worked went into liquidation. Plan "B" therefore entailed his attending Birmingham Polytechnic and Worcester College of Higher Education to escape from the mayhem.

Nigel was the Trade Union Education Officer for the General Federation of Trade Unions in London between 1978 and 1988 and a Labour Councillor in Haringey. He has been a Parlimentary Candidate at four General Elections since 1979 in Bodmin, Hastings, Wyre Forest and Worcestershire South. He is currently a District and County Councillor in Hereford and Worcester but fully expects the County to go the same way as his schools and carpet factory, very soon.

In 1990, Nigel was one of the Heinemann New Writers, with his comedy, "*The Tailers Dummy.*" He is currently working to produce his new comedy play, "*A Touch of Wilde Chekhov and Shaw*" with Provincial and London theatres.

STAR GARTER

BOOKS

1992

THOSE IN FAVOUR
by
NIGEL KNOWLES

Chapter One
The Election 1

Chapter Two
The Annual Council Meeting 12

Chapter Three
Characters of Crewdley 27

Chapter Four
The Garden Party 36

Chapter Five
An Outbreak of Paganism at Halloween 48

Chapter Six
The Trap.. 63

Chapter Seven
Octavia Bland is Unwell 77

Chapter Eight
A Most Peculiar Funeral.. 86

Chapter Nine
Twinning with Croutonne Lautrec 97

Chapter Ten
Puccini Shoots The Mayor 116

Chapter Eleven
The Great Wool Shop Scandal 130

Chapter Twelve
The Scales of Justice 136

Characters of Crewdley

Harold Presbyterian . . . . Mayor of Crewdley, representing
Crewdley Town Ward. (Elected in 1990)

Anton Robespierre . . . . The Mayors Chauffer, Valet
and Town Crier.

Bernard Beard . . . . Town Clerk, seventh generation

The Crewdley Town Councillors

Larry Blondel. . . . . Independent Crewdley Town
Ward (Elected 1990)

Mrs. Octavia Bland . . . . Independent Octogenarian,
representing Meadow Ward
(Elected 1987)

Mrs. Olivia Bland. . . . . Independent (as above) (Elected
1991 at a By-Election and
re-elected 1991)

Mrs. Enid Thomas . . . . Socialist, Riverside East Ward
(seeks re-election in 1992)

Mrs. Louise Evans-Jenkins. . . . . Independent Meadow Ward
(Elected in 1990)

Norman Bull . . . . Tory Crewdley Town Ward
(Elected in 1990)

Morton Muggeridge . . . . Conservative, Meadow Ward
(Elected 1991)

Arthur Hardie . . . . Socialist, Riverside East Ward
(seeks re-election in 1992)

Alan Arkwright . . . . Independent, Forest West and
Foreign Ward. (Elected 1989:
for re-election 1993 plus
County Election)

Mrs. Sylvia Smart. . . . . Conservative Riverside Ward
(seeks re-election 1992)

Citizens

Dorothy and Myrtle Flack......................	Spinster sisters and owners of The Wool Shop
Edwin Grimley	Funeral Service Proprietor
Horace Bramley	Crewdley Police Superintender
Natasha Hardie..............................	Young Socialist Academic
Rupert Beard................................	Rich, eccentric brother of the Town Clerk, lives in a tent.
Lord and Lady Crewdley	Of Crewdley Manor
John Doolittle & Henry Dash	Solicitors to The Council (Seventh generation)
Archibald McSnadden	Editor of "The Weekly Weave
Dr Jonathen Scargreaves	Medic and sage
Reverend & Mrs. Wilfred Wooly	Vicar of Crewdley and his loyal wife
Mrs. Pippa Monroe	Headmistress of Crewdley Comprehensive School, The Mayor's Mistress
Ronnie Bettinger.............................	Bookmaker owner of Crewdley Betting Shop
Seamus MacGurk	Landlord of "The Star and Garter"
Michael 'Smokey' Flint	Crewdley Fire Chief
Eric and Elsie Finney	Fish & Chip Shop Proprietor
Robert Potter................................	The Crewdley Tailor
Roland Jones	Bank Manager
Kevin Farquar...............................	Kissagram Toy Boy
Ms Annette Page.............................	Librarian
Susie Goodthigh	Temporary Secretary
Fiona Lumley	A Cheer Girls Hooray! Hostes
Marian Carter...............................	A red headed crochet-knitter
Sharon Hayes	Waitress at " Star and Garter"
Caroline Cresswell	Student of Crewdley Academy of Music (Harpist)

Visitors

Fredric Puccini	The English Documentary Film Company Director
Councillor Marcel Leotard	Mayor of Croutonne Lautrec
Florette Angou	Councillor of Croutonne Lautr
Marianne Limoge	Councillor of Croutonne Lautr
Angelique Pascal.............................	Councillor of Croutonne Lautr
Claude Molaire	Councillor of Croutonne Lautr
Henri Pugette	Councillor of Croutonne Lautr

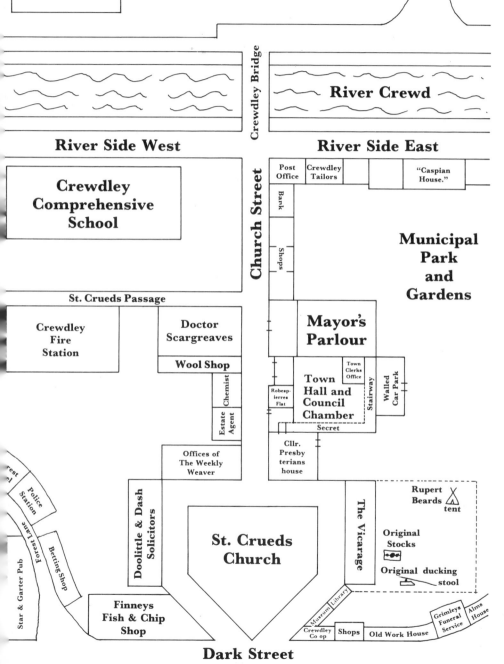

CREWDLEY

Crewdley Manor

River Crewd

Crewdley Bridge

River Side West

River Side East

Church Street

Post Office

Crewdley Tailors

"Caspian House."

Bank

Crewdley Comprehensive School

Shops

Municipal Park and Gardens

St. Crueds Passage

Crewdley Fire Station

Doctor Scargreaves

Wool Shop

Mayor's Parlour

Chemist

Estate Agent

Robespierres Flat

Town Clerks Office

Stairway

Walled Car Park

Town Hall and Council Chamber

Secret

Cllr. Presbyterians house

Offices of The Weekly Weaver

Rupert Beards tent

Original Stocks

Police Station

Forest Lane

Betting Shop

Doolittle & Dash Solicitors

St. Crueds Church

The Vicarage

Original ducking stool

Star & Garter Pub

Finneys Fish & Chip Shop

Museum

Library

Crewdley Co op

Shops

Old Work House

Grimleys Funeral Service

Alms House

Dark Street

CHAPTER ONE

The Election

The Mayor of Crewdley Town Council sat in his Parlour looking down at the people in the street below.

"Scruffy bloody lot," he thought to himself, "thank God none of them ever find their way up here."

Things had been going Mayor Presbyterian's way of late, and apart from the eternal irritant of Councillor Blondel, he fully expected a sweeping victory at the Municipal Elections which were being held that very day. He didn't give a damn about any other candidate he was "Independent", a term which in Mayor Presbyterian's case, was always taken literally. He was "Independent" of the three main political parties represented on Crewdley Town Council,"Independent" of policies forwarded by anyone other than himself and totally "Independent" from all moral and political responsibility to his electorate.

In the small world of the Crewdley Municipality, Mayor Presbyterian was "King". The only dark cloud on the distant horizon, apart from Councillor Blondel and he was neither dark nor distant, was the gnawing possibility that one day and he would never know when that day might come, if it were to come at all,Councillor Presbyterian, The Mayor of Crewdley Town Council, might actually lose an Election.

But not today. He'd done too much during his Municipal Year to let it slip now. Many palms had been crossed with silver, many babies had been kissed and The Mayor was certain that Victory would be his.

Each week without fail, at least one photograph of The Mayor had appeared in the local free newspaper,"The Weekly Weaver," showing him in various poses of civic grandeur, the high-light of which had been, without doubt, the photo of Mr Mayor and his entourage patting a rhinoceros at the local Safari Park.

In The Mayor's case, it had not been merely patting the pre-historic beast, but actually sitting astride the hapless creature dressed in full Civic Regalia. (The Mayor that is not the rhinoceros.)

At one stage of the ceremony, The Mayor had even put his noble Chain of Office around the horn of the timorous beast.

The beast, it should be said, was timorous for one reason only and that was because it had been drugged especially for the occasion by the Manager of the Safari Park who dared not turn down the "photo-opportunity" of the season.

True enough, takings at the turn-stile or more properly, the drive-thru family-car entrance did actually increase two -fold shortly after wards, when every son and daughter under twelve years of age demanded that they be given the chance to mount the now not so timorous beast in the same manner as The Mayor of Crewdley.

But The Mayor had been determined to increase his vote. A thousand vote majority may have seemed large to those not in the know, but The Mayor recognized a threat when he saw one.

It had been four years ago at his last election when The Mould had been broken. Until then, Mayor Presbyterian had always had a free-run, an "uncontested election" as political parlance has it. The dark cloud particularly took the form of a young and radical off-spring of Councillor Hardie, a Socialist who had been around as long as Presbyterian had himself.

The Mayor drew little consolation from the fact that young Natasha Hardie polled a mere 100 votes to his 1,100. He hoped to God that she was accepted to the furthest-flung university in the Kingdom and never heard of again. Unfortunately, he knew this was unlikely. The Hardies were notoriously difficult to budge.

But it still didn't alter the fact that he hoped she would never darken the doors of a Crewdley Polling Station ever again, or at least until he had been given a place in the House of Lords.

The Mayor spent the rest of that Thursday, Polling Day, pottering around his Mayors' Parlour, occasionally looking out of the civic window and often cursing the occasional constituent under his breath whom he knew would either not vote for Crewdley's finest son or would vote against him.

Natasha Hardie had indeed completed her University Degree and gained a sparkling Double First in Politics, but instead of zipping off to London or Brussels, she had returned to the fold.

Therefore, The Mayor had to endure an electoral challenge for the second time in four years, an unwelcomed irritant it had to be admitted, but he knew that the young woman's three years away at Oxford had denied her the opportunity of crossing palms with silver or kissing the dozens of assorted babies that he had kissed.

And here was another element of darkness that might one day cause the cloud to blacken even further. He firmly believed Natasha Hardie had no other motive for being an election candidate than to serve the people of Crewdley as their Councillor.

"My God!", he ruminated over a half-bottle of Civic wine, "what does she think Civic Life is all about! If Civic Life was all about "serving the people," and "doing one's best for others," where would I be? Anyone can do one's best

2

for others, it's doing one's best for oneself that keeps the system going!"

Mayor Presbyterian had had too much to drink, but others would do his work for him by knocking doors of those electors who had promised to vote for him and then taking them down to the Polling Station. So he settled down for a snooze in the Mayoral Chair.

He was rudely awakened by the Civic Chauffer, come Town Crier, come Mayors Personal Secretary, Anton Robespierre.

A word of explanation concerning the ante-cedance of Anton Robespierre at this juncture would perhaps not be amiss.

During the Napoleonic Wars, the men of Crewdley were whisked to far-off fields to serve under the flag of King and Country. Some of course, didn't come back and others came back who had not been expected.

A trickle of French soldiers had joined the forces of the wrong Flag, the wrong King and the wrong Country.

The ancester of Anton Robespierre was one such trickler, or "Tricoloure" as some called him. He had made his way to Crewdley and married a local girl. The rest was history.

"Mr. Mayor!" he shouted, "it's time to go to the Count." The Mayor woke abruptly from his sleep and allowed himself to be adorned by Robespierre with the Robes of Office to which he had become well-accustomed - first the Robe itself, then the White Laced Collar, next the Mayoral Chain of Office and finally, the Civic cocked hat.

"You look really nice Mr. Mayor," said Robespierre. "Let's go, and just make sure you take it easy in the Rolls," The Mayor grumbled, "I've got a bit of a head." Now the fact that the counting of votes for the Election would take place in the Town Hall itself and the Mayor's Parlour was situated but two flights of stairs above it, did not in any way deter The Mayor from arriving at the Count in the Civic Rolls Royce.

They would leave by the back entrance as usual, get in the car and drive around the town for as long as it pleased The Mayor. He believed in The Grand Entrance; and because he always had the element of surprise on his side and because Anton Robespierre was also the Town Crier, The Mayor usually gave a faultless performance.

Attention was guaranteed by the grating tones of The Crier who, though not a powerful man, could never the less muster quite a raucous delivery. Even this physical attribute had not escaped the attention of the towns inhabitants and it was assumed the lungpower of Robespierre had direct linkeage with the original 'turncoat' on the battlefield of Waterloo when he was yelling, "Surrender, Surrender" or whatever was the French equivalent.

The car stopped at the front of the Town Hall, Robespierre held the door, and Councillor Harold Presbyterian got out to do his Civic Duty, which was surely to be returned to his rightful position as Councillor for the Crewdley Town Council.

"I give you Mr. Harold Presbyterian, The Mayor of Crewdley," he called.

"Not for much longer!" came a voice from within a small group of people near the entrance.

"Bloody socialists," The Mayor muttered as he entered the Town Hall which was a relative hive of activity. People were clustered excitedly around the tables where the votes were being counted by the Council Staff and others hired for the day as Polling Clerks and Tellers by a grateful Council, fully committed to letting Democracy bloom at least once every year, even if it did mean a few pence extra on the Poll Tax.

The Mayor found his way to the table where the Crewdley Town Ward votes were being counted and sat opposite the young people who immediately took on a less jovial attitude.

His opponents, and he did have opponents both on the Council itself and amongst the staff of Crewdley Council, were divided on the reason for The Mayor's four-yearly implantation on the seat directly opposite to the Ballot Papers.

Some considered his tactics to be intimidatory - the Great Man would take special note of every vote cast against him and particularly watch for any sign of joy on the face of the young Counting Agents.

Others, and these were nearer the mark, considered The Mayor had drunk too much and couldn't get off the chair for love nor money, an unfortunate exaggeration actually as The Mayor would always rise to individual pecuniary gain.

However, there he sat as the votes piled up in his favour.

"Nice going Mr. Mayor," Robespierre whispered over his shoulder.

"She's got more than last time damn her!" he complained, "why didn't she go to Brussels like any normal bureaucratic careerist?"

The votes were put into stacks of 50 and then 100. He had won easily, but The Daughter of Democracy had made a reasonable showing.

"Ladies and gentlemen. I have the result of the votes cast for the candidates in the Crewdley Town Ward," said the Electoral Officer in a tone which gave nothing away. A hush fell over the Town Hall, Robespierre held his breath, and The Mayor held the corner of his cocked hat.

"The result is as follows ... Hardie, Natasha, Lara, Louise, one hundred and fifty votes" a small cheer was heard from the back and a few loud comments along the lines of, "Up Yours Presbyterian ..."

"Presbyterian, Harold ... one thousand and forty-nine votes."

"You're on the way out!" roared a voice from over The Mayor's shoulder, but this was partially masked by polite clapping from all corners of the Town Hall.

The Electoral Officer had not yet finished, "Spoiled ballotpapers seventy-two. I hereby declare that the under-mentioned Harold Presbyterian has been duly elected to serve as the Councillor for the Crewdley Ward of Crewdley Town Council..."

"Rubbish!" called another voice from the darkest corner of the Town Hall,"She'll win next time! Make the most of it Harold."

With that, the wholly expected and newly-elected Councillor for Crewdley Town Ward swept out from the very bowels of the Democratic Arena and back intoThe Mayor's Parlour where the Emigre from Waterloo and the Machiavelli of Municipal Politics opened a bottle of the very best Civic Champagne, then another and another until at last, as The milk-man trod once again on the tail of the Town Hall cat, Robespierre and The Mayor fell asleep counting bundles and bundles of juicy-white, healthy-white, nice-cold, ice-cold Votes.

Harold Presbyterian nearly always found the month of May to be most condusive to the life-style to which he had become accustomed.

Once the wretched Annual Municipal Elections were out of the way (though he, as was previously noted, like all other Councillors, had only to seek election every fourth year) Presbyterian could sit back and enjoy the fruits of his labour.

His eager Lieutenant Robespierre would faithfully bring to his notice the cause of any little wave on the Serene Civic Mill Pond. They would be bought off if they were business and laid off if in-house. The last decade of the 20th Century had not fully caught up with Crewdley. It had been given a Charter by Henry the Eighth which provided much scope for manoeuvre by the current incumbent of Crewdleys highest office. Parliament had on several unsuccessful occasions attempted to cut it down to size, but at the final moment, namely the outbreak of World Wars One and Two, the relevant legislation had been withdrawn in favour of more pressing and vital national work. The closest call had been during the reorganization of Local Government in the early 1970's, but the fall of the Government of the day put paid to that. Apparently, so the story goes, the relevant Minister of the time had saved Crewdley until last, thereby committing the fatal error of assuming the General Election was going to be called in 1975 and not as happened, in 1974.

The Prime Ministers prerogative of going to the country in March 1974 was nowhere celebrated with more zeal than in The Mayor's Parlour.

He had thought seriously about writing to the defeated and out-going Prime Minister and thanking him for sparing Crewdley in one of it's darkest hours. In the event, The Mayor settled for a gold-plated Civic Pen with the inscribed words emblazened on its side, "P.M. Prerogative, Crewdley's Salvation." So the tiny borough of Crewdley had been bestowed with much flexibility and freedom, relative of course to the crushing power of central government. But if one had lived ones life in Crewdley and no where else, then one accepted the "Crewdley Way." As far as it was possible, legislation from Government over the decades, and the centuries had been put to one side. Life went on, untrummelled by inappropriate Acts of Parliament which curtailed mid-English individuality and personal freedom.

Thus Harold Presbyterian had inherited, almost then by fate, a situation that was ripe for exploitation. The majority of Town Councillors were extremely laid-back, only the Socialists tended to rise to the bait cast by Central Government and their preference for local action was regularly thwarted by overwhelming apathy. The problem was, this benevolent apathy expressed in both the Council Chamber and in the street, had been co-opted by Presbyterian for his own ends. Centuries of relative equalibrium, even trust between the community and it's elected representatives provided The Mayor with a beautiful cover! For a Town Hall employee or mere voter to have attempted to alert the populace at large that its leading inhabitant was corrupt, would have had the effect of them being whisked off to a secure place of calm and tranquility.

No one would have believed them ... except the Socialists of course and few enough people believed them as it was.

No...The Mayor of Crewdley was in a strong position. Four more years in office would solidify his personal dynasty and help his bank-balance no end.

SoThe Mayor slept on, with the images of those glorious, fat bundles of votes filling his head, deep within a champagne stupor, until the noises of the milk man and the cat awoke Anton Robespierre with a start.

"Monsieur le Mayor!" Robespierre stuttered, "it's time to get up." Now the definate, French address directed at The Mayor by his faithful servant was but a distant echo of his ancestory which rarely showed itself.

It didn't happen often and when it did, Robespierre invariably apologized. But not on this occasion. The Mayor was beyond even crude detection of a French accent and so Robespierre was able to collect himself and try again. "Mr Mayor! Good morning Mr Mayor."

The great man stirred.

"Mr Mayor. It's me...Robespierre."

A cold eye half-opened before a slow-tongue offered recognition.

"Well of course it's bloody you. Who else?" he drawled. The Mayor sat up in the chair and felt the pressure in his head from his alcoholic indulgence. It was a grey day in the streets of Crewdley. He got up and looked out of the window. "Coffee!" he croaked. "Yes sir!" replied Robespierre, already on his way into the annexe of The Mayor's Parlour. Now the whole issue of the Mayor's Parlour, is itself worthy of comment. Very few people ever found themselves invited into The Mayor's inner-sanctuary. His "special friends" or "clients" were occasionally invited but those who crossed him were dealt with in the Town Hall, well away from his sanctuary. Once or twice, the odd visitor, usually American and even on one occasion the local tramp, had stumbled into the Parlour by accident. They were immediately got rid of by Robespierre who responded to the emergency red light in his humble quarters close by, with the zeal of a man possessed. A no-go area it was, and everyone who mattered had long since given up any idea of being cordially invited for after-meeting drinks in the Mayoral Chamber. Presbyterian treated the room as his own property and he had invested much of the citizens cash into providing their civic leader with a Mayors' Parlour worthy of the name. His 'little facilities' included a satellite TV and video, a direct intercom link to the local bookmakers and a folding bed which could dissappear into the wooden panels of the wall at the press of a button. A trouser-press had been given by a grateful local tailor for his 'cherished custom' and of course, his drinks cabinet was comprehensive. A further item of furniture had been positioned in the corner of the room, many years ago, by workmen under the direct supervision of The Mayor. The old, grey metal safe contained Presbyterian's insurance policy; not to provide cover to The Mayor against accident whilst on civic duty, rather the kind of 'insurance' guaranteed to get him out of any conceivable corner.

Enough evidence, and hard cash, sat in that untouchable depository for Presbyterian to consider it part of his very being, a weighty extension of himself. It had been so long since any other Crewdley Councillor had sat in the Mayoral Parlour, that some had probably forgotten its existence. For instance, Mrs Octavia Bland, the octagenarian Independent member for Meadow Ward, who sometimes seemed not only to forget the Council Chamber, but the Town Hall itself. However, she still managed to appear at least twice a year, the requisite required to ensure a by-election writ was not declared in her absence. As to whether her performance actually merited her being preserved as a Town Councillor or not, was an entirely different matter and one that would undoubtedly be settled by the constituents, or more likely, the Grim Reaper.

It would be true to say, that in the world of Mrs Octavia Bland, the issue of The Mayor's Parlour figured somewhat lower on her scale of priorities than did her council expenses. It mattered not a jot, a fact well taken by Presbyterian whose ideal would have consisted of eight other Councillors taking exactly the same appalling interest in his Chamber and the affairs of Council as the good

Mrs Bland. And so it was, that The Mayor was firmly established in his Chamber, unhindered by officials, councillors or constituents, all but Robespierre were unwelcome, with few amorous or financial exceptions. His eager Lieutenant did not, however have full knowledge of that non-civic room. In the darkest hour of the darkest day, were it to come to that, if husbands were to threaten or Inland Revenue press it's case to the very door of the Chamber, Harold Presbyterian would not fall prey to his enemies.

A secret door in the wooden-panels led onto a staircase which would take him quickly from his nemesis into the bedroom of the building adjacent to the Town Hall ... his very own house.

The key to Presbyterian's success had always been attributed to forward planning and ruthless persistence.

When an old and badly delapidated Georgian house had been put onto the market in 1969 at the modest price of £4,000, he had been the first to realize it's future potential and first to have his offer signed and sealed before ordinary mortals had had time to read the advertisement in the Estate Agents window. This period was most satisfactory for Crewdley's would-be First Citizen. Soon after he had purchased the house, a by-election was called after the death of 92 year old Councillor Badland. Harold Presbyterian over-spent the legal limit on advertising and election leaflets by the ratio of about ten, but victory was his. The rest would follow quickly with bribery, blackmail, bullying, flattery and quick-wittedness being used to install him as Mayor of Crewdley in record time, the next year in fact, as it corresponded with one of the quite frequent rows between the other Councillors as to who should be given the job.

Presbyterian had been the 'compromise candidate', and although one or two of the more conscientious Councillors had equally as quickly realized their mistake, it was too late. Presbyterian was home and dry. He had used the secret escape route only twice, but on each occasion, he considered himself lucky to have got away from men intent on doing him physical injury because of an assumed (correctly so) liaison with their wives.

Presbyterian was a batchelor by choice, Robespierre not so by choice, but rather on the explicit instruction of his employer "If you get married Robespierre, I'll have your cap and badge quicker than you can say Waterloo." The point was well made and well taken. Robespierre had little time for women. His world revolved around The Mayor and The Town Hall. His loyalty lay with the man who fed and clothed him and protected him from the world. Anton Robespierre was a loyal fool, defensive for his master and accomodating to the point of embarrassment. Even if by some mishap, he had discovered the secret stairway, he would not have told another living soul.

But Presbyterian was determined to ensure no mishap occured, and with the knowledge of the stairway, the safe and it's contents always tucked away in his mind, he could be doublysure of survival in almost any political or social scenario.

"Your coffee Mr Mayor," said Robespierre looking anxiously at his provider to make certain he was fit to face another day.

The Mayor slurped from the cup and indeed began to take more notice of his surroundings.

"The bitch!", he called suddenly, causing Robespierre to jump. "Who is Sir?" he asked. "Bloody Natasha Hardie standing against me. The Bitch!". Robespierre fussed around like an old hen dusting, cleaning, rearranging the furniture of The Mayor's parlour as the Great Man himself glanced through the morning papers. His face lit up with a smile when he finally got round to opening his post. The ordinary letters were pushed to one side as he gloated over one pink envelope and basked in it's smell of delicious perfume. Robespierre cast an eye towards him and knew by instinct who the letter was from.

The Mayor took a silver knife and opened it. A pink letter card sent off an aroma even Robespierre could smell. "I'm a much loved man Robespierre." "Yes Sir!". "Mrs Pippa Monroe loves me!". "Yes Sir!" The Mayor continued to stare at the card as if in a kind of pleasant dream, as Robespierre stood to attention near to the door and waited for instruction. "We'll sign the acceptance of Office forms later with that idiot of a Town Clerk," The Mayor murmured. "Yes Sir!" And so, for the next few minutes, Robespierre stood to attention, watching his master from a discreet distance. What really went on inside that Anglo-French head, no one really knew, but this epitome of discretion stood like a rock as the man in the chair slowly woke up and cleared his head. The Mayor of Crewdley was a big man, a big balding man, who filled the chair of office where others would have been physically lacking in this respect. He had a short moustache and his hair, although receeding was visable enough to be identified as once black but now rather grey.

He was over six feet tall and apart from being slightly overweight and slightly out of condition, Harold Presbytrian looked good. He had what is know in some circles as a "presence".... something he'd worked on for years, a certain charm even, when it suited him, which wasn't often when dealing with clients or clerks. Women were his special weakness, certain women in particular. At the moment, his especial, certain particular weakness was Mrs Pippa Monroe, the buxom Headteacher of Crewdley Comprehensive School and wife of Michael Monroe, a senior partner in a small oil company who spent most of his life pursuing his business interests in Scotland, Texas and most other places on the map, both East and West of Crewdley. While the cat is away, the mice will play! The Mayor's games with Mrs Pippa Monroe had taken place over a quite long period of time. They were discreet, but of course, tongues occasionally wagged as they did in any small community, though fortunately, the gossip never reached Michael Monroe because, as was stated, he was hardly ever at home. And so, much to The Mayor's delight, she had sent him a card on that pleasant Friday morning in May. His head slowly began to clear and Robespierre recognised the signs of imminent action. The Great Man stood up and walked over to the door, opened it and inhaled as though taking the perfume from the pink card into the very depths of his being. Robespierre smiled, for he knew well what was to come. "Beee-aarrd!" The Mayor boomed, "two minutes, your office!" Robespierre loved the way the Great Man treated Bernard Beard the Town Clerk ie, like some sort of lower-life, lower even than Robespierre himself. No respect, none whatever. Robespierre loved it, and could only smirk with delight at the denegration of the man, "The Pox Doctors Clerk," as Presbyterian called him often. "I thought you'd like that Robespierre, but don't get too confident or else it's back to Waterloo." Robespierre bowed his head and followed the Great Man down the old, wooden staircase into the Town Clerk's Office. Bernard Beard was already waiting, pen in hand and forms at the ready.

"Good morning Mr Mayor,"cringed the Town Clerk. "Yes, isn't it Beard, and particularly so on this fine day, the first day of my next four years of office." He looked Beard coldly in the eye and stared. Each knew the meaning of those words, four more years of subservient compliance for the small Town Clerk, always knowing his place on the scale, wherever he went, whatever he did, Bernard Beard was haunted by the weight and power of his boss, The Mayor. He had to tolerate the situation for some years yet, at least four, even if Presbyterian were to lose his next election. But retirement for Town Clerks seemed a life-time away in Crewdley. God! How Beard wanted early retirement and how The Mayor loved letting him know he couldn't have it.

"Shall we begin?" the Town Clerk asked, "Would you please read this paper?" He gave it to The Mayor who cast a cursory eye over it. "Would you please now read the document to me?" asked Beard with a timidity relevant to his station. The Mayor gloated as he delivered his monotoned reply, Bible in hand. "I Harold Presbyterian of Civic House, Church Street, Crewdley, do hereby solemnly swear to serve as an elected Councillor for the Crewdley Ward in the District of Crewdley Town, for a period of four years. I do accept the terms and conditions of office as laid down by The Representation of the Peoples Act 1983 and the Bye-Laws of Crewdley Charter of 1546." A benign smile crossed Presbyterian's lips before he continued the oath, "I shall properly serve all constituents to the best of my ability, irrespective of political or personal disposition and always for the public good and dignity of civic office." Robespierre grinned from ear to ear. "O.K Beard. That's all for now. Inform the Press that my Charity for this year will be directed into the Old Town Trust." "Again, Mr Mayor. Oh I'm sorry, I merely meant," the Town

Clerk apologised.

The Mayor was not amused and gave him one of his threatening looks reserved for occasions such as when a subordinate temporarily forgot himself and spoke out of turn. The Mayor swept out of the Town Clerks Office with Robespierre two steps behind. The thought of another glorious year of Charity filled him with joy. "Charity begins at home," he muttered, as they walked through the old carriage-way arch to the car park and the Civic Rolls Royce. "Yes sir," echoed Robespierre, "at home." Presbyterian laughed as he got into the back of the car. He could almost smell the money that the citizens would donate for the Crewdley poor. If they were lucky, they might even get a pound or two of it, depending whether or not The Mayor was in a particularly philanthropic mood. The car drew out into Church Street, Presbyterian sank back in the leather seat and Robespierre took the long route to the house of Mrs Pippa Monroe. "Come in Presy darling," she purred from behind her front door. "I've taken the day off." And so it was, that Harold Presbyterian spent the post-election weekend safely in the arms of his loved one, a coming together of the political and educational, in a honeymoon of perfume and pleasure. The Mayor was in his heaven and all was well with the world.

CHAPTER TWO

The Annual Council Meeting

Monday morning dawned and Pippa Monroe prepared for school. "Aren't you ever going to get up darling?" she teased Harold Presbyterian as he peeped from beneath the sheets. "I love watching you dress", he answered, "I'm such a lucky man." He attempted to grab the arm of the glamorous Headmistress, but she proved too quick, and he fell out of the bed onto the Persian carpet picked up by Mr Monroe in an Eastern Bazaar during one of his many quests for oil. "If your constituents could only see you now," she laughed, "what a difference without all of that Mayoral Regalia." "Please," he chided her, "no foul language in the bedroom. Any reference to constituents depresses me no end, especially when you look so ravishing. Give me a kiss." "Don't be so silly. I'm late for school. And shouldn't you be going to the Town Hall, it's nearly eight-thirty? Robespierre will be waiting," she reminded him. "He can wait," he shouted. "Let yourself out Presy darling and don't leave it so long next time, I'd almost forgotten what you looked like." Pippa Monroe slammed the front door hard behind her and all that was left was the delicious smell of her perfume which wafted strongly into Presbyterian's nostrils. "What a woman," he ruminated as he peeped through the curtains and watched her walking towards the school. He got dressed and then did the usual thing that he always did when he left her house after dawn, stepping quickly outside, closing the front door and knocking it loudly for a minute or two, until it was obvious to any passer-by or prying neighbour that he was merely calling upon the Head Mistress, but to no avail, because the good lady was not at home. He walked down by the River Crewd and took in the sweet May air.

The swans were gathering on the riverbank, a few mallards flew over head and one or two people passed him by with the greetings of, "Good Morning Mr Mayor," and "All right mate?" respectively. Presbyterian was still enjoying the blissful panorama when a voice from behind cast the first shadow on the day.

"I say Harold, don't jump old man, we don't want a by-election now do we?" "What are you doing here this early Blondel?" asked The Mayor. "I could ask you the same thing old man. You wouldn't have happened to have noticed whether or not the Postman has been down here yet would you? Or are you too engrossed in thoughts about the condition of the Comprehensive School and all of it's inhabitants to have noticed?" He looked Presbyterian in the eye and grinned knowingly.

"We batchelors should stick together old man, eh? See you later no doubt? Cheers for now."

Barry Blondel paced briskly away towards the town, smiling broadly as The Mayor, just for once, fumbled for a riposte.

"Creep!" he finally barked, as the tall, blonde figure of the irritant Councillor bounced out of sight.

Fortunately, on this occasion at least, out of sight, meant out of mind, Blondel's exit did indeed return The Mayors thoughts to the day ahead and he quickly regained his inner calm. He strolled quietly along, happy in the knowledge that another four years of civic opportunity lay before him.

Robespierre was waiting at the entrance to the Town Hall as the Great Man approached.

"Good morning Mr Mayor," he enthused, without daring to ask about his weekend, but nevertheless having a pretty good idea as to how it had actually been. "Morning Robespierre. Any messages?" The Mayor asked as he walked under the archway.

"Nothing yet Sir," replied the faithfull servant, "I'll make you a coffee." All was as it should have been in the Mayor's Parlour. Presbyterian sat at his desk and began to read some of The Municipal papers which had been given to Robespierre by Bernard Beard the Town Clerk, in the time honoured way.

"Coffee Sir." Robespierre placed the cup on the table and took two steps backwards. The Mayor took a decent drink and looked at him. "You're wondering if I had a good weekend, well I certainly did, I told you before Robespierre, I'm a much loved man. "Robespierre smiled until the second the telephone rang out, when he immediately resumed his official straight-faced impassive, frown, much in keeping with that of a Town Crier, come Chauffer come 'Aid De Camp'. "Hello," Presbyterian said into the instrument, "Oh it's you Beard. What do you want?" Robespierre adopted his briefly off-duty smile. "Of course everything is allright. Why shouldn't it be?" He put the reciever down with a heavy thud and turned again to Robespierre.

"Are you sure everything is allright Robespierre? I don't like that little twit ringing me up first thing Monday morning asking if everything is allright." "But everything IS allright Mr Mayor. I havn't heard a dicky-bird." "It had better be or one or two people will be seen to suffer."

Presbyterian had a gut-feeling that something was up, an animal instinct that said "beware" when everything in the garden looked rosy. However, he had absolutely nothing to go on, so for the time being he would take extra care and treat everyone, as he always did anyway, as individual threats to his existence. "And what about you Robespierre? What have you been up to since Friday?" he asked, not really expecting the first threat to come from his 'Batman'. He wasn't disappointed. "I went fishing Mr Mayor. I caught nothing, but I had a few drinks. It was a nice weekend, the river is very calm."

Presbyterian sat impassively for the next few minutes, listening to Robespierre reminisce about the one's that got way, until at last, he called a halt. "Listen," The Mayor growled, "you know what day it is, don't you?" "Yes Sir, it's Monday." "And!" barked Presbyterian. "It's the Annual Meeting of the Council."

"Right! The Annual Meeting of the Council. Now do you suppose Robespierre, that by this time tomorrow morning, I shall still be Mayor?" The colour drained away from Robespierre's face and he became as ashen as a pall-bearer. "My God Sir, of course." Robespierre was truly shocked by this hopefully-rhetoric question, his own future was inextricably linked with the fate of his Master, too many Councillors and Officials had grudges against him for him to contemplate keeping his job, if Presbyterian fell from power.

"Well keep your ear to the ground, something is up, I can feel it in my bones. I don't know what it is, but it's there all right."

"Sacre-bleu."

"Robespierre! No French!"

"Pardon Monsieur!"

The man was clearly rattled.

"Sorry Sir, Mr Mayor. I'll attend to it right away. Consider it done. If anything is going on, I'll find out what it is."

He dashed from the Parlour, the sound of his quick steps on the old wooden staircase gave comfort to Presbyterian. If it was there, Robespierre would find it. The Mayor went to the window and looked down across the street to the offices of "TheWeekly Weaver," for this would surely be the first port of call for Robespierre in his quest for information. True enough, the crow-like figure of Robespierre, dressed as he was in black clothing which hung on him like a coat of loose feathers, disappeared into the hub of Crewdley gossip.

As Robespierre entered, so a little old lady made her exit, content in the knowledge that her best hope of finding her lost cat lay now with the simple message she had placed in the columns of Crewdleys most read newspaper. Robespierre glanced around the sparten accommodation and sidled up to the counter, which he looked over in his usual, rather furtive manner. "Anything for me?" he whispered.

A ginger haired man turned around in his rotating-chair and confronted the interloper in his best Scottish brogue. "Aye laddie, ah have something feh yuh!" Robespierre raised his eyebrows. "What?" "A 'gude piece o' advice .... get lost!"

"But The Mayor asked......."

"I dunna care what The Mayor arsked laddie .... get Lost!"

14

"Thank you Mr McSnadden, and a very good morning to you,"replied the rejected representative of Crewdleys finest son.

"Ah ...away with yuh laddie. Ahm only kiddin'. Now what do yuh really want eh? I expect the old rogue will be wantin' the telephone number o' the lassie we met at the Chamber o' Commerce reception last week. Am ah right?"

"No, you're wrong," said Robespierre, "we want to know if you've heard anything particular to The Mayor?" He leaned even further across the counter and began to slowly cup his hand to his ear, in anticipation of news.

"I've told yuh before Robespierre laddie, dunnu' use the ter'rm wee. It puts me in mind o' Royalty and ahm inproperly dressed to receive 'em."

"Beg pardon Mr McSnadden," Robespierre apologized. What I meant was ...."

"Ah know what yu' meant laddie and ah have'na hearrd a dickie bird. Now good-day!" From past experience, Robespierre knew he would get nothing from the crafty Editor on that occasion, so he quietly slipped out of the hub of news-activity back into the street. He looked quickly up to The Mayor's window and was not in the least surprised to see the large figure of Harold Presbyterian hovering like a hungry vulture, waiting for the poor, skinny old black crow to admit failure and collapse onto the pavement in a permanent and final admission of defeat.

But each knew that Robespierre would continue in his quest until he had at least something to take back to his Master. Indeed, if he were to return empty handed, his Master would keep the door closed firmly in his face.

It was too early to contemplate tapping the drink-sodden grape vine of the 'Star and Garter' public house, or to meander in and out of the queue to Finney's fish and chip shop. In a desperate effort to discover the source of The Mayor's unease, Robespierre duly took his place in the waiting room of Dr. Scargreaves surgery. He had convinced the Receptionist of the urgency of his imaginery health problem, an acute pain in his knee, though after one and a half hours of being abused by pensioners who demanded every newspaper and magazine he picked up and young mothers who blamed him for causing their toddlers to trip over his feet and crash into the coffee-table, he was extremely glad to have escaped without seeing the Doctor by re-convincing the Receptionist of a miraculous return to knee-normality. Unfortunately, he had suffered a fruitless period of acute and barren frustration in Doctor Scargreaves surgery and was in sore need of quiet. The Library provided the perfect sanctuary. Many a tasty morsel had fallen Robespierre's way from behind the book shelves of Crewdley Library. There was the time he had heard Bernard Beard whispering his intent to find another job. It had been down hill for the unfortunate Town Clerk ever since.

On another occasion, Robespierre had listened intently, to the beginnings of an amorous affair between two of the newer Crewdley Councillors, a piece of information made much of by The Mayor, as a weapon of black-mail when required.

He settled down in the comfy seat near to the Reference Section and went quickly to sleep. It was some time later in the afternoon when Robespierre was rudely disturbed by one of the Librarians.

"Mr Robespierre," she whispered rather loudly, "shouldn't you be in The Mayor's Parlour or something? You're cluttering the place up." "Oh my God!" cried Robespierre, already in full flight, "I fell asleep." It was by now almost lunch time and Robespierre hurried quickly into the 'Star and Garter'. Seamus MacGurk pulled him a pint of best bitter which he drank almost at once.

"Whisky," he asked,"and have one yourself."

Robespierre adopted a nonchalant, laid-back attitude and casually said to the landlord, "Have you heard anything lately that could damage The Mayor?"

"Yuh what?" MacGurk growled (for he was a big man with a big voice) "Nawh, not me mate, what goes on at the Town Hall is nuthin' tu do wit me." One look into MacGurk's wild, black eyes was enough to convince Robespierre to search elsewhere. "I'll try the Lounge," he apologized.

His luck was in; sitting with their backs to the bar were the unmistakable figures of the Council Chambers illicit lovebirds, Councillor Mrs Louise Evans-Jenkins, a rather amorous and attractive young Independent, and Morton Muggeridge a mild mannered and wet Conservative theologian, filled with self-doubt about worldly politics but deeply infatuated with Louise Evans-Jenkins.

Robespierre quickly sat down, and picked up the copy of The Independent and hid behind it to listen.

He had been listening to their pathetic and trivial words of love for half an hour, suffering from severe cramp in both arms, when at last, they began to talk about the Annual Meeting of the Council.

"Yes, I did hear Hardie was going to do that and personally, said Muggeridge, "I think....."

"Robespierre!" boomed MacGurk, "are yoh havin' another or what?" Robespierre slowly lowered the newspaper and adopted a silly grin, as the love-birds turned around to confront the eaves-dropper.

"No thanks Mr MacGurk, I've got to be off," he exclaimed, cursing under his breath at MacGurks intervention at the very moment when it seemed all might have been revealed.

Robespierre spent the rest of the afternoon in various shops, Estate Agents Offices, and finally the Municipal Gardens, in his effort to gain the information which The Mayor considered necessary for their survival.

With heavy-heart, he trod the old wooden staircase up to The Mayor's Parlour.

A familiar voice greeted him.

"Where the hell have you been Robespierre?" "Sorry Mr Mayor," answered the faithful servant, "I've been everywhere. It's been very difficult Your Honour! But I did finally over hear something I think you will find interesting Councillor Muggeridge said to Councillor Mrs Evans-Jenkins"

"Forget it! I already know," snapped Presbyterian, "that idiot Beard brought me a note. Hardie is going to try and move a vote of "No Confidence" in me at the Annual Council Meeting."

"Yes Sir! That's it Sir! That's just what I was going to tell you!" Robespierre lied through his tobacco stained teeth, "What a terrible thing to do Sir."

"Precisely, never trust a bloody Socialist Robespierre. They're likely to turn on you at any minute. He's a sanctimonious swine, that Hardie, a bloody nuisance." The Mayor was clearly not a happy man.

"There's always someone Robespierre, who refuses to see the world as it really is," he added. "But I thought all Socialists were like that Mr Mayor," the Town Crier squeaked.

"I don't know about the rest. I just know about our two, well three I suppose, if you count his blasted daughter. Thank God she's not on the Council." Robespierre adopted his pall-bearers pose and looked suitably glum-faced.

"Yes indeed Sir, Thank God." "Just make absolutely sure that you never go into politics Robespierre. It's a thankless task. After all I've done for Crewdley. It's a pity we can't use the Ducking-Stool, I could try him for being a witch."

"Why not put him in the stocks, Mr Mayor?" "Because the Reverend Wilfred Wooly would never agree to it. There's another 'liberal' do-gooder. He's absolutely useless."

The reference to 'stocks' and 'ducking stools' was not that uncommon a riposte from The Mayor to his aid-de-camp.

Both implements were implanted on the lawns of The Vicarage, saved from destruction by a well-meaning Priest in the 19th Century who had been determined to preserve this dark shadow of Crewdleys past, as a reminder of mans inhumanity to man and how good would over-come evil. The redundant pieces of antiquarian torture had remained unused ever since, a glowing example of divine intervention and ecclesiastic far sightedness.

"No! I'll just have to sink him by other means," concluded The Mayor. And so, relative calm descended upon The Mayor's Parlour as Robespierre and Presbyterian prepared for 'The Big One'. Robespierre went out for two portions of Finney's fish and chips which they enjoyed with two bottles of the best Civic Champagne.

A distant bustle of near-activity could be heard in the rooms below as Robespierre began to dress The Mayor in his Civic costume .....first the Robe itself, then the White Laced Collar, next the Mayoral Chain of Office and finally, the Civic Cocked Hat.

"You look really nice Mr Mayor," Robespierre said in genuine admiration. Presbyterian was not impressed. "Just make sure you're ready to repond to any emergency, and I mean any, which might include your giving me the kiss of life if it's necessary to get the meeting abandoned."

"Sacre Bleau!" coughed Robespierre, "the kiss of life?" "No French!" the Great Man retorted, "how many more times?"

"Sorry Your Grace."

"That's better, now lets get down to the car."

They made their way down the stairs through the rear door of the Town Hall under the arches to the car park. Robespierre opened the rear door, Presbyterian got inside and off they went, into the very heart of the metropolis where ducking-stools and stocks played absolutely no part of Civic Life.

"Drive around the Church a few times," Presbyterian called, "then take it down by the River, and drive slowly Robespierre, I want them all to see what value they get for their Poll Tax money."

"And shall I drive past 'Caspian House', Mr Mayor?" Robespierre enquired.

"Of course, but don't stop. I haven't time," he replied as they went around St. Crued's Church for the second time. The occupant of 'Caspian House' could be seen behind the lace curtains as the car drove slowly past. So grateful was Mr Michael Monroe to his Middle Eastern Oil Trading Partners, that it seemed an obvious choice, to name his house after one of his favourite regions. As it was, Presbyterian had to no more than even mildly consider that part of the world, and his passion was sorely roused by the name-association between the Caspian Sea and his comely mistress.

"Not too fast Robespierre you fool," he insisted, blowing kisses to Pippa Monroe as the car rolled by. He took a last glance at her through the rear-view window and then resumed his up-right posture for the final part of their ritualistic journey. Robespierre drew the car up alongside the pavement directly outside the Town Hall and opened the rear door.

"Ladies and Gentlemen," he shouted, "Mr Harold Presbyterian, The Mayor of Crewdley!" "Do you have to shout in my ear mate?" asked an old man walking his dog, "it's bad enough with ice-cream vans and those bloody church bells."

Robespierre ignored him and slammed the car door then walked quickly behind The Mayor, under the arch-way of The. Town Hall where several people were milling around.

Presbyterian stopped at the old oak doors to the Council Chamber, as Robespierre collected The Mace from the office. Bernard Beard, the wretched Town Clerk, opened up the ancient doors, Robespierre entered the Council Chamber with The Mace, inhaled as deeply as he could and shouted at the top of his voice, "Councillor's, citizens and distinguished guests .... will you please be upstanding for Mr Harold Presbyterian, Mayor and First Citizen of Crewdley." The assembly stood, almost as one, though some were quicker than others.

Robespierre made his way to the top table and placed The Mace onto its stand. Presbyterian followed slowly, eyeing everyone, before taking his seat.

He delayed asking them to sit, an old trick he had developed over time, which he considered gave him a psychological opportunity to assert his dominance over any wavering officer or councillor who perhaps harboured, even yet, a small doubt concerning the ruthlessness or total commitment of The Mayor to hold on to what he had. Of course, his performance and the 'Grand Entrance' itself, cut no ice with the two Socialists, but the others certainly had no particular desire to make an enemy of 'The Great Man'.

At least, that rule had held until now. Presbyterian eye-balled every Councillor and made them remain standing as he looked into the soul of the seven whose votes would surely save him.

"Please be seated,' he said finally as old Mrs Octavia Bland was seen to be rocking to and fro, as if about to collapse.

Bernard Beard flapped around, tidying agenda papers as The Mayor continued his statesman-like posture and took in the atmosphere. The Council Chamber was full. The Officers were in place, the Councillors, the Press and even, on this occasion, members of the public who packed the small gallery to its full capacity of twelve.

His heart skipped a beat as the image of Sabrina, his 'Water Goddess' of the Caspian Sea, Pippa Monroe puckered her lips towards him in a beautifully submissive and seductive manner.

His passion was roused, and he felt a surging power rush through his body in the way it always did when she looked him like that. But he would not be diverted from the cut and thrust of the Meeting which lay ahead, nor indeed could he afford to be diverted from the Agenda. He had stayed where he was by being sharp and always having worked out the potential danger areas before the Meetings ever began.

As was his wont, Beard jumped up and called for the meetings attention.

"Mr Mayor, the Agenda papers have been properly circulated, and as you are no doubt fully aware an Emergency Motion has been received in the names of Mr Arthur Hardie and Mrs Enid Thomas."

The threat appeared real but Presbyterian ignored it. Instead, he stood up to his full height and cast his eyes down to the papers on the table.

"Thank you Mr Town Clerk, I am as you say, fully aware of the Emergency Motion. The Agenda is as amended then, Item One, A short address by Cllr Harold Presbyterian, the out-going Mayor of Crewdley; Item Two, Apologies; Item Three, Minutes of the last Council Meeting; Item Four, Matters Arising from the Minutes; Item Five, Correspondence (The Charity Letter) Item Six, the Election of Mayor; Item Seven, the Emergency Motion. "Is that agreed?" he asked.

Arthur Hardie got quickly to his feet.

"No it isn't agreed. The whole point of the Motion is to have a vote of "No Confidence passed in you."

There were gasps from the Public Gallery at this juncture, but Hardie continued, "If the Motion is carried, we intend to nominate someone else as Mayor, so lets have none of your tricks Councillor Presbyterian. I move that we take the vote of 'No Confidence,' before we elect a new Mayor."

"And I second that Motion," said Councillor Mrs Thomas.

Now, given the seriousness of the situation and the apparent lack of manouvre left open to The Mayor, it appeared to those present, that he would have no option but to put the Motion to the vote. However, he hadn't been at the hub of Crewdley politics for over twenty years, without knowing how to deal with an attempt on his political life.

We have then, to go back merely one hour before the Annual Meeting of Crewdley Council, to gain the benefit of listening to a telephone conversation, or rather several such conversations, made by The Mayor from his Parlour, to one or two people considered essential to the outcome of the debate.

Firstly, the telephone rang in the home of Councillor Mrs Octavia Bland. The conversation went much as follows: "Hello, this is The Mayor. I just wanted you to know Octavia, that I've been approached from Buckingham Palace regarding my thoughts on whether or not an M.B.E award would fit snugly upon yourself."

"Oh Harold!" she cried, "I do hope you were able to concur as much?"

There was a pregnant pause before The Mayor continued. "Well actually, as you know, these awards are deemed to be all about loyalty to the system and the establishment. As you are aware Octavia, in our own modest little way, given our seniority of rank by Charter of Henry VIII, we in Crewdley are considered part of the establishment. I have to tell you that the bloody

Socialists are going to move a vote of 'No Confidence' in my good self at tonights meeting."

"The swines!" she fumed. "Precisely! Such a move, if it were successful, would be seen to be a victory for the "Forces of Darkness!"

"It'll never happen Harold!"

"Good!" he replied and put the telephone down. The second call was to Councillor Morton Muggeridge. "Hello Muggeridge look, I hope it's possible to keep your little affair from the public gaze at tonights meeting?"

There followed a sickly groan and a deep sigh. "Oh dear no, what's happened? Is someone going to say something Mr Mayor?" Muggeridge asked dejectedly.

"I bloody well hope not, but the Socialists are moving a vote of 'No Confidence' in me, and you know how nasty a free-ranging debate like that can get?"

"Oh my God, one can almost imagine, oh my God. Please don't let it happen Mr Mayor, I beg you, do your best to stop it," he pleaded. It didn't take a genius to detect that the phone call had had the desired effect. Presbyterian could almost see Muggeridge shaking in his shoes.

"Well you just make sure that Hardie doesn't get his way and tell your lady friend to do the same understood?"

"Oh yes Mr Mayor, thank you, oh my God."

The receiver clicked and Harold Presbyterian took comfort from the knowledge that even in such a supposedly genteel and civilized place as Crewdley, a swift kick between the legs worked wonders.

The Mayor now required just one more vote to be cast against the Motion for the question of 'Confidence' to be a non-starter.

With Mrs Octavia Bland, Morton Muggeridge and Mrs Louise Evans-Jenkins in the bag, plus of course, his own vote, the total was already four against a potential six. However, Presbyterian needed but one vote to beat off the attack, because one more vote would make five and if the votes are tied, The Mayor, under proper statute, had the casting vote.

Without even breaking sweat, he received an undertaking from Councillor Mrs Sylvia Smart that she would not support the Socialists under any circumstances whatsoever (that made five votes and provided certain victory) but just for good measure, he co-opted Councillor Alan Arkwright, the amateur inventor and Independent, on the spurious grounds that a Government Grant was expected any day, which would be solely devoted to the development of new technologies and alternative sources of energy, under the auspicies of Crewdley Council, but on the specific understanding that the 'Grant' would be administered by the current Mayor, Councillor Presbyterian.

Arkwright virtually slobbered down the telephone.

"That's just up my street," he enthused. "Thought it would be. So just make sure I survive O.K?"

"Consider it done old chap. My Goodness! A development grant eh?" Presbyterian was almost embarrassed by the ease of his success. He didn't bother with Norman Bull or Barry Blondel, though each had their achilles heel. He would cut their tendons on another day, if necessary, with six votes against Hardie. The Mayor would not have been concerned if Bull and Blondel were to have been lost to the world in flames of spontaneous human combustion. The Annual Meeting of the Council would be yet another successful 'Coronation' of Crewdley's finest son. It was then, with certain confidence, that The Mayor resumed his setting-out of the Council Agenda. "Very well, it has beenMoved by Councillor Hardie and Seconded by Councillor Thomas that the vote of 'No Confidence' is taken as Item Six. Those in favour, please show." A hush fell over the assembly as The Mayor sat down. The two, lonely hands of Arthur Hardie and Enid Thomas were raised high into the air.

There was a gasp of recognition that the attempt had been lost, as Bernard Beard got to his feet to record the obvious vote.

"Those in favour, two, Mr Mayor, And those against,please show." The hands of Presbyterian's victims went up, plus his own.

"That is six against, Abstentions, please show." Councillors Blondel and Bull indicated their lack of concern by not even bothering to record their Abstentions.

"The Motion is clearly lost Mr Mayor. The Agenda will be taken as printed," said Beard.

Pippa Monroe gave The Mayor one of her most sensuous and provocative looks and he was almost lost in the amorous and generous curves of her body, until he broke away and resumed his composure. "Right!" he barked, "lets get on with it!" Robespierre shed an emotional, Anglo-Gallic tear into his handkerchief, with the blessed realization that they were safe for another year.

"How does he do it?" he blubbed quietly to himself, "what a man." Presbyterian rose to his feet. "Item one it is, a short address by the out-going Mayor of Crewdley." He beamed with delight as Councillor Hardie and Councillor Mrs Enid Thomas stared impassively ahead.

"This current Municipal Year has been one of immense satisfaction to me. We have seen our town continue to flourish in spite of the incompetance of the County Council and remote ineffectiveness of Central Government. Our community is blessed by nature as it is, tucked alongside the beautiful River Crewd, but a stones-throw from the joys of marvellous countryside and the magnificent Crewdley Forest. In these days of International tension and conflict and the juggernaught of legislation from Europe and Westminster, what a joy it is for us, the lucky few of Crewdley, to continue to have the favoured opportunity of living here in this wonderful place." "Three cheers for Crewdley and The Mayor!" yelled a voice from the public gallery, "Hip-hip hooray, hip- hip hooray, hip- hip hooray!"

"Thank you, thankyou," said The Mayor, "And I hope that beautiful moment of spontaneus joy will be captured forever in the pages of 'The Weekly Weaver', 'eh Mr MacSnadden?" The Editor scribbled away without looking up to'The Great Man' as he continued his orgasm of public adulation. "Thankyou Archibald, I know we can rely upon you to do justice to our Town. Now, Item Two. Apologies .... none. Item Three, Minutes of the last Meeting. Will someone move that they are a true record.?" "I move," said Councillor Mrs Smart. "And I second," added Councillor Octavia Bland, who was seeing an ever-more definate picture of an MBE before her eyes as she spoke.

"Agreed?" asked The Mayor. "Agreed!" came the reply.

"Thankyou, and Item Four, Matters Arising from the Minutes. Are there any?" He looked around for a hand to go up, but the hands stayed down.

"Very well, Item Five, Correspondence." The Town Clerk hovered like a honey-bee around the jam-pot and passed The Mayor a letter which he held up and read from without acknowledging the hapless Clerk.

"Ah yes, the Charity Letter." He smiled again, not of course because the idea of Charity appealed to his nature, rather the thought of the revenue which would go directly into his own Bank Account as the Sole Trustee of The Old Town Trust.

"I have decided, that were I to be given the honour of again being your choice as Crewdley's First Citizen...." "Oh you certainly will be Mr Mayor," Councillor Muggeridge concurred. The Great Man continued, "Then my Charity Appeal would continue to be directed to the benefit of 'The Old Town Trust'. They do a marvellous job and I think we should continue to support them." "Here, here!" shouted a voice, "You carry on the good work Mr Mayor."

"Indeed,"he said, "the letter is brief, it reads ...... Dear Mr Mayor, Thankyou so much for your marvellous efforts on our behalf. Without the money provided by the 'Old Town Trust Charity', the lives of our old folk would be so much the poorer. Please continue to help us, yours faithfully, Anthony Roberts."

Apart from The Mayor himself, Anton Robespierre alone knew the real non-identity of the illusive Mr Roberts, and the real meaning of the initials A.R a nice coincidence to a phoney signature Robespierre had perfected over the years, at The Mayor's instruction, by writing the assumed name backwards.

"I intend to write to Mr Roberts informing him of my decision. If Mr MacSnadden would kindly make reference to my Charity Appeal in 'The Weekly Weaver', it would help enormously."

There was some polite clapping from the gallery at this juncture, and entering into the spirit of the evening, Mrs Octavia Bland managed to get to her feet and clap for as hard and as long as it proved possible; a full three seconds before she dropped back into her seat with a bump.

"Charity is the downfall of the working classes," shouted Councillor Hardie, "Put that in your paper MacSnadden!"

"Now then Hardie," said The Mayor, "lets have none of your politics in here. This is a Council Chamber, not the bar of The Labour Club." "Here here, Mr Mayor!" shouted Beard, "it's not The Labour Club."

Presbyterian gave him a look that said it all, but he added, "Shut up Beard!" for good measure anyway, just in case the point were to have been lost on anyone.

"Item Six, The Election of Mayor," roared Presbyterian, "Do we have a nomination?" Councillor Mrs Sylvia Smart stood up and said quite loudly. "Yes Mr Mayor, we Conservatives take great pleasure in nominating you, Councillor Harold Presbyterian, as Mayor."

She sat down, also rather loudly. Next on her feet, very slowly and with effort, was Councillor Mrs Octavia Bland.

"The Independents have always thought highly of you Harold and I second the nomination." She eased herself back into her seat and exhaled in a rather undignified manner.

Beard jumped to attention and grinned foolishly, "Are there any other nominations?" he whined. There were not. "I shall put that to the vote then.

Those in favour of Harold Presbyterian, please show." Messrs Smart, Bland, Arkwright, Muggeridge, and Evans-Jenkins indicated in the affirmative, as of course, did Presbyterian himself.

"Those against, please show," said Beard. Councillor Hardie and Councillor Mrs Thomas reached for the ceiling.

"Abstentions?" asked Beard. Councillors Blondel and Bull again couldn't be bothered to record their indifference.

"That is carried. I therefore take great delight," Beard lied, "in declaring Councillor Harold Presbyterian to be the duly elected Mayor of Crewdley Town Council for this Civic Year." There was applause from many parts of the Chamber as Presbyterian stood to acknowledge his grateful public.

"I am deeply grateful," he called, trying not to stare at Pippa Monroe who was doing her best to indicate her pleasure by pouting and blowing kisses his way, in a not too discreet fashion.

"Thankyou," he said, "and finally, Item Seven, The Emergency Motion."
"Forget it!" Hardie yelled, "it's a waste of time. We withdraw it!"

"Excellent! In that case, I hereby close the Meeting. Thank you all for your attendance. Please give generously to the Old Town Charity box in the foyer and enjoy the rest of the evening."

The assembly began to melt away, until at last, Harold Presbyterian and Anton Robespierre were alone in the Council Chamber.. Robespierre collected The Mace and walked from the Chamber and up the old wooden staircase to The Mayor's Parlour, with Presbyterian two steps behind and grinning like a Cheshire cat.

"Put the bloody thing down Robespierre and open the Civic Champagne," instructed the Great Man, "then get down to that Charity Box and bring it up here, I'm a bit short of ready cash." "Yes sir Mr Mayor," Robespierre replied with genuine pleasure, "You look absolutely marvellous Your Grace. I'll just pour the drinks and then I'll get the Charity Box." The next few hours were spent in the usual way, with Presbyterian and Robespierre drinking their way through several bottles of champagne, until at last, the 'Great Man' got up from the chair.

"O.K Robespierre," he said somewhat less than one hundred per cent coherently, " get me into the bloody Rolls Royce."

" I've just had a fantastic vision of the Caspian Sea. Pippa Monroe loves me, Robespierre, so lets go!"And so, after his triumphant evening, Harold Presbyterian left the precincts of the Town Hall safely in the opulence of the Civic motor car. Although it was extremly dark and Presbyterian's faculties were less than perfect, he nevertheless rolled down the rear-window and stuck his head out to see the soft, yellow lighting of "Caspian House", but a few yards ahead. His passion was rising inextricably as the shadowy figure of Pippa Monroe could be seen behind the curtains.

His ardour suffered a severe and near mortal blow as the figure of a man materialized from the shadows. Mr Michael Monroe was making his way home, suitcase in hand, oblivious of either jetlag or time zone, as he himself also viewed the figure of his welcoming and faithful wife. Presbyterian re-wound the window and collapsed dejectedly into the leather seat.

"Sod it!" he cursed, "back to the Town Hall Robespierre. I'll have a cold shower and a cup of coffee." "Yes Sir, Mr Mayor," answered the chauffer, "shall I stop for fish and chips at Finneys?" The Mayor grunted. "You might as well," he groaned, It's the only pleasure I'm likely to get now, thanks to that oily twit!" "Oh very good Mr Mayor, I get it. Mr Monroe is in the Oil Business. Oily twit, ha, ha, ha." The Mayor was not amused and just to prove it, he made Robespierre eat his supper under the arch-way of the Town Hall as he crunched the last pickle and swigged the last drop of champagne.

25

The evening ended with a belch in The Mayor's Parlour as Presbyterian flopped onto the chaise-lounge. Some time later, Robespierre put his head around the door and saw his Master sleeping like a baby. He turned out the light and went to his own sparse and meagre quarters down the corridor, as the moonless night descended over Crewdley and Democracy fell asleep, until the dawning of a new day.

CHAPTER THREE

Characters of Crewdley

As the citizens of Crewdley slept in the safety of that black and starless night, before the sun once again would rise over the River Crewd to paint the old walls of The Town Hall a dappled and honest yellow, bringing a sparkling, and fresh newness to the ancient town, we shall look through this window of opportunity provided by this interlude, to consider a more detailed deliberation of Crewdley and it's people. Given that buildings usually endure so much longer than the people who built them, perhaps our thoughts should necessarily go firstly to the town itself? Crewdley is not particularly remarkable in any way, being as it is, a rather typical and small mid-English town; and old settlement built around a river, a nice enough place in which to live, but lacking either excitement or the real sophistication of some of it's larger and altogther more grand neighbours. The Church of St. Crued occupies more or less, the pivotal position in the town. Although the building itself is but a few hundred years old, church historians are certain that previous and ancient churches were in evidence on the site.

In fact, evidence suggests that not only Medieval Christian and Saxon Churches existed before the present building, but perhaps even pre-Christian Pagan places of worship occupied the same, central area of Crewdley. Church records, once kept in the old oak chest of St. Crued, but now safely in the small Museum opposite, indicate that the early English and little known St. Crued, was the person responsible for stamping out Paganism and bringing Christianity to the people, after the Romans had left. The present holder of the title, Vicar of Crewdley and therefore the occupier of St. Crueds, was the Reverend Wilfred Wooly, of whom more later.

Perhaps the most important building, or more accurately structure, in Crewdley after the Church, is Crewdley Bridge. Again, records tell of previous wooden structures occupying the same shallow spot in the River Crewd, but many wooden bridges were washed away before the present bridge was constructed by the Engineer Thomas Telford in 1790 after a prolonged and ultimately successful appeal for Public Subscription.

Since that date, generations of Crewdley folk have passed over its rather spendid stone arches, to and from their little town. Although the terrible floods continued to occur until quite recent times, the bridge held its place and it is now as familiar a feature of Crewdley as the Church.

The town itself fans out from the main Church Street, which occupies the area from Crewdley Bridge down the main shopping area, before dividing each side of St. Crueds Church, and running into Dark Street.

To this day,Dark Street remains the subject matter of some occasional debate. Was it named thus because it truly always was a "Dark Street", running as it did in the narrowest of gaps between the centuries-old housing ? Or, did "Dark Street" have a much more sinister meaning, relating back to the Pagan days of Pre-St. Crued enlightenment?

This latter interpretation was preferred by the Reverend Wilfred Wooly, who always considered "Man's Fall from the Garden of Eden", if not to have actually first occured in Crewdley, then certainly somewhere nearby. "Dark Street" for him, was the Pagan's Retreat, where the Godless sought refuge from "The Light". Most of the houses, shops and buildings in the central area of Crewdley were mid 17th Century, and Dark Street had its share of houses of that time.

Crewdley Co-op occupied one of the corners of Church Street which ran into Dark Street, though the ground-floor accomodation of the shop was fitted out in a modern style. The other corner was the site of Crewdleys busiest nocturnal food outlet, after eleven o' clock at night when the pubs had closed. Finney's Fish and Chip Shop was an institution.

Eric and Elsie Finney were less concerned about the origins of Dark Street than receiving a regular supply of potatoes, fish, flour, oil and lately, kebabs and cans of pop.

The Western end of Dark Street ran into Forest Lane, with Bettinger The Bookmakers shop on the right and 'The Star and Garter' Public House directly opposite.

Ironically, the Police Station was situated adjacent to Bettingers, a fact which had over the years, suited some of the young Constables with a penchant for gambling, and often had been the time bets and a stake were placed under a helmet until the owner was safely off-duty and could take his place at the counter with the rest of the punters. The Eastern side of Dark Street, which included the shops, houses and buildings which ran away from the Co-op, were interesting and unusual.

The Old Crewdley Workhouse had been empty for as long as almost anyone could remember, but it still cast a shuddering shadow over the older people, some of whom remembered it being open for business. From the records kept in the Museum, it was obvious, that in bygone days, quite a few of the ancestors of present day inhabitants had spent various periods of time in Crewdley Workhouse. For some of the working class people at least then, Dark Street had a particular meaning which had little to do with either Paganism or lack of light. The spectre of dread conjured up by The Workhouse for Crewdley's past unfortunates, could only have been made worse by the positioning of Grimley's Funeral Service in the Building next door. Grimley's had been established during a particularly bad out-break of cholera in 1746, the same year as The Workhouse; obviously, 1746 had not been a good year for the people of Crewdley.

However, Grimley's had remained open ever since and never had a year passed since without their Services being called upon to ensure the departed were ready to deny the long, Pagan shadows of Dark Street which sometimes seemed to fall across the steps of the premises, and deliver them instead to the safe and eager arms of the Church of St. Crued for decent, Christian burials.

Next door to Grimley's were the old Almshouses, the last refuge of the Crewdley's elderly poor. Again, the irony of their position was noted by most thinking people . The Almshouses had been established for over three hundred years by a Trust Fund Endowment in the last Will and Testament of Lucy Baxter, a wealthy widow whose husband had been an early trader of tobacco from the American Colonies.

Presbyterian had spent much time studying the Deeds of the Trust, before he had been able to syphon off much of the money from the Trust into his own Bank Account.

But of course, the elderly occupants were always pleased to see him on one of his occasional visits, when he made much of his concern for their welfare and security of tenure, not a great distance to travel to ensure twenty votes would be cast for him at Election time.

At the opposite end of the town from Dark Street, were River Side West and River Side East, roads which ran away from Crewdley Bridge; the West past the site of Crewdley Comprehensive School, whilst various houses, many quite pleasant, were positioned along the Eastern Road. Some four houses down from the Post Office on the corner of Church Street, was "Caspian House", the home of the Headmistress of both the School and The Mayor's Parlour. Whereas Dark Street hardly ever seemed to enjoy the full light of day, the children of the school and the occupants of River Side East, were blessed with both the pleasing aspect of the River Crewd and the wide, open spaces provided by the Riverside Promenade and the splendid view across the River to Crewdley Manor, West of the Bridge. In days long since past, the River Crewd had been the main means of communication for local people. It was a working river, where traders loaded local produce such as timber, leather, iron ware, cereals, rope, hats and even livestock from the rich Crewdley pastures. The goods were shipped down-river in the flat-bottomed boats or trows, peculiar to Crewdley and a few other river-side towns in those mid-English county districts through which the River Crewd made its way from its source in the Welsh mountains and out into the Celtic Sea.

The boats made the return journey loaded down with imports from the West of England, Ireland, France, Germany, and Spain and according to ancient records, the Mediterranean countries and those of the old Roman

Empire. Various artefacts had been discovered around the confines of Crewdley that indicated it had fared well in previous ages, as well as our own. It should be noted that in addition to settlement by past invaders, that this influx of foreign trade had resulted in at least some of the men and women involved, actually settling in Crewdley.

A Crewdley person could therefore be dark and rather short Mediterranean type or taller and more fair, as is similiar to central European peoples.

However, the Riverside was now a place of relative quiet and pleasantness, with fishermen and the occasional drunken swimmer being the only sources of activity, however subdued or infrequent, sometimes each launching themselves into their favoured occupational pastime, fishing or swimming, from a small rowing boat or coracle- like craft, almost guaranteed to take even a sober person to the bottom of the River.

If Dark Street was considered gloomy and River Side agreeably pleasant, then Church Street could be agreed by all to be where the majority of Crewdley business and shopping was carried out.

Church Street was dominated by St Creuds Church near Dark Street, the Crewdley Bridge at its River Side end, and The Town Hall situated as it was equi-distant between them and on the Eastern side.

Many of the buildings in Crewdley were but centuries-old structures built upon the sites of even older and earlier ones.

The Town Hall was one such building. Although its origins were not certain (Rupert Beard, brother of the Town Clerk, maintained it was first a Roman Temple) the foundations indicate a building of definite antiquity. However, the most widely accepted version acowledged nothing in particular being built on the Town Hall site before about 1500, when it was considered quite likely that a market and row of butchers shops seemed to have been there. The present building was erected in the year 1760, that is to say, after Grimley's and the Workhouse, yet a few years before the construction of the Bridge.

It was a fine building of soft yellow sandstone. At its centre was a large archway, high enough for a coach and horses to enter. A smaller arch was positioned on either side of the main one, all three being hung with rather beautiful iron gates, which when closed, gave the impression of an extremely secure stronghold, rather in the fashion of a small fortified castle. However, the three high windows on the first floor directly above the arches, belied that impression. Over the River Side arch and behind the high window, was The Mayor's Parlour. Above the Church Side arch, a pleasant room with oak-panelling, behind which was Presbyterian's secret stairway between his own adjacent house and his Parlour.

At the rear of the main arch-way was the entrance to the Council Chamber and to it's left, a small office suitable in size and position for the Town Clerk. At the front of the building, at ground level, was a small flat provided for the Mayor's Chauffer, Anton Robespierre. At the rear, through the central archway and past the Council Chamber, was a walled car-park which once had been a stables, but was now used to house the Civic Rolls Royce. The Town Hall was one of those buildings considered by many members of the public to be , "a no-go area". They were not, by and large, welcome guests to either The Mayor's Parlour or the Council Chamber. Perhaps, if a very special reason presented itself for instance, the Council was considering compulsory purchase of their house and intended knocking it down, then a member of the Public might actually have presented themselves into the 'Bowels of Democracy' for an explanation.

Even the Mayor-making ceremony, an annual event throughout the centuries, would not in itself have been considered sufficient reason for attendance. More likely that friends or relatives of Councillors would have been asked to be there to observe, some would argue, the mindless ritual of dressing up in strange clothes and acting like pompous asses. Reference has been made to the house adjoining the Town Hall, and the far-sightedness of its purchaser and owner, Harold Presbyterian, Mayor of Crewdley for over twenty years.

It was now, after having been restored by Presbyterian, an excellent property, constructed in the traditional mid-English style with heavy oak beams openly displayed between the brick walls which were painted white, under a red-tiled roof, giving the overall picture of prosperity so coveted by Crewdley's First Citizen.

Next to "Civic House," as Presbyterian had ostentatiously named it, was The Vicarage, a large and splendid building positioned directly opposite to St. Crueds Church and set in its own grounds.

Even Presbyterian envied the Reverend Wilfred Wooly for having the honour of living, at least temporarily, in Crewdley's finest house. The Mayor occasionally hoped for the Church to go out of business and for The Vicarage to be put on the market, but Christianity was for the moment, managing to hold off the Pagan Forces of Darkness. The Vicar himself was an Oxford graduate, a man nearing sixty years of age, rather tall and of a nervous disposition. His belief in the Fall of Man from the Garden of Eden was both sincerely held and particularly related to Crewdley.

For Wilfred Wooly, the living proof of human infallability was everywhere and he had been engaged in a mortal battle against lethargy, greed and Aetheism for all of his life. He feared that he himself might slip into that Godless position, and so the internal and external fight for Salvation needed to be fought on a permanent basis. This struggle did not however prevent the

Vicar from being a charitable man. His motto, or one of them, "Charity begins at Home," was put to the test when Rupert Beard, the eccentric and rich batchelor brother of Bernard, the hapless Town Clerk, was evicted from the family home some years before and he turned up on the Vicar's doorstep.

Wilfred Wooly took him in, but after a particularly exotic display of behaviour on Beards part, he was put out of The Vicarage and into a tepee-tent in the garden where he remains in residence.

The poor man considers himself to be encamped on a reservation, the 'Wild West' being represented by the Municipal Park and Gardens, just over the wall of the Vicarage garden.

Adjoining the garden, was the Library, a very modest affair indeed, believed by some to have been used as a mortuary in the past. Others, less charitable, considered it was still in use as a mortuary, given the dead-pan expression and lack of life of the staff and many who used it.

Between the Co-op and the Library was a small Museum, which generated slightly less interest than the Library. Its prime display was a Saxon sword which was found on the river bank near Crewdley Bridge in the last century.

The Museum also held the records of Crewdley Workhouse and some other important civic and church papers, but apart from the occasional scholar or tourist, few local people ever bothered to visit the little building.

The other side of Church Street contained only five buildings, which included the Offices of Doolittle and Dash, Crewdley's only firm of Solicitors (seventh generation); the offices of 'The Weekly Weaver', an Estate Agents, a Chemist and on the corner of St. Crueds Passage, Doctors Scargreaves Surgery.

St. Crueds Passage was the only other street in the central area of Crewdley. It led off Church Street and onto Forest Lane, and was dominated by Crewdley Fire Station, the occupants of which, enjoyed a pleasant view across the Passage over to Crewdley Comprehensive School and Crewdley Manor beyond.

And so here, in gentle mid-England, the people of Crewdley lived their lives, unfettered by war or famine and almost any other known deprivation, stimulation or conflagration. There were churchgoers and frequenters of Public Houses, though usually different groups of people, some managed to straddle the Great Holy-Alcoholic divide with ease.

Seamus MacGurk did as much business from behind the bar of "The Star and Garter" on Sunday as the Reverend Wilfred Wooly did from the Pulpit of St. Crueds Church. The rest of the week was a 'no contest', MacGurk won easily.

It was true, that arguments and fights occured as frequently in Crewdley as elsewhere and these did not all originate in "The Star and Garter".

Doolittle and Dash had been kept busy for over seven generations with the trials and tribulations of Crewdley folk their property, their marriages, their divorces, their last wills and testaments... but never could it have been suggested by anyone, even an outsider, that Crewdley people were debauched, aggressive or even dishonest.

Unfortunately, the citizens of Crewdley were on the whole, far too trusting, far too passive and far too unsophisticated to tackle the systematic embezzlement being perpetrated by its leading citizen.

They didn't want to know, they couldn't have cared less and neither could seven other elected representatives. Why should they? Most of them had relatively well paid employment if they wanted it, the Council still provided homes for those who couldn't afford to become full participants in the property-owning democracy and of course, television sets were in every living room . Why then, with all of these comforts, would any Crewdley citizen feel inclined to participate in the full and demanding process of active democratic politics, of which the key words were, "Electoral Vigilance?"

One or two people, now and again, did actually attempt to rouse the sleeping citizenship to what had befallen them. Unfortunately, the Councils two Socialists, Arthur Hardie and Mrs. Enid Thomas, were considered eccentric, rabble-rousing and even unpatriotic by the rest of the Council and most of the populace. Perhaps some members of the public did indeed take more notice of the Civic 'goings on' than was realized, yet maybe even these people considered that on balance, even if all was not entirely well, Presbyterian was still ,"good for the town", the best test of which was to rejoice in the anonymous vacuum which guaranteed Crewdley never made the headlines on National Television or the Press.

During the period of Presbyterian's reign, Crewdley had undergone some changes to its physical make-up and population, though the town centre had been left virtually untouched.

Various roads leading into Crewdley had had to be widened and improved to accomodate the vast increase in motor traffic. Within the confines of the District of Crewdley, but out in the 'Foreign Parish' region and not in the town centre, quite a number of new houses had been built to accomodate the mostly young and upwardly mobile people who had turned their backs on life in the City for the assumed-tranquility and isolation of rural Crewdley.

These detached and large houses usually had two garages and the purpose-built nursery-room cum creche was quickly turned into an extra study to accomodate his computer and her filofax collection of useless information relating to intending purchasing power of anyone between the ages of 18 and 88 who might conceivably be interested in purchasing double-glazing, stone-cladding, sophisticated all-in-one French kitchen equipment capable of peeling carrots, potatoes and tomatoes and then spontaneously combusting in a ball of flames, so that the lucky subscribers would have to buy another one. However, to suggest that these people would be committed enough to leave their houses ten minutes earlier for work usually at around 6.20am to take the time to vote at a Crewdley Election, would be to stretch the realms of possibility and credulity altogether too far. A postal vote maybe, if the idea was sold to them that to,"vote postal" was the trendy, if not environmentally-friendly, thing to do. Alas,no one from Crewdley Council would be bothering them with such frivilous choices. And so, it seemed likely, The Mayor would continue to enjoy and benefit from, the benevolent apathy of the people of Crewdley. Of course there were irritants, Councillor Barry Blondel for instance had the knack of annoying 'The Great Man' whenever he could, but Presbyterian was a serious and avaricious politician, whereas Blondel remained a cheerful and politically-ineffective womanizer. Hardie and Mrs. Thomas were irritants to Presbyterian, but always seemed destined to play the role of 'also rans' when trying to defeat The Mayor.

The young and academic daughter of the Socialist did concern Crewdley's Machiavelli, but she could only present a serious problem and real match for him if she were ableto get elected onto the Council. He sincerely hoped that she never would and had lately taken to sending her various job-prospectus leaflets and University Doctorate enrolment forms anonymously through the post. The Editor of 'The Weekly Weaver' of some five years standing, was the clever Scot, Archibald MacSnadden, a man well-able to make trouble for anyone if he wished, but under strict instruction from the owner of the newspaper to present Crewdley in as positive fashion as was possible...... quite a challenge for an advocate of hard-hitting journalism who found himself, at the whim of the owner in the journalistic back-water of Crewdley.

But MacSnadden knew his place, and if he was ever to make it to Wapping and a big National Daily Title, he'd have to bite the bullet.

Of the other, more prominent citizens of Crewdley who might have been vaguely interested in politics if the need ever arose, several are worthy of mention.

Doctor Jonathen Scargreaves was well respected in the town and probably knew more confidential and personal information concerning the majority of Crewdley people than anyone else, partly because of his long and comprehensive list of patients and secondly because of his quite pleasing bed-side manner. However, the various oaths of confidentiality and propriety, prevented him from spilling the beans, not that he was indeed ever likely to spill the beans, it was merely that Presbyterian knew any exercise or bribe aimed at prizing the information from him, would have been absolutely fruitless.

34

The Solicitors, Doolittle and Dash, were mild men, capable in their own way, but never likely to seek election. Indeed, much of their business was dependent upon Crewdley Council. Many contracts emanated from the Council Chamber in general and The Mayor's Parlour in particular. The prospect of losing any of that highly valued trade filled them both with horror. The Mayor was their most valued client. Many things therefore could be forgiven, forgotten or ignored.

Seamus MacGurk would be about as likely to give up trading on Sunday and advocate that his customers went to Church instead, than consider going near the Town Hall. For him, politics was a word with roughly the equivalent stature of 'free beer'.

And so, there it was. A little town filled with people intent on going about their own business, with a Mayor dedicated to self-help and the maintenance of political power, supported to the best of his ability, by a descendent from the battlefield of Waterloo, whose ancestor had shown exemplary courage, not in fighting for his newly created Republic, but in turning his coat inside out and joining the band of Crewdley Fusilleers who carried him aloft before setting him down, with them and their women, on the gentle banks of the River Crewd.

Robespierre's ancestor had spurned Napoleon in favour of Wellington and Anton Robespierre himself had long ago thrown in his lot and his destiny, with that of Crewdley's own Wellington, Harold Presbyterian. This seemingly unstoppable combination of military and political prowess, looked set to reign supreme over the little town, unless calamity befell The Great Man through 'Divine Intervention', 'National Disaster' or 'Invasion' by a Foreign Power. None of these things seemed in the least bit likely as Crewdley slept on in that black and starless night, before the Sun would once again rise over the blessed and tranquil River Crewd and the Citizens would awaken to meet, at least, the prospect of a challenge posed by the new day.

CHAPTER FOUR

The Garden Party

The mild days of May and Presbyterian's Coronation, were succeeded by a most pleasant early period of Summer, with sufficient rain to have pleased even the farmers in the countryside surrounding Crewdley and quite long periods of warm sunshine, which put most people in good heart for the anticipated pleasantness of July, August and September. The Mayor was standing near the window of The Parlour looking cautiously down into Church Street. He spotted Seamus MacGurk walking from the bank with an empty bag tucked beneath his arm, having no doubt divested its monetary contents into his account.

"MacGurk makes a heck of alot of money from that pub of his Robespierre," he said enviously. Robespierre sniffed. "Yes sir, he does. " Presbyterian began to walk around The Parlour, as a lion paces its cage whilst waiting for food.

" It ' s time we had a Garden Party." "Yes sir," Robespierre answered as he stood to attention, straining his eye-balls to follow each step taken by The Mayor.

"And I mean a proper Garden Party, where the tickets cost £100 each and all of the food and drink is donated by the likes of MacGurk, " said Presbyterian.

Robespierre grinned, but maintained his statuesque pose, as The Great Man walked back to the window, hands in pockets and a cigar in his mouth.

Robespierre tried to hide a smirk as he spoke, but the pleasure was too much.

"Will it be for the Old Town Trust Charity, Mr Mayor?" he asked eagerly.

Presbyterian turned to face him. "Of course it bloody well will be. I need the money, "he coughed.

And so, the Vicarage was made available for Saturday 7th July. Wilfred Wooly was pleased to have been able to comply with The Mayor's request. Robespierre spent many days selling tickets with a contrived Uriah Heep expression on his face and an outstretched hand for the £100 privilege of attending a function in the presence of Royalty.

For many, parting with £100 was a cheap price to pay for getting rid of Robespierre. The business Community, as a body, considered the pathetic figure of The Mayor's Lieutenant, standing in the door-way of their premises, to be extremely bad for trade. The man simply wouldn't budge without selling the ticket. Other citizens who came into the category of non-business, but able to pay, also parted with their money easily. These included the Fire Chief, the Police Inspector, the Vicar himself, the Librarian, Doctor Scargreaves and the Editor of The Weekly Weaver, Archibald MacSnadden. On the explicit instructions of The Mayor, Robespierre hand delivered a complimentary ticket to Pippa Monroe, but to make up the income lost by such benevolence, Presbyterian instructed Robespierre to charge Lord and Lady Crewdley two hundred pounds for each of their tickets.

"Very nice indeed," Presbyterian smiled as the full total of all the ticket receipts became apparent. "Sixty three tickets at £100 each, that's £6,300, plus two at £200, making a grand total of £6,700."

Robespierre stood to attention as The Great Man approached him.

"Here's £10 Robespierre, think yourself very lucky that I'm in a good mood." Robespierre held out his hand to take the bank-note.

"Thankyou, Your Grace, you're a gentleman," he grovelled, putting the money into his pocket.

"Right, now take £6,690 down to the Bank and put it into the Old Town Charity Trust." The Mayor passed a leather money-bag to his loyal servant, who took it and headed for the door.

"And Robespierre!" The Mayor called, "I want a receipt!"

The Mayor went to the window and watched Robespierre walk to the Bank, an old black, scraggy crow with a tasty morsel for the nest. He had a vision of the Caspian Sea, which quickly gave way to the soft, fullness of Pippa Monroe, as low and behold, the elegant woman was indeed passing by in the street below.

"My God you're a beauty," he murmered, his breath already steaming up the window, as his mistress quickly disappeared into St. Crueds Passage. He retained his composure and turned his thoughts instead to the Garden Party. There would, of course, be no Royal Guest, but he had gained particular pleasure from the pathetic display of excessive reverence given to the assumed-visitor by several of his fellow Councillors. Sylvia Smart had virtually snatched the ticket from Robespierres hand, and Octavia Bland obviously considered the Royal Guest would be making a special announcement concerning the award of MBE to herself. True to form, the Socialists had refused to part with their money and had told Robespierre to "get lost." However, matters were well in hand, large quantities of food had been promised by the Co-op and one or two other little shops. As expected, MacGurk would supply all of the alcoholic and soft drink refreshments. With one week to go, The Mayor was pretty pleased with himself. The idiot Councillor Arkwright would shortly be ascending in his hot air balloon, "The Spirit of Crewdley," in an attempt to raise more money for The Old Town Trust with a sponsored sail around the district. Apparently, for each photograph taken of the houses of each sponsor, Arkwright would receive £10. Presbyterian doubted if the man could even take a proper picture of the sky above him without a problem occuring, but he was nevertheless shortly to join Arkwright and his balloon in the Municipal Gardens to officially launch the flight.

He waited for a minute or two until Robespierre rejoined him in The Parlour. "Receipt!" said The Mayor curtly.

Robespierre passed the receipt of an entry for £6,690 into the Old Town Trust Charity and grinned foolishly.

"Come on get me dressed!" The Mayor called out, "That fool Arkwright might just provide me with a few hundred pounds."

Robespierre went to the cupboard and took out The Mayor's clothing. Presbyterian took a deep breath and the faithfull valet began to adorn his "Wellington" ... first the robe itself, then the White Laced Collar, next the Mayoral chain of Office and finally, the Civic Cocked Hat.

"You look fantastic Mr Mayor," Robespierre opined with genuine admiration.

"And you don't unfortunately," said Presbyterian, allowing himself a rather long look in the mirror, "let's go." They walked down the old wooden staircase into the Foyer of the Town Hall, then out into the walled car park at the rear of the building. Robespierre eyed the heavy wooden door in the wall which led directly into the Municipal Park and Gardens. Presbyterian shook his head, "No, I want to go in the 'Rolls'. I might be able to give a lift to someone who is extremely beautiful and makes me feel young again."

Robespierre held open the rear door of the car and The Mayor got inside. The warm, embracing waters of the 'Caspian Sea' seemed to engulf him, as his passion was sorely aroused as Robespierre drove the Civic car under the Town Hall arch-way, slowly into Church Street, past St Crueds Church and into Dark Street, before turning left again and stopping at the entrance to the Park.

Robespierre opened the car door and shouted loudly, "Ladies and Gentlemen, will you please make way for The Mayor of Crewdley, Mr Harold Presbyterian?"

"Thankyou Robespierre," The Mayor said quietly, in a matter of fact way, "You do realize there's no one within fifty yards, don't you?"

Robespierre grinned sheepishly, "I always like them to realize that you are here, Your Grace," he apologized.

They wandered slowly along the path between the flowering shrubs and the beautiful horse-chestnut trees. The pleasant smell of freshly mown grass filled The Mayors nostrils as he walked nearer to the crowds of people who were gathered around, "The Spirit of Crewdley, which was tethered firmly with ropes that looked strong enough to tow a tank.

"Just look at that clown," The Mayor scoffed, "who does he think he is, Phillias Fog?" Robespierre smirked and bleated an appalling sound that in no way resembled honest, clean laughter.

"Passporteau more like," he conflicted. Presbyterian gave the man a cutting look. "That's almost funny Robespierre. Have you been drinking?", he asked sarcastically.

"No Sir," replied the would-be comedian, "I just thought ...." "Shut up Robespierre!" demanded The Mayor, "and keep close to me!"

The Mayor mingled in and out of the crowd and being unable to resist, kissed the hand of Mrs Pippa Monroe.

"You look divine," he told her. She winked seductively and he almost melted into the soft, green grass.

"I'd like to give you a lift home in the Rolls," he wheezed. "I'll try," she purred, "but I must be careful Pressy darling, we never know who might be looking now, do we?"

"Oh sod it! I don't care if the whole world wants to look. I could make love to you right here in this gorgeous grass and still run a hundred metres in ten seconds."

He tried again to grab her by the hand, but the elusive HeadMistress was too quick. "My word Pressy darling, you are keen, aren't you?" She hurried away and Presbyterian kicked out at a turf, as she scampered off.

"Mr Mayor,!", shouted Robespierre, "Councillor Arkwright would like a word." Arkwright stepped forward with outstretched hand and grasped The Mayor, who was still staring at Pippa Monroe as she disappeared into the crowd.

"Thanks awfully for coming Mr Mayor. I'm off as soon as you've said a few words," he said with enthusiasm that Presbyterian found almost repulsive.

"Mm, well there's no point in keeping everyone waiting, is there? Get in the basket Arkwright and I'll get you off."

Arkwright lept into the basket of the hot-air balloon and Presbyterian stood back and took a deep breath.

"Dear Friends," he began, "I thank you all for coming. I sincerely hope everyone has sponsored Councillor Arkwright? We wish him well and 'Bon Voyage', Off you go then Arkwright."

With both hands firmly on the basket, Arkwright excitedly began to shout instructions to his assisants.

"Release the ropes!" he called, "and make sure they're free from the pegs!"

Various people began to pull the pegs from the ground as Arkwright moved around inside the basket like a cat on a hot tin roof. The craft began to slowly rise into the air. "What's that?" The Mayor boomed, pointing to a large leather case on the grass. "It's my camera!" yelled Arkwright, some two feet from terra-firma. Robespierre grabbed the camera case and in one heroic movement, passed it to Arkwright, as the balloon ascended quickly.

"Got it! Thanks old boy!",

Arkwright yelled, "Bye.......eee.......ee!"

The Mayor watched "The Spirit of Crewdley"rise above the trees. "What a bloody fool," he said to Robespierre,"come on, I've seen enough." They re-traced their footsteps along the path, and sure enough, when they got back to the car, Mrs Pippa Monroe was already waiting in the comfortable opulance of the rear seat.

"My God Robespierre," said The Mayor, "just keep driving around." And so it was, that The Mayor of Crewdley was driven around the district for quite some time. With the blinds pulled firmly down. Harold Presbyterian was in Heaven itself as Arkwright sailed over the old, tiled roofs, clicking away at the houses of his sponsors. The Mayor's car finally came to rest outside 'Caspian House'. After a final and lingering, succulent kiss, Pippa Monroe got out and moved her three middle fingers quickly in a kind of peculiar wave at Harold Presbyterian who remained in a state of absolute bliss as Robespierre closed the door.

He put the blinds up and Robespierre headed for The Town Hall.

"My God! What a woman!" he growled through the now opened window between his chauffer and himself, "If you have any friends in Saudi Arabia Robespierre, who could possibly dig a deep hole for Michael Monroe to fall down, there might be another tenner for you." As they approached The Town Hall, Presbyterian saw a large crowd of people gathered around St Crueds Church. "What are that lot doing blocking the road Robespierre?" he asked, straining his neck to see. The sheer numbers of people involved caused the car to stop.

"I'm going to walk Robespierre," said Presbyterian, "put the car away and I'll see what's happened." The Mayor got out into Church Street and immediately saw the attraction. "The Spirit of Crewdley" was firmly tethered to the top of St Crueds Church spire. The weather-vane, shaped into the form of a beautiful, golden cockerel, was being strangled by Arkwrights ropes.

"That bloody fool couldn't earn £10 if someone gave him £9.99 pence! "ARKWRIGHT!!!!!," he boomed, "What are you doing!!!" The timid figure of Alan Arkwright lent over the edge of the basket and with a rather week voice replied,

"Oh hello Mr Mayor sorry. I seem to be rather stuck." "Get it loose you fool!" roared The Mayor. "Sorry. No can do," came the reply. The Mayor was not pleased, and Wilfred Wooly himself was less than enamored. "What are we going to do?" asked The Vicar, "that cockeral was especially commissioned." "Yes Vicar, I know. Now just leave everything to me. Robespierre!!!" he yelled, "leave the car and come here." Robespierre left the car where it was and dashed over to The Mayor. "Go and get the Fire Chief. This is their department", he told him. "Right away Sir," Robespierre panted wheezily, as he turned on his heels and headed for St Crueds Passage.

The Mayor stared up at Arkwright, as the crowd enjoyed the impromptu performance of Crewdleys very own piece of Street Theatre.

Robespierre and the Fire Chief 'Smokey Flint' came trotting like two 'Peelers' out of St Crueds Passage.

"Ah! There you are Chief. You can see the problem. Get him off the Church spire, will you?" asked The Mayor. "No problem!" said the Fire Chief, "I'll have him off in two minutes." "Good!" The Mayor replied, "and don't be too concerned about Arkwright's safety either. Just be careful with the cockerel."

"It's specially commissioned," concurred The Vicar. The Chief drew his axe and dashed towards the Church, The Mayor quietly cursed under his breath and Arkwright waved graciously at his adoring public. The Fire Chief finally emerged on the roof of St Crueds, as the crowd grew restless for action. He began his long, slow and arduous climb up the ladder of the Church spire. "May the Lord protect him," said the Vicar.

"If you mean protect him from Arkwright Vicar, I agree with you. The man's a menace," The Mayor fumed. The Fire Chief was now almost at the top of the Church Tower, and the rope from "The Spirit of Crewdley" was within his reach. The crowd gasped as he swung the axe at the rope and the balloon seemed to flutter like a huge butterfly. The axe was wielded again and again as Arkwright shouted encouragement and the Fire Chief hung to the ladder for grim death. "The Spirit of Crewdley," shuddered and fluttered again, until at last, the rope was severed and it ascended quickly up into the air. The crowd began to cheer, which Arkwright took to be a sign of gratitude for his own salvation, but it was the Fire Chief who received the praise of his back-slapping fellow citizens on his return to earth.

"Good work Flint," The Mayor shouted loudly to be heard above the noise from the crowd.

"Thanks! said Flint, "now if you don't mind Mr Mayor, I'm going for a pint at The Star and Garter. It was bad enough being a hundred feet up that tower without having to pose for photographs for that idiot!"

Smokey Flint headed for the pub and the hot-air balloon headed West towards the Sun, though Presbyterian considered it too much to hope for, that

Arkwright might be blown out into the Atlantic Ocean or further. The whole issue had somewhat marred the extreme state of pleasure and ecstasy that he had enjoyed with Pippa Monroe, just a short time before. And so, The Mayor retired to the quietness of his Parlour and was joined some time afterwards by Robespierre.

"I have a message from Councillor Arkwright Mr Mayor, " he said rather breathlessly. "What do you mean to tell me , he's still in the land of the living?" The Mayor remarked.

"Yes Sir! He came to rest in the Municipal Gardens and wanted you to know that he fully expects at least three pictures to be good enough to actually receive money for, including one of the Fire Chief."

The Mayor said nothing, but instead walked to the window and looked down into Church Street.

"Next Saturday Robespierre , just you make certain that the idiot is kept well away from The Vicarage." In the meantime, make yourself busy. There's still a week to go. Try and sell some more tickets."

Robespierre padded dejectedly back down the old wooden staircase. He could sense The Mayors eyes burning him on his back as he went into the street. He stood on the pavement, eyeing up would-be purchasers of The Mayor's Charity tickets, as The Mayor himself picked up the hot-line between The Mayor's Parlour and Bettingers The Bookmakers.

"Hello Ronnie. Two hundred pounds to win on "Caspian Beauty" in the four o' clock at Worcester. I'll send Robespierre round for my winnings Ronnie. It can't lose!"

The Mayor of Crewdley was many things, but gambling was not really his most successful indulgence.

"Caspian Beauty" came a very poor last, but by one of those pieces of luck, that even the most hardened and persistently bad gambler needs from time to time, two hundred pounds was put into his hand within the hour, by a rather fed-up Robespierre who had managed to sell two Charity tickets to two American tourists who firmly believed that the money was to help The Mayor of Crewdley get over an individual financial problem, hence he needed a Charity. In a way of course, they were right, but it wasn't that The Mayor was impoverished, destitute and in dire need; merely that he was a cheat, a fraudster and the most greedy person in town. However, the official activities of Crewdley Council during that next week, could properly have been described as 'light', that is to say, apart from the bureauracy pushing paper in its normal way, nothing else actually happened. Decision making (or lack of it) was safely in the hands of Crewdleys First Citizen, who took the opportunity to visit the Race Course twice in the Civic Rolls Royce. Although, on each occasion, he had lost money by gambling unsuccessfully on horses which on reflection, would have been better employed pulling milk-carts, Presbyterian enjoyed himself, claiming expenses for meetings which didn't take place and a large hospitality allowance which provided expensive lunches and dinners for him at an out of town Restaurant in the company of Pippa Monroe.

Having pocketed the £6,690 provided by receipts from the Old Town Charity Trust Appeal and delegated arrangements for the Garden Party to The Vicar, Presbyterian gave the event virtually no thought at all until the sun peeped through his window on the actual day. He walked the few yards from 'Civic House' to the Town Hall and went to The Parlour to study the form of horses that would race again at Worcester later in the day.

Ronnie Bettinger, was pleased to pick up 'The Hot-Line' and take his bet. Robespierre commented politely that he had overheard someone mention at The Star and Garter that a Head Stable lad had visited there the previous evening and sang the praises of a horse called "Big Pink Racer".

The Mayor suggested that Robespierre put his own wages on 'Big Pink Racer' and he would leave his money on 'Stolen Fruit'. Some time later Bettinger came through on 'The Hotline' to tell The Mayor that 'Stolen Fruit' had gone lame before the race and if he wished to change his bet, he would be happily accomodated. 'Big Pink Racer' was duly nominated, it duly came in last and Robespierre would have £10 stopped from his wages by Presbyterian, who took real exception to being given such a dubious tip on heresay by his 'Aid de Camp'.

It was two o' Clock when The Mayor left The Parlour for the thirty-yard trip to The Vicarage in the Civic Rolls Royce. As usual, Robespierre was instructed to go past The Vicarage and to drive several times around the town, until the car duly stopped outside the actual venue.

He held open the rear door as The Mayor got out, immaculately dressed as always, in the Civic Cocked Hat, Mayoral Robe, Chain of Office and his fetching White Lace Collar.

"Ladies and Gentlemen!" roared Robespierre, "I give you Mr Harold Presbyterian, Mayor and First Citizen of Crewdley!" One or two people in the street looked rather bewildered as they made their way into the Library, "Thankyou Robespierre', said the 'Great Man',"and once we're inside, stay close to me." The large and imposing front door of The Vicarage was already ajar, and Wilfred Wooly put out his hand to The Mayor.

"Lovely to see you Mr Mayor," he enthused, "we're already well under way, please come through." Presbyterian followed The Vicar into the hall-way and through the house. The Mayor looked anxiously around and seemed uneasy.

"Is everything all right Mr Mayor? You look rather worried,' enquired The Vicar.

"Are you certain that Rupert Beard is well out of harms way?" "Oh yes! I made him go to stay with Lord and Lady Crewdley at The Manor. He went yesterday," answered The Vicar, "and I haven't seen him since." The Mayoral Party moved on and The Vicar smiled broadly. "I expect we shall have him back tomorrow, and he'll soon be tucked up safely in his own little tepee."

The Mayor looked sternly ahead, "Yes I suppose we shall", he replied.

The Garden looked exceptionally nice and under the shade of a weeping willow, Presbyterian caught his first glimpse of his Goddess from The Waters of The Caspian Sea, sipping a cocktail, as was absolutely appropriate. He made a bee-line for her, leaving both The Vicar and Robespierre in his wake.

"You look absolutely gorgeous!" he declared. There was no point in her pretending that she either hadn't heard the eager politician or that he was guilty of mistaken identity. "Oh hello Pressy darling," she purred with a warm charm which left The Mayor quite weak at the knees. "Lets go into the potting-shed", he growled. Pippa Monroe looked cautiously between the green boughs," There isn't one my love. Have a drink instead," she purred, offering him a small glass of something resembling fruit salad, which was in fact, The Vicar's very own interpretation of a 'Summer Punch'. The lawns of The Vicarage had rarely been decorated with so many fine men and women, dressed as they were in greys, blues, whites, yellow, red, orange and purple.

"My God Pippa, it's like a film set here. Can't we go somewhere quiet?", Presbyterian urged her. The temptress melted away between the tables with their starched, white sheets touching the green grass with their edges. She picked up a small sausage roll and popped it into her mouth as The Mayor felt a passion in the very essence of his soul which would not be subdued by The Vicars punch.

Several of the Crewdley Councillors were already performing their rituals of hand-shakes, toasts, and forced pleasantaries with each other and anyone else within sight.

Octavia Bland was seated in the shade of The Vicarage and was watching a butterfly on a tablecloth with such an intense stillness, that Presbyterian wondered if she had died.

Apparently, this was a view shared by Edwin Grimley, the Funeral Service Proprietor who appeared to be giving her the once-over. Councillor Barry Blondel was busily talking to any woman under sixty who would listen.

Mrs Sylvia Smart seemed to be giving a lecture on economics.

The Estate Agent could be seen, and heard, touting for business, but the market was currently pretty flat and she seemed depressed.

The good Doctor Jonathen Scargreaves was trying his best to convince 'Smokey Flint' to give up smoking and was singularly unsuccessful.

Doolittle and Dash, Solicitors to the Council, were smiling graciously as Mrs Wooly offered them sandwiches. All seemed well, but Presbyterian still had to deal with the question of the absence of the Royal Visitor.

He would wait until Lord and Lady Crewdley arrived and then let everyone down as easily as possible. Robespierre seemed to be enjoying himself, and so The Mayor made him stand on his own, under a tree without a drink. Presbyterian was watching Pippa Monroe who was in light conversation with The Vicar's wife, when The Vicar called out as if struck by lightening. "Aaahhh! Lord and Lady Crewdley! What a pleasure," he shrieked.

It was the opportunity that The Mayor had been waiting for, and as telepathic as ever, Robespierre took two steps forward nearer to the Municipal Machiavelli, from under the boughs of the tree.

Presbyterian walked to where he considered was the centre of the lawn, inhaled deeply and with each hand grabbing a Mayoral collar, began his address.

"My dear friends and colleagues! I wish to say a few words as we enjoy this marvellous hospitality on this pleasant afternoon. First of all, I know that you will wish me to extend our thanks to our hosts, the Reverend and Mrs Wooly for their magnificent Garden Party?" There was polite clapping, during which time one or two sandwiches and several sausage rolls fell to the ground, as participants tried to clap with one free hand being used against the other, which held the food plate. The Mayor was sure he could detect something of a heat-haze rising gently from the gathering, a heat-haze which contained a strong vapour of alcohol.

Obviously, some of them had been drinking since mid-day or before, a factor which suited Presbyterian, who would now endeavour to manipulate the apparent collective feeling of warmth and goodwill.

"As we eat, drink and make merry," he continued,"let us, the 'Favoured few', remember for whose benefit it is that this Garden Party is actually taking place." He snatched a glass from the nearest table and held it aloft.

"The poor of Crewdley salute you!" he shouted, "and the occupants of The Alms Houses asked me to toast your health .... Cheers!"

There was the sloshing of drink and cries of "Here, Here! ....

Thank you Mr Mayor!" and of course, more sandwiches dumped on the grass.

"I have one announcement to make. Because of an Emergency Meeting of the Privy Council, which incidentally I am assured is in absolutely the strictest confidence, our 'Royal Visitor' is unable to be with us this afternoon."

"Oh dear! What a shame!" came the reply. "However, I have been asked by our absent Royal Guest, to tell you that on this occasion, she wished especially to be represented by our very own, Lord and Lady of Crewdley!" There was more clapping and The Crewdleys performed a gracious bow and courtsey respectively for the gathering.

"And so!", continued The Mayor, "You who are at the heart of the political, economic.. (and now he gazed deeply at Pippa Monroe) and Educational life in Crewdley please enjoy the festivities."

There was a spontaneous cheer, followed by the rather loud and extremely rustic sounds of drinks being consumed, as The Mayor retired beneath the weeping-willow to the luscious presence of Mrs Monroe.

"I'm bored by all of this nonsense," he murmered,"wouldn't you like to come for a ride in the Rolls? We could go to the forest and pick mushrooms?"

"No well not yet anyway Pressy. I'm enjoying myself, she answered.

The eating, drinking and laughing continued, and the alcoholic heat-haze rose more densely from the lawn.

Councillor Barry Blondel and an attractive young woman from the Estate Agents were sitting astride the Ducking- Stool, much to the consternation of The Vicar, and some how or other, a group of revellers had managed to put Bernard Beard into the Stocks.

Seamus MacGurk arrived pushing a large trolley filled with crates of alcohol, a sight that was greeted with whoops of delight by everyone except Councillor Mrs Octavia Bland, who was still asleep .

MacGurk distributed the fresh supply of drinks and even The Vicar replemished his glass. On the periphery of the exotic scrummage, Harold Presbyterian was about to steal a kiss from his "Lady of The Deep." Suddenly, the bizarrely-dressed figure of a strange man appeared on top of the wall, after apparently having climbed it from the Municipal Park and Gardens side.

"Stop! " he yelled. The crowd immediately fell silent, for the man was dressed as an Apache Indian, with beads , buckskins and brightly painted face . Even these embellishments may not, in themselves, have been sufficient to have gained the revellers attention as instantly as occured . Yet, not only had the evicted squater returned to claim his rightful home, Rubert Beard was armed with a bow and arrow which he aimed at everyone and anyone.

"Get down off t ' wall yuh fool ! " shouted MacGurk. "White man kick Indian Brave off Reservation. Ancesters say The White Man must go back across The Big River and let Indian hunt the Buffalo and live with squaw and papoose in tepee ! " Octavia Bland awoke with a start and where a butterfly had nestled on a starched, white table-cloth, her eyes now focused on a fullblooded, vigorous and hostile Red Indian.

"Aaaaaaaahhhhhhh! " she screamed, "take him away. " The Vicar took a step forward. "Oh my God Mr Beard ! Please come down, " he called . The

Apache pulled back the string of his bow and adopted the statuesque pose of a Bohemian archer. "The Pale Face must leave Indian Reservation or Apache Warrior take many scalps !" roared the Mighty Brave. "I can explain everything," shouted The Reverend Wilfred Wooly, "it's my fault ! I told him to go ...... just for today . "

"He's never been the same since he received the final demand for his Poll Tax," added Mrs Wooly, rather sympathetically.

As the strain of the moment began to bite, a shadow fell across one corner of the lawn, then even the gloss-white of the starched table cloths seemed to turn grey before the Garden Party was cast into almost total darkness. The alcoholic heat-haze rose to meet the rapidly descending "Spirit of Crewdley" as it touched down on the hallowed turf, in a confusion of wicker-basket, and huge mass of nylon envelope. Rupert Beard fired his arrow into the hot-air balloon which gave out an awesome hiss of gas and caused the political, economic and even educational, cream of Crewdley to scatter. The Indian Chief disappeared back over the wall and was immediately followed by many of the younger participants. The Mayor and Pippa Monroe made a hasty exit, as Councillor Alan Arkwright began to haul-in the canopy of his grounded vessel. Robespierre was already at the wheel of the Rolls Royce as the First Citizen and his Mistress flopped into the soft, leather rear seat and drew the blinds of the windows. "To the Forest Robespierre," yelled The Mayor, "we're going to pick some mushrooms!"

CHAPTER FIVE

An Outbreak of Paganism at Halloween.

The Summer of 1990 had been particularly pleasant in Crewdley, but the long, hot sunny days were giving way to the prospect of a rather beautiful Autumn.

With the exception of a very brief and uncontroversial Council Meeting at the end of September, The Mayors political activities had been minimal. He had however enjoyed several pleasurable functions and Civic Engagements, including a Banquet at Crewdley Manor, a party on board "The Trow of St Crued", with a subsequent trip down the River, and a Mayoral Reception for the leading citizens of Crewdley: not much to tax the sharpest politician in the region, but Presbyterian had learned the valuable lesson of seeming to be 'Off duty' and approachable (though hardly affable) when in fact every move and sentence was being noted and filed away inside the personal dossier that constituted his permanent Insurance policy against any attemped coup.

And so it was, that during the golden days of October with its Seasonal mist and occasional light frost, the children of Crewdley began to prepare for the festivities of Halloween and Bonfire Night.

The local shops began selling 'rubber bats' (of the non-cricket kind), plastic spiders, tall witches hats and various masks that resembled particularly gruesome examples of horror-movie characters. One week (and many sales) had past before the same shops supplemented their Sections devoted to "Trick or Treat at Halloween", with a vast array of Fireworks, Sparklers, Rockets, Catherine Wheels and concoctions of gunpowder in multi-coloured packages of cardboard and paper that made the 'Guy Fawkes' collection seem tame by comparison.

The first broken boxes and pieces of wood were placed in the middle of The Municipal Park by eager participants in the yearly ritual of 5th November, who would take great delight in seeing 'Guy Fawkes' perish in The Bonfire lit by The Mayor.

From the rear window of The Town Hall, Presbyterian watched the daily procession of children placing their offerings of branches and wood onto the growing pyramid.

Like everyone else, Presbyterian had been pestered by vigorous exponents of 'Trick or Treat' throughout the last week of October, and was rapidly losing patience, particularly as three children of around twelve years of age (though it had been difficult to judge, given the repulsiveness of their masks) had got to the very last stair leading to The Mayors Parlour, before they were stopped and sent on their way by Robespierre.It was on Monday 22nd October, that events took a real turn for the worse. In the gathering gloom of a cloudy and moonless early evening, the Councillors were assembling in the Town Hall for a meeting, and The Mayor was about to bring down the ancient wooden hammer on the table, when one of the strangest events in the history of Crewdley took place.

"Good evening!" he called loudly, yet before even the lackey Bernard Beard could issue a subservient reply, there came into the Chamber, something or someone who caused the whole assembly to stand in open-mouthed silence. A huge noise filled their ears, as a physical being, hardly human, came thundering in on cloven-hooves, in the form of a creature on hind legs, with tail and fur, bellowing like a moose, antlers aloft and clipping the chandelier-lighting, nostrils fuming and eyes so wild that Octavia Bland yelled in horror.

"Uuuuuuuuuuuuuuummmmmmm!!!!" roared the Stag.
"Aaaaaaaaaaaaahhhhhhhhhh!"yelled Councillor Octavia Bland.

"Crewdley is a Pagan Place and I have come to reign!" the Stag bellowed. "Oh my God!" the Councillors called out, as the beast ran swiftly to the top table, grabbed 'The Mace' bellowed again at The Mayor and dashed out into Church Street, leaving The Council Chamber in total chaos, with several Councillors in various stages of unconsciousness and disbelief.

"What's that! What's that!" Councillor Muggeridge shouted, as he held firmly onto the arm of Councillor Mrs Evans-Jenkins. "Good Lord! What's going on?" said Hardie," who was that?"

"Robespierre .... get after him!", The Mayor shouted, "don't let him get away!"

The surprise had been so great, and the event so disruptive to the normal psychological processes of everyone, that not only did Robespierre leave The Council Chamber, but so did everyone else.

"Stop! Stop!", they yelled as they paraded into Church Street, looking in vain to the Church and the Bridge for the Medieval Incarnation of ways long past. But it was too late. The 'Spirit' in Animal form had disappeared into the black, swirling mist of the night, yet a faint and distant roar suggested that the ancient Forest of Crewdley had swallowed the evidence of 'The Beast', witnessed as it had been, with their own eyes just a few short moments before. The mist and fog from the River seemed to thicken even as they stood in the street, bewildered and defeated by the powerful, stark image of Hell on a Cloven Hoof.

"He's gone!' said The Mayor, "Everybody back inside!" His words were like a siren through the watery environ; the bewildered remnants of Crewdleys thin grey line ambled back towards The Council Chamber, where they found Octavia Bland in a state of complete shock. Robespierre was ordered to retrieve a bottle of whiskey from The Mayor's Parlour (a magnanimously generous act on behalf of The Mayor) and the good lady was finally revived sufficiently enough to continue where she had left off.

"Aaaaaaaaarrrrrrgggghhhh!" she yelled, "it was horrible!", a sentiment echoed by everyone present.

"It was an outrageous act of terror inflicted by.... "The Mayor's words trailed off, as he realized that the culprit was, as yet, unknown. But he and some of the others certainly considered someone they all knew to be the most likely culprit.

"Robespierre go into the Park and then climb over The Vicarage wall".

Robespierre sprang to attention.

"Yes Sir!" His normally sanguine expression turned to blank.

"Why Sir?" he asked. "Because I want you to look inside that bloody tepee. See if our demented friend Rupert Beard is in situ or parading around the garden dressed as the Stag at Bay".

"Yes Sir! Right away Sir!" Robespierre dashed from the Council Chamber with all eyes upon him. "I'm not having this!" said Councillor Hardie, "I'm not having Paganism in here, or outside for that matter either." "Here here," echoed Councillor Muggeridge, still hanging on to the arm of Councillor Evans-Jenkins.

"I think you can safely say Councillor Hardie, that that is a view shared by us all," replied The Mayor, turning around to address the gathering. It was then that he realized that The Pagan Stag had stolen The Mace.

"He's got The Mace! Robespierre he's got 'The Mace!'"he called. "Well that's it," Hardie said dejectedly, "we can't have a Council Meeting without The Mace." "What are we going to do? There's a maniac on the loose and he's got The Mace..... Oh God!" shrieked Councillor Mrs Smart.

Presbyterian didn't like it.... he didn't like it one little bit. The Stag was a challenge to his authority, he would have to be caught.

"The meeting is adjourned", said The Mayor, "if anyone wishes to wait until Robespierre returns, I'm sure the Town Clerk will arrange some refreshments." "Yes Sir," replied Bernard Beard, already feeling totally guilty in the assumed knowledge that his brother Rupert was indeed the source of their woe.

He left the Chamber to return a few moments later with a tray of glasses and two bottles of alcohol. The Councillors were imbibing to the limit when a breathless Robespierre burst in.

"He's there Sir, Mr Mayor, in his tepee he's there!", he panted.

"He's what! " The Mayor boomed, fully expecting a totally different and condemnatory answer which would have settled the issue at a stroke.

"He's sitting in his tepee reading a book Mr Mayor." The Mayor was not amused. "Then who the bloody hell was that?" The Meeting was duly called off, and the assembly left The Chamber leaving only The Mayor and Robespierre to contemplate the shocking event.

"Pour me another," said The Mayor. Robespierre poured the drink and gave it to him and then looked longingly on as he downed it in one. "Well go on, have one yourself," he chided, "and I'll have another."

The drinking persisted until the image of The Pagan Stag mellowed just a little. They retired to The Parlour and continued with a variety of malt whiskies, best brandy and finally, well after midnight, sank several glasses each of Russian Vodka. The first light of day peeped through the windows of The Mayor's Parlour and Robespierre walked through into the ante-room to make tea. He re-entered to see The Mayor still fast asleep on his chaise-lounge.

"Monsieur Maire..... oops.... pardonne..... Good morning Mister Mayor," said Robespierre, "your early morning tea, Your Grace."

The Mayor opened half an eye-lid and squinted at his valet.

"Did I hear French?" he asked accusingly. Robespierre hung his head, "I'm sorry Your Eminence." The Mayor sat up, "Robespierre you're beginning to sound like an advert for one of those awful hotels that takes great pleasure in waking you up to tell you your credit card is out of date." He drank the tea quickly. "He's got to be found," he said, getting to his feet, "it's going to require some serious thought." Robespierre smiled, "Yes Sir, serious thought Sir."

"Let's just consider the facts," The Mayor went on, "we, The Council that is, assembled last night for our October meeting."

Words failed him, for once, "What am I talking about? We all know what happened. But if it wasn't Rupert Beard, who was it?"

Robespierre looked glum and offered no answer, as The Mayor continued, "It doesn't make sense. I know the children like Halloween and of course, the Shopkeepers make a lot of money selling bloody awful masks, but this is different." Robespierre allowed himself a half-grin. "Perhaps it was a joke?" he said with some trepidation.

"Hhmmmmphh!" snorted The Mayor," of course it wasn't a joke. Paganism is a very sore point with Crewdley people. It was slightly before the time, even of your illustrious ancester from the fields of Waterloo, but believe it or not Robespierre, some people even today, continue to tell the tale of The Godless Western Side of the River Crewd being a place of refuge for outlaws and refugees from Religious persecution."

Robespierre adopted his pall-bearers expression, as The Mayor breathed in deeply before continuing his explanation.

"So you see, whoever that was last night, has raised a terrible spectre. Good God we don't want Paganism re-emerging in Crewdley, even on the Western bank."

He got up and walked to the window, as Robespierre stood to attention "Come along Robespierre, we've got work to do," he said, leading the way to the old wooden staircase and down into the foyer of The Town Hall. The Town Clerk, Bernard Beard, was in deep contemplation and staring hard at the outside wall near to the main gate-way.

"Oh Mr Mayor, just look!" he moaned, "isn't it awful?" The reason for his depression was immediately obvious. Daubed on the wall, in red letters two feet high, was the word PAGANS. "Damn it!" cursed The Mayor. "Oh here, here," echoed Beard.

The Mayor turned and looked Robespierre in the eye, "Go and get Flint and tell him to bring paint-remover." "Yes Sir!" replied Robespierre, already turning on his heels and heading for the Fire Station. The Town Clerk took out his handkerchief and began to dab pathetically at the offending word.

"Don't be so bloody silly Beard. It's dry..... havn't you any work to do?" The Mayor said in his most cutting style.

Beard looked timorously at his wrist-watch, "Well it is rather early actually Sir," he stammered.

"Don't be impertinent! Go to your work!" demanded Crewdleys Chief Citizen. Beard slunk away to his office like an animal that had returned to its lair to find another had moved in with its mate, and yet was far too timid to retaliate and turn on the intruder.

Robespierre returned with Flint the Fire Chief, who immediateiy got to work on removing the paint from the wall of the Town Hall.

"Well done Flint," The Mayor said as the Fire Chief worked with various sprays, cleaners, cloths and buckets of water. The Mayor was about to go inside, when a man driving a milk-float, pulled up alongside the pavement and leaned out to speak.

"Mornin' Mayor......I left yuh' milk."

"Yes I know,' replied The Mayor still walking towards the foyer.

"Who was that then I saw running around here this mornin?" asked the milk-man, "was it someone who's going to be in the Carnival?"

"What are you talking about? The Carnival is held during the summer," The Mayor answered.

"Oh well, there was someone running around here by these gates, dressed as a deer..... it might have been a stag, I don't know, but it certainly had antlers

52

and a long tail..... I thought it was one of your fund-raising people .....I had to laugh, the cheeky devil took a pint of milk from my float."

"Only one pint? You surprise me," said The Mayor," didn't you see him painting the Town Hall wall?"

"No Sir, I didn't," replied the milk-man," but now that yuh mention it, he had got a paint-pot hanging from his antlers, but I never looked at the wall. Ah well, nice to have had a chat with you Mr Mayor, but I'll carry on with my milk round now if you don't mind. Got to keep the customers satisfied hey! You don't think the Stag was a rival salesman from another Dairy? They're always trying new gimmicks to pinch our customers."

With that , he set off towards Crewdley Bridge to complete his mornings work, pleased at having had his little chat with Mayor Presbyterian, yet rather confused about the subject matter of their discussion. "You'll be on guard tonight Robespierre," The Mayor indicated to his faithful servant.

"I assumed that I would be Your Worship," he answered, " and will Your Eminence be calling in the Police?" "No I shan't! The last thing that I want, is Superintendent Bramley and his merry band of flat-feet banging about all over the place. No ....it's down to you Robespierre, and you had better grab him."

He searched in his pocket and took out a whistle, "Here!" he said, giving it to Robespierre, "when you catch him, hang on to his antlers and blow this. I shan't be far away and when I hear it I'll ring for Bramley ....understand?"

Robespierre seemed less than enamoured, "Yes Sir" he said in a reluctant tone which properly summed up his mood, "thankyou for the whistle Mr Mayor."

Presbyterian spent the rest of the day telephoning various Councillors and prominent citizens in an effort to discover the identity of The Pagan Stag. None of them had any inclination as to the name of the culprit and no one had noticed particularly strange behaviour in members of their families, their friends or colleagues at work. Robespierre had been sent off to frequent the usual haunts of potential information in times even vaguely like the present one. MacGurks Pub proved fruitless, although Robespierre took full advantage of obtaining as much courage as he could from the various bottles and barrels of "The Star and Garter." The Library had only one customer during the hour and a half that The Mayor's representative spent there, the offices of The Weekly Weaver were closed for essential repairs to be carried out and, as usual, the Museum had a small cross-section of students, visiting American tourists and the nephews of Eric and Elsie Finney who seemed intent on smoking themselves to death away from the sharp eyes of the Fish and Chip Shop proprietors. The day drew on, and an ominous mist engulfed the Town Hall. At 4.30pm a weary Robespierre returned to The Mayor's Parlour and gave his report.

"Nothing Your Worship, I'm very sorry," he apologized, "absolutely nothing at all to report," "Mmmm, by the smell of your breath, Robespierre, most of your time was spent in the "Star and Garter."

Robespierre didn't deny the charge and dropped his head submissively to his Master. "Now listen," said The Mayor, "have you still got that whistle?"

"Yes Sir! it's right here Sir!" replied the faithful valet. "Good! It'll be dark soon with this mist over the town, so here's what I want you to do."

Robespierre stood to attention and held his head up straight, as The Great Man instructed him for his nights work. "You may or may not have noticed, but I've had one of those large, yellow grit-boxes placed directly outside the Town Hall?" "Yes Sir, I did Sir," answered Robespierre.

"Good, nice to know you're being observant', The Mayor added,"however, what you don't know Robespierre, is that I've had the grit taken out of the box, and two small holes drilled into the lid." He paused and Robespierre sniffed.

"That yellow box marked "Grit", is therefore now empty and large enough for someone to get inside, and prepare for a long,and hopefully uneventful, night Robespierre." He looked the poor man in the eye and smiled, "make absolutely sure of two things," he said, "firstly, make sure the eye-holes are permanently occupied by your own very open eyes." "Yes Sir Mr Mayor." "And secondly, don't lose that bloody whistle!"

"No Sir Mr Mayor."

"Right! Then why are you hanging around here when there is a job to be done?"

Robespierre left the room and shuffled away down the stairs. It would indeed be a very long night.

The Mayor retired onto the chaise-lounge and, un-noticed by the citizens of Crewdley, Robespierre retired to the plastic yellow grit-box.

It was in the wee, small hours when Robespierre heard a mysterious shuffling outside his plastic cocoon. Unfortunately, as he knew it would certainly be, it was far too dark to see who it was, though he squinted and peered through the eye-holes of the lid for all he was worth.

The shuffling grew louder and Robespierre's heart was beating like a drum as he fumbled for the whistle.

A cold panic swept over him as a shadowy figure kicked the box with a thud and lifted the lid.

Robespierre froze like a rabbit in the headlights of a car and prepared for certain death inflicted by The Pagan Stag.

The Town Drunk relieved himself over the petrified figure of Robespierre for what seemed like an eternity, before he slammed down the lid and shuffled off home. The frozen, wet valet found the whistle and, still in the dark and with the lid closed, blew it as hard as he could.

"Ppprrrrsssshhhh! Ppprrrrssshhh!", but the pea was rotating in a watery wet whistle that was useless for the purpose and tasted of salt and best bitter.

Robespierre sprang up like a Jack in the Box, sending the lid flying backwards with a bump.

"Monsieur Maire!!!", he bawled. "Heeeelllp!" The Mayor slept on, as Robespierre crawled out of the Grit-Box and staggered through the gates of the Town Hall Foyer, in a painful, bent stooping position.

"Monsieur Maire! Vite Monsieur!" The Mayor finally heard the rantings of his aide-de-camp. He went to the top of the old wooden staircase and shone a torch onto the bedraggled and wet source of the noise.

"Monsieur Maire!"

"English!" The Mayor demanded.

"I was in the box Monsieur," he stammered, "Oh pardonne, Oh sorry Sir, I was in the box......."

"I know you were in the bloody box Robespierre. What happened?"

"The Public Toilets are closed Sir. Someone relieved themselves... in the box..... I'm soaking wet."

"Where's your whistle man?" The Mayor shouted.

Robespierre put the whistle to his lips and blew. The pathetic, wet, gush of air caused a minor vibration between mushy pea and metal, a noise which hardly carried the length of the staircase, to the expectant ear of The Mayor. "I don't know. I give you a nice simple job to do, and what happens?" The Mayor shone the torch at his watch. "My God! It's three o' clock," he said walking down the stairs, "Who was it?"

"I think it was just a drunk Sir," replied Robespierre, "what are we going to do?" "You'd better have a shower, you smell like a cess-pit. I'll keep an eye on the street from my window," Presbyterian answered. The rest of the night proved uneventful and by the time the milkman had stopped his float outside the Town Hall shortly after seven am, The Mayor fell asleep in The Parlour. He was woken later by the Town Clerk knocking at his door. On principle, Presbyterian would not let him in. "Mr Mayor! It's me, Bernard Beard!" he called out nervously.

"Wait in your office Beard I'll be with you shortly," the First Citizen chided him. Presbyterian washed his face at the sink, then went downstairs into the Town Clerks office.

"Well?" he enquired, "what do you want?" The Town Clerk adopted his usual glum expression, "I'm afraid there has been some more trouble in the night Sir," he confessed, "the childrens bonfire was set alight." "Huh!", The Mayor snorted,"is that all? It was probably some kid playing with matches." Beard remained uneasy, "Well, I suppose it could have been Mr Mayor, but someone has daubed paint on the Civic Motor car."

The Mayor exhaled loudly, "Don't tell me! Let me guess. The word, 'Pagan' comes to mind." "Unfortunately, yes Sir." said Beard, "I've already taken the liberty of instructing one of our men to remove it. Whoever did it, must have got over the wall of the car park Sir." The Mayor seemed singularly unimpressed by the man's logic. "Yes, unless the 'Pagan Ghost' can walk through walls, but somehow I don't think so."

The Town Clerk shifted from one foot to the other and seemed hesitant to speak, but he finally plucked up sufficient courage and said quickly. "I also telephoned Superindendent Bramley."

"You did what!" barked The Mayor. "I telephoned the Police Superindendent," he stammered, "to get back The Mace, Mr Mayor. They're going to search Crewdley from top to bottom, 'No stone will be left unturned,' Mr Bramley said." Beard knew he'd over stepped the mark.

"That was an executive decision Beard," said The Mayor coldly,

"You don't take executive decisions Beard I do!"

"Sorry Mr Mayor .... I panicked. It's just that The Mace is so precious to the Town. I remember as a little boy, being told by Grandfather Beard how he would sometimes clean The Mace with a special mixture of olive oil and bees-wax to give it a particularly splendid shine and he always said...."

The Mayor leant over Beards desk and looked him in the eye.

"Beard! Shut up and get on with your work!" he snapped, and left the office as quickly as he had entered it, to return to The Parlour.

He stood for a considerable time looking out of the window into Church Street and at the people of Crewdley going about their daily business. Two policemen were going into and out of various shops and offices, no doubt in search of The Mace.

"Stupid idiots," mumbled The Mayor, "they're about as subtle as a sledge-hammer." Some time after that, he was joined by Robespierre, who had donned a fresh, black suit and white shirt.

"You smell a little better," The Mayor reassured him, "I hope you've got the whistle Robespierre, I'm still depending on you to catch him. Look at those imbeciles out there!" Robespierre glanced through the window at the police, who were busily questioning everyone who went within ten yards of where they stood.

"Crime fighters! Look at them! Completely inept! They couldn't catch a cold! Why we pay them good wages I'll never know." The Mayor was by now in a wretched mood. "Who the Hell would want to dress up as a bloody Stag and frighten everybody half to death?" he cursed, "What sort of society are we living in?" The hours dragged on without a positive word from the police or anyone else. Darkness again came early at around 5.30pm and one or two fireworks were already being set off by the children of Crewdley.

"I'll have dinner in here," Presbyterian said to Robespierre, "on a tray. Put the chair near to the window. I want to carry on looking." The Mayor ate his meal in the dark with the tray balanced precariously on his knees, as he stared down into the street. The children were running around with sparklers and others cruised along the pavements on skateboards, wearing grotesque masks in preparation for 'Trick or Treat.'

It was after eight o' clock when The Mayor broke his silence. "Something tells me, that the answer to our little problem will be found in the vicinity of the Municipal Park and Gardens."

"Really?" said Robespierre, "thank goodness, Mr Mayor." "So what I want you to do, is to stay in there tonight. Take the torch and your whistle and get into the shrubbery. I'll keep watch from here."

Robespierre groaned, " Oh dear! I was hoping for a good nights sleep your Worship."

"Don't you dare complain ! None of us can sleep with that maniac on the loose!" The Mayor shouted, "You've had it too easy lately Robespierre, that's your trouble. Now go to it!"

The hapless valet retired to his quarters and reluctantly changed into old, warm clothes then made his way to The Municipal Park and Gardens. It wasn't particularly cold, but the last thing Robespierre wanted to do, was spend the night inside a rhodedendron bush. But duty called, and he slowly walked into the shadows and sat beneath the ever-green boughs, pulling his coat tightly to his body and sinking his neck down into the collar. He felt like a hibernating hedgehog, yet, given he had no option but to stay there until dawn, his only wish was that the town drunk did not discover him.

Meanwhile, The Mayor took another long drink of beer from his pewter mug and enjoyed a long, lingering vision of Pippa Monroe being pampered in her bath by hand-maidens dressed in their kimonos and splashing fragrant perfumed scents of rose and heather onto their fruitful,bountious mistress. It was too much, even for him. "Damn it!" he fumed, "I've got to see her!"

And so it was, that Harold Presbyterian made his way towards 'Caspian House' as the clock struck midnight. As usual, some of the street lights were out and Presbyterian cursed when he caught his toe in a loose paving-stone. He stumbled on, filled with passion and fire, and even broke into a gentle trot. It was as he was crossing the road, that he noticed a set of antlers appear over the shadowy sky-line of Crewdley Bridge.

"Oooooohhhhhhhh!" bawled The Creature, galloping down the street. "Good God!" bawled The Mayor, as he turned to gallop after it. "Pagans! Pagans! Pagans!" shouted The Stag as he ran.

"Robespierre! Robespierre! Robespierre!" gasped the Mayor in hot pursuit. They galloped past The Town Hall and around St Crueds Church, The Mayor being unable to gain a single yard on the fleet footed beast. They turned left into Dark Street at a steady pace. All thoughts of Pippa Monroe were erased from The Mayors mind as he stuck to his task and watched the mighty antlers swaying backwards and forwards as The Pagan Deer showed him a cloven pair of hooves.

The narrow confines of Dark Street seemed filled with the noise of hooves and groans, the swishing of a hairy tail and the panting breath of the hunter and the hunted.

The Stag increased its pace and made a dash towards the fence of The Municipal Park and Gardens. It threw itself onto the fence and scrambled up,but its hind-quarters seemed reluctant to breach the obstacle. Moreover, its antlers seemed to have caught in the over-hanging trees and its tail appeared entwined in the railings. Presbyterian bore down on the Pagan Beast, but as he desperately grabbed at the twisting, turning creature, it lurched to safety over the fence.

The Mayor did his best to scramble up after it but the panic that had spurred The Beast was not there for him. Finally, The Mayor scaled the heights of the fence and dropped down onto the ground.

He was deep inside the shrubbery of the pitch-black Park, and extremely disorientated. He stood still to listen for the noise of the galloping deer, yet it was difficult because he was breathing loudly and hard after his chase.

The sound of a snapping twig made him jump around to face the enemy, but instead of being confronted by The Stag at Bay, a hedgehog burrowed deeper into the leaves at his feet. Yet, other leaves rustled and the sound of branches being disturbed, indicated that there was indeed something moving close by. He moved slowly nearer to the sounds and a shadowy figure suddenly stood up directly in front of him.

"Ooh!"it called. "Gotcha!" said The Mayor as he hurled himself forward into the void and landed heavily on top of something barely human, momentarily causing his flesh to creep when he touched the cold, wet, scrawny figure. "Mon-Dieu!" it yelled, "Je Serendre! Serendre!"

"Robespierre! Bloody typical! Surrender indeed!" puffed The Mayor, "what the hell are you doing here? It went that way!" The two men got to their feet and tried to walk out of the shrubbery. "Come on Robespierre! He's not far away. Get your torch out and hurry up!" They scrambled through the bushes onto the lawns of The Park. "It's pitch black, shine it over there!" The Mayor demanded, already striding purposefully after The Beast.

"Look! Over there!" Presbyterian exclaimed, "Follow me!" He quickened his pace, as the bushes ahead were noisily disturbed. "It's him, come on!"

Robespierre shone the torch onto The Mayor as they moved towards their quarry, "Not on me, on him, you fool!" roared The Great Man.

A strange shape was at last caught in the yellow beam, antlers could be seen with the fullness of a Pagan Stag beneath,frantically trying to out-run his pursuers. The Stag was desperate and crashed through the thicket, as The Mayor and his Valet gained ground.

The Beast lept up a solid brick wall and scrambled over the top, closely followed by The Mayor and Robespierre.

"We're in The Vicarage Garden," said The Mayor, "can you see the Stag?" Robespierre shone the torch around the vaguely familiar garden, finally settling on the primitive structure of poles and canvas that formed the tepee, as the flap to get in moved gently in the night breeze.

"We've got him now follow me!", The Mayor called exitedly as he ran towards the wig-wam and dived into the flap, with Robespierre following on all fours.

"Right! Where are you?" asked The Mayor, "Give me the torch Robespierre." He took the torch and shone it into the middle of the tepee, where a huge pile of blankets appeared to have sprouted a tree.

"Ooooooohhhhhh!" the blankets moaned. "You can cut that out," said The Mayor, "Robespierre! Unmask The Pagan Stag of Crewdley!"

"Ooooohhhh!" it went again. "I hope you're not going to resist Beard," The Mayor shouted loudly, "Robespierre is a Black Belt in Hakimoto."

"Beg pardon Sir?", asked the strictly-braces Valet. "Get on with it man!" urged The Mayor, pulling the blankets from the Beast. Robespierre grabbed at the antlers and Presbyterian pinned the creature around the waist, as all three bodies twisted and turned, grunted and moaned, kicked and yelled, until at last, Robespierre held the decapitated head and antlers of the defeated creature.

"Hold him! I want to see his face!", said The Mayor shining the torch directly at his opponent.

"Aargh!" he whinced, I don't believe it."

"I still can't see Sir!" said Robespierre.

"Good Grief! It can't be!" Presbyterian gasped in horror, "It's it's .....It's The Vicar!!!!!"

"Oooohhhh!" The Vicar groaned, "what have I done? Oh why, Oh why? It's The Pagan Spirit of Halloween you see...... I've always fought against it, but this time it was too strong," he said mournfully un-wrapping his tail from the disgarded antlers, as Presbyterian and Robespierre looked in amazement.

"But you're The Vicar!" The Mayor reminded him, lest he had forgotten, in this, his darkest hour. "I know," blubbed the fallen Guardian of St Crueds Parish Church,

"You just don't understand someone like you ....," he stared hard at the torch, ..."someone as honest and decisive as you Mr Mayor, who never has a moments doubt about which side to back......good or bad, virtue or sin ..."

"Oh, I wouldn't say that Wooly," answered Crewdley's Finest Son," "it's not easy for any of us ......even Robespierre has his moments, don't you Anton?"

"Yes Sir, Mr Mayor, but being so close to you Sir, keeps me on the right track," he cringed.

The Vicar started to sniffle again, "Ohh .....I'm ruined.... a hopeless failure... I'll be cast out of the Church oh dear."

"Who says so!" Presbyterian challenged him, "who says anyone has got to know?" His razer-sharp mind had seen a way forward, advantageous to both The Vicar and himself. "Just you give us back The Mace old boy, and we'll forget all about it."

"B.. b... but..... Mr Mayor", Robespierre stammered, "he's The Pagan Stag!"

"Shut up Robespierre ....speak when you're spoken too," The Mayor chastised him.

"No! He's right, I'm not worthy to be The Vicar of Crewdley. The forces of darkness are too much."

"I'll decide that," Presbyterian said quickly. "But it's like this every year, I always feel the same urge to paint myself in wode and bay to the moon. Bad spirits are everywhere," The Vicar said fearfully.

"Speaking of bad spirits and war-paint, where's Beard?" asked Presbyterian. "I don't know .... I scared him half to death when I came in here."

"He got out from under the canvas", The Vicar replied, "Oh dear, what am I going to do?"

"Well, first of all you'd better get out of that piece of fancy dress, and then I shall require re-possesion of The Mace," The Mayor answered firmly. "Thank God you caught me at it. Heaven knows what I might have done next. Actually even now I feel a compulsion to run into St Crueds Church and chant a Pagan oath that I read as a boy, I really want ...."

"Quickly! Grab him Robespierre, he's going again," Presbyterian shouted, "lets get the deer skin off him!" "Oooohhh!" The Vicar moaned, "Darkest night when ghosts do walk, wing of bat when spiders talk........ "

"Pull his legs out!" The Mayor called desperately, "he's regressing back to Paganism." "Hocus, pocus, slimy toad, hairy human, painted wode," The Vicar chanted seeming'y lost in the nether world of Pagan ritual.

"Quickly! Undress him!", yelled The Mayor, "we've got to keep him in the land of the living." After a slightly surreal struggle, The Vicar was shorn of his Deer skin and left wearing only his cotton combinations and dog collar.

"You're wearing your dog collar!", Presbyterian accused him. "Yes," said Wooly, "it was my only link with all that is decent.. were I to have gone without my Holy Collar, I really believe I would have been lost forever in the nether-world of Paganology."

"Sacre-Bleau!" Robespierre declared, "Mon Dieu!" "English!", said The Mayor, "I don't want you regressing Robespierre. Now! Get up and hold that bloody flap open and we can all go home ... that is when The Mace has been returned, now where is it Wooly?"

"In a pile of leaves by the Ducking Stool," The Vicar answered, "I was going to take it to Crewdley Forest and offer it to the Tree Spirits, but it's a long way and the Deer skin was rather uncomfortable and the hooves used to pinch my feet." He laughed manically as the three figures walked across the lawn towards The Vicarage, "Heh, heh, I suppose that's a strange thing for a Vicar to say really isn't it Mr Mayor? But worst of all was the tail. You wouldn't believe how difficult it is to sit down to dinner with a tail."

"Oh my God! You don't mean to say you wore The Pagan Deer skin in the house? With Mrs Wooly there? My God!" Presbyterian said painfully.

The Vicar giggled again, "Heh heh! No - she's gone to her mother's in Much Hemlock .... I mean Much Wenlock." "Hold him still Robespierre, and I'll get The Mace," The Mayor instructed his nervous Lieutenant, taking the torch from him and walking towards the Ducking Stool. He put his hand into the pile of leaves and pulled out The Mace.

"Got it!" he said, "O.K Robespierre, put him to bed." Robespierre escorted Wilfred Wooly into The Vicarage and up the stairs to his bedroom. Presbyterian watched the light go out and he was quickly re-joined on the lawn by his throughly depressed servant.

"We can either go back the way we came, or spend the night in the tepee," he said. "Why can't we go out through The Vicarage Mr Mayor?" Robespierre asked hesitantly.

"Because when you were putting Wooly to bed, I heard noises from Church Street. It's probably that idiot Policeman Horace Bramley. So what's it to be Robespierre, the wig-wam or the wall?" The Mayor stepped solidly into the small of Robespierre back and pulled himself up over the wall.

"Come on Robespierre get up!" he called shining the torch at his servant who was squatted on all fours in the dirt. "I can't move Your Worship! Go without me! I shall crawl into the tepee." The Mayor stared at him for a moment or two before dropping as silently as he could into the Municipal Park and Gardens. There was some mild excitement in Church Street as two police officers grappled with a very irate Rupert Beard, who was protesting his innocence with vigour.

"Let him go officers, you've done your duty, but it's perfectly all right to return Mr Beard to The Vicarage. He does have a key, so you needn't disturb Mr Wooly." "Yes Sir," replied the officer releasing his hand from Rupert Beard's collar, "and a very good night to you Mr Mayor. Still no sign of The Pagan Stag, I'm afraid Sir."

"No! Well lets hope we've seen the last of him eh? And by the way, please tell Superintendent Bramley that I have found The Mace," The Mayor said boldly, "and tell him someone had left it in a litter-bin in Dark Street and I'm extremely disappointed that it wasn't spotted by the Police." He walked off quickly, and just for a change, went into 'Civic House' to spend the night alone, but wishing with all his being for the company of Mrs Pippa Monroe.

He fell asleep as the clock in St Crueds Church was striking one ... Robespierre heard the same chime then two, later three, and four chimes, as he lay on the damp grass inside the tepee.

"Mon Dieu," he mumbled, "why did my ancestor leave the field at Waterloo?"

And so ended a most strange episode in the history of Crewdley and its people. The next day, Presbyterian restored The Mace to its proper place at the top table of the Council Chamber and on the following Monday, the Council resumed its adjourned Meeting, attended by The Reverend Wilfred Wooly who said a special prayer for all sinners at Halloween.

It was only afterwards, when Members of the Council were having sandwiches and refreshments that The Mayor saw his first sign of absolute guilt expressed in The Vicar's face when he was addressed as 'dear' by Councillor Mrs Octavia Bland. He turned as red as a beetroot until the moment passed and the official party dispersed, leaving only The Mayor and Robespierre to finish the Civic wine.

But The Mayor would never forget Wooly's 'little failure,' and of course, proper account had been made already and placed in the secret safe in his Parlour. It would surely prove to be a most difficult year for The Vicar of Crewdley? Yet Presbyterian had considered how catastrophic a repeat performance might be for The Vicar. He might suggest a Caribbean holiday for Mr and Mrs Wooly..... one outbreak of Paganism at Halloween was quite enough and The Vicar would surely be guided by Crewdley's Most Famous Son, unless he was prepared to be de-frocked, and Wooly was a timid man.

CHAPTER SIX

The Trap

Horace Bramley, the Superintendent of Crewdley Police, was not a particularly intelligent man. True, he was a big man, but not an intelligent man. Some would say he had indeed found his real level at Crewdley, where he had enjoyed his present position for some ten years. He would soon be retired, a prospect he looked forward to every day of his life. The contingent of Crewdley Police was not large; two female typists worked two shifts throughout the week, but not at weekends, two Constables also worked shifts, a Sergeant shared various hours of duty with them and supplemented his time in the police Station, which left Bramley free to flit in and out when he chose. The Station was not manned on Saturday or Sunday, unless Bramley wanted to use the telephone to speak with members of his family in Australia, in which case he would spend an hour or two in the Station drinking and playing games on the National Police Computer. Like most senior Policemen in similiar positions, he was extremely bored and, some would say fortunately, extremely under worked. This supporting pillar of The Crewdley Establishment was living out his time in office, knowing how virtually every day would be, having spent the last ten years engaged in virtually identical pursuits. Civic functions would be attended, local school children talked to twice a year, Church services patronized and regular support given to most of Crewdley's Charities (particularly The Old Town Trust) and of course, old ladies were sometimes helped across the road.

Much of Crewdley's crime, and it had hardly ever been a ripple, let alone a wave, eminated from patrons of the Public Bar of 'The Star and Garter ' who often let drink cloud their judgement. Yes, motorists occasionally ran into one another or stole each others vehicles; yes wives and husbands fell out and threw things at each other; children broke windows, dogs fouled footways, fishermen didn't pay licence-fees, and once in a while, burglaries occured.

There was therefore, sufficient crime to keep the whole thing ticking over, but nothing more. Yet in spite of all this, Superintendent Horace Bramley longed for, "The Big One," that special case which other Police yearned for, which becomes folk-lore in the annals of crime. He wanted the one that would put him apart from other Provincial Police, so that at any Gala ball of County or even perhaps Metropolitan Police, Bramley would need no introduction, because "That Case" had occured in his Crewdley patch. But it didn't happen; month after month, year after year was the same and Bramley would soon be gone from the Force, without a single, memorable case to his name.

The first few years of his time at Crewdley had been taken up ensuring that he had got to know every nook and cranny, every twist and every turn in his patch. Bramley wanted to be able to rely on those people near to him, to be sure of them sufficiently well he need never have a single doubt about his colleagues and the various Civic Dignitaries of Crewdley.

And this was how it had proven to be.... he had those upon whom he could rely and he himself could always be relied upon. And yet..... and yet Horace Bramley harboured a grudge, a rather serious grudge that indicated a malevolent streak and a probable dis-regard for his ultimate welfare. After ten years his grudge, his burning desire for a settling of accounts, could hardly have been called impetuous.

But his desire and need for "The Big Case" had led him down a particularly difficult path filled with possible danger as well as the prospect of glory. Unfortunately, the twin harbingers of danger and disaster did not register on his mind as strongly as the need for glory.

The source of Horace Bramleys discontent was no mere petty pilferer, no benign centre-half guilty only of a slide-tackle off the ball: Bramleys target was a formidable player at the centrestage for whom the professional foul was a neccessary part of his repertoire, and that made his quarry an eminent and worthy target, capable of snatching victory from the very jaws of defeat. The Mayor didn't know it yet, but Horace Bramley was out to get him.

Mention has been made of the fact that Bramley was no Einstein; however he was a Superintendent of Police, and therefore could lay claim to a particular level of consciousness, nouse and perhaps more importantly, a large reserve of animal cunning.

However, the prospect of failure filled him with dread and caused him to have an upset stomach for several days past. But the thrill of the chase..... the danger of the opponent.....   the smell of victory .....these things led him to conclude that he must act decisively and follow the matter through to its conclusion.

Given his safe position in the Police Force and Presbyterian's continued use of dubious, and devious methods, even out and out extortion to keep in power, perhaps the Superintendent had underestimated the fighting abilities and desire for self-preservation of The Mayor from the outset? Not that he would have held back; his destiny called and the thought of his own elevated position in Police history (and even the prospect of an honour) were too much to resist.

"I'll have that bugger!" he told himself, "we'll see how he stands up to a real opponent!" He had, by this time, assembled what he thought would be a case to answer against Crewdleys Finest Son, but had kept it strictly to himself.

For quite a while, Horace Bramley had taken a particular interest in The

Mayor's activities. Instinct told him all was not as it seemed, yet proof was a very different and difficult matter. His interest focused around Presbyterian's Business and Financial Affairs, but the real problem facing Bramley was how to get access to certain papers and documents without blowing his would-be case wide open.

He had approached Robespierre, but found the man to be totally loyal to his boss. After regular bouts of mutual drinking in "The Star and Garter" all that Bramley obtained from treating The Mayor's chauffer to countless drinks, was an extremely large bill. He talked endlessly to Crewdley Councillors, but apart from the two Socialists, Arthur Hardie and Mrs Enid Thomas, who regularly referred to Crewdley's First Citizen as "a shark willing to sell his own Grandmother if the price was right," no one else seemed particularly bothered about the activities of Harold Presbyterian, whether political, sexual or financial. The Business Community took a likewise attitude, but Bramley didn't trust them particularly either, though he did admire one or two of them in spite of that, for making so much money. The Public at large, even voters in particular, seemed reticent even coy, about their Mayor. Perhaps this was because, even after ten years, he was considered still to have been an outsider.

Perhaps it was because he was a policeman or even perhaps because he had B.O. For whatever reason, the Public seemed ill disposed to talk to Harold Bramley, or more particularly, reluctant to tell him what he wanted to hear.

One irksome aspect of his almost private investigation, had been the annoying way in which some working-class people had spoken about Presbyterian in such glowing terms, to the extent that Bramley considered himself to have been in the wrong job, though this feeling soon disappeared when he contemplated the coming pleasure of "nicking" The Mayor and putting him away. His cause was now an obsession, nothing else mattered, even crime in Crewdley, as all of Bramley's efforts were directed against Harold Presbyterian. Colleagues had perhaps noticed a glazing-over of his eyes whenever The Mayor's name was mentioned, but even they had no appreciation of his commitment to bring him down.

Bramley had been floundering on an ice-cold trail for almost the limit of his patience, when at last, he got his first lucky break.

An out of town builder had been drinking rather heavily in the Public Bar of "The Star and Garter," complaining that the Crewdley system of Contract Allocation seemed very peculiar. Bramley bought the man a whisky, then took him into a quiet corner of the lounge, and bought him another.

"So you think you should have won the contract for laying the tarmac in Dark Street?" he asked the increasingly drunk builder for the third time. "I told you," said the man, "I did bloody well win it, and then he took it off me."

Bramley had played this game before, "Oh I see.. a bad loser are you?"

65

"No I'm not. I put in the lowest price £8,888.88 pence .....buuuttt" his speach was by now not the clearest, "buuuttt then he goes and gives it to somebody else."

Bramley winced sharply, "Tcchhh .....that's a serious accusation you're making Mr ...er'mmm- I didn't catch your name?"

"Smith..... Bert Smith , " he answered,"sherious or not,it happened."

"But how do you know it happened?" asked Bramley, leaning forward so as not to miss any evidence that might be offered through the alcoholic-stuper of his only likely source of information.

"Because ," he hesitated and looked over his shoulder,

"I don't know whether I should be tellin' yuh this," he wavered.

"Oh, you don't want to win Council Contracts in the future then, do you?" Bramley baited him.

"Course I do, it's a bloody fix."

"Well then explain," urged Bramley, "but not so loud."

Smith lent closer and nearly fell off the stool.

"The bloke who won it told me his price it was £6,000......"

Bramleys face lit up, "Oh was it now...... and would he swear to it in a court of law?"

The man breathed in deeply, "Dunno, but I'd like a whisky when you're ready."

The policeman duly obliged, but unfortunately for him, it proved to have been the one which put Bert Smith beyond understandable dialogue and Bramley had to let him go. But, at last Bramley had a lead; there was a crack in The Mayors armour and he had found it.

He had a name and a strong accusation, but he needed much more than that, so he telephoned Bert Smith and arranged to see him again, this time, down by the River near Crewdley Bridge.

"O.K Smith I want the name of the other Contractor," he said, almost a l'a Bogart.

"It'll cost yuh," answered Smith, "if you cross The Mayor and don't win - well no one's ever beaten him yet and there's plenty thats tried for good reason."

"I'm different," Bramley replied, "I'm a man with a mission." "Oh bloody hell, you're not religious are yuh?" Smith enquired.

"No I'm not, but I'm going to have him if it's the last thing I do," answered Bramley, "now - who was the other man?"

"What's in it for me? It'll have to be more than Council Contracts,

I can tell yuh ..... I want cash, up front .."

Bramley was desperate, "You'll get this in your ear if you don't talk," he threatened, holding a large, clenched fist menacingly at the smaller man.

"Bloody Hell! I thought this was Crewdley, not Chicago!" he whined"no violence please - it was Tom White." Bramley resumed his normal posture, "Thats better.....just as long as we understand each other. Theres a lot riding on this case."

It was a cold December day and obviously Bert Smith was not enjoying himself. He strongly regretted his loose-talk in "The Star and Garter," but now that Horace Bramley had got his hooks into him, it was too late.

"Here's what I want you to do," Bramley said with just a hint of menace, "when the next Council Contract comes up for tender, let me know." "They're meeting tomorrow, the 5th December," Smith answered, "I put my tender in last week."

"Pity it's so soon," Bramley grumbled, "never mind .... now who else has put a bid in for the work?" "We're not supposed to know,"answered Smith coyly.

"Listen! I shan't ask you again," Bramley said threateningly, "Who are they!"

"Dear, dear," Smith replied, "and I thought our Police were wonderful. O.K, Riverside Road and Pavements Ltd, Crewdley Builders and me."

They continued to walk along the River Bank and Bramley was determined to get a result, so he issued his instruction in a calculating and deliberate tone.

"Here's what you do. First of all, tell me what the job is?" "Repair work to Crewdley Bridge," answered Smith.

"What was your price"? asked Bramley. "£7,000 exactly, that was my price." "And the others"?

"Well, Riverside Road and Pavements put in for £6,900," replied Smith, "but I don't know about Crewdley Builders." "I should bloody well hope not. What sort of a racket have you lot got going anyway"? Bramley challenged him.

"What do yuh mean? It's custom and practice in the trade to know other blokes prices. If we didn't, we'd all go out of business. It's buggin's turn if yuh take my meaning ..... I win one, Tom White wins the next .... The trouble is, bloody Crewdley Builders are winning everything. It aint right Mr Bramley, you've got to get it stopped, " Smith implored him.

A thin smile appeared on Bramleys lips, he was winning, it was going his way, he was almost there. "Now just you listen carefully to me Smith. When you go from here, I want you to go and see Tom White.

Get him to write down his price, then you write yours down on the same paper. Then, post that letter to me at the Police Station, do I make myself clear?"

"Yes Sir," said Smith, "very, but what happens then?" Bramley's smile increased, "You just make sure that you do your part properly - now hop it!"

They parted company and Bramley returned to the Police Station in a more positive frame of mind than he'd been in for years. He would have to work quickly, and had already devised a plan which he was determined to carry through, entirely alone.

The Contracts Committee was to meet at 6pm in the Council Chamber, under the Chairmanship of The Mayor. The public, as was quite right and proper and in full accordance with Local Government rules, would be excluded from attendence at the Meeting, given the confidential nature of the business.

Bramley guessed that apart from the other Committee members, Councillor Barry Blondel and Councillor Mrs Sylvia Smart, only The Town Clerk, Bernard Beard would be present. It was mid-day and Bramley picked up his bugging-device, an expensive Japanese model called 'The Whisper Listener', which consisted soley of a small, plastic case about as large as a matchbox and a monitor receiving apparatus which he would keep with him. This monitor had an inbuilt Recording System and a set of head-phones for what was described in the instruction book as 'Surveillance Personnel', ie, himself.

The 'matchbox' microphone could be attached, 'quote', "beneath a table or even inside a large vase of flowers, giving perfect reception, in the knowledge of comlete certainty that it can be neither seen or heard by uniformed observers or participants, "unquote'.

He put, 'The Whisper-Listener,' into his brief case, and left the Police Station for The Town Hall. The Town Clerk was working in his office and looked up at Bramley as he came under the arch and into The Foyer.

"Good afternoon Superintendent", said Beard, "is everything allright?" "Oh yes Mr Beard, there's no need to worry, I'm merely going to carry out a security check inside the Town Hall. I think that incident concerning The Pagan Stag unnerved a lot of people. Incidentally, we're still looking for the perpetrater of that dastardly deed. I don't suppose you've heard anything at all on the grapevine - you know, idle chatter, the inadvertent naming of probably perfectly innocent individuals, that sort of thing?"

"No no I havn't," replied Beard, "not a thing, it's still a complete mystery. But thank God that The Mace was returned virtually unmarked. Do you know my Grandfather used to clean it with a special mixture of olive-oil and bees-wax?"

"Did he now?" Bramley replied sarcastically, "how very interesting. I must get on Mr Beard - duty calls." "Yes of course Superintendent, please carry on," replied Beard, with his nose already back at his books.

The Superintendent stepped briskly into The Council Chamber, feeling much like Wyatt Earp staking out an ambush for Jesse James, or perhaps it was the other way round, but either way, the adrenalin was flowing and he was high on the buzz of entrapment. He went quickly over to The Mayors top table and felt underneath. He took out the "Big Ears" Transmitter and positioned it at arms length beneath the surface of subtle green leather and the rests in which The Mace was positioned at Council Meetings.

"Don't let me down," he said quietly as he resumed his upright posture. The old photographs of past Mayors of Crewdley looked down at him from the four walls and of course, the largest one in the most ornate frame, was of Harold Presbyterian. Bramley smiled and could imagine the photograph on the wall of his own sitting room, with the words beneath, "Arrested and convicted on the sole initiative of Superintendent Horace Bramley." He left The Council Chamber and returned to The Police Station. Shortly afterwards, he rang Bert Smith at his office.

"Hello, this is Superintendent Bramley. Have you done what I told you to do?" he asked. "Yes," replied Smith, "I've posted it already, just like you said."

"Good," said Bramley, "you can relax now, and leave the rest to me." He put down the receiver and poured himself a drink, and in the privacy of his own office, he took 'The Big Ears' receiver from his case and set it up on the table. He turned it on, and low and behold, distinct voices could be heard from the very bowels of The Council Chamber itself.

Beard could clearly be indentified instructing some Junior Clerk with regard to the filing system, recently augmented by an expensive computer which Beard himself did not understand. The next part of Bramleys Trap required him to go back to The Town Hall with the skeleton- keys he legitimately kept in his possession for Civic emergencies when the Police might have recourse to enter The Town Hall, perhaps to use it as a refuge for towns folk threatened by floods after The Mayor and all of the Council had been swept to their deaths by the raging torrents of the River Crewd, or for the more likely event of Robespierre losing the keys, which until then had certainly never occurred. Bramley knew that Beard would be at lunch, so he picked up a relatively-small Instamatic Police Authority camera and set off for Beards office. Sure enough, there was no sign of The Town Clerk. Bramley let himself in with the skeleton key and went straight to the desk, where three large brown envelopes had been left near to the telephone. He took out an especially-sharp and thin-bladed knife, slit the envelopes open, and photographed the contents one at a time.

Each letter was headed with The Crewdley Council motif, and were the particular bids of Riverside Roads and Pavements Ltd, Bert Smith Master Builders Ltd, and Crewdley Builders Ltd. As Smith had told him, his price-bid for the work was exactly £7,000, and Riverside Road and Pavements £6,900.

Bramley smiled when he looked closely at the bid from Crewdley Builders. "The crafty sods, they havn't filled it in," he chuckled, "lovely job! I can't fail now." He replaced the letters, licked the envelopes and stuck them down, placing them back very carefully near to the telephone. He let himself out and went to 'The Star and Garter' to celebrate on his own. Two whiskies continued his elation as he laughed quietly to himself at his own cleverness. The Mayor would later open the envelopes and fill in the price-bid for Crewdley Builders; probably £6,800, he thought.

He reflected over the next two whiskies.... no, The Mayor wouldn't be as foolish as to fill in the bid himself ....

Robespierre would do it ..... yes, that is what would no doubt occur before six o' clock that evening.

But however Presbyterian arranged the actual fraud, Bramley would nail him.

The trail would lead directly to The Mayor's Parlour, the Police would confiscate his Bank Accounts and have details of every transaction between him and Crewdley Builders..... Robespierre would crack under severe pressure and questioning in "The Dock".... other citizens would no doubt come forward to testify that The Mayor was indeed corrupt, once it appeared safe to do so.

All he had to do was wait and he enjoyed the rest of the afternoon in the familiar and alcoholic-hazed surroundings of "The Star and Garter," even buying Seamus McGurk a double Irish whisky, in anticipation of wrapping up "The Big One."

Bramley finally returned to his own office in the Police Station at around five o' clock and set out the 'Big Ears' receiver on his desk. He looked contently at the Instamatic photographs of the price-bids of the three Building Companies.

"Lovely job," he repeated, "Sherlock bloody Holmes was an amateur compared with me." He counted the chimes of St Crueds Church clock as it struck six, and listened intently as the meeting of the Contract Committee was called to order.

"Good evening colleagues," The Mayor was clearly heard to say, "we have only one item of business before us, as printed on your Agenda papers, and that is to award the contract for necessary repair work to be carried out to Crewdley Bridge. The Town Clerk has informed me, that three envelopes have been returned from the list of our approved Building Contracters. Mr Beard, would you please therefore open the envelopes and read out the bids?"

"Yes, go on!" said Bramley, lets hear the good news." There were some peculiar noises which Bramley assumed related to Beard undoing the envelopes, but then the unmistakable voice of The Town Clerk came over very loud and clear.

"Thankyou Mr Mayor. If Councillors could please take note of the following price-bids for the Crewdley Bridge contract." "Get on with it!" The Mayor chastised him, "we havn't got all night."

"Sorry Mr Mayor, the first bid then is from Bert Smith the Builders and the figure is £7,000." "Lucky seven eh?" said a voice that Bramley recognized as that of Councillor Barry Blondel. "The second bid is from Riverside Roads and Pavements and the figure is £6,900."

There were more peculiar noises before Beard resumed, "And finally Mr Mayor, the third bid is from Crewdley Builders and the figure is £6,850."

"Gotcha!!!," yelled Bramley. "I say, that was close," said Councillor Mrs Sylvia Smart. "Gotcha! Gotcha! Gotcha!," Bramley shouted again, "Lets see you get out of this one Presbyterian." He tried hard to regain his composure as the voices continued to discuss the bids.

"Need we say anymore?" The Mayor asked," Crewdley Builders bid is the lowest at £6,850. Would someone please move that they be awarded the contract?" "I move!" answered Councillor Mrs Smart, "And I second Mr Mayor," said Councillor Blondel.

"Good! Is that agreed then? Those in favour, please indicate." "Huh! Pity I havn't got a television link," Bramley complained, "I could see them putting their paws up."

"Thankyou, that is carried," said The Mayor, "the contract will be awarded to Crewdley Buliders at £6,850. I hereby close the meeting - Robespierre!" Bramley listened intently, "Robespierre - please bring some wine. Would anyone like a sandwich?" "I have to be off," said Councillor Mrs Smart, "bye bye everyone."

"I'll just have a quick one added Councillor Blondel, "I'm off to Worcester in a few minutes." "Oh what a shame," answered The Mayor, "I expect you'll be going to see someone's wife 'eh Blondel?"

"Now, now Harold, don't be jealous, we can't all restrict ourselves to the confines of Crewdley, can we? Oh thankyou Robespierre Cheers!"

Bramley listened in for a few more minutes then switched 'Big Ears' off. He poured himself a large whisky then another, and another, before finally closing his office and going home.

Presbyterian could wait; Bramley preferred the drama of a dawn arrest, so he set his alarm for five am and after another hour or two of drinking whisky, he retired for the night.

At 5.45am on Thursday 6th December, Superintendent Horace Bramley, the Chief of Crewley Police knocked loudly on the door of 'Civic House.'

He stood back onto the pavement and looked up to the bedroom window. The light went on , the curtains moved and the window opened. Harold Presbyterian was not pleased.

"What the hell do you want Bramley?" he called down to the figure below. "Sorry to trouble you Mr Mayor, especially so early in the morning, but it's an emergency. Could you let me in please and I'll tell you all about it?" Presbyterian put on his dressing gown and went downstairs to the front door. "Come on in Bramley - what on earth is the problem?" The moment that Superintendent Horace Bramley had yearned after for so many years had finally arrived. He put his hand quickly onto The Mayors shoulder, "Harold Presbyterian, I arrest you for conspiracy to defraud Crewdley Council of monies properly due to it, for criminal deception, larceny and embezzlement of Public Money. You do not have to say anything but anything that you do say will be taken down and may be used as evidence against you."

"You've been at the magic mushrooms Horace, havn't you? You're out of your mind. Why don't you go and catch a real criminal? The Pagan Stag for instance, he ran rings around you and you still havn't a clue." "Ah, but I have caught a real criminal and he's The Mayor of Crewdley. Now! Are you coming quietly to the Police Station with me or are you going to resist arrest and add to your catalogue of crime?", Bramley said firmly. "Are you proposing to take me down to the Police Station in my dressing-gown?" The Mayor asked, looking him straight in the eye.

"No, but no tricks mind, you can go upstairs and get dressed. I'll wait here, but don't be too long or I'll be up after you." The Mayor walked slowly upstairs under the watchful gaze of Superintendent Bramley, thinking with each step about his predicament, and concluding before he reached the bedroom door, that Bramley must somehow have taped the Contract Committee meeting and had probably nobbled one of the other contractors, almost certainly Bert Smith, he thought.

There was always the secret passage -way through into the Town Hall. He could get dressed, use the exit, then escape through the rear door and into the Civic Park and Gardens.

"Not too long now," called Bramley, "two minutes at the most or else up I come." Presbyterian was dressed in less than thirty seconds and walking down the secret passage to the Town Hall. Robespierre was still sound asleep in his room, so The Mayor went quickly into The Parlour, slid back the wooden wall panel and opened the safe. He took out various papers, documents and photographs and was about to leave the room when he was confronted by

72

Robespierre.

"Monsieur!" he called out in alarm, "What is wrong?" "English!" demanded The Mayor, "nothing is wrong, but that idiot Policeman Bramley thinks he's going to ruin me. Go back to bed Robespierre." He watched him go back to his room before he returned along the passage into his own bedroom and opened the door to find Bramley coming up the stairs.

"I was just coming," he said rather breathlessly, "come on, it's time to go." "Yes, of course," Presbyterian replied, "but I think we both need a drink first."

"Oh no you don't, "Bramley said impatiently, "I'm taking you down to the Station." "But I've got something that I'd like you to see," said The Mayor.

"I'm not going to accept any bribe that you could offer," Bramley snapped, "so forget it." "Well, it's a great pity that your career will be ruined merely because you refused to have a drink with me," Presbyterian answered, "I've got some photographs that I think you'd be interested in."

He offered a photograph to the Police Chief, who took it and gasped in horror. It was a picture showing him in a very compromising sexual position with a hotel maid.

"My God!" How did you get this?", he fumed. "It's very good isn't it? I asked one of my employees to make full use of an excellent camera with a long-range lense. Marvellous shot, there's no mistaking you, is there Horace?"

Presbyterian walked into his lounge and in spite of the early hour, poured two glasses of whisky, and offered one to Bramley who had followed limply in in a state of shock.

"That was five years ago" he protested.

"There are others," replied Presbyterian, "of course, you may wish to contest your divorce, but I want you to look at these." He passed various papers to the policeman. "These are telephone bills," he croaked.

"Yes, that's right. A mere snap-shot of your telephone calls to Australia from the Police Station..... specimen items, you might say Horace. They go back a long way though, don't they? About ten years I'd say. Yes..... I've got a very good friend at the Telephone Exchange."

"Bloody Hell!" Bramley called out, as he read through them, "Bloody Hell!"

"You're quite impressed by those then, are you Horace?" said The Mayor in a manner that indicated perhaps worse was to come, "I thought you might be. Now do you see what I meant when I mentioned us having a little drink together before you did anything rash?" "Swine!" said Bramley in sheer disbelief, but knowing that The Mayor had probably only just started to dig the knife in.

"Yes, it's a tough old world we live in Horace, isn't it? For instance, it must have been tough on the previous land-lord of 'The Star and Garter' when you

73

offered to turn a blind eye to various matters concerning illegal drinking and keeping a disorderly house. It cost him a lot of money keeping you quiet Horace, didn't it? I've got signed statements of course, and if necessary, he'll come back from Spain to give evidence against you, but I told him years ago, I didn't think it ever would be." "Bastard!" Bramley seethed, "you lousy rat!"

"Now now Horace, all is fair in love and war my friend. I've got some more specimen items here .....look! For instance, 7th March, 1981, documented evidence recording that £1,200 was raised from the Police Gala Charity Ball, but only £800 was finally handed over..... no prizes for guessing who it was who actually collected the cash 'eh Horace?"

The Superintendent sank deep into the chair, as Harold Presbyterian warmed to his task.

"Oh look, here's another one! 10th March 1982 ...your claim for expenses and petrol allowance £73. 80 pence ......now I believe that you had lunch paid for by one of the Reporters on 'The Weekly Weaver'.... I've got a Statement.... I think I mentioned that I needed to know you're favourite food so that I would be sure to please you when you came to my Charity Evening at The Town Hall..... that's right, he paid the bill..... gave it to me in fact.... kept a copy for his boss of course.... oh yes, he took you around the district all day in his car Horace, so unless you did forty miles in your garage, I firmly believe that you fiddled your expenses. Here's another one .....I thought at the time that this was actually quite enterprising of you Horace .....3rd September 1983..... you were paid £100 by Rupert Beard for allowing him to fish in the River Crewd ..... you told him that you were responsible for distributing a Special Licence which gave him the right to fish at night.... he could actually have bought one for £2..... there's another....." "No! Don't!", shouted Bramley, "I've heard enough!"

"Yes and so you should have Horace, old boy, so I'll tell you what I want you to do. Are you listening?"

"Yes yes, I'm listening," answered Bramley.

"Good, it's quite simple. We go to the Police Station right now and you give me two things..... first the tape and the other half of your listening- device, and secondly of course, the copies you no doubt have of the Contract- bid papers."

Bramley was shattered.

"I can't compete with you Presbyterian. I'm not in your league," he moaned.

"Don't take it too badly Horace ......better men than you have tried and failed. Come on, it'll be light soon and it wouldn't do for The Mayor of Crewdley to be seen going in to The Police Station at this hour, would it? People might start to talk."

The two men set out for the Police Station in the cold, early morning. Bramley was totally depressed and moaned persistently, and was almost incoherent by the time they got inside his Office.

"Here," he said "this is the listening-device..... and the photographs of the Contract bids."

"Play the tape," Presbyterian demanded, "and hurry up Horace, I'm ready for my breakfast." The Superintendent ran the machine and Presbyterian smiled as the voice of The Town Clerk read out the bids.

"O.K, put them into a bag for me Horace ... Oh here's a nice one, I'll take this," Presbyterian exclaimed, knowing full well to whom the case belonged.

"But that's my own case," answered Bramley. "Yes, that will do nicely thankyou Horace," said The Mayor, He snapped the case shut and stood with his hand on the handle of the door. "I expect it won't be too long before you're retired, 'eh Horace? Don't worry, if you're a good boy for the rest of your time in the job, I expect your pension will arrive on time without any problems. But do behave yourself Horace, people expect a lot from someone in your position and I would be loath to be the one who blew the whistle..... good morning Horace".

With that, The Mayor of Crewdley left The Police Station and returned to The Town Hall where Robespierre was cooking breakfast.

"Ah, there you are Mr Mayor," he said, "I knew you wouldn't be long. Will bacon, eggs, tomatoes, mushrooms and fried bread be alright Sir? I'm afraid we havn't got kippers, but I'll get some from the Co-op later today." "That will be fine thankyou Robespierre, I think it looks like being a rather nice day in spite of a chilly start."

And so it was that Harold Presbyterian began yet another day as Crewdley's First Citizen. His duties were light, a few official letters were signed, one or two telephone calls answered and The Town Clerk handed him an invitation to The Christmas Dinner Dance of Crewdley Police. He looked down into Church Street and smiled as a young policeman was putting a Parking Ticket on an offending lorry. Quite suddenly, the warm waters of The Caspian Sea seemed to wash over him and his passion was roused for his "Mistress of The Waves", but just as suddenly his ardour was depressed by the realization that Pippa Monroe was probably teaching thirty children the origin of The English Civil War. "Robespierre!" he called, "go round to 'Caspian House' and leave my visiting-card. I shall require the Rolls Royce this evening. I want a mid-night picnic by moon-light with Pippa Monroe at my side. We'll go up to Crewdley Forest, make sure you pack a decent food hamper and some whisky,..... oh and put a small electric fan-heater in the car will you? I wouldn't want her to catch a chill."

At nine pm precisely, Mrs Pippa Monroe stepped into the back of The Civic

Rolls Royce.

"Hello Pressy darling," she purred, "I hope you're going to keep me warm on such a frosty, cold night?"

"Have no fear of that you gorgeous girl," he answered, pulling down the blinds, "I thought it would be nice to begin Christmas early, so I bought you a present...... look....... I know how much you adore jewellery."

"Oh Pressy", she said, kissing him tenderly, "it's just what I've always wanted."

"Drive on Robespierre!" he called. "To the Forest and sound the klaxon as loudly as you like when we go past the Police Station. Superintendent Bramley will no doubt still be at his desk and I'm sure he knows the klaxon well enough to realize we're saying hello."

The car pulled away from 'Caspian House' and The Mayor was soon in Paradise and all was well with the world. Robespierre sounded the klaxon as The Mayor made passionate love to Mrs Pippa Monroe.

Horace Bramley cursed as the car sped past The Police Station and he tried unsuccessfully to re-light the gas fire which had gone out several hours before. His lighter was empty and as he stood looking at the cold, metal bars of the fire, the lights went out. It had not been at all a good day for Police Superintendent Horace Bramley, in fact it had been a lousy day, an awful day. He would never forget Thursday 6th December. The Trap had indeed been sprung, but against his own throat, and the feeling was extremely bad.

CHAPTER SEVEN

Octavia Bland is Unwell

As all good students of Local Government are aware, The Municipal Calender is radically different to the ancient Julian, or even current Gregorian versions. Whereas our modern calender year naturally begins on 1st January and ends on 31st December, The Municipal Year is peculiar, in that the cycle relates to the Financial Year and culminates with the Budget Meeting at the end of March.

Several factors complicate the 'Annual Political Clocks' of the elected Councillors and Officers, though the effect on Rate Payers, Poll-Tax Payers, Voters or mere ordinary members of the public, may be considered as perhaps rather negligible.

Firstly, Municipal Elections are held in May and The Mayor is elected as soon after that as is possible at the first Full Council Meeting of the new Municipal Year.

Secondly, the Councillors and Officers are, in the main, rather ordinary people who look forward to, and enjoy, the 'natural breaks' to the calender provided by Easter, Christmas, New Year and all other bank Holidays.

This second set of complicating factors, relating as they do to holiday periods, coupled with the third factor,'The Budget Making' process, which as mentioned culminates at the end of March, tends to create a hiatus of activity at times in the calender when other social and economic groups of people are already well into their year of work. It is true that a tenuous comparison might be drawn between the calenders of local politicians and the farming community, though of course, rather than ending their year like politicians with the Budget, farmers end it with the harvest.

To this day, scant regard is given to our Gregorian Calendar by the farming communities of some Scottish Islands including Orkney and Shetland, because the rigours of the seasons demand that the Julian calender with its New Year beginning on the 7th January, is preferable to one imposed from London. Therefore politicians and Council Officers (even farmers themselves) tend in practice, to consider Christmas as the end of the year, when most things Municipal come to a pleasurable halt.

The Councillors and Officers of Crewdley are indeed unexceptional in wishing to scale down their Municipal activities for the Christmas Holiday. Apart from the Contract Committee, Crewdley Town Council held one full Council Meeting in December, a very relaxed and sparse affair, spoiled only for some of them, by Council business, the majority preferring the festive activities of eating, drinking and making merry in the Town Hall, after the Meeting had finished.

It was during this period of pleasure, that Councillor Mrs Octavia Bland first complained of feeling unwell. At eighty nine years of age, she was no 'Spring Chicken'; yet it is perfectly possible that some of her voters considered her to be of the age she looked in her Election Photograph - around forty. When old Councillors begin to fade away, they do not generally knock every door touting for votes. Therefore, because Octavia Bland was virtually house-bound, many of the non-active citizens were unaware of her true age.

But no one lasts forever, not even Crewdley's eldest and seemingly most indestructible Councillor. Although Octavia Bland could remember most of the years of the 20th Century, her political development was curtailed extremely early upon her marriage to the late Herbert Bland, Banker of Crewdley and one of the most un-political of people ever.

Octavia was the eldest of the two Llewellyn sisters in the long established Crewdley family of Drapers. Her younger sister Olivia had also remained in Crewdley, and after decades of rather uneventful marriage, each of them had settled sedately into widowhood. Octavia Bland sat on Crewdley Council as an Independent. Not for her, the thrill of having once belonged to The Suffragettes or Independent Labour Party; her idea of political activity favoured opening a Jumble Sale, selling Raffle tickets or attending a Meeting of the Council like the ones held in December, rather than deal with nasty, contentious economic and political items. In spite of her Conformist and Pro-Establishment attitude, Octavia Bland was a quiet individualist, not it seemed at all Bohemian, but rather a character all the same. Her fellow Councillors were used to her funny little ways, which might indeed have appeared very strange to out-siders.

For instance, she was in the habit of attending Winter Council Meetings wrapped in a thick blanket with a hot water bottle and a hip-flask filled with whisky. She liked the £21 Attendance Allowance, but not the business of the Meetings and had lately developed a habit of listening to all sorts of music, including Rock and Roll, on a 'Walkman' headset.

Hardly anyone ever disturbed her, there was no need. Votes went in the usual way, usually seven votes to two, or if she happened to notice, eight votes to two. She rarely made speeches, but occasionally she did rise to her feet and participated on the dangers of traffic in Crewdley, irrespective of whether the debate was concerned with Housing, Planning, Contracting, Education, or even Fishing in the River Crewd. It always ended up with Octavia Bland talking about Traffic- no one minded; she was a harmless, 89 year old woman and her interventions and her presence were taken as part of the fabric of the Council.

However, her illness persisted throughout that December Meeting and for the remainder of the Christmas Holiday. Dr Jonathan Scargreaves was quite concerned, and advised her to cancel all Social Engagements and remain indoors, which she did.

The next full Meeting of Crewdley Council, was scheduled for Monday 21st January 1991. The Mayor had called the Meeting to Order when he was disturbed by noises outside the Council Chamber. The doors were forced open by a nurse who was pushing Councillor Mrs Octavia Bland in a wheelchair.

"Goodness Gracious!" said Presbyterian, "Councillor Mrs Bland.... we weren't expecting to see you tonight..... there was really no need..... please pass the Expenses Sheet to Councillor Bland Mr Beard ..."

There were many gasps of astonishment from those present, not merely at the sight of the old lady being pushed into the Chamber by an Agency Nurse, a bad enough shock in itself, but an intravenous drip complete with suspended bottle and tube was attached to her arm. To make matters worse, the 'Walkman' head-set was in place and with the cocoon of blankets, foot-warmers and gloves, Octavia Bland gave the impression of appearing as trapped and helpless as a shrivelled old fly in a spiders web.

"Oh! Please take her home nurse. She's surely too ill to be here?" said Councillor Mrs Evans- Jenkins.

"It's pathetic!" replied Councillor Hardie, "it's not as if she needs the money." "It's horrible !" added Councillor Morton Muggeridge, "do we have to endure this Mr Mayor?" he asked.

"We have to endure you Muggeridge, so please sit down and stop babbling. Let's get on with the Meeting." "No! No! I can't ! I won't," shouted Muggeridge, "it's positively indecent! Look at her! she's half dead!" "Which half is alive?" asked Councillor Blondel," she's been like that for years, what's the difference?" "The difference is she's very ill," answered Hardie, "she should be in hospital"

"Well, she isn't .... she's here instead," The Mayor said coldly, "so let's get on with it shall we? Agenda Item One ....is Prayers... Will you say Prayers Reverend Wooly, to set us on our way?"

The Vicar of Crewdley stepped forward, held up his Prayer Book, then promply put it down, as he began to speak.

"Lord .... please watch over this, our Council, as we go about our Civic Business .... encourage us to take wise decisions for the benefit of us all and ...." He stopped and looked with real concern at Councillor Octavia Bland , "and please God that our much loved eldest Member, Councillor Mrs Octavia Bland, is soon resumed to full and sparkling health ..." (It seemed most unlikely, even with the helping hand of Providence) The Vicar continued,

"Dear Lord, in this the first Meeting of Our Council in the New Year, please hear our Prayers .... we Pray for Peace in the World,..... we ask for your continued help in achieving the stability and goodwill that we need to help our Local Government be a success......."

He glanced across at Councillor Bland who seemed to be in a peculiar state of suspended animation, and then to The Mayor who was already looking at his wrist watch, "Amen," he concluded quickly.

"Thank you Mr Wooly," said The Crewdley Colossus, "Item Two... Apologies for absence..... none..... Item Three..... To receive questions submitted by Members of Crewdley Council and the replies of the Chairmen of Committees...."

"As printed Mr Mayor," shouted Beard.

"Is that agreed then?" The Mayor enquired.

"Agreed!" came the collective reply.

"Item Four..... to confirm the Minutes of the Meeting of the Council held on the 17th December 1990 .... would someone care to move them as a true record?" he asked, in a matter of fact tone.

"I move Mr Mayor," responded Councillor Mrs Enid Thomas.

"And I second that proposal," concurred Councillor Arthur Hardie.

"Is that agreed?"

"Agreed!"

"Thankyou..... Item Five..... then Communications to The Mayor.... yes, a letter signed by Anthony Roberts on behalf of the residents of The Almshouses, expressing their thanks to me as the Administrater of The Old Town Charity Trust for their Gifts at Christmas..... next various letters from local Business men and women wishing a Happy New Year to myself and all Crewdley Councillors; finally, a package of Crime Prevention posters and Information from Superintendent Bramley, who would like the Council to display the relevant Public Items on our Notice Boards and in our Council premises..... that will be done .."

A smile spread over Presbyterian's face as he considered the irony of his own position and that of Bramley, who was no doubt pleased to have made it into the New Year without seeing his name spread over the pages of 'The News of The World,' and who was now totally subservient to The Mayor on each occasion they met, both publically and privately.

"Item Six..... to consider any Motions in the Order in which the Notice has been received..... there are none "

"Item seven ."

"Uuurrghh! uurrghh!", came a noise from the spiders web.

"Councillor Mrs Bland do you wish to speak?" The Mayor enquired with curiosity.

The Agency Nurse leant over her charge and put her ear between 'The Walkman' and the old lady's mouth.

"She wants to tell you all it's her birthday, said the Nurse, "she's 90 today."

"Good Gracious....Happy Birthday Octavia!" yelled Councillor Norman Bull, "Absolutely splendid old girl, well done!"

Councillor Mrs Sylvia Smart promply left her seat, went over to the Birthday Girl and, after finding a way between the tubes and wires, kissed her firmly on her cheek. The Mayor looked down on the scene with trepidation. Disorder was about to break out, but he was worried about something potentially much more threatening, as would no doubt be revealed in the fullness of time.

"Item Seven...... any other business" "Happy Birthday!" someone shouted."I herby close the Meeting!" said Presbyterian loudly to make himself heard against the growing noise.

"Robespierre!" he called", bring in some refreshments!" Within a minute, Robespierre had returned with a large tray and glasses, which he put down on a table, before leaving The Council Chamber again to collect several bottles of wine and spirits which he placed on The Mayor's table.

"Help yourselves," Presbyterian shouted, "and I'll have one with Octavia, please Robespierre." He took his large whisky and went over to Councillor Mrs Bland. Robespierre passed her a rather small whisky and soda, which she took without emotion.

"Cheers!" said The Mayor, "Happy Birthday Octavia," The old lady switched off her 'Walkman' head-set and let it fall to her lap. "Have you heard from the Police yet?" she asked weakly.

"The Police?" The Mayor enquired, "Oh- you mean about your   oh- No I'm sorry Octavia, not yet, I expect it will be soon."

She knocked back the whisky and began to splutter. "Oh dear. I hope that wasn't alcohol", said the Agency Nurse.

"Well of course it was," Presbyterian answered sharply, as the venerable and ancient Councillor coughed and gasped for air.

"Robespierre, you'd better go and get Doctor Scargreaves, and be quick, I fear time is of the essence," said The Mayor.

The old lady coughed and spluttered, gasped and wheezed until she was extremely red in the face. She held on to the nurse's arm and coughed again, then quite suddenly, took a very deep breath before exhaling noisily. Various Councillors gathered round, "Give her air," cried the Nurse."

"Give me another whisky," croaked the patient.

"You must not," the Nurse implored her, "please let me take you home." "Whisky!" she implored back,"whisky!" Unaccustomed as he was to the role of waiter, Presbyterian poured another drink and offered it to her. She stretched out her feeble arm to take it through the web of wires. All eyes were upon Councillor Mrs Bland as the glass was moved towards her lips. It was as if time itself stopped for a moment and the scene was merely a photographic portrait of still-life, there in the Chamber she knew so well. A wild look lit her eyes, the glass dropped to the floor and the coughing re-commenced, but this time with a particularly intense ferocity. She gasped for air like a landed fish and the Councillors became alarmed. The nurse undid what clothing she could get at beneath the tubes and wires, as Robespierre came crashing back into the Chamber. "He's on his way Mr Mayor," he panted, "Just getting his bag!"

Councillor Mrs Octavia Bland was struggling for breath and the Agency Nurse began to fan her with a Council Agenda.

"That's no good!" said The Mayor, "she's sinking fast." "Oh my God! What shall I do?" pleaded the Nurse, "I'm still on probation."

"Yes, that's bloody typical of this system," Hardie shouted, "Private Nursing is a scandal. I expect you've got a day job ..... hey .... havn't I seen you behind the counter at Finneys?" "Oohh! Help!"cried the Chip Shop Medic, "it's not my fault, I wanted to better myself."

With that, Councillor Morton Muggeridge threw himself upon Octavia Bland and began mouth to mouth resuscitation. "Good on you Muggeridge," said Councillor Arkwright, "but if I were you, I'd certainly use a mouth- wash afterwards."

"It's horrible!" shrieked Councillor Mrs Louise Evans-Jenkins, as she watched her lover snogging and grunting with the old lady as if there was no tomorrow, and it certainly seemed a strong possibility that there wouldn't be for the recipient of his reckless attempt at the kiss of life. Doctor Scargreaves hurried into the melee of the scrum. "What the hell is going on?" he asked, "What are you doing Muggeridge? Leave it to me please."

Muggeridge broke his hold and retired gracefully to hold hands instead with Councillor Evans-Jenkins, as Doctor Scargreaves got to work on his patient who had suddenly gone extremely quiet and still. Scargreaves put his stethoscope on her chest and demanded that the assembly was quiet. He moved the instrument quickly from one place to another, then opened an extremely large case and took out a Heart-Resusitation Appliance which he attached to the ghostly form of Octavia Bland. He flicked a switch and a massive "ppuumpphhh!!"echoed across the Chamber, he flicked the switch again, "ppuumpphh!" and again "ppuumpphh!"

"She's going fast, I'm afraid," he said to the onlookers, "Ppuumpphh!"

"ppuumpphh!" The wretched figure of Councillor Bland jumped up several inches each time the machine was used. "Oh stop it!" yelled Councillor Smart, "The old girls had enough!"

"Yes, I'm afraid she has," the Doctor replied, "she's gone." "Oh God. It was her birthday," said Muggeridge. "Poor old thing," rasped Councillor Bull, "but what a splendid performance on the old girls part 'eh?"

"It means a bloody by-election," The Mayor whispered to Robespierre, "why couldn't she have hung on until May, she was up for election anyway then?"

"It was the whisky! She shouldn't have had the whisky!" complained Councillor Louise Evans-Jenkins. "Wouldn't have made the slightest bit of difference," said Doctor Scargreaves, "she had a weak heart."

"Ooohhhh!" cried the Agency Nurse, "ooohhh! I'm not going to do this anymore .... can I go home please Doctor?" "Yes, there's nothing anyone can do for her anymore. Now Mr Mayor, if you would be kind enough to either telephone Mr Grimley or send someone round to tell him, I would be grateful."

"Of course," Presbyterian replied with phoney concern, "Robespierre! Go round to Mr Grimleys Funeral Chapel of Rest and explain what has happened." He turned to face his fellow Councillors and caught a final glimpse of the Agency Nurse heading for home.

"O.K everyone. Unfortunately, we have lost our most loved colleague, Octavia Bland.

As a mark of respect, could I ask that you please leave the Chamber in a quiet and orderly fashion?" The Councillors fell silent and began to decant from the Chamber, one or two of them taking a final look at their colleague, before Doctor Scargreaves covered her with the blanket.

"Would you care for a wee dram Doctor? Dear Octavia was extremely partial to whisky. It was one of her pleasures", suggested The Mayor. "Oh very well, there really isn't anymore that we can do, except wait for Edwin Grimley. What a shame," he said taking the drink, from The Mayor, "on her 90th birthday too - your very good health, Mr Mayor."

"And yours," replied Presbyterian downing his drink with one swallow. The Doctor sipped his whisky, "It's the end of an era isn't it? She's been around for as long as anyone can remember."

"It certainly seems so," said The Mayor, "she was elected onto the Council in 1926 that's sixty four years, it must be a record. It's longer than Queen Victoria's reign.

"Yes, but only just, Victoria ascended the Throne on the 20th June 1837 and died on the 22nd January 1901 .... that makes sixty four years and five months,

Octavia Bland was elected on Tuesday 6th May 1926 .... I reckon she wins by two months and 18 days."

"Good Grief! How did you know that?", asked The Mayor. "Well as I said," replied Scargreaves, "she had a weak heart and could have gone at any time, so I looked up her dates and Victoria's to see who had 'reigned' the longest. Octavia was ahead from about October I think. A remarkable effort, don't you agree Harold?"

"I do, I do indeed," he answered, with his mind firmly on the By-Election, "But we've all got to go sometime I suppose?" The Doctor smiled, "Not her though it seems."

"What are you talking about? She's dead isn't she?" The Mayor asked inquisitively, topping up both of their glasses.

"Can't say I'm afraid.... not yet at any rate..... oh good here's Grimley."

"What do you mean you can't say?"

"Oh sorry,..... yes ....she's certainly dead, what I meant was that I couldn't say about the other thing .... now then Mr Grimley .... she's all yours," said the Doctor.

The Mayor shook his head and wondered what the Doctor had meant.

"Dear me, " said Edwin Grimley the Undertaker, with just a glint in his eye, "Poor old Mrs Bland gone at last eh? I sometimes wondered if she'd ever go, and if she ever did, whether she'd go before I did..... ah well .....I 've got the Hearse outside. Would it be all right to bring it through the gates and into The Foyer Mr Mayor? It would make life alot easier .... except for Councillor Bland that is, if you know what I mean .... she is dead isn 't she Doctor? " he asked lifting the blanket and staring at the assumed-deceased client, "only, and , you'll pardon me for saying this, it's sort of difficult to tell with her somehow .... do you know what I mean? When we were at The Vicars Garden Party, she was sitting in her chair for hours as still as a stone .... I .... could hardly detect whether she was with us or not."

"Yes .... yes, she' s dead alright Mr Grimley .... you can be sure about that."

"Oh Good ! " said Grimley, "Oh Dear ! I'm sorry, you know what I mean Doctor, don't you? It's the shock of seeing her like this. I've known her all of my life, since I was a boy ...she's always been here in Crewdley, hasn 't she Mr Mayor?"

"She certainly has Mr Grimley. We won't see her like again, she was a one-off, " he answered still considering the implications of the By-Election and trying to work out all of the possible scenarios . Grimley assembled a mobile aluminium stretcher and wheeled it beside the body of the now confirmed, late Councillor Bland. "Would you mind giving me a hand with her please Robespierre, there's a good chap?" As was absolutely apt, Robespierre adopted his best pall-bearers posture and expression and assisted Grimley with the body.

"Pull the blanket over her will you Robespierre, then we can wheel her into the hearse?" asked Grimley, warming to his task. "There' s nothing else for me to do Mr Mayor, I'll write the Death Certificate later, cheerio" said the Doctor, struggling with the large case of equipment. The Mayor watched Grimley manouvre the aluminium stretcher out into The Foyer as Robespierre held the door open. He poured another drink and cast his eye at the Minutes in The Council Agenda and looked at the names of the Councillors, trying to assess the health and strength of each one. None of them were super fit, which was just as well, he thought.

No one was aged more than about sixty, so perhaps 'The Grim Reaper' would not strike again until they were all as old as Councillor Octavia Bland? The last By-Election had been in 1969 and was caused by the death of the ninety two year old Mrs Eugene Badland; bad luck for her but good luck for the thrusting, young and ambitious Harold Presbyterian.

Yes....... the very thought of the coming By-Election worried him, but for now he left The Council Chamber and witnessed the final departure of Octavia Bland as she was put into the hearse.

"I'm going home Robespierre," he said, take the night off." He then leaned forward and whispered so that Grimley shouldn't hear,"I was looking forward to visiting 'Caspian House,' but I'm not in the mood anymore." "Good night Mr Mayor," replied his Faithful valet, "I'll lock up."

"Well of course you bloody well will it's your job!" The Mayor scolded him," and don't be late in the morning!"

CHAPTER EIGHT

A Most Peculiar Funeral

News of Councillor Bland's death spread quickly throughout Crewdley, and although many people were unaware of exactly who she was, these would have included the seventy and sometimes eighty per cent who couldn't be bothered to vote for her or anyone else; for others, the opinion leaders, her passing was quite a talking point.

It was mentioned in the Co-op, throughout the Offices of The Council, in the bar of 'The Star and Garter,' at the Post Office and of course, amongst the congregation of St Crueds Church.

Her funeral was to be held on Friday 25th January 1991. Although Presbyterian was really not at all interested in the disposal of her mortal remains, unfortunately matters had been taken out of his hands by the explicit detail contained in Octavia Bland's last Will and Testament. There could be no equivocation on his part; he was to be totally involved, and refusal, even for him, would not be politically survivable: it was too specific...... "The Mayor shall take necessary measures...... The Mayor will then ensure ....to be undertaken solely by The Mayor of Crewdley..... etc, etc, etc......."

He would therefore have to comply with the old lady's instructions.

It depressed him slightly and he was missing the company of Mrs Pippa Monroe. However, duty called.

The Mayor had been given The Will on the morning after the demise of the aged Councillor by John Doolittle and Henry Dash, Crewdley solicitors of long-standing who considered the matter so important as to warrent their joint deputation.

"The Will is in two parts," Dash had explained, "this .... the Civic Part, concerns Funeral Arrangements..... the Second Part is concerned solely with bequethement of property and effects......"

A special meeting of The Council would have to be called Robespierre hand-delivered the Notices that same afternoon..... .... carpenters would have to be instructed forthwith ...The Vicar would have to agree....., Civic and Statute Law would need to be referred to, as well as her sister Olivia.

Presbyterian had realised for some time that Octavia Bland had been 'whacky' or 'eccentric' as they no doubt preferred to call it in more refined circles, but with this new evidence, 'bizarre' might have been nearer the mark.

Wednesday was to be the day of the Special Council Meeting and it was well below freezing as Presbyterian and Robespierre prepared to go into The

Council Chamber. The Mayor was being dressed by his valet..... first The Robe itself, next the White Laced Collar, then the Mayoral Chain of Office and finally, the Civic Cocked Hat.

"You look really nice Mr Mayor," said Robespierre.

"Thankyou," he answered, "I wish this wasn't happening, all the same." They left The Mayors Parlour and descended the old wooden staircase into The Foyer. "I assume you wish to go by car, Your Excellency?" asked Robespierre rhetorically.

"Certainly, value for money that's what they want let 'em see what they get for their Poll Tax," replied The Mayor.

They circled the town twice before Robespierre drew up outside The Town Hall, nipped smartly out to the rear door and held it open for The Great Man.

"Citizens of Crewdley!", he yelled to no-one in particular, "I give you The Mayor of Crewdley, Councillor Mr Harold Presbyterian, Thankyou very much, God Save the Queen!"

"Thank you Robespierre and hurry up, it's freezing," The Mayor remarked as he walked towards The Town Clerks Office. Robespierre gathered up The Mace and went through the doors into The Council Chamber as Beard held them open for The Mayor.

"Will you please be upsatanding for The Mayor of Crewdley, Councillor Harold Presbyterian!" Robespierre yelled again as he placed The Mace upon its stand at the top table.

The Mayor took his place and surveyed the scene.

"Please be seated," he said, "Reverend Wooly, will you please say prayers?"

The Vicar got to his feet and smiled ridiculously as he began his prayers.

"Dear Lord, we are gathered here today to join in matrimony." "Wooly! This isn't a wedding ceremony!", The Mayor said sharply. "Oh my God! I'm so sorry .... I was miles away ... please forgive me. It's the shock of her passing away, as she did here in this very Chamber and.... "

"Mr Wooly! Will you please get on with your Prayers for our Meeting?" Presbyterian rebuked his man of the cloth.

"Dear Lord, we Pray for Peace and Happiness in the World and for our Meeting tonight. Forgive our human frailty, yet please give us the strength Dear Lord to serve you so that we may serve others in our Community who need strong leadership and guidance. We Pray for the soul of our dearly departed sister, Octavia Bland and are thankful for her life and long service of Public Duty in Crewdley.

May we, your humble servants, be blessed with wisdom as we consider that dear lady's wishes, so that the people of Crewdley may benefit from her anticipated benevolance...... Amen."

He sat down meekly as The Mayor rose to his feet to speak.

"Thank you Reverend Wooly," he said coldly and stared at the hapless man with a look that Wooly knew was filled with distain, and just for a moment, The Vicar put his hands to his head to reassure himself that no trace of either antlers or fur remained from Halloween.

"Fellow Councillors," The Mayor said seriously, "Thank you for your attendance here tonight on this sad occasion." He looked at the assembled representatives as they held their heads low in pious contemplation. A feeling of contempt caused him almost to rebuke them, but he refrained and stared again, as he considered how easy it was to outwit them and how advantageous that he had enough information on all of them, except Hardie and Thomas, to put them away.

"Councillor Octavia Bland served the people of Crewdley from 1926 until January 1990 - a remarkable achievement for anyone," he said, pausing for a moment to consider her last years when it had been difficult to detect life itself in the old girl, unless either the whisky bottle was produced or someone mentioned that a visit from Royalty was imminent.

"Her last act was to attend a Council Meeting, when it was painfully obvious that she did not have long to live. This is not a Memorial Meeting, it is an Extra Ordinary Meeting of the Council, called for the sole purpose of reading the Civic Part of Octavia Bland's Last Will and Testament."

Not a sound could be heard as the Assembly listened intently, hanging on The Mayor's every word.

"The document reads as follows; 'I Octavia Bland, being of sound mind....'

The Mayor coughed awkwardly before continuing, 'do hereby declare this to be the Civic Part of my Last Will and Testament, the other part to be read at a proper time and place to members of my family, in the presence of my Solicitors John Doolittle and Henry Dash.

It is my especial wish, that an Extra Ordinary Meeting be called of Crewdley Town Council at the earliest possible time after my death. The Mayor shall then read this Will to those who are present.

My dear Colleagues, I have served our Council for sixty years and enjoyed every minute. I dearly loved the people of Crewdley and wanted always to be in their midst. My only wish is that for this to continue in perpetuity. I therefore ask that the following decision be taken in the name of the Lord and our Community. Please, please, please, I implore you, may I not be buried, nor burned nor put into the River Crewd! It is my sole and lasting wish, that my body be preserved for eternity by Edwin Grimley and placed in a glass case in The Foyer of The Town Hall."

"Aargghh!!!," shrieked Councillor Muggeridge, "it's too horrible." "My God! It's a sick joke," shouted someone else.

"Mr Mayor! I really must protest!" Councillor Hardie protested, "this can't be!" "Uurgh! How absolutely vile! Uurgh! Stuffed and put in a box like an old ferret!" yelled Councillor Bull.

"No No! We must not," said The Vicar, "it's an act of sacrilage." "Let me finish!" shouted The Mayor, "The final sentance reads ...... 'When this matter is successfully accomplished, a sum of £100,000 will be placed into the coffers of a newly-created fund, entitled, The Octavia Bland Memorial Fund for the Welfare of Past and Present Councillors of Crewdley..... Thank you all so much, Heaven waits for our return, signed this the 20th of July 1989, by Octavia Bland, Councillor for the Meadow Ward of Crewdley, God Bless our Town, it's Councillors and our Mayor Vox Populi, Vox Dei ,...... The Voice of the people is the voice of God,'"

"That's it!" said The Mayor, "in a nutshell, that's it! She wants to be mummified and put on display in The Foyer...... she's willing to pay and I for one, don't think we should dismiss the suggestion out of hand. Oh yes, there is a P.S which reads, 'I ask only that my preserved body be uncovered for Public Display once each year upon my birthday the 21st January in memoriam'.

So that it is! Any comments?" said The Mayor hurriedly, "or shall I put it straight to the vote? I think it's a goer, but how about everyone else?"

There was a pregnant pause as the Councillors drew breath. "It's absolutely beyond belief," said Councillor Mrs Sylvia Smart, in a state of obvious nervousness, "it gives me the creeps. How could she do this to us....... how ...tell me ...HOW!!"

"Fine..... Right...... Let's think it over," The Mayor responded, perhaps a little awkwardly, "and as we do so, I must tell you, that I have asked the Carpenter to make up a large, wooden box, rather like a sentry-box one might see outside Buckingham Palace - as we all know, Octavia was a true Royalist - it has a glass-window at the front and shutters which open back for the one opening-day of the year. Any how it's all ready for Members to inspect. She would be quite snug sitting there, on guard as it were, keeping a watchful eye on us, those who remain, as we go about our Council Business.

Now, what do you say colleagues?" he asked firmly.

"I always thought she was disturbed," replied Councillor Arkwright," but I never realized quite how much. If that's what she wants .... maybe we should let her have her way? You never know, it could be a Tourist Attraction, and we could do with the extra revenue in the town."

"Well!! What a mature attitude Alan", said The Mayor, "I must say that's incredibly mature of you. Will you move it?" "I will" he replied, having thought long enough about the prospect of the £100,000 for their own use.

"Is there a seconder?" asked The Mayor. "Yes, I'll second the motion," said Councillor Blondel, "I can't imagine anyone else wanting to follow suit, and after all, she did serve Crewdley for over sixty years. Yes, I'll second it."

"I must object Mr Mayor," Councillor Hardie said abruptly," The Public Health Department will close us down. We can't agree to this - surely?"

The Mayor watched as Members fidgetted uncomfortably in their seats, wrestling with their consciences as they considered the grim prospect of being greeted by the mummified form of Councillor Octavia Bland, if only once a year in her full glory, against the entirely condusive thought of £100,000 being placed in the Collective Kitty to draw on when necessary. In this respect, The Mayor not only had a mutual interest, but an overwhelming advantage because, of course, he would be the Sole Trustee of the Memorial Fund.

"It's not nice," wailed Councillor Mrs Smart, "why couldn't she just go quietly like everyone else?" " I shan't want to attend any more meetings," moaned Councillor Muggeridge, "I've got a weak stomach and a very vivid imagination!"

"Now come along!" said Presbyterian, realizing the issue was in the balance, "It's what Octavia wanted! And of course, there is a precedent". He didn't have to wait long for the bait to be taken. "A precedent for this? Never Sir!"roared Councillor Bull, "with respect Mr Mayor, you are surely mistaken?"

"Not at all, even discounting Lenin, who was a Russian and could not therefore be considered a fair example, there exists in the Foyer of the University College, London, the mummified remains of the Philosopher Jeremy Bentham. I am assured he has been there since 1832. No one objects to his presence, not even the students who go about their business quite un-worried. In fact, as Councillor Arkwright suggested, the remains of Jeremy Bentham have become almost an attraction, part of the very fabric of the building. Councillor Blondel also made what I consider to have been an extremely valid point, when he said no one else would wish to join her. That's true for me. How about anyone else?" "You must be joking Mr Mayor," said Councillor Mrs Smart, "Octavia was definately a one-off!"

"Oh Good," Presbyterian replied a la mode, "Just for a moment, I thought we were about to be inundated with volunteers."

Councillor Arthur Hardie got to his feet. "Mr Mayor, the peculiarities of this Council never fail to amaze me. Here we are, nine reasonably intelligent people apparently seriously considering having one of our recent number embalmed and put on Public Display. I personally can't think of one reason why we should agree to her request, but I can think of a very good reason for some of my fellow members agreeing to it. In one word Mr Mayor - Money!"

"Shame on you for making such an improper suggestion," yelled Arkwright, "we're trying to do our best for Octavia."

"Here, here," added Councillor Mrs Smart, "whatever we decide, it will be for humanitarian reasons only and certainly not for monetary gain."

"The whole damn thing is very peculiar," Councillor Bull suggested, "it's bloody ridiculous. I mean, cats and dogs can slip in through the railings of the gates. They get into The Foyer, they'll be peeing up the bloody thing."

"It will be properly mounted, I assure you Councillor Bull," replied The Mayor, "every hygenic precaution will be taken." "Can we have your word on that old boy?"asked the doubting Bull.

"Certainly!" The Mayor assured him, "Absolutely - any other comments or shall I put it to the vote?" "Well, I certainly shan't be supporting the motion. She was a deranged old woman," said Councillor Mrs Enid Thomas, "we all knew that. Surely, it's not legal? What do the Solicitors to the Council say?"

"Mr Dash..... how about it?" The Mayor asked.

The Solicitor got up and shuffled a few papers, as Solicitors do before replying, "It's perfectly legal Mr Mayor, that is to say, both the arrangements for the preservation of her body and the creation of her proposed Welfare Fund."

"Thank you ...any thing to add Mr Doolittle?"

"No Sir," he replied, "it is as Mr Dash has stated."

Councillor Hardie waited for a moment or two for others to speak, but no one did, so he rose again.

"Mr Mayor, I know the Members of this Council very well indeed and from what's been said already, and what's not been said by one or two who should have at least said something, that you might be about to take the most ridiculous decision you have ever taken. The whole thing is preposterous! It could only happen in Crewdley! My God! She even mentioned the prospect of her not being put into the River Crewd. Did she think it was The Ganges? Our Solicitors say everything is alright. Tell me Mr Mayor, was there a particular fee given to them when the old lady made her Will?" He took his seat and waited for an answer. The Mayor looked to Doolittle and Dash and then back to Hardie.

"Yes, a fee will be paid, as in any legal transaction," said The Mayor firmly. "And didn't they consider their loyalties might have been divided, as they tried presumably, to weigh their fee against the legal position of her Will, and the moral position, in my opinion. Can I be assured that the Solicitors to the Council were not influenced by any motive other than the legality of the Will?" demanded Hardie, "and I want to hear them answer for themselves Mr Mayor."

It was obvious the Councillor was annoyed and he sat down with some indignation, frustrated by the lack of support from his colleagues. Dash stood up to address the Members, with the confidence of one well-experienced in such matters. He bowed his head slightly towards Hardie, who glared straight back at him. "Mr Mayor, I can reassure Council of our absolute impartiality and integrity in this matter."

"Of course you can, and thank you Mr Dash," said The Mayor, "Now, are we ready to vote? Those in Favour, please show" His own hand was the first to go up, and it was followed by the hands of Messrs Blondel, Evans-Jenkins, Bull, Muggeridge, Arkwright, and Smart. "That is seven in favour Mr Mayor," said Beard.

"Those against," The Mayor asked. Hardie and Mrs Thomas raised their hands. "That is two," counted Beard.

"And that is carried," Presbyterian added cheerfully, "Thank you colleagues. We have only tomorrow remaining to prepare for Friday's funeral. With your permission, and as described in the pre-amble of the Will, I shall make the final arrangements." "What funeral? It's not any funeral a normal person would recognise Mr Mayor," shouted Hardie, "it's more like keeping her in a cupboard. You'll be telling us next she's going to do a Walt Disney."

"What are you talking about?" demanded Arkwright, "sorry Mayor, through you of course. What do you mean Councillor Hardie, a Walt Disney?" "Bringing her back to life when they've got the technology, that's what I mean," answered Hardie, "I hope we're not going to dabble in that sort of nonsense as well, are we Mayor?"

"Don't be silly Arthur, of course not," he answered, "Any more questions? Good! I can advise everyone that the time of Councillor Bland's funeral will be at 9.22 am precisely on Friday morning," said The Mayor, "and before anyone asks, 9.22am precisely was the time Octavia was born into the world..... a nice, if somewhat unusual request I thought."

"It's bloody bizarre," Hardie answered, "well in keeping with the rest of it."

"Would Councillors therefore be at their places for 9.15am? " The Mayor asked, ignoring this last, provocative remark, "I declare this Extra Ordinary Meeting of the Council closed. Goodnight, have a safe journey home. Robespierre - The Mace, if you please!"

Robespierre picked up The Mace, bowed to The Mayor and all of the Councillors stood as The Mayoral Party left The Chamber, but instead of going straight up to his Parlour, Presbyterian stopped abruptly in The Foyer.

"Do you have your driving gloves with you Robespierre?" he asked casually. The Chauffer almost puckered his lips as he answered, "Yes I have, Mr Mayor. Will it be a short drive down to the River Sir?"

"Yes, I'm sure it will be Robespierre. Park the Rolls discretely near to 'Caspian House' and then I suggest you go and get yourself a pizza...... I might be some considerable time."

Robespierre parked the Rolls near to the quay at the River side.

The Mayor had dis-robed in the back of the car, he slipped out quickly and knocked the door of 'Caspian House'.

His Lieutenant smiled coyly as he sat behind the wheel watching his Master waiting for the door to open. It soon did, and the comely figure of Mrs Pippa Monroe could be seen in the hall light.

She lent forward and kissed The Mayor fully on his lips, and just for once, Robespierre wished that he too had a lady friend who would risk all for a stolen kiss. However, he locked the car and went for a pizza, as instructed.

This was followed by a long stint at 'The Star and Garter,' where one or two of the Councillors were drinking quite heavily and talking very loudly above the noise of half of the citizenship of Crewdley getting drunk. "Here's to Councillor Mrs Octavia Bland! May she rest in peace in The Foyer of The Town Hall," Robespierre said to himself, "Thank God it isn't me!"

Friday the 25th of January 1991 was an extremely cold day. It was just before 9am and in The Mayor's Parlour, Harold Presbyterian was being dressed by his ever faithfull man-servant, Anton Robespierre: First, The Robe itself, then the White-Laced Collar, next The Mayoral Chain of Office, and finally, The Civic Cocked Hat. "You look really nice Mr Mayor," said Robespierre.

"I know I do Robespierre," replied The Great Man, "I'm value for money." They left The Parlour down the old,wooden staircase and The Mayor walked nervously behind the still-closed iron gates of The Foyer, then turned to inspect the footings in the corner, onto which Councillor Bland's Casket would be mounted.

"Take the key from Beards' Office and open the gates," he said, "I'll be glad when this is all over. I don't like funerals, especially ones where the 'Star-Turn' refuses to go properly." Robespierre opened the massive iron-gates and The Mayor stepped out onto the pavement. "Good morning Mr Mayor," Councillor Blondel called out with a mis-placed enthusiasm which grieved The Great Man.

"Hello Blondel. What brings you here so early? Did her husband arrive home unexpectedly or have you been walking the streets in pursuit of Crewdley's women of the night?" "Fat chance," Blondel replied, "all is temporarily quiet on the feminine front I'm afraid Harold. We can't all have a regular place at night-school, can we?"

The other Councillors began to arrive and a few people gathered across the street in anticipation of the event. Beard was flapping about in his office and The Reverend Wooly took up his position at the entrance near the gates. It was 9.21 am when the horse drawn glass-sided hearse came into view around St Creuds' Church.

Two of Bramley's Constables halted all of the other traffic as Edwin Grimley drove his horses sedately into Church Street. "Here comes Snow White," mumbled Councillor Blondel, "waiting for her Prince to give her 'The Kiss of Life' which will return her to her beautiful, previous self."

"You're a sarcastic swine Blondel," The Mayor mumbled back, "that's one woman even you wouldn't want to kiss."

Grimley eased the horses gently over the pavement into the confines of The Town Hall Foyer. The horses were beautiful and black as the night. They stepped from one foot to another and the clacking of their hooves echoed around the ancient stone walls as Grimley drew them to a halt. A crowd of spectators had by now assembled outside on the pavement, and the eager ones were inquisitively staring through the iron bars of The Town Hall Gates.

Grimley secured the brake, and stepped down from the hearse, whereupon four young assistants, dressed as black as the horses, stood two by two at the rear. The Reverend Wooly kept a tentative and reverent distance from the hearse until the four young Pall-Bearers had managed at last to get Octavia Bland's Grand Casket down to the stone pavings. He made the sign of the cross, as much for his own reassurance as for the soul of the departed, before taking the few steps to the footings where he opened the Bible. Robespierre, in complete harmony with the occasion, adopted his best Poll-Bearers countenance as The Mayor took his place next to The Vicar of Crewdley. Presbyterian stared at The Casket. It was huge and over-bearing, rather in the fashion of a Sentry-Box, yet with the slightly bowed middle and arched top, it rather resembled a large and demented Portuguese wine barrel. It was gruesome; a dormant Jack-In-the Box lying on the stones like a felled tree, waiting to be up-lifted once again, so that its branches might grow with the sun and the rain. But it remained rooted to the spot as Reverend Wooly began to chant his Prayers and Presbyterian considered the proud people of Ghana who buried their dead in their 'occupational coffins' - beautiful wooden Ghananian Peanuts, painted yellow with green leaf motifs, a Wooden Tuna Fish, resplendent in hard-wood, honed between tailed-fin and sharp-nose in varnish and bright colours of the sea and sun, an Eagle for a Keeper of Birds, even a modern, wooden model of a motor car for a taxi-driver going on his last journey, the long and noisy way to the cemetary. No, the comparison was not a good one. A wall-safe for keeping Council Expenses money would have been more apt, The Mayor thought, or even the replica of the picture-postcard Dolls House Cottage where she lived on the outskirts of Crewdley.

Wooly droned on for what seemed like an eternity, until at last he uttered the words, "And now Lord, we commit the body of our dearly departed sister, Octavia Bland, Councillor of Crewdley, safely to the footings of this, her last resting place, in permanent memory of a life spent selflessly in Public Service, an example to us all in these dark days of temptation and sin, Amen!"

Grimley's morbid quartet tipped the Casket upright, much to the annoyance of Grimley himself who ordered them to put it back flat on the stones, so that they might each lift at a corner and thereby perform their duty. This was done, and the Civic Party watched with fascination as they shuffled the huge box along the Foyer floor and into the corner.

"Right! Gently raise it up again," said Grimley through clenched teeth. This, they did, then man-handled the coffin safely onto its stone footings. "Amen!" Wooly repeated with trepidation, "is that all Mr Mayor?"

"No it isn't. I have been instructed to open the front for a few minutes so that Civic Dignitries may view their late colleague," answered The Mayor, "so let's get on with it." He stepped smartly up to the coffin, placed his hands onto the two handles, and forced open the doors.

"Robespierre!" he snapped, "do your duty." His aide-de-camp threw the doors wide open to reveal the awful figure of the late Councillor Octavia Bland, squatting behind glass on a wooden chair, engaged in knitting a woollen scarf. "Good God!" She looks more alive than she has done for years," Blondel blurted out. "Oh dear! I'm afraid I don't like it at all," Councillor Muggeridge moaned, "please close it Mr Mayor, it makes me feel quite ill." Octavia Bland was wearing one of her best flowery dresses and a large straw hat.

Her glasses were positioned impishly at the end of her nose and she had adopted, or been given by Grimley, a peculiarly demented smile.

"Mmm not everyone's cup of tea, I grant you", replied Councillor Norman Bull, "but the old girl doesn't look too bad does she?"

Various Councillors drew nearer to inspect the mummified body of the Member for Meadow Ward. The Vicar was obviously nervous, Robespierre had hoofed it to the very back of The Foyer and was doing his best to blend with anyone and everyone. Only Councillors Arkwright and Smart kept a respectable distance between themselves and the corpse.

"Close the doors Robespierre! That will suffice until the 21st of January next year; her Ninety First Birthday Anniversary, I believe? Thank you everyone for your attendance," said The Mayor," Goodmorning!" He walked quickly up the stairs to The Parlour, followed by Robespierre, who looked round for one final glance at the Crewdley Funeral of The Century. It was not a pleasant sight.

Four weeks later, on Thursday 21st February 1991, Octavia's younger sister,

95

the eighty eight year old Olivia, was swept into Office on an over-whelming tide of apathy to serve on Crewdley Council as the new Member for Meadow Ward, in an un-contested By-Election as the single Candidate, (Natasha Hardie was by this time studying for her Doctorate in Politics at Oxford).

The turn-out figure was eight percent of the Electorate who were eligible to vote. It was almost as if Octavia had never left, with her mummified remains in The Town Hall Foyer and younger sister Olivia having taken her place in The Council Chamber, who could have noticed the difference?

CHAPTER NINE

Twinning with Croutonne Lautrec

It was just after the Annual Elections of 2nd May 1991 and the newly re-elected Members of Crewdley Council were extremely pleased with themselves. The two lovers, Morton Muggeridge and Mrs Louise Evans-Jenkins, were returned unopposed. They were rejoined by Olivia Bland, the recent By-Election victor, now elected for the second time in less than three months, at the age of eighty eight. She would therefore have to offer herself again to the Electorate in 1995, her ninety third year.

Councillor Olivia Bland was not to be offered the usual Life Insurance normally provided for the Councillors of Crewdley, but nevertheless she seemed to be enjoying the whole thing, positioning herself exactly where her late sister Octavia used to sit in The Chamber, rejoicing in the fact that Octavia's Civic Robe fitted her perfectly and smiling serenly beneath her Civic Cocked hat for the Councillors Photographic Portrait.

A pleasant air of relaxation was abroad and all seemed well with the world in Crewdley. The Annual Meeting of the Council had been held later that month and Presbyterian was duly re-elected as Mayor, without the challenge of a 'No Confidence Motion' as had occured on the last occasion, one year earlier. It was Monday 3rd June and The Mayor was sitting quietly in his Parlour as Robespierre polished the gold plated Civic Pen provided by The Great Man to celebrate the fall of a Government in 1974, committed to scrapping Crewdley's privilaged position in Local Government. The words, "P.M Prerogative, Crewdley's Salvation." could be very clearly seen by the faithful valet, even after 17 years of use at The Mayor's hand.

"The pen is beautiful," remarked Robespierre. The Mayor gave a cursory glance at the man and replied casually, "Yes, it has a charmed existence as an executor of the 'Common Good' Robespierre, matching exactly, the purpose of its humble owner."

Robespierre put it down onto the table and adopted his best Pall-Bearers expression, "Yes Sir, indeed .... its purpose exactly."

"There is altogether too much frivolity in Crewdley at the moment," The Mayor said quickly, "I don't like it. It's unnerving. They all seem to be enjoying themselves...... could be dangerous."

"I don't understand Your Honour," Robespierre replied.

"No, I don't suppose you do. Let me put it this way. Just because the weather is exceptionally good and the people seem to be happy as larks, we must not forget, that beneath the sickly facade, there probably lurks a major

problem, just waiting to erupt.... Life has taught me that much Robespierre.....
never get complacent or you're finished."

The Pall-Bearer looked even more morose, as he rubbed a soft cloth on the
windows overlooking Church Street.

"Did Sir have anything particular in mind?" he asked, knowing full well
that if he did, (and he almost certainly did) that sooner or later, (almost
certainly sooner) the problem would surely come his way, as well as The
Mayor's.

"Yes -tonights Meeting of The Council," answered Presbyterian, "that
stupid, interfering busy body Councillor Sylvia Smart has introduced an
Agenda Item that I don't like at all." Robespierre continued to clean the
windows.

"She's raised the idea of 'Twinning!'" The cleaner stopped abruptly and
looked to his Master, "Twinning Sir?"

"Yes, Twinning Robespierre." "Who with Mister Mayor?"

"A French town," he answered curtly. The colour drained from
Robespierre's face and the strength ebbed visibly from his body. "Non
Monsieur! It can not be!"

"English damn you man!" rapped The Mayor. 'Pardon Monsieur! A French
Town! Oh God!"

"Robespierre shut up!! I feel the same as you do." "But Monsieur! Pardonne
Mr Mayor, but why a French Town? Why not a German town or a Duch town,
why a French town?" The Mayor looked sternly at his disintegrating Batman.
"Pour the drinks and we'll talk this thing over in a calm manner." "Yes Sir,
certainly Sir, a whisky for both of us Sir."

He poured the drinks and sat down heavily opposite The Mayor, "That's
better Robespierre, take it easy. As I said, I dislike the idea as much as you do,
but even I can't stop her putting it on the Agenda."

Robespierre was still in shock. "However," said The "Mayor, "I can
probably get it defeated." "Thank you Your Grace. You know that for me, the
whole issue of my 'French Connection' is rather delicate."

"I am very well aware of that Robespierre, but personally, I think you are
far too touchy about your ancestor." The colour returned to Robespierre's face,
before turning bright red, "Qui Monsieur, sorry Mr Mayor."

"Look, you're no good to me in your present state, have the rest of the day
off." "Thank you Sir," he said without enthusiasm.

"But don't be late for The Council Meeting tonight." "No Sir," he answered,
already putting on his coat and disappearing through the door.

Presbyterian heard his quick footsteps on the old wooden staircase and drank the whisky that remained in his glass. He sat there for quite some time, drinking whisky and smoking a large cigar. Occasionally, he got up from his opulent leather chair to look out of the window at the people below, until he tired and resumed his seat. Certainly, the people seemed glad to be alive as they went about their business beneath blue skies and bathed in warm sunshine.

He had, of course, known of the existence of the special Agenda Item for a week, as per Standing Orders, but had been most relunctant to divulge the information to Robespierre, in anticipation of the bad effect it would surely have upon him. Presbyterian had been right in that respect and he was equally sure that Councillor Mrs Smart's reason for suggesting the wretched Agenda Item, was because she wanted to go to France on a regular basis, and she was too mean to pay for herself. A Civic Twinning would therefore achieve both objectives for the grabbing Member for River-Side East Ward. Presbyterian considered his options for that nights Meeting. He could refuse to take the Item relating to Twinning on the grounds that it was of such importance the legality of any such proposal would have to be personally vetted by The Lord Chancellor, but that was such a potentially good tactic he would keep it in mind for future use for a more serious issue, if necessary. He could claim not to have been given the statutory seven days notice of the Item, but several people knew that not to have been the case.

As a last resort, he could have attempted to seduce Councillor Mrs Smart, buy her a set of exciting French undies and taken her for a dirty weekend in Paris. Alas .... even he wasn't up to that. The Agenda Item on Twinning would be taken, but her suggestion would not recieve over-whelming support. He knew exactly which Councillors would support such an idea, and those who would not. Those in Favour were easily named as Messrs Smart, Arkwright, Blondel, Muggeridge, and Evans-Jenkins. Councillor Arkwright was a Hot-Air Balloon fanatic who made regular visits to France to participate in various Balloon Festivals, so his support would be certain. Blondel would go half way around the world in search of feminine company..... the prospect of numerous French women being presented to him as an honoured guest by the grateful inhabitants of a small French town, would guarantee his over-whelming support.

Muggeridge and Evans-Jenkins would delight in taking illicit trips abroad together on the legitimate basis of Civic Duty.

He smiled as he delighted in counting the opposition.

Bull was a bigot who hated the French and Olivia Bland disliked them intensely for ditching the Monarchy and starting a Revolution.

That left Councillors Hardie and Thomas, the token Crewdley Socialists, who would definately refuse to support any and every idea which entailed spending one penny of Rate Payer's or Poll Tax Payer's money on absolutely anything, except Direct Services for for The Town.

Presbyterian chuckled as he counted the votes .....5 In Favour, 4 Against ...It was beautifully poised, marvellously balanced..... excitingly close.....

If he was to vote 'In Favour' Councillor Smart would win, if he Abstained, she would still win but - and it was a very important but, if The Mayor decided to vote Against, the votes in The Chamber would be cast equally..... an interesting scenario because as every student of Local Government knows, in the event of a tied vote, someone very special has the chance to vote again..... The Mayor has the 'Casting Vote'!

Therefore, the success or failure of Councillor Sylvia Smart's Agenda Item would be utterly dependent upon her receiving his support.

He picked up the telephone and dialed a number he had little occasion to bother with in the normal course of events.

"Hello Sylvia, it's Harold. I think we need to talk about this evening's Council Meeting and your Agenda Item on Twinning - might I suggest lunch? Good! Shall we say one o' clock at The Forest Hotel? Excellent, I look forward to it Sylvia goodbye."

Needless to say, their rendezvous did take place, but the details of their conversation might best be considered under the heading of 'Private and Confidential'.

As instructed, Robespierre returned to The Mayor's Parlour at 5.30pm, in good time for the Council Meeting at 6pm.

He was dressing Presbyterian with the Robes of Office, in the time honoured way..... first The Robe itself, then The White Laced Collar, next The Mayoral Chain of Office and finally, The Civic Cocked Hat.

"You look spendid Mr Mayor," said The Civic Servant without his usual enthusiasm.

"Look Robespierre, stop worrying about this stupid Twinning. You're making me nervous. I can read you like a book, so behave yourself and concentrate on your Civic Duties, which as you are aware, relate entirely to my preservation and well being, so buckle up man and smile damn it!" He stared hard at his long-suffering aide de camp, who straight away lifted his chin and grinned foolishly as they prepared to leave The Parlour. Robespierre opened the door then stepped smartly ahead of The Machiavelli of Local Politics. The old wooden stairs creaked as they descended towards The Foyer and the Bowels of Democracy , but of course, did not yet enter that spendid Chamber, The Mayor choosing, as always, to be delivered to The Meeting in The Civic Rolls Royce. After two circuits of the Town, the car finally came to rest at the pavement directly outside The Town Hall. Robespierre opened the rear door for Presbyterian and shouted loudly, "Citizens! Will you please make way for your Mayor, Councillor Harold Presbyterian!"

"Thank you Robespierre, beautifully said," The Mayor congratulated him, "Now please get The Mace from Beard's Office and lead me in." Robespierre did just that, pausing only at the very door to The Council Chamber to call again, "Ladies and Gentlemen, would you please be upstanding for The Mayor of Crewdley!"

The Assembly stood as one, waited patiently for Robespierre to put The Mace in its position and then for The Mayor to take his place.

"Please be seated," he said, "The Agenda is as printed. Item One, Prayers .... Two, Apologies for Absence, Three, to confirm the Minutes of our last Meeting, Four, to receive such Communications as The Mayor of The Council may desire to lay before The Council...... Will you therefore begin our Meeting for us Reverend Wooly?"

The Vicar of Crewdley got to his feet and with a little cough, looked slowly around The Chamber, as if in some kind of dream.

"Dearly Beloved.....we are gathered here...... as Councillors and Officers of our beloved Parish .....to continue the work begun by our Forbears..... generations of Crewdley people have lived, worked and served in our little Town.....(he started again, almost as if he were a condemned man on a scaffold)..... We are all weak and humble in sight of The Lord, yet He leads us to a Promised Land .... Dear God, bless us, your humble servants, in this, their meagre place of Civic Meeting and decision ..let them agree what is best for the people of Crewdley, and be guided by your hand .... Amen." He sat down with a bump.

Prebyterian gave him a cursory look and wondered if it was perhaps time for The Vicar to take that holiday.

"Thank you Vicar. Item Two..... Apologies ..there are none, Item Three..... to confirm the Minutes of our last Meeting ..... will someone move acceptance?"

"I move Mr Mayor," shouted Muggeridge. "Second," said Councillor Louise Evans-Jenkins quickly.

"Thank you ...is that agreed?"

"Agreed," came the collective reply.

"Good....... on to Agenda Item Four..... Communications to The Mayor..... yes..... I have received a Communication which I intend to place before you now. It is a letter from Councillor Mrs Sylvia Smart. In fact, I think I would actually prefer to ask if Councillor Smart would perhaps para-phrase the letter herself and give everyone the benefit of its contents?"

"Certainly Mr Mayor," she answered already getting to her feet.

"The floor is yours," said The Great Man.

"Thank you Mr Mayor. Dear Colleagues.......my letter to our Mayor was not a long one, but it is rather important. I have been asked to para-phrase, so I hope that you will bear with me?"

She smiled peculiarly, her red lipstick framing her teeth, like sugar-cubes in a bed of strawberries, "For quite a number of years, I have sought to propogate the name of Credley wherever I have travelled. Many of you will be aware that France has been my favourite port of call since 1981, when I was lucky enough to have won a weekend for two in Paris." Robespierre looked impassively ahead as Councillor Mrs Smart drew breath and continued, "Since that time my husband and I have often followed the course of the beautiful River Seine on our return journey to Crewdley." There was still not even the suggestion of a blink from The Mayor's Chauffeur though Councillor Mrs Olivia Bland seemed to have lost interest. "It occured to me Mr Mayor, how much it might benefit the people of our town, if others were given the opportunity to do as I have done? You did ask me to para-phrase my letter Mr Mayor and so I shall. What it comes down to is this........after several years of personal association with the people of one small town in Northern France, a town I might add remarkably similiar in both size and appearance to Crewdley, and after much discussion, informal of course I assure you, I am convinced that the time is perfect for us to consider Twinning with Croutonne Lautrec!"

Robespierre sank deeply into the seat and seemed to pass out as Councillor Smart's words rang in his ears.

"I therefore propose Mr Mayor, that we send a fact-finding party to Croutonne Lautrec with the specific purpose of clearing the way for a Grand Twinning between our two towns; to take place as soon as possible."

"Have you any particular dates for us to consider?" The Mayor asked knowingly. "Ah yes," she answered, returning once more to the script, "I propose Mr Mayor, that we visit them on Sunday 14th July, that is Bastille Day Your Worship, and that if all goes well, the French attend our next Council Meeting on Wednesday 31st July."

"Thank you Coucillor Smart..... does anyone wish to speak?" The Mayor asked somewhat cautiously, fully realizing what was to come.

Councillor Bull rose to his full height as Robespierre disappeared under the table. He placed one hand on each jacket lapel and breathed in deeply, going redder by the second. "I do!" he roared as he exhaled, "This is an outrage! How dare you bring such a matter before this Council Madam," he fumed, "have you no shame?" "Here, here!" squeaked Councillor Olivia Bland, "they're horrible Revolutionaries who ditched the Monarchy. A pox upon them all!"

"Charming!" someone called out, in mock astonishment, but in a tone that clearly asked for more.

"Now now," said The Mayor, "all comments are to be directed through me, if you please." Councillor Bull took another deep breath, "Does Councillor Smart know anything at all about our history? Is she aware of the dastardly role of the French after hundreds of years of treachery, deceipt, Jacobianism and debauchery of our women?" "I say Mr Mayor," Councillor Muggeridge interrupted, "they were our Allies in the War weren't they?"

"Huh! You must be joking!" Councillor Bull bellowed, "You know nothing! Between 1940 and 1944, we were Occupied by the buggers. They were here, in this very town." "Oh what's he going on about Mr Mayor?" asked Councillor Mrs Louise Evans-Jenkins, seeing the prospect of illicit Civic weekends in France with her lover in the next seat being snatched away by the Roaring Bull.

"There you are! Too young to know, but never interested sufficiently to have found out bugger-all about the Dark Days of the Forties," Bull retorted angrily. "I stand accused Mr Mayor," said the guilty young woman, "I'm so sorry I wasn't born at the time Councillor Bull .....matters were entirely out of my hands."

"Humph!" Bull snorted, "ignorance is bliss I suppose. Now let me tell you and the other Councillors who weren't here exactly what happened. Permission to speak Mr Mayor?"

"Oh, please carry on Councillor Bull, I certainly think that we should have an open and honest debate about the issue," he answered, knowing full well the venom that was to follow.

"Thank you..... Councillor Mrs Smart suggests we Twin with the French, I suggest that we give her a one-way ticket to the wretched place and declare a By-Election!"

"Don't be so bloody ridiculous Norman. What on earth is the matter with you?..... sorry, through you of course Mr Mayor," said the staying-put Member for River Side East Ward.

"The French! That's what's the matter with me..... it's a stab in the back! You're asking us to Twin with the bastards!"

"Language, please Norman," said The Mayor, "lets keep it clean, shall we?" "But the French!", the Bull snorted, "they were here in Crewdley..... the Free French, DeGaulles Fornicators. This was their bloody headquarters! They started to change our way of life, they were actually holed-up here for four years with their wretched parades, wearing their bloody berets and stupid striped jerseys. They sold onions from bicycles Mr Mayor, they played accordians, ate snails and garlic, they smoked foul French cigarettes, drank French wine and I can't stress this too strongly, they actually spoke in French!

"They put French frogs in the pond to remind them of home, they had never heard of cricket, they drove on the wrong side of the road and they played The Marseillaise every time it bloody well rained!

"They organized the most degrading social evenings and clamoured after our women. Our whole way of life was under threat. Thank God the Americans came to help us out!"

"I'll take that as a speech against the proposal, "The Mayor said with a certain degree of understatement, " anyone else?" Yes Mr Mayor, I feel I must speak out against this anti-French hysteria. As Members may know, I have often visited France to participate in various activities relating to Hot-Air Ballooning. In fact, Croutonne Lautrec was the venue for one such Festival. It was marvellous! The people made me so welcome."

Robespierre sank deeper into his seat.

"In fact, I always hoped that someone would take the initiative. Twinning is all the rage you know Mr Mayor. Everyone is doing it. Haringey has Twinned with somewhere in Jamaica and Sheffield has Twinned with some city in Northern China! So what's wrong with Crewdley Twinning with Croutonne Lautrec?"

"They're French! Thats what's wrong!" roared Councillor Bull "Well, I think you're stupid," Councillor Mrs Evans-Jenkins shouted loudly, "bloody stupid."

"At least I know my history Madam!"

"You're pathetic," she retorted, "You're out of date and pathetic!"

"Wait!" called The Mayor, "it's all getting rather silly. Now, Councillor Blondel, you have had your hand up for quite some time. Do you wish to speak?" "Yes Mr Mayor," answered the rather elegant and dapper Member for Crewdley Town Ward. "I really don't know what all this fuss is about. It's surely just to say the occasional hello to our friends across the Channel? After all, their food and drink is first-class and the people are awfully nice. I must admit to still being a little in love with Bridgette Bardot Mr Mayor, but am I the lesser man for that? I think not actually.

Then there's the extra revenue that will be generated when the French come over to see us ......the Local Business people will like that and so will I. It seems to me, the English have trouble enjoying themselves..... too inhibited if you ask me, whereas the French, well! They really know how to let go, particularly the women, I've noticed. Yes Mr Mayor! Count me in! I'm all for it!"

"I rather thought that you might be Councillor Blondel," said Presbyterian, trying to keep a protective eye on Robespierre, who seemed to have recovered slightly from the initial shock.

"Anyone else?" he asked. "Yes," answered Councillor Mrs Enid Thomas, "I am certain that someone as politically adroit as yourself will already have worked out our attitude to this proposed piece of extravagance Mr Mayor."

"Indeed," he replied.

"Yes I thought so..... Councillor Hardie and I are concerned at the cost of Twinning to the Poll Tax Payers..... not only that, we question the motives of one or two Councillors who seem rather keen on the sexual and social possibilities, and not the cultural and fraternal."

"I say Mayor," said Blondel, "can she say that?"

"She already did!", snapped Hardie, "junketing on the Rates, that's all it is. We're against it on principle!"

And just for good measure, Councillor Mrs Olivia Bland summoned up enough breath for one, good, loud shout of, "Jacobins!!"

"Mm, I wonder if we're ready to vote?" asked Presbyterian. Councillor Muggeridge jumped up quickly to his feet. "I think we should go and see them in Croutonne Lautrec. I like the French!"

Robespierre slid under the table and The Mayor took his cue.

"Those in Favour, Please show." Councillors Smart, Arkwright, Blondel, Muggeridge, and Evans-Jenkins indicated their approval, but The Mayor's hand stayed down.

"And Those Against," The Mayor asked. Bull, Bland, Hardie and Thomas raised their hands, and the Town Clerk Bernard Beard called with enthusiam, "Those in Favour five, Those Against, four."

"And I shall Abstain," said The Mayor. "Thank you Sir," replied Beard, "the Motion is carried in that case by five votes to four with one abstention."

"Very well colleagues, we have agreed to send a fact-finding party to Croutonne Lautrec to investigate the possibilities of a Grand Twinning between our two towns. The date mentioned was Sunday 14th July, Bastille day, and we shall invite a Civic Party from Croutonne Lautrec to attend our next Council Meeting on Wednesday 31st July. Any volunteers?" asked The Mayor. The same five hands were raised as for the affirmative first vote, but again The Mayor's hand stayed down.

"Thank you. I suggest our Civic Party consists of Councillors Smart, Arkwright, Blondel, Muggeridge and Evans-Jenkins," said The Mayor.

"And yourself Sir?" Beard asked cautiously.

"No, no not on this occasion, I am more than confident that Councillor Mrs Smart will do a marvellous job in representing Crewdley."

Robespierre couldn't believe his ears...... The Mayor was declining to represent Crewdley on an Expenses Paid Trip abroad ..... Councillor Mrs Smart was certainly confused by The Mayor's performance and Councillor Bull was already dis-robing in The Town Clerks Office.

"Thank you Colleagues," Presbyterian called cheerfully,"I hereby close the Meeting. We shall assemble again on Wednesday 31st July ... Good Night, have a safe journey home."

Robespierre collected himself and The Mace then led The Mayor from the Council Chamber. He deposited the Symbol of Office on Beard's desk and dashed breathlessly up the old, wooden stairs to The Mayors Parlour.

"Mr Mayor..... you didn't vote against," he rasped.

"I never said I would Robespierre. When people come up with ideas, particularly when Councillors come up with ideas, which isn't very often I must admit..... but when they do Robespierre, one has to be extremely circumspect. It's all about instinct for survival, so I'm not going to commit myself For or Against the idea of Twinning at this stage; it's too early, things can go wrong, events can get out of control if the idea has come from someone else. So I'll have to let it run I'm afraid .... free-wheel so to speak, to make sure we're on the winning side at the end Robespierre, just like your ancestor, you understand?"

"But Monsieur!"

"English!"

"Mister Mayor, Mrs Smart said Crewdley would be Twinned with Croutonne Lautrec."

"That's right Robespierre, what about it?"

"But that is the town of my ancestors Mr Mayor!" he said with alarm.

Presbyterian watched his aide de camp trembling before him. "Pour the drinks and sit down," he said firmly, "you look a little perplexed."

They each drank a whisky before Robespierre helped The Mayor to disrobe.

"I don't know why you're so concerned Robespierre. It was all such a long time ago after all," The Mayor said as he downed another drink. Robespierre was by now shaking like a leaf. "It is bad My Lord, very, very, bad, "he quivered.

They drank more whisky and Robespierre calmed down. The Mayor knew his man as a time-keeper knows his watch. There was something more between Robespierre and that little French Town.

"Have you told me everything about your ancestor?" he asked him. Robespierre gave a silly, non-convincing grin.

"There's nothing to tell Sir..... it was as you say, a very long time ago."

Exactly five weeks and five days later, the Civic Party set off from Crewdley in a Mini- Bus to the Provincial Airport and the hour's flight to Paris. The Mayor wished them Bon Voyage from The Town Hall Foyer and saw the look of anxiety on the face of Robespierre when Councillor Blondel promised to look up his relatives in both Paris and Croutonne Lautrec. "If they're French and they're called Robespierre, I'll definately give them your name Anton,"he said, "you never know, when they find out about you and your esteemed position in Crewdley, it might just be the thing that will swing this Twinning lark for us eh?"

Robespierre spent the remainder of that weekend in a kind of limbo as he waited for the Civic Party to return. It was late on Monday evening when the Mini-Bus came quietly over Crewdley Bridge. The Councillors disembarked to make their weary way home. Anton Robespierre watched the scene from the privacy of his apartment, and cursed as Councillor Mrs Sylvia Smart waved to the driver. "Damn her," he said, "she's even brought back a Tricolour and a string of onions!"

Tuesday 16th July was a most beautiful day, the sun shone, the birds chirped and the good people of Crewdley were majoritively content. The Mayors Parlour was quiet and only the rapping of Presbyterian's fingers on the table disturbed the silence. It was just after 8am, but The Mayor had now to take the initiative, and so after checking a telephone number in his book, he pressed the buttons and waited as it rang out.

"Hello..... ah Sylvia, a very good morning to you, sorry it's rather early .....I thought we should have lunch Sylvia and you can tell me all about Croutonne Lautrec..... oh good..... yes The Forest Hotel, shall we say 12.30pm? Bye Sylvia, look forward to it..... yes..... indeed au revoir as they say in France."

Robespierre pulled up outside The Forest Hotel at 12.15pm and Presbyterian instructed him to wait.

"I might be an hour," he said coldly, "but it's your own fault Robespierre. I just couldn't possibly trust you within twenty yards of Councillor Mrs Smart with your attitude problem to this Twinning issue.

You can have one drink at 'The Star and Garter' , I shall be watching from the Restaurant, so just make sure you're no longer than twenty minutes." He went inside and took his seat at a table near to the window. Councillor Mrs Smart entered the Restaurant as he was finishing his third gin and tonic.

"Ah Sylvia, please come and join me," he said as convincingly as he could, "you look extremely well..... France must have agreed with you Sylvia."

"Oh it did Harold..... it did," she sighed, "it was wonderful."

He ordered more drinks, and after a period that was rather too long to have indicated maximum efficiency, the waitress finally came to their table. After making little jokes about the absence of L'escargot and frogs legs being on the menu, they each settled for Dover Sole.

"So how were our French cousins?"asked Presbyterian, with by now a slight alcoholic glint in his eye. "Absolutely marvellous," she answered, "so courteous it was almost embarrassing. They are extremely keen to Twin with Crewdley as soon as possible."

"Oh good!" replied The Mayor, doing his best to pretend that she had not, in truth, confirmed his worst fears. Their lunch lasted almost exactly an hour, during which time Councillor Mrs Sylvia Smart behaved in a more liberal manner than The Mayor had ever witnessed. She seemed almost like a school-girl on her first date and he found her most disconcerting. They said farewell in the car park and he watched her drive off towards the town. Robespierre pulled the Civic Rolls Royce alongside his Master, brought it to a halt and got out to hold the door.

"Caspian House Robespierre .....I happen to know that Mrs Pippa Monroe has a half day off ...park near the Bridge and wait, I might be quite some time."

Harold Presbyterian was as good as his word. The moon had long risen when he reappeared from the front door of Caspian House, grinning like a Cheshire cat.

"Cheer up Robespierre," he chided, "look life in the face and smile." "Yes Sir," he answered, looking for all the world as if he was about to attend his own funeral,"I'm as happy as a lark Sir, or perhaps a Night Owl would be more apt?"

"That's it Robespierre, cheer up .... there's everything to play for. Life is extremely good. You can have tomorrow morning off, how's that?" "Thank you Sir, but I was going to ask you for it anyway."

"Oh! And why's that?" asked The Mayor as they approached The Town Hall. "I have a terrible toothache, Your Worship. I must visit the Dentist." The Mayor exhaled in exasperation. "Take the whole day off then Robespierre in that case. We musn't have you miserable on the job must we?" His look at The Mayor in the rear view mirror spoke volumes as his tooth throbbed with pain and a gnawing fear in his stomach made him wish Croutonne Lautrec had been covered by the cruel waves of La Manche at a date not entirely dis-similiar to 18th June 1815.

The French arrived in Crewdley on Tuesday 30th July, in good time for Wednesday's Meeting of the Council. Beard had booked them into 'The Forest Hotel,' where they would be joined for dinner by the Crewdley Civic Party, led by The Mayor. Robespierre had asked The Mayor for the night off, claiming his tooth had once again become a source of agony, a request to which The Mayor reluctantly acceded; not that he had believed Robespierre, far from it, but because he knew very well that his valet did not wish to attend. Robespierre would be allowed his absence from the dinner, but his services would definately be required the next day, whatever he said or did.

A happy coincidence was apparent with regard to the number of Councillors attending the dinner. Crewdley was represented by The Mayor of course, with Councillors Smart, Arkwright, Blondel, Muggeridge and Evans-Jenkins; six in all which perfectly matched the French Party's number. However, the French were divided equally between the sexes, with three male Councillors and three female. They were Monsieurs Marcel Leotard, Mayor of Croutonne Lautrec, Henri Pugette and Claude Molaire, so elegantly complimented by the presence of Madames Florette Angou, Marianne Limoge and Angelique Pascal.

A most pleasant evening was enjoyed by all, with the possible exception of Bernard Beard, the Town Clerk, whom The Mayor forced to stand to attention between courses as a kind of makeshift Robespierre who could be called over by anyone to attend to their needs. Degradation was the name of the game, and Beard was redder than the Lobster Entree, as he stood between Roast Beef, Apple Tart, French coffee and Napoleon Brandy. The "Pox Doctors Clerk" wished the ground would have opened up, but it didn't and he had to take it like the wimp that he was. The big day arrived and Presyterian had arranged for the French to attend a Reception prior to the Council Meeting, which as usual, would commence at 6pm. A Red-Letter Day indeed, particularly as the Reception was to be held in The Mayor's Parlour. Robespierre had ensured that a torrent of drinks were available, with sandwiches and various cheeses of France and England. Presbyterian noticed particularly that Robespierre had disappeared the second the French arrived, but he was caught up in the melee of Gallic greetings and could not conveniently break free to reprimand his absent aide de Camp.

Unfortunately for Robespierre, the strain of the last few weeks was to prove too much. He locked himself in his quarters and drank a whole bottle of the best Civic Red Wine. Presbyerian was not unduly worried by his non-appearance, though he would later fine him at least a months wages. The Council Meeting was about to begin, Beard was again called upon to carry out Robespierre's duties, and he placed The Mace firmly on the top-table with a defiant thud. The Mayor got to his feet, breathed in deeply and looked carefully around The Council Chamber. The Press were present, as were a good number of the public. The French Party were seated in the places of the absent English Councillors, Hardie, Bull, Thomas and Bland.

"Dear Friends!", The Mayor began, "it gives me great pleasure to welcome you all to tonight's meeting of Crewdley Town Council. In parlticular of course, on behalf of us all, may I extend a sincere welcome to our French guests, the Councillors of Croutonne Lautrec and their Mayor, Monsieur Marcel Leotard?" There was polite clapping around The Chamber and several waves of ackowledgement from the French at this announcement.

The Mayor continued, "Tonight's Meeting is therefore both extra ordinary and unique in the history of our Town. We have a few items of ordinary business to conclude before we officially welcome Monsieur Leotard and our French guests. The Agenda then is as printed; Item One, Prayers; Item Two, Apologies for Absence; Item Three, to confirm the Minutes of the Meeting of the Council held on the 3rd June 1991; Item Four, to receive such Communications as The Mayor of The Council may desire to lay before The Council; Item Five, Twinning with Croutonne Lautrec.

Will you please say Prayers then, Reverend Wooly?" "Certainly Your Worship," replied Wooly with a ludricrous grin, "Dearly beloved we are gathered here today in the sight of the Lord our God. May it please the Lord as we attempt to serve our people in the certain knowledge that He watches over us all and His is a Forgiving and Kindly Presence. Dear Lord, we welcome our guests from France..... may their time with us be both happy and fruitful; may our two Towns prosper from their association and their Churches be blessed with virtue and rightoeusness."

For a moment, Presbyterian saw The Vicar resplendent in Stags Antlers, a phenomenon experienced also by the culprit himself. Their eyes met and each knew what the other thought, before Wooly regained his composure and ended the Prayer with a "Thank you God, Amen".

"And thank you Reverend Wooly," said The Mayor, truly thankful indeed that the man of the cloth had not shouted,"Paganism lives in Crewdley" in his moment of near-weakness.

"Item Two, Apologies for Absence." "Yes Mr Mayor, there are four apologies from Councillors Hardie, Thomas, Bland and Bull," said Beard without explanation as to their reaons why.

"Item Three; to confirm the Minutes of the Meeting of The Council held on 3rd June 1991 - would someone please move that I sign the Minutes as an accurate record?" The Mayor said. "I move Mr Mayor," said an ebullient Councillor Mrs Smart, "And I Second," added Councillor Arkwright.

"Is that Agreed?" enquired The Mayor. "Agreed!" came the collective reply.

Thank you ....Item Four; to receive such Communications as The Mayor of the Council may desire to lay before The Council," he said breezily, "Yes, there is a letter from Councillor Bull which, given the Public nature of our gathering tonight and the presence of our guests, I propose to consider at a future meeting. Needless to say, it is a letter very much in keeping with Councillor Bull's considered opinion on the issue of bi-lateral Civic Connections."

There were some puzzled expressions on several French faces and The Mayor moved quickly on.

Item Five; Twinning with Croutonne Lautrec. Councillor Mrs Smart will now address The Council. The floor is yours Madame," he said with panache.

The Ambassador for Goodwill stepped forward, dressed resplendently in a blue suit with its lapels pinned back with the badge of a French cockerel and a Fleur-de Lis respectively. Her head was covered with a wide brimmed white hat which cast a smokey shadow over her face yet gave an atmospheric and contrasting effect to the blood-red blouse of the finest shiny shot-silk. She had certainly entered into the spirit of the event. "Thank you Mr Mayor," she began nervously, "it is a great honour for me to welcome Monsieur Marcel Leotard, The Mayor of Croutonne Lautrec and his fellow Councillors to Crewdley."

She smiled approvingly at the applause this brought and waved her fingers in the general direction of the French. "I am truly honoured to have been asked to give this address. May I first of all thank Councillor Leotard for the magnificient hospitality which he provided for our Civic Party on our Official visit to Croutonne Lautrec on the 14th July, Bastille Day?"

She stopped and smiled again as a few more claps echoed around The Chamber. She was beginning to enjoy it. Quite suddenly, the doors flew open and the drunken figure of Robespierre came falling into The Chamber. There were gasps of anguish from all sides at the appearance of the man. "My God!" said Councillor Mrs Smart, "what is he doing?"

"Robespierre!" The Mayor shouted, "what's the meaning of this?" "Vive Crewdley - Vive Croutonne Lautrec!" he yelled, oblivious to them all.

The Mayor's reputation as a quick-witted Politician was put to good effect.

"I hereby Move Standing Order 13 - is there a Seconder?" he barked. "Which one is that?" asked Councillor Muggeridge.

"Exclusion of the Public!" he replied.

"Then I Second".

"Is that agreed?" asked The Mayor in near desperation.

"Yes!!!" came the reply, "Yes!!!"

"Beard!! Clear the Gallery!" roared The Mayor, "we shall adjourn for fifteen minutes!" Robespierre staggered around The Council Chamber as members of the public and the Press cleared the Gallery.

"And the French!", The Mayor insisted. Beard reluctantly urged them into The Foyer as pandemonium broke out. "Robespierre!" yelled a voice that was not local. "'eet ez Robespierre!!"

"Get the French back in," yelled The Mayor,"we'd better settle this thing once and for all!" Beard did as he was told and as the last of the French were safely back inside The Chamber, he closed the door.

Madame Marianne Limoge grabbed Robespierre by the collar in a manner befitting the occasion, "Eet' eez Robespierre," she gasped, "look at eez face!" The whole assembly was unfortunately already doing just that as Robespierre grinned like a Court Jester. "Monsieur Maire!", he blubbed.

"English!" demanded The Mayor.

"I am soree," explained Madame Limoge, "but I am doing mei bezst."

"No, not you dear lady," he apologized, "Robespierre - what the hell is going on?" "Theur portrait en Croutonne Lautrec," said Councillor Molaire, "eet ez 'im."

"Who?" The Mayor demanded. "Robespierre!" the French yelled back. "Ee eez theur exact likenez ov Maximilien Marie Isidore Robespierre," added Councillor Marianne Limoge, "I am an 'istorian - I know my 'istory."

"Well I don't", said Blondel.

The contemporary version of the man in dispute swayed quietly to and fro, incommunicado entirely with the physical exception of the.fingers of his right hand, which were formed into a victory 'V' sign. "The Revolution!" said Councillor Pugette.

"The execution of Louis the 18th!", added Councillor Angelique Pascal.

"My God, what does it all mean?" asked Councillor Mrs Smart. Councillor Florette Angou was the next to speak, "For us, 1789 is both 'thur end and 'thur beginning of France. Bastille Day is like a volano! 'E must be related to the Revolutionnaire Robespierre" "Hoorah!" roared Angelique Pascal, Marianne Limoge and Mayor Leotard. "Merd!" shouted the others. "You see?" said Councillor Florette Angou, "we are divided still."

"Eez ancestor was given much jewellery and gold by the Monarchists," said Councillor Henri Pugette, "but the bastarde ran off weeth the treasure and joined the Revolution! In Croutonne Lautrec, ee eez 'ated by Monarchists."

"And loved by Republicans!" Mayor Leotard exclaimed defiantly. "And then," said Marianne Limoge, "Robespierre was a Captain in Napoleon's Army, 'ee changed sides at Waterloo and joined 'thur Eengleesh." "Napoleon was a dictator," said Mayor Leotard, "he was still a hero of the Republic!" "He was the most controversial man in our 'istory," added Councillor Marianne Limoge, "I gained my Doctorate een ez life... eez biography az you say."

"And this man 'eez is an Officer 'en Crewdley?" asked Henri Pugette.

"Yes!" said The Mayor, "but a very minor one indeed. "Oh! But theese makes 'eet very difficult for 'uz," answered Florette Angou. "Surely not," Councillor Mrs Smart said with a hint of desperation in her voice, "it was all such a long time ago after all."

Mayor Leotard's expression became grave, "In France Madame Smart, 'thur Revolution is everything, in England 'eet eez not ' thur same. Our community was divided, thur wound was verey deep. And now, to find Robespierre 'eer like theese."

"But he's just the chauffer," said Councillor Mrs Smart, "the chauffer that's all, in fact, he isn't even that because he is dismissed from his employment as from now."

The chauffer in question didn't seem to care about the terms and conditions of his contract at that particular juncture, and continued to sway to and fro, with his arm outstretched resembling a demented stork.

"He is certainly not dismissed," Presbyterian insisted, "Beard! Would you please be kind enough to take Mayor Leotard and his Party into your office for a few minutes? We need to talk."

With some difficulty, Beard managed to convey the essence of The Mayor's request to the French, and in a most agitated manner, they followed him out of The Chamber to The Town Clerks Office. "You swine Robespierre!" shouted Councillor Mrs Smart," you're going to ruin everything. Consider yourself sacked!" "Vive Crewdley!", garbled the source of discontent.

"Shut up Robespierre," demanded The Mayor, "I'll speak with you later. In the meantime, sit down over there and don't move!" "He has to go!" shouted Councillor Mrs Smart, "it's all his fault!"

"Ah, now that is a most interesting point for discussion," replied The Mayor, "particularly in view of the fact, that it was you Councillor Smart who suggested Twinning with the French in the first place."

"How dare you - he's your chauffer and he's drunk!" she yelled.

"That is absolutely correct on both counts," said The Mayor, "however, Robespierre has been under the most severe strain ever since you first mentioned the idea of Twinning." "So it's all my fault?" she enquired incredulously.

"I am merely stating the facts. But whatever happens, Robespierre stays," said The Mayor. "Oh dear, things seemed to be going so well, I was so looking forward to Twinning with a real French town," said Councillor Mrs Louise Evans-Jenkins.

"Yes me too," added Councillor Muggeridge, secretly squeezing her hand. "Very bad form Robespierre old boy," Councillor Arkwright confirmed turning to the miscreant, "he's absolutely blotto". "Whatto!" answered Robespierre, attempting to enter into the spirit of the occasion.

"Shut up," snapped The Mayor "now listen everyone. Nothing has changed. I am going to recall the Meeting to Order, the sooner we resume, the better."

"But it has changed!" Councillor Mrs Smart asserted, "we have got a drunkard who just happens to be our Chauffeur and Mace Bearer to The Mayor of Crewdley. The French won't want to know us. What a pity there isn't a guillotine out there in the Park!"

"Beard! Ask the French to come back in and make sure no one from The Weekly Weaver is present. It could be quite an awkward meeting" said The Mayor.

The French returned, still deep in animated conversation.

"Please be seated everyone," said The Mayor, "let me first offer an apology to you and your fellow Councillors Monsieur Leotard, on behalf of of all, including Robespierre." All eyes turned again to the hapless individual, who now seemed to have slipped into an alcoholic stupor.

"Councillor Mrs Sylvia Smart had begun her Civic Address to our friends from Croutonne Lautrec and I now propose to allow her to continue. Councillor Smart, would you therefore kindly carry on with your speech?"

As she was rising, the sullen figure of Councillor Marcel Leotard, Mayor of Croutonne Lautrec, also stood up to speak.

"Ah, you wish to speak Marcel," Presbyterian enquired, "I did intend to call upon you to reply to Councillor Smart's welcoming address, but if you wish to say something now, please do." "Monsieur Maire," he began, "when Councillor Madame Smart came to 'uz in Croutonne Lautrec, we 'wur veery plezed to see 'ur. We wur knowing that many French people were 'en Crewdley in the War. The Free French were 'erre and per'aps we should 'ave kept 'en contact long before now?"

There were a few polite shouts of, "Here, here!"

"But but now 'eet ez de'ferent," he said "Robespierre 'ez 'ere. 'Ee 'az, 'ow you say, opened up a can 'ov wurms.

"Oh God!" said Councillor Mrs Smart, "I knew it."

"I 'em sorry Madame Smart,"he added, "but now we 'av a division in 'ower delegation. Some of 'uz are indeed Republicans 'oo approved of Robespierre. But 'othurs .... for some 'ov our Party, thur pain 'ov thur Revolution 'ez still too much. Per'aps et waz fate that brought us to Crewdley? Monsieur Mayor .... Croutonne Lautrec 'ez very much like Crewdley. Our town 'ez 'undreds of years old. But 'thur community 'ez divided. Some people want to keep 'thur Republic, 'othurs want 'thur Monarchy to be restored. It 'ez unfortunate that Robespierre 'ez 'ere among you still. In ow'er Town 'all, are two portraits. One 'ez 'ov King Louis 18th and the 'uther 'ez Robespierre. Our Community 'ez balanced between those two men .... we could not disturb 'thur balance, else catastrophe would befall Croutonne Lautrec. Therefore, Monsieur Mayor, we cannot agree to Twin with Crewdley!" "Robespierre has to go!", shouted Councillor Mrs Smart. "But no Madame," answered Mayor Leotard, "may I suggest that your balance also needs to be kept, 'az 'en Croutonne Lautrec?"

"Quite so," said Presbyterian, "that was my decision precisely. We must maintain the status quo at all costs." "Alas Monsieur Mayor," said Mayor Leotard, "I think that now we must return to France. Everyone 'ez welcome to visit 'uz, but I think it is best that Monsieur Robespierre stays 'ere 'en Crewdley."

"Most aptly put," replied Presbyterian, "Well colleagues, I do believe that this would be an appropriate time to end our Meeting? May I in turn, extend the hand of friendship to all citizens of Croutonne Lautrec and ask that they visit us soon, but not perhaps all at once?" "Ha, ha, most humerous your Worship," said Beard inappropriately. One look from The Mayor was sufficient to force a meek apology.

"I hereby close the Meeting," The Mayor called out in a rather up-beat tempo, "Good night and thank you all for your attendance." The next issue of "The Weekly Weaver," was extremely devoid of real detail concerning the abortive Twinning Meeting of The Council. It certainly contained reference to the bizarre appearance of Robespierre and the fact that The Meeting had suddenly been declared closed to the Public.

However, a telephone call from The Mayor, to McSnadden the Editor, in which he tactfully reminded him of the Newspaper Proprietor's commitment to and demand for, a Newspaper that engendered a feeling of well-being, patriotism and commitment to the status-quo, was enough to have ensured a personal foot-note in the Newspaper from The Editor that quote,

"It is understood that a Spokesman from The Mayors Office suggested the man's apparent lack of decorem was precipitated by a combination of food poisoning, stress and medication being taken as a painkiller against tooth-ache," unquote. The Editorial article also insisted that an extremely fraternal relationship existed between the Councillors of the two towns and future reciprocal visits were planned. Councillor Mrs Sylvia Smart was determined to visit Croutonne Lautrec as soon as was possible after The Council meeting, which she did on Friday 2nd August. It was rumoured that she was met at the Airport by a most distinguished looking gentleman who strongly resembled Councillor Henri Pugette. It was further suggested (after many off the record conversations between The Mayor and various Councillors and leading members of the Business Community) that perhaps, after all, Councillor Mrs Sylvia Smart's interest in Twinning with Croutonne Lautrec, had been entirely personal if not to say amorous?

CHAPTER TEN

Puccini Shoots The Mayor

The Summer of 1991 had been a good one in Crewdley and by the end of September, its people were in the majority in good spirits. Carnival produced a record amount of money to be channelled into The Mayor's personal bank account via The Old Town Charity Trust.

The Mayor had suggested that the Reverend and Mrs. Wilfred Wooly take a long holiday to put all thought of Paganism and Heathenism out of his mind. After three weeks, he received a post-card from the Caribbean island of St. Vincent which read, "Dear Mr.Mayor, We are having a wonderful time. The island is covered with banana plantations, such a change from the wheatfields and forests of Crewdley. The people are wonderful, and a sight more Christian than even some of my own flock. There are ten small churches in the village of Biabou alone, though some of the Parishioners seem to find Religious peace by smoking a most peculiar weed called "ganja." I have tried this weed myself but it merely induced visions of a Pagan Stag and I have not therefore over-indulged in this practice. However there is a local drink for which I have developed a particular liking. Liberal amounts of rum are tipped into a fresh coconut. Absolutely marvellous! Must dash to catch the post and then we're off to a beach party. Au Revoir, Reverend and Mrs.Wooly."

"My God," The Mayor mumbled to himself, "if he comes back saner than he went, it will be a miracle."

Presbyterian was in a particularly good mood. After years of fruitless enquiry and application, he had at last, received a very special letter from The Lord Chancellors Office in London. Instinctively, he had realized its contents and a reading had confirmed his intuition, "I hereby authorize that Harold Presbyterian of 'Civic House', Crewdley, be appointed to serve as a Justice of the Peace and to sit in the Crewdley Division of the Mid-Shires Assizes. God Save the Queen."

Moreover, because of the increase in crime across the nation in general, and in the Crewdley area in particular, an extra Court would be held in Crewdley itself. The Lord Chancellor's Office suggested the Court be constituted on a regular monthly basis in Crewdley Town Hall. The Mayor was delighted and agreed to ensure the correct specifications were carried out to modify the Council Chamber. A fee was paid to the Council in The Mayor's name, and the cheque duly found its way into his bank account.

The increase in the crime rate, although disturbing, was related mostly to increases in convictions for drinking offences, numerous driving infringements and various people refusing to pay their taxes (particularly the Poll Tax). It had once been a delicate calculation for Presbeterian, whether or not, the value of becoming a Magistrate outweighed the loss of votes from some of the people he would no doubt be looking at across The Bench. However, years of experience had indicated that A - most of the petty criminals did not vote and B - he could win without their support anyway (as previously mentioned, as well as petty criminals not voting, the majority of Crewdley citizens didn't vote either.)

A few people in particular, would no doubt raise an eye-brow when the news of Presbyterian's appointment became public. Police Superintendent Horace Bramley would be one. Ronnie Bettinger, the Crewdley Bookmaker, would be another. He knew enough about The Mayor to realize his contributions to The Old Town Charity Trust would now have to be increased. Seamus McGurk would have to be extremely careful about after-hours drinking and no doubt, the Vicar (already petrified in the knowledge that The Mayor knew him also as The Pagan Stag) would probably walk over red-hot coals in a fiery furnace to keep on the right side of Harold Presbyterian, the wielder of so much power in his Crewdley Fiefdom.

The Mayor had arranged to celebrate, as it were, with Mrs. Pippa Monroe, and so they set off for a picnic in the Civic Rolls Royce, heading in the direction of Crewdley Forest.

She squeezed him in a very susceptible part of his anatomy and purred, "Mmm, Pressy darling so much power...... all in one person..... what are you going to do with it?" "Robespierre!" he boomed, scrambling to pull away the blind between them and the Chauffer, "pull into the Forest and go for a long walk - quickly!"

And so once again, as Mr.Michael Monroe was no doubt striving to increase the oil-sales revenue for his Middle Eastern Company somewhere in Algeria, The Mayor was making love to his wife in the back of the Civic Rolls Royce.

As was usual on such occasions, Robespierre did as he was told and walked away from the car and into the Crewdley Forest, where he sat down on a grassy slope beneath an oak tree, took out a can of beer and some sandwiches from his bag, and relaxed in the warm sunshine to eat his lunch.

During the two months since his ordeal in the Council Chamber he had had time to reflect upon the whole ghastly episode. In a strange, alien kind of way, he almost enjoyed the notoriety that had emanated from the debacle. It could not be said anymore, that Anton Robespierre was an insignificant nobody. It was established beyond all reasonable doubt that he was the direct descendent of Anton Jaques Robespierre, the notorious and opportunist turn-coat brother of Maximillian Marie Isidore Robespierre, the undisputed and ruthless Leader of the French Revolution who was executed in 1794. In fact, since, "The

Twinning Incident," Robespierre had taken the opportunity to visit Crewdley Library on his days off to read up on 18th and 19th century French history. What he read was extremely bloody, extremely dangerous and extremely exciting. He conjured up a picture of his ancestor and was fascinated by the details of the period. His imagination ran riot as he sat on the grassy-slope; he was almost there in the Paris of 1789 with the carbines firing around his head, he was one of the first to storm The Bastille; again on the battlefield at Waterloo, he bravely changed sides against the despot Napoleon, for Liberty, Fraternity and Equality!! Vive Anton Robespierre!!!

"Robespierre! Robespierre! "Robespierre!," shouted a voice he knew only too well, "where are you Robespierre?"

It was The Mayor, "Come along man, its time we were off," he called to his aide de Camp, from beneath the bough of a chestnut tree.

"Pardonne Monsiur Maire," he answered blatently as he rose to his feet. The Mayor watched Robespierre as he gathered up his belongings but refrained from chastizing him for using French.

Even he now realized that things were different with his man and he would let things settle for a while. He may or may not allow Robespierre to use a little French in future: it depended entirely on local reaction. After all, a mere two months had lapsed since Robespierre's ancestor had become rather prominent amongst Crewdley Councillors, though the public remained as yet in the dark. Inevitably the public would become aware of the incident, but by that time, the issue would have been put into its proper perspective and no threat would be perceived. The Mayor would make sure of that, uncertainty and turmoil were the last things he would allow, his position depended upon it. They returned to the car. It was hot and Mrs.Pippa Monroe was drinking champagne. "Have a strawberry Pressy darling," she smiled, "they're gorgeous with champagne."

"Mm," he agreed,"its one of the bottles the French brought over in July, what a combination." He was lusting again, and she dropped a strawberry inside her blouse, "would you like one?" she purred.

A beautiful, exquisite image of the Caspian Sea engulfed Crewdley's First Citizen in a wave of passion. "Drive slowly Robespierre," he said with heavy breath, "and take the long way home, we're going to have strawberries and champagne - close the blinds and put the Elgar tape on..... periods in heaven are infrequent enough in our harsh world, they need to be savoured and lingered over."

She kissed him heavily with a fresh passion that excited him and caused him to tremble.

"Fantastic!" he shouted, as the first notes of Elgars Cello Concerto wafted through the speakers, "Wunderbar! Mama Mia! .... Ole!"

The elderly sisters, Dorothy and Myrtle Flack, seemed to have had more customers at their wool shop during the last few weeks than ever The Mayor could remember. He stared down from the window of his Parlour and watched three young men go into the shop opposite. It was very strange, he thought, that they should require mohair, merino or even Kashmir wool, unless the under 18's had suddenly taken up knitting. However, teenage fashion preferences seemed to him so bizarre as to hardly now be worthy of comment. After all, green mohican haircuts, punk-rag clothing, mini-skirts, drainpipe trousers, winkle-picker shoes and even inflatable trainers had all been worn during the last few years. If young boys wanted to buy wool to knit "sloppy-joe" sweaters, then so be it! At least they weren't charging around Crewdley dressed as Pagan Stags like the Reverend Wooly. He had just lit a large cigar when the telephone rang. "Yes, this is The Mayor of Crewdley speaking. Who is it?", he asked. "It's The English Documentary Film Company," replied a voice, "I'd like to arrange a meeting Mr.Mayor, as soon as possible please."

"Why?"

"Ah! Well thats exactly what I'd like us to talk about ... it would certainly be to your advantage Mr.Mayor. I've heard a lot about you..... your reputation preceeds you," the voice said knowingly. "Shall we say the lounge of The Forest Hotel in about twenty minutes? My name is Fredric Puccini. You can't miss me, I'll be wearing a white suit, Panama hat and a bow tie."

The Mayor was instinctively suspicious, but the phrase, "to your advantage" rang a bell. A man dressed as he had described himself should prove no problem, he thought, he sounded one step up from skate-boarding punks at Halloween.

"O.K. - I'll be there. I'll give you no more than ten minutes," said The Mayor, "and it will be entirely off the record." Fredric Puccini was drinking a pint of lager when Presbyterian went into the lounge of The Forest Hotel. It would indeed have been difficult, if not impossible, to have missed him or mistaken him for anyone else. He was a peacock where others were grey and drab. His white suit and hat were set off with a pink bow tie and his beard was as red as Fire. "Ah Mister Mayor!" he said loudly getting to his feet, thanks a lot for joining me. I know you're a busy man .... a very important one too .... I'll get straight to the point," he added taking his seat, "what's your poison?"

"I'll have a large whisky," The Mayor answered, " so what's this all about?" "Waiter!," bawled Puccini, a large whisky and another lager if you please, for me and The Mayor."

The Mayor cringed at his crassness and wondered if he'd made a mistake. Puccini lit a large cigar. "Like one?" he offered. The Mayor took a cigar and Puccini lit them both with a gold lighter. "I'll get straight to the point," he said,

"The English Documentary Film Company would be very interested in making a film about Crewdley."

"Oh really, and why would you want to do a thing like that?"

"Because its so English," said Puccini, it's absolutely marvellous." "Yes it is and that's just how we want it to remain - marvellous and quiet", said The Mayor. "I can assure you Mr.Mayor, that we treat all of our projects in a most discerning way. Our audience is a very select one. We're talking about a quality product. My last film was short listed at Cannes, " he said without batting an eyelid.

The Mayor had heard enough. "Now look here Mr. Puccini, " he said sternly, "unless there is an extremely good reason for saying otherwise, I really don ' t think this conversation is going to be at all fruitful. " "I'll pay £15,000 straight into your bank account if you'll give me your support. " "Done! " said The Mayor, "when do you want to start filming?" Puccini grinned around the cigar, "Excellent ! As soon as possible, " he answered. "Yes ... as soon as possible after the money goes into my account." The Mayor reminded him. "Of course, of course Mr.Mayor. It will be a marvellous film. I am an artist ! It will be an historic document..... a genuine glimpse of a late 20th century English country town in all its glory ... my word, the Japanese are in for a treat. I want to capture every marvellous moment before we all become European. "

"Just make sure the money is in Pounds Sterling Mr. Puccini, else Crewdley will be a no-go area for you. I hope that I make myself clear? "

"As a bell, Mr.Mayor, as a bell, " he replied.

"Good, you ' ve got time to draw it this afternoon and give it to me this evening, " said The Mayor ungenerously, "so lets say cheerio for now Mr. Puccini, and I'11 see you tonight in here at 8 . o' clock . "

With that, The Mayor got up and left the restaurant with the warm feeling he always got when big money was due to come his way .

At eight o'clock precisely, Harold Presbyterian, The Mayor of Crewdley, re-entered "The Forest Hotel" to find Fredric Puccini chatting to the head-waiter about the evening's menu. "Ah Mr.Mayor! Won't you please join me? he exclaimed,"I am going to enjoy the nut-loaf. Would you like to try it?"

"Not on your life," answered The Mayor, "I'll have roast beef and Yorkshire pudding." He sat down and watched the waiter disappear into the kitchen, ""That is, if you have the money Mr.Puccini? If not, then regrettably, I shall have to bid you goodnight." "I have the money here", Puccini replied, opening a small leather case, "Look!" he said. The Mayor was pleased. Bundles of bank-notes were piled into the case. "Excellent Mr.Puccini. I think I'm going to enjoy the meal after all."

After one or two drinks, the meal was served and Puccini began to discuss the film project with enthusiasm. "All I want" he said, "is to be able to film life in Crewdley and its Council of course." "Yes," The Mayor answered sternly, "I'm still a little concerned about. You'll have to be extremely discreet." "I shall be, Mr.Mayor, I promise, the boys and girls in my crew are absolutely marvellous. You won't know they're here." "What! Here?" The Mayor asked, "you don't mean to say they're in here filming us now do you?" Puccini grinned widely, "Just a few shots of your good self entering the Hotel Mr.Mayor." "I've a good mind to charge you an extra £50 for that Puccini - we hadn't agreed a damn thing before dinner."

"Sorry Mr.Mayor, but I did fully expect us to agree terms and conditions," Puccini said in his best Uriah Heep fashion. The Mayor was not convinced. "Look - quite frankly Puccini, I don't want to see you around Crewdley after 31st October. Do I make myself clear?" "Extremely Mr.Mayor - would you prefer apple-pie or Fruits of the Forest?"

Presbyterian had a particular preference for Fruits of the Forest, which related to his carnal activities with Mrs.Pippa Monroe, and so the choice was easy. He stared at Puccini as they ate and drank their brandy. "No better than a skate-boarding punk," he mused "except he's loaded with lovely money."

October was a beautiful month, but The Mayor kept a particularly close eye on The Vicar as Halloween approached. Wilfred Wooly seemed to be holding his nerve and keeping The Pagans at bay with extra religious services throughout the period to give him extra fortitude.

Meanwhile, The Mayor had also noticed the continued activity both into and out of the Wool Shop, by the young people of Crewdley. But for all of their undoubted purchases of wool, he'd yet to see a hand-knitted "sloppy-joe" jumper.

Robespierre was still in a kind of dream and often resorted to using French phrases when The Mayor had occasion to speak with him. However, because of his peculiar condition, which The Mayor considered as being somewhere between a state of ecstasy and idiocy, Anton Robespierre, descendent of Waterloo and The Bastille remained unpunished.

In spite of Puccini's assurances to the contrary, his filmcrew were not particularly discreet. Wherever The Mayor went, representatives of The English Documentary Film Company seemed to have arrived there first. Presbyterian had availed himself of the opportunity to let the Coucillors know that Puccini was in the area and would be filming around Crewdley. He let that idea ferment for about a week and a half before he mentioned, in a very casual manner indeed, that Puccini would like to film a session of Crewdley Town Council. The reaction was predictable. Councillor Mrs.Sylvia Smart was extremely keen and pressed The Mayor for permission to spend Civic Money on a new Robe for herself. Councillors Mrs.Louise Evans-Jenkins and her lover

Morton Muggeridge were also delighted at the prospect of capturing their love forever (albeit discreetly) on the silver screen. Alan Arkwright was determined to encourage footage both inside and outside of the Council Chamber, and particularly wanted Puccini to film him rising over The Town Hall in his hot-air balloon. Unfortunately for Arkwright, October proved to be a difficult month in which to demonstrate his aero-nautical accomplishments, and after several unsuccessful attempts to get air-born and the final admittance that his equipment was faulty, Arkwright had to concede defeat.

Enid Thomas and Arthur Hardie were not particularly concerned at the prospect of a Council Meeting being filmed, but nevertheles wondered why anyone would first of all be interested enough to want to film it, and secondly, what sort of person would be interested enough to watch it. Councillor Barry Blondel considered the prospect of his performing on film, to be wholly beneficial for his chances of romance. The film would be shown to hundreds if not thousands of attractive women, all over the world - a dating-agency with its own free Civic, publicity. It was on that basis that Blondel extended warmth and hospitality towards Fredric Puccini, insisting as he did, that his left side gave the best profile and if Mr.Puccini wanted, "exciting, pensive, natural or even humorous," film close-ups, he would be delighted to accomodate him. Finally, The Mayor informed Councillor Norman Bull about Puccini's film-crew, and true to form, (after being firstly assured they weren't French) he could not have been less interested. Beard was given strict instructions to comply with all reasonable requests from Puccini and only to speak when spoken to. One or two important business people and, reluctantly, The Vicar, were also informed, but apart from that, Puccini went around Crewdley filming the town and its people in a now rather proficient and capable manner. Police Superintendent Horace Bramley attempted to raise the issue of Puccini and his cameras constituting a public nuisance, but The Mayor (Crewdley's newly-created Magistrate) took great delight in telling him to address himself to solving and preventing crime in Crewdley and to keep his nose out of Civic affairs.

The Mayor was in his Parlour and looking down through the window into Church Street. "Robespierre," he said, "what the hell is going on in The Wool Shop?" Robespierre joined him at the window and stared across the street. "I don't know Your Worship," he replied, "is something wrong?"

"I'm not sure, but I'm becoming suspicious about the number of young people going inside. Its been happening for weeks. I can't understand it. Find out exactly what its all about."

Robespierre did as he was told and wandered off towards The Wool Shop. Two teenage boys were leaving the premises and hurried quickly away when they saw The Mayor's Minder.

Briefly considering The Wool Shop to be the walls of the Bastille itself, Robespierre went inside. Dorothy and Myrtle Flack each gave him a smile worthy of the ones used by nursery supervisors to greet a newly-introduced child. For a moment, they were uneasy, nervous even, as Robespierre stood there, seemingly waiting to hand them his little coat for labelling and hanging-up on a brightly-painted clothes peg. Myrtle Flack broke the ice, "Aah, Mr.Robespierre, how nice to see you," she said. "Good afternoon," he replied, looking around the shelves as a tourist might look up at the gargoyles on the walls of a Cathedral. "Would you like some wool?" asked Dorothy, "its very good value for money. You could knit yourself a nice scarf for the Winter Mr.Robespierre. It would keep you warm when you were waiting in the car for The Mayor," she smiled again. Robespierre smiled back and furtively looked around the counter, as he walked slowly to and fro. He didn't reply, then with one, long look towards the doorway of their living accommodation,he made his exit into the street.

"Nothing to report," he explained to The Mayor, who had watched his performance with interest, "except -," he hesitated. "Yes?," The Mayor enquired.

"Well, its just that somehow - ." He stopped again.

"Go on! said The Mayor impatiently. "Somehow, they seemed, I don't know, a bit suspicious, ... sort of guilty Mr.Mayor. It was very strange." "They're up to something alright, but what? The Senior Citizens of Crewdley don't usually welcome teenagers with open arms, especially if they own a Wool Shop. Ah well, it'll have to wait Robespierre. I'm seeing Puccini in a few minutes about filming the next Meeting of Crewdley Town Council. Get the car out and I'll be down directly." After visiting the toilet, Presbyterian went down the old wooden staircase, through The Town Hall Foyer and got into the Rolls Royce. "The Forest Hotel," he called through the driver's window," and sound the klaxon when we go past the Police Station, just to remind Bramley who's in charge." He saw Robespierre smile into the rear-view mirror, and it wasn't long before the eager Chauffeur sounded the klaxon four times as they past "The Star and Garter" and then the Police Station.

"Go round again," The Mayor shouted, "I need time to think." Robespierre travelled on for a few hundred yards before he turned the car around and drove back through Crewdley, circled St.Crueds Church, and once again headed for "The Forest Hotel." The Mayor had felt a lot easier about Puccini's film, since receiving a Company Search on The English Documentary Film Company. He discovered that its owner was a Lord Nigel Rice Knowles, a well known rich, eccentric member of the aristocracy who thrived on lost causes and preservation of the English way of life. His track record in the film industry indicated that he didn't care a fig if he sold more than ten copies of a video, or if his film extravaganzas, documentaries and even Spaghetti

Westerns, were watched by more than three people.

Obviously, he was indulging Puccini to make a little documentary on a typical small English Town ..... The Mayor enjoyed the meal at The Forest Hotel (pea-soup, steak and Fruits of the Forest) was bored by Puccini and his small-talk about the Film Industry (particularly as he'd already been paid) but was in heaven some half-hour later when Robespierre dropped him off outside "Caspian House" and into the arms of Mrs. Pippa Monroe.

It was a few days later and Presbyterian was sitting at his desk in The Parlour reading a book, when Robespierre burst in. "Mr.Mayor! Disaster!," he yelled, "The Sisters Flack!" "Calm down Robespierre, for heavens sake. And what disaster has befallen the Sisters Flack, as you call them?", The Mayor asked impatiently. "It's Superintendent Bramley My Lord. He's arrested them!" "What! He's what?" "Arrested them Your Worship," spluttered the Boy from the Bastille. "He can't have. They're harmless old women," said The Mayor, "I knew this would happen. It was just a matter of time before Bramley or the Vicar went off their heads, it seems Bramley has got there first. Unless....."

"Unless what sir?" prompted Robespierre.

"Unless .... it doesn't bear thinking about, but all those teenagers going into The Wool Shop..... it must be that!"

"Bramley is in the Wool Shop now ...Vite! Vite! Monsieur Mayor," Robespierre urged his master.

They made their way quickly down the old wooden staircase.

"I might as well mention now Robespierre," The Mayor said through gritted-teeth as they scampered into The Foyer, "I'm not happy about your increased use of French."

"Pardonne Monsieur," replied the culprit, already dashing out into the road to hold up the traffic so that The Mayor might cross safely.

"Oh My God!" The Mayor shouted, "he's called a Black Maria!"

Indeed, a police-van was parked on the double-yellow lines outside The Wool Shop. The Mayor hurried across and into the shop. Bramley was grinning like an idiot, as two young police women were standing extremely close to Dorothy and Myrtle Flack, as if they were about to ask them to dance. "Bramley!" The Mayor shouted, "What the Hell is going on here!" There was madness in Bramley's eyes as he revelled in the situation and gave up all the pretention of propriety. "Its nothing to do with you! They're nicked I'm taking them down the Station . It was a fair cop. They're just getting a few things together and we're off. The sooner people like them are put under lock and key the better," he ranted, "We've all got the right to walk the streets in peace. Take 'em away officers." He glared menacingly at Myrtle, "Go on .... go on, I dare you .... resist arrest .... please! Go on .... make my day." The policewomen escorted the Flack Sisters out of The Wool Shop and placed them in the back of The Black Maria and it roared off a la down-town New York. "Bramley! Bramley!'yelled The Mayor, "have you gone mad?" It was too late. Bramley was psyched-up by the thrill of the Big Kill and defiantly swept several balls of wool off the counter as The Mayor and Robespierre watched in amazement, before the wretched Police Superintendent slammed the door and left them open mouthed in the deafening silence of The Wool Shop.

After much threatening by The Mayor, Bramley finally allowed him into the cell to speak with the Sisters Flack. "Its all a misunderstanding," bleated Myrtle," we were only selling home-made wine." Despite the strongest of protests, Bramley kept the sisters under lock and key, and The Mayor was forced to retire from the Police Station, with the pathetic cries of Dorothy and Myrtle ringing in his ears. Robespierre chauffeured him back to "Civic House", and Presbyterian spent an uneasy night wondering whether Bramley had really flipped his lid or if he had truly uncovered the centre of an international crime-ring. On balance, the first consideration still seemed the most likely. He would tackle Bramley again the next day and hoped the hours of darkness would provide time for the misguided Policeman to reconsider his actions and listen to reason.

Presbyterian went back to Crewdley Police Station at 9.00 a.m. and walked straight into Bramley's office. "OK Bramley, its time we had a talk," he said, sitting down near to the broken gas fire. "I don't think there is anything to say on this one," Bramley answered in a strange tone, "its cut and dried. They're as guilty as Hell and I for one can't wait to see them carted off to Holloway. There's too much of this Pensioner delinquency. They're corrupting our youth. If we were in Ancient Greece, they'd both be stoned to death." The Mayor was finding it extremely difficult to get into the conversation. "Look Bramley, I think you need a holiday," he said. "No! No I don't! I'm going to retire soon, and that'll be one long holiday. Everything is fine; what we've got here, is a nasty case of serious crime." "What we've got here Bramley," asserted The Mayor, "is a nasty case of a Policeman exceeding his duty." "Oh no Mr.Mayor, the Flack Sisters broke the Law. Its a straightforward case. They were making their own wine and selling it without a Licence." "Bramley!" said The Mayor. "Yes," he answered strangely. "Bramley .... you're not hearing me, are you? Let me spell it out. There is no case to answer against the Flacks."

"Yes there is!" Bramley snapped, "they've confessed everything."

"No there isn't and you'll tear up their statement and let them go right now. Do you understand?" The Mayor asked, "I'm taking them out of this Police Station in about three minutes time." He stared Bramley in the face, "Look, if it makes you happy, I'll let you give them a caution, OK? Bramley seemed in a world of his own. "Just give them a caution and I'll wait for them outside," said The Mayor.

With that, he got up and left Bramley staring at the gas-fire, contemplating the prospect of defeat yet again. Presbyterian stood near to the entrance of the Police Station and within three minutes, he was joined by Dorothy and Myrtle Flack. "Thank you so much Mr. Mayor," said Dorothy, " my word, such a to do about hardly anything at all."

"Please ladies, just sell your beautiful wool. Believe me, there's no future for you in moonshine liquor," he told them.

"Oh absolutely," agreed Myrtle, "we wouldn't care if everyone in Crewdley signed The Pledge of Abstinence, would we Dorothy?"

"Thanks again Your Worship. It was very kind of you to help us like that," added Dorothy, "we won't forget to vote for you at Election time, will we Myrtle?" He watched them walk arm in arm towards the town, "My God," he said quietly, "the things I do for Crewdley."

The Mayor was not pleased to have received the second telephone call in almost as many minutes from Councillor Mrs.Sylvia Smart. "It's awful Harold The Council Meeting is just a few hours away and that wretched little man at the Tailors hasn't finished my Robe yet.

Olivia and I were about to leave home for the shop ... I'm taking her down in my car Harold, she's not up to driving herself since the accident. Anyway, I was virtually out into the street when Robert Potter telephoned to say the Robes aren't ready. What are we going to do? I want to look my best for Mr. Puccini don't I Harold?"

"Leave it to me Sylvia, but please don't ring again, I'm extremely busy. I'll tell Potter to pull his finger out . If he doesn' t finish them, I'll take The Council's account off him - hows that? "

"Wonderful . . . thank you Harold . . . see you tonight . . . bye! "

The Mayor did indeed make the required threatening telephone call to Robert Potter, proprietor of The Crewdley Tailor and Outfitters. It had the desired effect and he quickly went back to reading his sports paper. He perused the horse-racing for that day, Monday 21st October, with no particular interest, until with a casual glance, he noticed a name which he couldn't ignore. Lucky streaks had to begin somewhere and the omen looked good. It was too much of a coincidence for a race-goer to turn down. He reached for his telephone-link with Bettingers. "Ronnie - I'lJ have £300 to win on Movie Premier in the 3 o'clock at Worcester . "

"Its 20 to 1," Bettinger gasped, "that's £6,000 minus tax." "Yes, you ' re quite right, but make it £400, I feel lucky . " "Puhh! I hope the bloody thing falls at the first Fence." "Now come on Ron, will you take it or not? " The Mayor asked. "Yes, " he answered, "and if it wins I shall personally demand a dope-test. "

Movie Premier ran a spirited race until the last fence when the horse stopped suddenly as if its hooves had been attached to magnets. The Mayor switched off his T.V. as the jockey was in solo-flight over the hurdle. "It's a mugs game, " he said ruefully, "why do I bother? "

It was just after 5.25 p.m. and Robespierre was dressing The Mayor in preparation for the Council Meeting - first The Robe itself, then the White Laced Collar, next The Mayoral Chain of Office and finally, The Civic Cocked Hat. "You look magnificent Mr.Mayor," said Robespierre, "absolutely superb!" "How right you are Robespierre. Value for money, that's me." After two circuits of the town, Robespierre parked The Civic Rolls Royce adjacent to The Town Hall. He quickly stepped out and held open the rear door. "Ladies and Gentlemen, please make way for Councillor Harold Presbyterian, Mayor of Crewdley Town Council," he said loudly.

"That's great! I think we got it first time," said the by now familiar voice of Fredric Puccini," what an entrance!" "I can't wait to see the back of him," The Mayor said quietly to Robespierre. "Thank God he hasn't asked to film Octavia Bland!" Puccini followed The Mayoral Party into The Council Chamber, gesticulating frantically for Robespierre to hold The Mace up higher and to keep his shoulders straight. The film-crew had taken root in various strategic positions in The Chamber. The Mayor noticed two cameras initially, and of course Puccini was flitting around like the demented participant in a game of hide and seek, with his red beard appearing to cover his own camera in the way that a Daguerre would have been covered inside a tarpaulin sheet in days of old.

The assembly stood as The Mayor took his place. "Good evening, please be seated. Welcome everyone, to this rather special meeting of Crewdley Town Council which is being recorded for posterity by Mr.Fredric Puccini and The English Documentary Film Company. I have been asked to stress that Mr.Puccini would wish us to be our normal selves, and not to pose for the cameras in the way that seems to occur in The House of Commons."

"Here, here Mr.Mayor!", someone shouted. All eyes turned to the hapless Town Clerk, Bernard Beard, "Oops sorry Mr.Mayor," he apologized, "awfully sorry."

The Mayor gave him a stern look before he continued," The Agenda is as printed; Item One; Prayers." He smiled directly at the camera being operated by an attractive young woman. "Reverend Wooly would you kindly say Prayers for our Council Meeting tonight?" The Vicar grinned an even wider grin as he stepped forward. He seemed transfixed by the cameras and frozen to the spot. "Wooly," The Mayor whispered, "Your Prayers." The grin continued," Dear Lord, Bless us, your servants, who seek to follow the path of righteousness." He paused to grin again directly at the cameras. "Help us to spurn all that is evil in the world, deny our excesses and help us to reject all Craven Images and lewd pleasures of the flesh. This is the time of year Lord, when harvests have been reaped and offerings made to you. It is a season of mists when the Pagan images of the Dark Ages attempt to raise their evil reincarnation." "Wooly," growled The Mayor,"you've said enough." "Images of Godless creatures seeking a way into the souls of men and women!"

"Wooly!"

"Wooly!"

"Before the long,dark,cold nights of Winter throw a black-cloak over those who are struggling against the Forces of Darkness!"

"Wooly! Sit down!" "Oh Dear Lord our God, bless the people of Crewdley and its Councillors ... let all Pagans and Heathens be cast out from our midst, that we might live in Your House ...Amen ...sorry Mr.Mayor."

For Presbyterian, The Vicar's words had obvious meaning - he was still struggling desperately with The Devil, but to his audience, it must have seemed a rather embarrassing case of showing off in front of the cameras. A quick look at the film crew certainly indicated this to have been the case with Puccini. He was loving it and now urging The Mayor on to greater, more demonstrative things. "Item Two;To receive Apologies for absence," he said calmly. "There are none Mr.Mayor," Beard announced, trying not to look directly at the cameras, for fear of incurring The Mayor's wrath.

"Quite so Mr.Beard ...we are all present and correct ...

Agenda Item Three   "

And so it went on, item after item of the usual Crewdley Council business. Councillor Mrs.Sylvia Smart, dressed almost immaculately in her new, blue velvet Robe which was finished by Potter just moments before the Meeting, made several long contributions entirely for the benefit of Fredric Puccini, whom she now considered to be rather attractive in a Bohemian kind of way. Barry Blondel used every precious moment to show himself off to his adoring foreign and domestic female admirers and Morton Muggeridge gave the kind of looks to Mrs.Louise Evans-Jenkins which indicated, at least to them, that their love was eternal, if necessarily discreet.

The highlight of the evening was a debate about the roads and footpaths of Crewdley, in which Arthur Hardie and Enid Thomas made solid speeches on the need for increased financial expenditure to be made readily available for repair and improvement. Councillor Olivia Bland made a startling intervention just as Hardie was summing-up. "The trouble is with all this," she asserted, "even if we did repair the roads, the wretched motor-vehicles would spoil it all again in no time at all." It was if her elder sister Octavia had never left, not in the physical sense as her mortal remains were still in-situ in The Foyer, but in the social sense that Olivia was incapable of making genuine reference to the needs and issues of the late 20th century and would of course, have been happier under the blanket of a Daguerre Camera with her young husband in the 1930's. Councillor Bull seemed unimpressed by the whole thing and actually fell asleep during one of Sylvia Smart's more flowery contributions. Arkwright was absolutely fascinated by the cameras and spent virtually the whole meeting attempting to become Chief Engineer to Puccini's film-crew and through sheer persistance, persuaded the young woman to let him film part of the proceedings. At just after 7.30 p.m., The Mayor concluded the Meeting and retired to his Parlour with a rather sullen Robespierre, who resented having been prompted so many times by Puccini to keep his shoulders back during long-shots of The Mace and The Mayor's top-table. They settled down to enjoy some serious drinking and Presbyterian took solace from the fact that Puccini now had the film in the can and there could be no conceivable reason for seeing him around Crewdley after the end of that week. They each drank to that prospect time and time again.

It was after midnight when The Mayor demanded that Robespierre should cook an omelette, which he did and they ate it with relish. Their meal was accompanied by a best bottle of Civic Claret which the French had brought from Croutonne Lautrec. Unfortunately for The Mayor, his reference to the origins of that delicious nectar, brought a flood of tears from the emotional refugee from Gaul. This deluge inspired another such bottle. At four a.m. Robespierre made his unsteady way along the corridor to his humble quarters and Presbyterian stretched out on the Chaise Longue. "Bloody Puccini," he mumbled,"Bloody nut-loaf .... bloody red-beard."

CHAPTER ELEVEN

The Great Wool Shop Scandal

The final days of October were filled with anxiety for The Mayor of Crewdley. He was concerned that The Vicar did not succumb to The Pagan Spirits of Halloween, that Police Superintendent Horace Bramley did not arrest half of the population merely for breathing and he was anxious that Fredric Puccini finished filming and went quietly on his way. There was also the nagging doubt about the Flack Sisters. Their deviation from the straight and narrow had not been properly explained and Presbyterian was in a rather edgy condition.

The Vicar was placed under virtual House Arrest and under strict instructions to contact The Mayor immediately, if The Pagan Spirits aroused him. Robespierre spent many hours of the days and nights sitting in the Civic Rolls Royce outside The Vicarage.

Bramley was told in no uncertain terms to spend the remainder of his time as a Policeman, in deep contemplation of matters legal, by reading all of the books on Case Law, Jurisprudence, The Criminal Mind and The Role of the Police in Civic Society.

Puccini was still filming in the town, but everything was pretty low-key and the people seemed to be enjoying it. In between Sentry-Duty outside The Vicarage, Robespierre had been instructed to keep an eye on The Wool Shop. The Mayor had been distinctly unsettled by Robespierre's first report of increased activity in the shop. His second report sent alarm bells ringing.

"Now Robespierre, are you absolutely sure it was the Bank Manager who went into The Wool Shop with dark glasses and wearing an old raincoat?"

"Yes Sir"

"Oh my God! Something is definately going on," The Mayor groaned, "what on earth could be the matter with them?" Robespierre looked from the window down to the street. "Mister Flint has just gone in Sir."

"Oh no! That settles it. It's a well known fact that the Fire Chief engages in many social activities, but knitting is definately not one of them.

You'd better abandon surveillance of The Vicar and transfer engagements to The Wool Shop." Robsepierre was not enamoured with that prospect. "Can I ask an obvious question Your Worship?"

"No!" replied The Mayor. "But surely if you suspect criminal activities are occuring in The Wool Shop Mr Mayor, the Police ought to be informed?"

"Now look Robespierre, I have done my best to ignore some of the more recent failures of your duty."

He eye-balled his man as a ferret transfixes a rabbit-

"I make policy around here, not you." The chastened employee dropped his head. "I'm extremely sorry Your Grace, I apologise for over-stepping the mark."

"I should think so indeed. Where would we be if it were you who made policy Robespierre? Pretty soon, you'd be sitting in my seat and I'd be just about to go out and keep an eye on The Wool Shop." Robespierre turned and left The Mayor's Parlour. He knew his place, but after The Bastille Revelations, he was unfortunately becoming rather prone to forgetting it. Robespierre went to his quarters and changed his clothes. The transformation was startling. The Civic Servants gentle persona had been replaced by the menacing appearance of a refugee from World War Two. On his head was a leather flying-helmet complete with loose-flaps which gave the wearer the demeanour of a hound-dog.

A ridiculous black-beard complimented the dark glasses so that his face was indeed extremely unrecognizable. An Army Great Coat, brown leather boots, and a walking stick completed his attire, and after turning up his collar, Robespierre stepped back into the corridor.

He was confronted by The Mayor who was open-mouthed in astonishment."'You're not intending to leave by way of the Foyer, are you Robespierre?" he asked. "No Your Worship, I was just about to go out through the Car Park," answered the Master of Disguises as he trotted down the stairs. Presbyterian returned to The Parlour and kept watch on the street below. Within a few minutes Robespierre had taken up his position outside The Wool Shop. To acknowledge that the strange figure looked suspicious, would have been to have admitted the truth. Pavement pedestrians quickly began to give him a wide-bearth as he tried to glimpse furtively through the window of The Wool Shop.

The Mayor looked on as Robespierre walked up and down the pavement. Finally, 'Smokey' Flint the Fire Chief emerged from The Wool Shop and quickly disappeared down St Crued's Passage, presumably either on his way to work or to begin knitting a woollen cardigan.

Robespierre waited a few more moments before crossing the street to return to base, via The Municipal Park and Gardens. It was after one am when The Mayor and Anton Robespierre, having now reverted to his normal clothing, approached The Wool Shop. "Is this really wise Mr Mayor?" he asked tentatively.

"I'm not really sure, but it's better than waiting until Bramley makes another lightening raid on the Flack Sisters," The Mayor answered, already ringing the bell.

The small figure of Myrtle Flack put her head around the door. "Oh I say, Good evening Mr Mayor. Or should it be good morning? I've lost track lately. I'm quite surprised to see you .... oh and Mr Robespierre as well .....Won't you both come in?"

They walked through the dimly-lit shop as Myrtle Flack locked the door. "There's no escaping now, is there Mr Mayor?" she laughed, "I've got the key."

"I don't like the sound of this at all Robespierre," whispered The Mayor, "I've got an awful feeling that something is very wrong." "Follow me," said Myrtle, as she began to climb the stairs with a definate spring in her heels.

The Mayor and Robespierre walked carefully between the bundles of wool and boxes of cotton, as Myrtle skipped over the landing and onto the second flight of stairs. The sound of voices could be heard, laughter even and things were going bump in the night. "Visitors!" screeched Myrtle, "come along you two, hurry up. You only live once you know, so make the most of it and enjoy yourselves." And with that, the little old woman disappeared into some room, spirited away as if by magic from under the noses of Crewdley's First Citizen and The Boy from The Bastille.

"Struth! I must be dreaming," gasped The Mayor as he reached the top of the second flight of stairs. "I couldn't stand another Pagan Stag Mr Mayor," said Robespierre, "especially if it looks like Dorothy Flack."

The Mayor grimaced at the very thought as he slowly turned the handle of the door. "Come on in!" shouted someone who sounded vaguely familiar. The noise increased as The Mayor and Robespierre virtually fell into the top-most room of The Wool Shop, positioned as it was in the highest part of the roof beneath slates of red clay and the spendid oaken-eaved timber from the ancient Forest of Crewdley.

They went in and were shocked, for here was a different world, a debauched cabal of sinners, a rampant clutch of revellers, wallowing in their depravity and lust.

"Hells Bells!" The Mayor shouted, as the naked back side of The Bank Manager disappeared over a settee.

"Good Grief!"

No one seemed to notice the latest house-guests. A naked young woman was kissing Councillor Blondel and a Kissogram Toy Boy seemed at one with an older woman with flaming red hair. "Sacre Bleau! Mon Dieu! Pardonne Monsier Mayor. It's an Orgy!" Robespierre blurted out, still not believing his eyes. Morton Muggeridge and Louise Evans-Jenkins were cavorting to the rhythm of the music, oblivious to everyone.

"I've seen enough!" said The Mayor.

"I think we are obliged to check the other rooms Your Worship," Robespierre suggested, "it might be worse."

It was! They were greeted by the sight of The Vicar being caressed, fondled and worse, by a young woman unknown to either of them, "Wooly!" was all that The Mayor could muster, so he said it again, "Wooly " "Push Off you creep," The Vicar of Crewdley demanded, "go and put your head into a bucket of something nasty." Smokey Flint was lying on a couch with Lady Crewdley, exhausted by their love making, they were now stretched out together and seemed to be asleep. Henry Dash ran from the room, pursued by a very eager Elsie Finney from the Fish Shop, "Come here, you gorgeous solicitor,"she cried, "I'm going to make a man of you," John Doolittle came in by the same door, arm in arm with one of McGurk's waitresses from 'The Star and Garter'. The place was alive with people. The Mayor had never seen anything like it.

"Stop!" he yelled, "this is Crewdley, not ancient Rome!" No one took the slightest bit of notice.

"Robespierre!" he called, but his man had been lost in the sea of passion and abandon. The Mayor staggered from room to room, deeply shocked by what he saw, and occasionally catching a glipse of The Madames Dorothy and Myrtle Flack, who seemed to be issuing instructions and collectlng money. Half the town seemed to be there, dozen after dozen of local worthies, rural interlopers and delirious strangers.

Suddenly, very suddenly, a massive and heavy banging and bumping began to invade their ears. Threatening voices were heard, alien noises were ruining the night. "Nobody moves! This is a raid!" The Mayor froze to the spot as Police Superintendent Horace Bramley shone a torch in his face. "You're nicked Presbyterian!" he yelled with total joy, "Take him away officers, do your duty!" Two burly policemen grabbed The Mayor and began to forcibly walk him down the stairs. They were strangers from another Division and obviously unaware of the identity of their charge.

"Bramley! I demand to be released !" shouted The Mayor. "Quiet you! You're coming with us!", a policeman answered menacingly. They each took an arm and lifted Presbyterian down the first stair. "Be a nice gentleman and behave," said the other one.

"I'm The Mayor, damn it!" "Yes, and I'm The Emperor Nero. I've already seen King Henry 8th and Lady Godiva on the way up."

The Mayor was ushered down the stairs and across the landing, through dozens of revellers and police intent on arresting them. The Wool Shop was by now fully lit-up and the scene resembled the first day of a Harrods Sale.

The counter had gone over, the shelves were knocked out and bundles of wool and cotton were every where.

"Shop! Shop!" someone was shouting, "Are you open?' asked another. "Good night Mr Mayor," squeaked a voice. He looked round to see the tiny figure of Myrtle Flack, crouched behind what was left of the counter. "Thanks for calling," added Dorothy, taking a moment off from her telephone call to her Lawyer, "I'll tell Mr Robespierre you've gone on ahead - nightie, night!" Presbyterian was bowled out of The Shop and into Church Street, where at least a dozen Policemen were waiting. "Here we are Sir," said the one who had lifted him down the stairs, "You're going for a ride in our nice Police Van. Isn't that nice?" He smiled sarcastically at his prisoner, "Get in!" The Mayor climbed into the van and the door was slammed shut. A small figure cowered on a seat and tried to hide under a blanket.

"Who's that?" The Mayor asked, lifting the blanket roughly. "Beard!" "Yes, I'm afraid so Your Worship," replied The Town Clerk.

"Disgraceful! What are doing here?" The Mayor demanded to know. "I might perhaps ask you the same question," Beard answered, obviously dejected and without his usual deference.

"Now look here, Robespierre and I went to that wretched Wool Shop to investigate what was going on. That's all!" Beard looked mournful. "If you say so Sir," he bleated.

"I certainly do say so Beard. But why were you in there?"

The Town Clerk shrugged his shoulders. "It's so bloody boring in Crewdley. All that crap about Protocol and Duty. It's too dry! I wanted something else, so I went to The Wool Shop. That's where all the action is."

"Where all the action was you mean," The Mayor corrected him, "The Flack Sisters have been well and truly busted." He shuddered at the thought.

"And I have just been appointed a Magistrate." "Oh dear. I do see your problem," said the brazened employee.

"Oh do you! And I can certainly see your problem Beard and it's going to take some rectifying on your part, I can tell you."

The Mayor and The Town Clerk were quite quickly joined by other customers, clients, revellers and perhaps even the odd innocent abroad, from The Wool Shop.

These included the Bank Manager (though his innocence would surely be difficult to prove), the librarian and Mrs Finney, who seemed to have developed a passionate attachment to the Chief Representative of local Banking Affairs.

The Mayor looked out of the van window as it passed The Town Hall. "This is going to take some sorting out," he said to himself, as Mrs Finney bit the Bank Manager's ear. "Sound that bloody siren!," a voice boomed out from the other side of the driver's partitian. A little window was opened and a large,red face peered in at the prisoners. The siren cut through the night air as the van rounded St Crued's Church, "And keep it on as loud as you like. I want everyone to know just who we've got in here!" Superintendent Horace Bramley cackled through the little window, then slammed it shut. It hadn't been a good night for The Mayor of Crewdley, and things looked set to deteriorate.

"Name!" a Sergeant demanded, as Presbyterian was brought to the counter inside the Police Station.

"Harold Presbyterian," he answered, "And I suppose you're another one of Bramley's imports?" "If you mean that I'm from another Division Sir, that's correct. We pride ourselves on doing a job properly. That's why he brought us in."

The entrance lobby was suddenly filled with people, extremely noisy people who seemed to have thought that the Party was still going on. "Keep them quiet!" the Sergeant demanded.

The Bank Manager pushed to the counter and swayed dangerously on his heels. "I'll have a pie and chips! Plenty of vinegar, not much salt!" "Naughty boy," shouted Mrs Finney,"You shouldn't push in like that, there's a queue." "Constable! Take Presbyterian down to the cells and I'll book this lot. Right - who's next?"

And so it was, that in the early hours of Thursday 31st October 1991, Harold Presbyterian, Mayor and Magistrate of Crewdley, listened to the distant chimes of St Creud's Church clock as he tried to sleep on a hard bench, deep in the cells of Crewdley Police Station.

"I'll fix you this time Bramley," he murmured, "just you wait when I get out of here."

CHAPTER TWELVE

The Scales of Justice

It was after 10am when Presbyterian was released. There had been no sign of Bramley, as the Sergeant sent him on his way and things were quiet in the Reception area of the Police Station. He breathed deeply as he took his first steps of freedom outside in the cold morning air and walked towards The Town Hall, past Finney's Fish and Chip Shop. He glanced through the window, taking care not to stop, but there was no sign of Crewdley's own Mae West, ... for which he was grateful and breathed a sigh of relief. Crewdley seemed exactly as it always was, an old and quiet small English town, but a twisted reality had kicked it in the teeth. The Mayor crossed Dark Street onto the pavement outside Crewdley Co-op, but was struck by the awful truth that The Vicar would probably have to be locked up for his own good and that of the community, and so he crossed back over Dark Street to avoid The Vicarage.

Unfortunately, as he walked in the lea of St Crueds Church, the premises of Doolittle and Dash, Solicitors to The Council and Notaries Public, came quickly into view and he wished he hadn't crossed over after all. He hurried past the offices of 'The Weekly Weaver' and held his breath, before crossing Church Street directly opposite The Town Hall.

He didn't dare look back to The Wool Shop, and hurried quickly into the Town Hall Foyer and up the old, wooden staircase to his Parlour. Robespierre was waiting. "Mister Mayor - thank goodness you're alright. Bramley refused to tell me what had happened to you. I even took the liberty of asking Mrs Monroe."

"Good! It's about time you used your own initiative Robespierre. Come on in and tell me what she said." They went into The Parlour and Robespierre closed the door. "Mrs Monroe had no idea where you were Mr Mayor. She told me to tell you that she spent a quiet evening at home watching television, and please would you telephone her as soon as possible?"

The Great Man did exactly that, "Pippa yes, I'm perfectly alright. I was arrested by that great oink Bramley, ... it's a long story darling and I haven't debriefed Robespierre yet, so I'll call back later .... bye bye sweetness."

He turned to The Boy from The Bastille, "Right! Now what happened to you when I needed you Robespierre? One minute you were at my side and the next you were gone." "Sorry Mr Mayor. I was pushed into a room filled with people. I couldn't get out, then I heard the Police arrive." He stopped as The Mayor scowled at him. "And?"

"And so I managed to get out on to the Fire-Escape Your Worship."

"And?"

"I found my way down the iron steps in the pitch black of the night, it was very difficult. I went down the alley between Doctor Scargreaves and the Fire Station and escaped down St Crued's Passage

"Oh bravo Robespierre!" The Mayor said sarcastically, "quite the little cat-burglar aren't we? Then what did you do?" "I went into Forest Lane and I intended to go back along Dark Street and return to The Wool Shop, but the Police vans started to come round the corner, so I hid behind a dustbin by 'The Star and Garter.'

"Absolutely marvellous! I suppose you spent the rest of the night trying to get into the pub?" "No Sir, I kept watch the whole time. I counted nine vans Your Worship, but I didn't see them take you into the Police Station."

"No, because I was in van number three, that's why. They'd already taken me inside by then." "Sorry Sir."

"Never mind" said The Mayor, "I suppose you did your best?" "Well Mr Mayor, if you remember, I did actually suggest going to The Police before all this trouble began?"

"It wouldn't have made the slightest difference. Bramley is crazy. He wants to go out with a bang," The Mayor answered, "but now, we've got a real problem because I think he arrested half of Crewdley last night Robespierre." "Yes Sir, I believe he did. Mr Beard is absent and somebody rang to ask if we could locate Councillors Blondel, Muggeridge and Evans Jenkins. The Bishop was asked to guarantee The Vicar's conduct, Mr and Mrs Finney have had a big fight, Doolittle and Dash have disappeared and so has the Bank Manager."

"Is that all?" said The Mayor. "No Sir, McGurk has sacked his waitress at the insistence of his wife, the Librarian has resigned and Lord and Lady Crewdley are going to be divorced. And oh yes..... The Fire Chief has gone on sick leave, he claims to have pulled a muscle."

"I'm not surrprised. Now, are you quite sure that's everyone?" The Mayor asked impatiently. "No Sir, it isn't. I'm not sure what has happened to The Sisters Flack."

"Oh them! They've probably been transferred to Chicago to pick up where Al Capone left off. Crewdley today, an International Crime-Syndicate tomorrow. I'm sure they've got a great future. Thrre's plenty of opportunity for two of the best front-women in the business.

My God! Butter wouldn't melt in their mouths! Two little grey haired old ladies eh? Fantastic, isn't it Robespierre? We're wasted here, serving The Great Crewdley Public. We should open a Wool Shop and make some real money!" "You are upset Mr Mayor?"

"Yes, I'm upset Robespierre, extremely upset. As you are aware, I like to be in control of events, not picking up the pieces after disaster strikes. I've got to put this thing back on the rails by fair means or foul!"

Robespierre gritted his teeth, "There was someone else at The Wool Shop who I forgot to mention Mr Mayor," he announced. The Mayor breathed in deeply, "Go on." "Well apparently, Fredric Puccini was filming the whole thing, answered Robespierre.

The Mayor held his head and sat down heavily in the chair.

"Oh marvellous! Well that's it then! The whole world can watch Crewdly's "Den of Sin" in their living rooms. No doubt he will produce exciting video's at £50 each .... and picture postcards..... then there's the Academic Market! Oxford University, Sociology Examination, Paper One, First Question ...What turns a typical English Town into a late 20th Century Model of Sodom and Gommorah overnight? Dicuss .... you may refer to the video and consult the notes made by witnesses who were there and actually participated in the down-fall of civilization."

The telephone rang.

"Make breakfast Robespierre," said The Mayor, "fried eggs, mushrooms, tomatoes and chips. And lots of coffee!

"Hello, this is The Mayor, who is that?" There was a pregnant pause before a familiar voice began to speak. "It's me Mr Mayor."

"Beard! Where are you?" "I'm in a telephone box near the Police Station. Can I please come in to work Mr Mayor?"

"Get round here double-quick!" he answered, "You're already over an hour late. What ever else happens, you will certainly stay at your desk until 6.30pm tonight." "Thank you very much Mr Mayor. It will be a pleasure and an honour." The Mayor slammed down the telephone, paced two circuits of the room and picked it up again to ring The Police Station.

"This is The Mayor. I want to speak to Superintendent Bramley , hello hello Bramley ...."

"Take a running jump Presbyterian," said Bramley. I don't care what you do now. I've got the lot of you .....Blondel, Beard, Lady Crewdley, The Vicar all of them, including you, so sod off. Why don't you go and open a fete or something while you've still got the chance? It's the end of the line for you.

" I'm going to bring the whole house down, it's corrupt everybody is on the fiddle and some of their personal habits are disgusting."

"Listen to me Bramley, if you pursue this, I'll break you. No pension .... career in tatters .... think about it." "I already have," he shouted and put the phone down.

The Mayor went over to the window.

"It'll have to be Plan B then, Robespierre," he said. "Bramley can't say I didn't warn him."

A wicked grin spread across Robespierre's face, "Thank goodness for that Your Honour. I was beginning to get worried."

"Look! Here comes Beard," said The Mayor, "that's one sheep back in the fold, because Plan B Robespierre, is to get everything back to normal - Beard at his desk, Blondel and the others into the Council Chamber, The Vicar back into the Church, though unless that man has a complete change of character, it might well be a temporary stay......"

He circled the room, arms behind his back, working out a strategy as he spoke, though of course, it would all be written down later, checked and crossed-checked, tested and finally, put into operation. Robespierre felt easier as he watched the familiar, physical part of Presbyterian's ritualistic method of problem solving when his survival was under threat.

If The Mayor was safe, then Robespierre would survive also. He waited patiently as The Mayor walked the floor, until he came to an abrupt halt.

"You'd better try and locate Puccini, I want to know exactly why he took his Film Crew to The Wool Shop," he said. Robespierre stood to attention, "Yes Mr Mayor." He looked puzzled.

'Where shall I look Your Worship?"

"You could start at The Police Station, if he's not there, go to The Forest Hotel. If he isn't at either of those places, you'll have to use your initiative. Don't come back without something positive."

Robespierre disappeared down the old wooden staircase, but a few moments later, he was back, breathless and already exhausted. "The mushrooms are frying Mr Mayor and the eggs will be ready. Would you please help yourself?"

"You stupid man. Of course I will. Go and find Puccini, and don't worry, your breakfast won't be wasted, because I'll eat it." Robespierre made a quick exit and The Mayor walked through to the kitchen and prepared his breakfast. He took the food on a tray and sat near the Parlour window.

His 'Salvation Plan', like all good plans, was relatively simple and involved the Salvation of many, though perhaps not all, of those who had fallen from the lofty heights of civic respectability and social normality. They would have to be rehabilitated quickly into the main-stream of life in Crewdley, else the whole structure would rapidly begin to crumble. It was not that Presbyterian particularly liked the Councillors, the Bank Manager or even the ludicrous Vicar, merely that the fire-storm which would surely come if he refused to intervene, would turn Crewdley into ashes.

The easy, but mistaken way, was to save only himself. This could have been achieved, no doubt, by the threats against, and bribery of, innocent people who would then have sweared on oath that The Mayor was not only of good character, but was the epitimone of virtue itself. However, he had long discovered the sweet irony that it was often more difficult to prove that someone was telling the truth, than to prove they were lying. And so Presbyterian had found it necessary to resort to illegal and threatening tactics to get the truth from a rival or someone he wished to intimidate on a permanent basis. It was simply the case that many people who occupied senior positions in Crewdley society, seemed to have skeletons in the cupboard, whereas the ordinary members of The Great Crewdley Public didn't seem to care who said what about them, or even whether it was true or not.

Therefore, although he could no doubt have obtained a 'not guilty' verdict on his behaviour that night, his would have been the only one, and it would not have been sufficient to have saved the good name of Crewdley, when taken with the dozen verdicts of 'Guilty' being ascribed to The Vicar, Lady Crewdley, the Fire Chief, the Bank Manager and the others.

These worthies who were about to fall would be saved and their guilt carefully sealed and put away in the wall-safe of The Mayor's Parlour. His Insurance Policies would be stronger than ever, his Portfolio of Incriminating Evidence and Confessions as solid as The Bank of England (and more so since the Banks subjugation into the European Exchange Rate Mechanism) Perhaps the Court would need a few sacrificial lambs, such as McGurk's Waitress, the Kissogram Toy Boy, even Mrs Elsie Finney? Yet, that scenario raised the key question - would the case go to Court at all? If it did, the lambs would have to be sacrificed to save the Civic Aristocracy, but this option would remain a second choice. Harold Presbyterian telephoned the offices of 'The Weekly Weaver' and demanded to speak to The Editor.

"Hello McSnadden ... listen, you must have heard rumours about last night in The Wool Shop....."

"Rumours man? It's true! It was the biggest Police Raid in the history of Crewdley," McSnadden answered.

"Not a word about it in your paper I'm afraid McSnadden. I've informed your owner and he agrees with me that this isn't the sort of thing that he wishes to see his syndicate giving coverage to .... all that valuable Advertizing space would be lost, wouldn't it Archie? A nd not only that, as you know, your owner likes to run nice, friendly little newspapers in towns like ours. A scandal like this would definately be against all our interests. Do you get the picture Archie? You've gone all quiet".

McSnadden replaced the telephone receiver. Presbyterian could almost see the disappointment on his face. Of course he hadn't spoken to the owner, there was no need. The threat was sufficient to keep McSnadden quiet. Well paid jobs were hard to get and harder to keep. If McSnadden was a good boy, then one day, he just might be given a job in Wapping, but if he upset decent people in small towns like Crewdley, he'd find it impossible to even get a Valentine message published in the Kidderminster Bugle.

His next port of call was to Lady Crewdley. She was most upset and the prospect of a court appearance, coupled with her impending divorce had made its mark.

"Sod the lot of them!" she cried, "I'm bloody annoyed! One little slip, and complete disaster befalls one."

"Please don't upset yourself," said The Mayor, "it won't find its way into the newspapers, I give you my word on that. I've had a chat with the owner and he's told McSnadden in no uncertain terms not to touch it with a barge-pole."

"Thank you Harold."

"I'm working hard to get the whole case dropped, but that lout Bramley seems unable to exercise even his one, single brain cell away from causing havoc. But don't panic Lady Crewdley, his head will be placed on the highest spike in town by next week, I promise. Bye for now and please give my regards to Lord Crewdley."

"He's going to divorce me," she said tearfully.

"Tell him it was all a mistake. You were merely a participant in a little 'Drama' initiated by Fredric Puccini."

"I can't."

"Well, that is going to be our collective defence Madam, so you'll have to lump it. Everyone else will testify to that, so unless you genuinely want to throw in your lot with Smokey Flint... you were possibly playing the role of someone in a Ken Russell film, but I'll leave the details to you.

Bloody Aristo's," he mumbled, "absolutely useless in a crisis. What does she expect me to do, shoot Bramley or burn Crewdley to the ground?" He poured another coffee and slumped into his favourite leather chair. A telephone converation with Lord Nigel Rice-Knowles revealed that Puccini had not been sanctioned to film activities in The Wool Shop. Although Rice-Knowles was rather taken with the idea, a threatening reminder of his own past indiscretions was sufficient to disown the rampant Director.

"No, no..... do with him as you will my good man," he said, "I want no part of it."

"Excellent," replied The Mayor, "and of course, I shall treat the issue of your past little problems in the strictest confidence I assure you."

He couldn't resist a final dig," By the way, have you ever been back to the Convent since then?" A long and pronounced silence indicated that Lord Nigel

Rice-Knowles still found 'The Incident' difficult to speak about.

"Never mind, no one is perfect eh? Least of all you - cheerio!" said The Mayor. He began to write notes on 'The Great Wool Shop Scandal'.

"Not at all a bad start for the defence," he said quietly, "but the Home Office might be a problem." After having his call transferred through three Home Office Departments, he was finally put through to a Senior Civil Servant with special responsibilty for Court Administration.

"Yes, that's correct..... I've just recently been appointed the Magistrate for Crewdley ....I want to know when I'm sitting."

"You can't do that without attending our Intensive Training and Induction Course here in London..... we wouldn't want you sentencing people to death for parking on double-yellow lines, would we?"

"Oh I don't know. There are one or two persistant offenders who need teaching a lesson," said The Mayor. "Hah, hah! Naughty, naughty! That would never do, would it? No ! You must be made properly familiar with all of the rules and regulations, it's most important. Now, we have a short course beginning tomorrow. Would you like to join us?" the man asked.

"Very well, the sooner the better I suppose?" "Quite so," answered the Civil Servant, "It's Room 6, Floor 3 of the rear wing in the Administration Block down here in Whitehall. Have you got that? We start at midday and go through until just after lunch on Sunday."

"I'll be there," said The Mayor," I shall be bringing my Chauffer. How are you fixed for parking?" "Oh absolutely spendidly, thank you. I have my own place in the Courtyard. Those who are attending the Induction Course however, have to park in the street. Please make sure you have plenty of change for the meter and oh yes, I almost forgot, we charge your Local Authority £700 for accomodation. I shan't be there myself ... golfing in Portugal - goodbye, nice to have you aboard old man."

"Typical", The Mayor said to himself,"an over-paid bureaucrat totally cut off from the real world .....sounded Chief Secretary to the Cabinet material to me."

He added a few more lines to his Salvation Plan.

"Mmm... apart from anything else .....we're going to need a new Librarian."

He wrote out a small advert for the local and provincial press, put it in an envelope and actually took out a stamp for it from his own wallet. If things were to be put back into place as quickly as possible, the Crewdley Bureaucracy would have to be short-circuited and it was quite likely that after his fall from grace, Beard would be about as much use to the Council as the imposition of a new Poor Law.

After yet another cup of coffee, The Mayor put on his overcoat, looked at himself in the mirror and set off for The Vicarage. The nettle would have to be grasped. "Oh please come in Harold," said a tearful Mrs Wooly, "I just can't imagine what's happened to Wilfred. He's consumed with self-doubt and worse. Now he tells me that he spent most of last night in The Wool Shop. He keeps babbling on about some wretched young woman he refers to as his Golden Nymph."

"Yes, he seems to be at a very difficult stage of his career, doesn't he, and it's about that very point I want to talk to you," he said, taking a seat near to the window in the lounge. Mrs Wooly looked blank.

"Obviously, The Bishop has been informed?" he asked.

"Oh yes," she acknowledged.

"And your husband's position ultimately rests in his hands?" She forced a smile, "Yes ...."

"Will you take some sound advice from an old friend?" he asked again. Mrs Wooly nodded and held her smile.

"Keep the silly old sod under lock and key until this thing is all over." "I shall do my best Harold," she answered, "but it's awfully difficult. He has to fight the Forces of Darkness, you know."

"Mmm, well at the moment, I should say Lucifer and Beelzebub are winning hands down, wouldn't you?" He saw himself out, and as he did, heard the awful moans from the bedroom of Crewdley's Vicar of Darkness, apparently failing miserably in his fight for Eternal Redemption and Blessed Grace.

The Mayor walked the few yards back to The Town Hall and looked up and down Church Street for Robespierre, of whom there was no sign. He took his Personal Bleeper, pressed a button and casually ascended the old, wooden staircase to The Parlour. He'd been sitting in his favourite leather armchair for about a minute , when the sound of fast moving footsteps became louder and heavier. Robespierre burst in, gasping for breath. "Here I am Sir," he panted, "the Bleeper went off and I ran back all the way."

"Heh! Good!," said The Mayor, "and where were you?" "In the toilet at 'The Star and Garter,' Your Worship."

"Mmm..... so I see look at you..... your flies are undone.....You're a disgrace to your profession," said The Mayor, "Get dressed —

We're going to London!"

"When ?" asked Robespierre.

"Now! You can tell me all about Puccini in the car, so hurry up and make sure you wear your best suit. I want to make a good impression in Whitehall."

They were well on the way to London in the Civic Rolls Royce when The

Mayor condescended to speak to his Chauffer.

"We're a day early actually, but I think some of the Citizens of Crewdley would appreciate their First Citizen being absolutely on top form for the course. Besides, I want to give them the benefit of a period of quiet and calm after The Wool Shop debacle.

Things need to settle down in Crewdley, and I shall appreciate a break from idiots like Beard and nincompoops like Mrs Wooly." "Yes Sir," said Robespierre, eyeing his Master through the rear view mirror. " About Mr Puccini, Your Eminence."

"It hardly matters actually Robespierre," answered Crewdley's Great Man, "he's irrelevant .... in the bag, you might say, and all because someone I know spent a few hours in a Convent."

Robespierre looked bemused and the furrows on his brow indicated he was at a loss with regard to this last comment. "I think Mr Puccini has flipped his lid Your Worship," he finally said, "I could see him through a window in the Police Station. He was standing on a table and singing Ave Maria."

"I don't suppose you happened to see Mrs Finney did you Robespierre?", asked The Mayor, "She seems to believe that she's Mae West. Be careful the next time I send you for fish and chips."

The London Course was extremely boring. Presbyterian did his best not to interfere or comment unduly about the Lecturers, but he found the whole episode almost as bad as a session with The Vicar's wife. However, it did provide him with the necessary ground-rules for a) committing people to prison b) defending himself from personal attack in Court from guilty defendants and their relatives and c) using the system for his own advantage and not being unduly fettered with red tape from the Judiciary and the bureaucrats in Whitehall.

Presbyterian was asleep in the car for most of the journey home, having been unable to have slept a wink in the peculiar Ministry accomodation. Robespierre saw the lights of Crewdley come into view at a little after eleven pm and called out to The Mayor as they were driving over Crewdley Bridge. "We're home Your Worship ,and I think my Personal Bleeper is on the blink. It's buzzing like a wasp," he said.

"Throw it away," The Mayor answered drowsily, "it was a gift from Crewdley Electrics. He's touting for trade. I'll tell him it was rubbish. He'll have to try harder if he wants any favours from me." Robespierre pulled in at the pavement outside 'Civic House'. The Mayor got out rather unsteadily and made his way inside.

A hundred and fifty mile journey, even in a Rolls Royce, wasn't his idea of enchantment, and after making himself a cup of coffee, he retired to his bedroom and without putting on the light, he got straight into bed. "I let myself in Pressy darling," purred his favourite person, "I hope you don't mind?"

Monday 4th November 1991 was a rather cold and horribly wet day. Presbyterian peered from the Georgian window panes of 'Civic House', and watched the rain falling hard onto the pavement. It was seven am and his mistress was already cooking breakfast in the kitchen.

"Come on Pressy .....time to eat," she called. He dressed quickly and joined her at the table.

"So tell me all about London," she asked, "I suppose you've already applied to be The Lord Chancellor or The Chief Judge of England?"

"Mmm, chance would be a fine thing Pippa darling," he answered. "in the meantime they've made me solely responsible for the Administration of Justice in Crewdley .... not bad for starters eh? Tell me is there anyone you would like thrown into prison at all? Your husband perhaps? How about fifteen years, with no remission Right of Appeal and mandatory divorce from you by the middle of next week?"

"Splendid," she said, "but don't you think the cells will be filled up with most of the Crewdley notables and a rather bizarre selection of other people, including McGurk's waitress? What on earth went on last Thursday Harold?"

"I love it when you call me Harold," he blushed, "oh - and Pressy as well of course........but it's just the way you say Harold! Where was I?"

"Just about to tell me exactly what happened at The Wool Shop," said Pippa firmly.

"Oh that .....where to begin," he replied, cutting up his eggs, "not much to tell really darling. Apart from The Flack Sisters becoming the Proprietors of Crewdley's very own Moulin Rouge, most of our prominent citizens becoming totally debauched overnight and Bramley organizing the biggest raid since the British burned Washington ...absolutely nothing happened."

"That's not what I heard Pressy," she insisted, "I heard Dorothy and Myrtle Flack have been running a Den of Vice for about six weeks."

"Who's saying disgusting things like that my darling? Give me their names and I'll have them flogged."

"Mrs Wooly," said Pippa.

"Oh her! She's bonkers .....almost as mad as The Vicar himself."

"She seemed pretty sure of her facts Harold. The Vicar confessed everything and he made Mrs Wooly dress up as a 17th Century Priest when he did it."

"He'll have to go," said The Mayor, "he's as nutty as a fruit cake ... .bats in the belfry ......a hopeless case."

"'Now come on Harold..... you're hedging ....what's going on?" she pleaded.

"O.K Here's the low-down. Unless I'm as sure-footed as a mountain-goat during the next few days, Crewdley will be finished." "You're joking aren't you Pressy darling?" she asked.

"No - no I'm not actually," he answered, "if all of this is made public and the Legal System gets its hooks into some of my Councillors and leading members of the Professions, Central Government will almost certainly intervene. They'd probably abolish Crewdley Council and disperse it to the elements. A whole way of life would disappear. It would be as if the River Crewd had flooded its banks and submerged everything and everyone beneath its icy waters." "Oh dear," exclaimed Pippa, "I didn't realize things were quite so serious.'

"I'm afraid they are, but don't worry you gorgeous Head Mistress, I'm going to smash Bramley and put everything back in its place," he promised. "And I love it when you take command Harold," she purred, "lets go back to bed?" A passion ran through him like 10,000 volts, but at the very last moment he regained control and bit his lip.

"My God Pippa .....I'm sorely tempted, but really I have much important work to do......." , he said with real regret.

The remaining period of their breakfasting together, was almost an anti-climax.

Presbyterian did his best to tell Pippa Monroe all about Puccini, Lord Nigel Rice-Knowles and how he would settle his account with Bramley. She flitted from room to room, collecting things she had left on the last occasion, and finally, at just after 8.15am, Mrs Pippa Monroe, Headmistress of Crewdley Comprehensive, left 'Civic House' by the back door and made her way to school.

There were several letters on the hall floor, but Presbyterian put them all to one side except the one with the emblem he recognized as belonging to the Home Office.

"Excellent," he said, "Friday 8th November..... my first sitting as a Magistrate .....plenty of time to secure any of the loose ends...."

He put on his coat and walked the short distance to The Town Hall.

Robespierre was waiting inside The Foyer and grinning at Beard who appeared to be hard at work in his office.

"Come on Robespierre," said The Mayor, "there's work to be done." "Yes Sir," replied The Boy from the Bastille, falling into line behind The Great Man as he went up the stairs to The Parlour two at a time. "Did Sir happen to have seen Mrs Monroe since we arrived back from London?" he asked, closing the door behind him.

"You don't miss much, do you Robespierre? Listen .... I want you to give me a full report on the whereabouts and welfare of everyone who was arrested in The Wool Shop." Robespierre stood to attention, "Yes Your Worship. Does that include The Vicar?"

"It particularly includes The Vicar .... and Lady Crewdley .... all of them. You can have a working lunch at 'The Star and Garter', but no more than two pints or else!" "And what time am I to report in Sir, now that my Personal Bleeper is kaput!"

"When you've finished your report of course," The Mayor answered, knowing full well that if Robespierre got home before midnight, he would have been guilty of rushing things.

"So don't cut corners Robespierre and make certain that your facts are facts and not figments of your frenzied imagination.

Now buzz off..... I need time to think."

A few moments later he rang the Police Station and asked to speak with Horace Bramley, but as expected, the Superintendent had gone to ground, realizing no doubt, that if Presbyterian could get at him before the Court Cases, he would probably come out second best.

"Good! If he's in his bunker, he won't be able to intimidate any of the defendents before Friday," Presbyterian said to himself with a wide grin, ...but I will."

Lady Crewdley was next on his list of people to be contacted. Robespierre would indeed probably attempt to speak with her himself during the course of the day, or at least spy upon the occupants of Crewdley Manor through field-glasses or even from behind the drawing room curtains, but he was generally about as subtle as a sledgehammer, and The Mayor wanted reliable, first hand information from several of Crewdley's accused leading Citizens, so he telephoned her himself.

"Lady Crewdley...... how are you today?" he asked.

"Bloody awful! One insisted one was merely playing a small part in Mr Puccini's film, but Lord Crewdley won't have it!" she responded with angst.

"Oh won't he? Mmm .... In that case, I'd better come round and speak with him. Lets say about twenty minutes. There is one slight problem, in that I haven't had a chance to speak with Puccini, but I believe that I will be able to convince him to see things our way."

Unfortunately for The Mayor, Lord Crewdley was not in a passive or receptive mood. "It's no good Presbyterian!", he shouted, "it doesn't explain why that lout Flint was lying on top of Lady Crewdley when the Police raided

147

The Wool Shop."

"They were filming 'Women in Love'," said The Mayor.

"In Crewdley?", asked the Lord of Crewdley Manor, "this used to be a decent, respectable little town where a chap could rely on not having his wife accosted by a lecherous fireman."

"And it still is Lord Crewdley. You have my word on it," insisted The Mayor, "the issue has been extremely badly handled, but from this moment, I'm personally taking charge of the whole affair." "But you were one of those who was arrested!", Lord Crewdley retorted, "It's jolly well not good enough Presbyterian."

"I can assure you," The Mayor insisted, "that both your good Lady and I are innocent." "He's being a pig!", shouted Lady Crewdley, "an absolute pig and a very boring old pig at that." "I beg your pardon madam!", said the accused. "You're being a boring old pig," she insisted.

"Actually, I do have another appointment," The Mayor interupted, "I'll see myself out."

"A pig, a rotten, mean swine!"

"Rather a pig then, than a harlot!"

"Monkey - Ape-Pig, Pig, Pig, !!"

Presbyterian closed the door of Crewdley Manor behind him, "Bloody Aristocrats, they can't even swear properly!"

His thoughts turned next to John Doolittle and Henry Dash, Solicitors to the Council, whose firm was a local institution and a by-word for propriety and respectability. The present incumbants were the seventh generation to hold such offices, and on paper at least, seemed beyond reproach in all matters legal, civil and social .

A cold wind blew as The Mayor walked over Crewdley Bridge. He looked down to the icy waters of the River Crewd and imagined whether it might just be possible for Bramley to launch himself into it from the highest parapet, witnessed by the whole of Crewdley as atonement for his sin of threatening their social cohesion and belief in all of those he had arrested and accused.

Unfortunately, he doubted the chances of it happening. He walked on and into Church Street and caught a glipse of Robespierre in hot pursuit of Councillor Barry Blondel "Idiot!", he called out, "don't waste your time on him! Get after The Flacks, you fool!"

Robespierre acknowledged His Master's Voice, gave up pursuing Blondel and ducked into St Crueds Passage, presumably to interview the Fire Chief, but with Robespierre, he could just as easily have been going the long way round to Finney's Fish Shop to spy on Mae West.

The Mayor made his way past Doctor Scargreaves Surgery and the wretched Wool Shop (which was closed). He continued on past the Estate Agents, "The Weekly Weaver," and finally, he went into the pleasantly furnished offices of Doolittle and Dash. The Receptionist looked up at him over her horn-rimmed glasses, just as the telephone rang. She immediately picked it up and ignored the visitor. "Good morning - Doolittle and Dash - I'm Susie - how may I help you? Yes......that's right...... I'll tell him... have a nice day - byee!"

After typing a few more words, she finally condescended to address The Mayor, "Yes?"

"Yes indeed," The Mayor answered, "you're new here aren't you?"

"Yes I'm temping."

"And I'm tempted," he said enthusiatically. "Beg pardon?" she asked.

"Never mind..... what's a beautiful young woman like you doing in Crewdley?", he enquired of the young maiden from the Waters of The Caspian.

"I'm temping!", she repeated.

"My God, you certainly are," he acknowledged, "if ever you need a job, come and see me, I'm just over the road." "Oh thanks," she smiled, "I'll buzz Mr Dash .... who shall say is calling?" Presbyterian breathed in deeply and stood up to his full height, "The Mayor of Crewdley," he answered, "Harold Presbyterian in person." "Right oh .... I might take you up on that one these days," she replied, buzzing Dash as she spoke.

"Excellent .... I'm sure I could find a most comfortable position for you over at The Town Hall, Miss .....?"

"Miss Goodthigh," she answered without emotion, but the emotion was all with The Mayor.

"Please go through," she said huskily, "perhaps I might come over to see you later on?"

"My God," said The Mayor, realizing now exactly how curvaceous and attractive Miss Goodthigh was, "It would be a pleasure." He exited left and into the corridor looking for Dash's Office.

"My God!" he mumbled, "she was beautiful .... absolutely beautiful!" "Come in!", Dash called, "What do you think of our new temporary Secretary?"

"There ought to be a law prohibiting young women like her," answered Presbyterian.

"Mmm ....I agree, but much better than the other one eh?"

"Incidently," Presbyterian asked, "what exactly happened to the other one?" "She walked out last Friday!" Dash said assertively and without regret.

"Yes .... last Friday .... more precisely the late hours of last Thursday and the early hours of Friday morning." "That's exactly why I'm here," The Mayor reminded himself, just as Miss Goodthigh seemed to be undressing in front of him. "My God!" he repeated, "why the Hell did you take her on? Don't you find her distracting?" "Yes .... fantastic isn't it?", Dash replied with relish.

"Well if you want to swap her for Robespierre, it's fine by me," said The Mayor.

Dash was grinning a wider span than Crewdley Bridge and for what seemed like an eternity, The Mayor stared at his stupid teeth, caressing and kissing Miss Goodthigh and finally rolling over and over with her in a field of brazen-red poppies, smelling for all the world like those on banks of The Caspian Sea. Then, after a Gargantuan Effort, he snapped out of it and regained his self-control.

"Look here Dash," he said roughly, "I take back what I said. She's a complete distraction. I came here to tell you exactly what's going to happen on Friday."

"Oh really! I thought we were all just going to plead guilty and get it over with!", Dash answered flippantly.

"Certainly not! What's the matter with you Dash, have you lost your mind?", asked The Mayor, "we've got to defend this case and we've got to win." "Why?", asked Dash.

"Why? Well I'm surprised that you of all people have to ask that," The Mayor answered. "Why?" The Mayor was becoming exasperated? "Because we've got to defend Crewdley's honour, that's why, you bloody foolish Solicitor you! Do you want to lose everything you've got? Your good name, your position in the Company, maybe even your wife and family? Come on man, buck up! It's your own affair why you went into The Wool Shop, but I'm not having Bramley dictate terms and conditions to me or anyone else for that matter. I'm going to nail him to the wall!" "Oh good! It's about time things livened up in Crewdley," said Dash.

"Yes .... I was speaking metaphorically of course, about the nailing to the wall. But nevertheless, he's not having half of Crewdley convicted for visiting a Vice Den," The Mayor insisted.

"Why not?..... It's true ....and we weren't just visiting either,"
Dash countered bravely.

"Don't start that again. This is very serious. And where's Doolittle? I havn't seen him since Friday morning in The Wool Shop," asked The Mayor. "He's out with Mrs Finney," Dash replied, "he's taken quite a liking to her."

"Oh God!", moaned The Mayor, "this is going from bad to worse!" Susie came in with two cups of coffee and put them on the table, making sure as she did so, that her loose blouse became even more loose, giving The Mayor a full view of her breasts.

"Thank you Susie," he said weakly, watching her every movement, until at last she disappeared back to the Reception desk.

"It's no good. I can't stay in this place any longer. But take good notice Dash," said The Mayor, "this is the story and make sure you stick to it. You were invited to The Wool Shop by Puccini. He wanted to Screen-Test various citizens of Crewdley for parts in a film, have you got it?"

"Oh, I suppose so," said Dash already losing interest and sounding extremely unenthusiastic.

"Excellent, and Doolittle is to use the same story. I'll leave the details up to you. You're usually pretty good at waffling on for hours at a time without saying anything of substance or incriminating yourself. But pull yourself together! You seem to have lost all sense of purpose," said The Mayor. "Sorry - I'll try," replied Henry Dash, "and you're quite right. Susie is an utter distraction ......but what a magnificent creature she is."

The Mayor almost tip-toed past the temporary Secretary as he made his way through the Reception area.

"You're off then Mr Mayor? If you need anything .... anything at all," she simmered, "just give me a call- byeee!"

He went out onto to the pavement, dashed across Church Street, up to The Mayor's Parlour and had a cold shower, which he rather quickly turned up to hot, as the vision of Susie melted into the white tiles of the cubicle. He had dressed and was tying his shoe laces when Robespierre tapped on the door,"Mr Mayor ... it's me."

"Come in Robespierre. What news from the front?", The Mayor asked. "McGurk's Waitress seems to be under the misapprehension that Mr Doolittle has committed himself to her, regarding certain favours of a financial and sexual nature."

"Marvellous," The Mayor exclaimed tersely.

"And ......Mrs Finney is accusing the Bank Manager of two-timing her for the waitress."

"Of course she is! What else?" "It's quite a long story," Robespierre said, looking at The Mayor for permission to sit down.

"Go and make some tea and then we'll talk," The Great Man conceded, "you look as if you've just taken part in a free-fall parachute landing and the silk refused to open."

"It's a long story Your Worship...... " The Mayor pointed to the door, "Go and make the tea!"

They spent the next hour going over the information which Robespierre had gleaned from The Accused. He seemed to have concentrated almost naturally and exclusively on the people who best equated with his own social class.

McGurk' s Waitress, Mrs Elsie Finney, the two young women who had adopted The Vicar and Councillor Blondel respectively, and finally, the woman with flaming red hair. "I couldn't find the Kissogram Toy Boy," he had explained, a point for which, given all the circumstances, The Mayor had been relieved to hear. Proof of the social theory of like staying with like in Crewdley Society (except in matters sexual) was confirmed by Robespierre's total failure to have spoken with anyone from the Middle or Upper Class. Again, The Mayor was thankful his man hadn't managed to get an interview with Lady Crewdley. That scenario might just have been suffient to have pushed Lord Crewdley over the edge. A clear picture of wanton and pre-meditated debauchery was painted by Robespierre, who seemed once or twice to have been irked by not having been there earlier himself.

"But what about The Flack Sisters?", The Mayor asked earnestly. "They've gone - disappeared from the face of the earth," answered Robespierre dramatically, "It's a mystery Your Honour. I looked everywhere."

"Yes, all right," The Mayor interrupted,"you don't have to convince me, I believe you,"

He looked at The Boy from The Bastilie, "And I don't want to hear any comments about you, leering after McGurk's Waitress. "I wasn't Your Grace!" Robespierre pleaded.

"I saw the way that you were looking at her. It doesn't become you Anton..... Your position is most important to the people of Crewdley. We can't have you leering after young waitresses."

Robespierre stared at The Mayor opened mouthed.

"What's the matter Robespierre? You look as if you've seen a ghost," said The Mayor. "You called me Anton, Your Worship," Robespierre said softly.

"Oh sorry Robespierre," he replied, "I'm under a bit of pressure at the moment." "It's perfectly alright Sir," he said, "it just surprised me rather."

It was by now, late afternoon, "We'll go out to The Forest Hotel for dinner tonight. They've got venison on the menu, and we might hear one or two snippets about our little local difficulty," said The Mayor.

Robespierre chuckled to himself.

"What's the matter with you?"The Mayor asked him. "I was just thinking Your Worship, wouldn't it be funny if The Sisters Flack had transferred engagements to The Forest Hotel and it was raided again by Bramley?"

The Mayor looked grim, "Robespierre..... that's not funny..... that's not funny at all."

At just after midnight, The Mayor of Crewdley and his faithful servant returned to The Town Hall, and having put away the Civic Rolls Royce, Robespierre joined The Mayor in his Parlour. It was after 2am and several bottles of the best Civic wine later, when Robespierre made his weary way down the corridor to his rooms and The Mayor sprawled out on his Chaise Longue to settle down for the night. He rolled over and a watery vision of Susie came slowly into focus. She was looking up at him over horn-rimmed glasses in a field of red poppies.

"A beautiful distraction," he murmered, "I bet she can't type though ..but she doesn't need to,does she?"

Tuesday 5th November seemed a miserable day to The Mayor as he looked from The Parlour window. He could smell eggs and sausages being cooked and the clatter of cups and saucers indicated that Robespierre was pouring the coffee. "Good morning Your Worship," he said, putting the drink onto the table, "breakfast is nearly ready. I'll bring it through in a moment."

"Thank you Robespierre," he answered, "I'm hungry." "The children have finished making their bonfire Mr Mayor," added Robespierre, "I can see it in the park from the back window."

"Mmm, thank God they havn't gone mad with the Fire Works so far this year. I don't think some of The Accused could stand the shock of the bangs, particulary Lady Crewdley and Mrs Wooly, although it's not her who is being accused! I'm sure that the foolish woman would volunteer herself to face the Court instead of The Vicar. I'm surprised she's stayed with him for so long. He doesn't deserve her! She's extremely loyal, which is quite something nowadays, wouldn't you say so Robespierre?" "Yes Mr Mayor. Loyalty is a prime virtue," Robespierre agreed, "It is to be valued above all else, I think," he said impassively.

"Yes I suppose you're right," said The Mayor watching his man as he walked back through to the kitchen. "Your own loyalty and service to The Council are much appreciated," he called.

"My loyalty is to you above all others," Robespierre replied, placing the breakfast onto the table, "as for the Council, I only serve it so that I may serve you, Your Worship," he said awkwardly.

The Mayor looked long and hard at his faithful servant. "I can read you like a book. The only reason why you said that, was because I caught you oggling McGurk's Waitress!" Robespierre retired from The Parlour to the temporary solitude of his own room. The Mayor had struck a chord, but he would be loath to admit it.

It was some time later that morning when Robespierre parked the Rolls outside Crewdley Fire Station for The Mayor's appointment with the Fire Chief. A fireman was cleaning one of the tenders when he saw The Mayor come in. "He's in the office", he said, squeezing his rag out in a bucket of soapy water. Flint was reading a book, but he got up and offered a chair to his guest as he came in. "Friday is the big day then Mr Mayor. Everybody is for the high-jump eh?", said Flint with a certain resignation to his fate.

The Mayor looked him straight in the eye, "That's not quite how I see things panning out actually Flint. But let's be clear, unless you're prepared to plead, 'Not Guilty,' I suggest that you have got a most serious problem regarding your employment in Crewdley."

The point was well made and the impact sufficient, "Oh - I'm not guilty Your Worship - certainly not." He paused, "The trouble is," he paused again, "the trouble is, Bramley arrested me with Lady Crewdley."

"What do you mean - 'with' Lady Crewdley?"

"Well ...erm.... well..... lets say, we had been getting to know each other."

"Yes, I had the gross misfortune to have witnessed part of that sordid scene with my own eyes. Whatever possessed you Flint? You're not even in her class," The Mayor reminded him.

"No that's just it..... I always fancied her, just because she was an Aristo, I suppose. We're the same age you know."

"How touching ....Let me remind you Flint, that if the truth comes out, not only will you be sacked, you'll probably end up as a wall trophy at Crewdley Manor."

"No I don't think she fancies me enough to do that," Flint answered, obviously still not thinking the thing through.

"It won't be her you fool, it will be him! Lord Crewdley holds the only licence in the area permitting him to use an elephant gun." "Oh, I see what you mean. Like that is it?", asked Flint.

"Yes, exactly like that. So this is the story and you'd better stick to it. Fredric Puccini went to The Wool Shop to audition various people for a film he wanted to make."

"Who's Fredric Puccini?", Flint asked again.

"The flaming film maker , that's who! The man who has been filming in Crewdley for the past month...... the man with the red beard .... a white suit and a red beard. You must have seen him ?"

"I don't think so - oh wait a minute. There was someone who came into the Fire Station and asked to film us going out to a fire. I expect that would have been him, eh?"

"Yes!" said The Mayor.

"He hadn't got a red beard and he was wearing a light brown suit ... no....
no..... wait a minute ......you're right of course.

Sorry Mr Mayor, I'm colour-blind .... yes, you'd be about right, red beard
and white suit...... I'm with you now!"

The Mayor was getting rather agitated and trying hard to keep his temper.

"Forgive my asking Flint, but if you're colour blind, how come you're the
Fire Chief? I'm certain we don't allow people who are colour blind into the
service." "Quite right Mayor. I was serving my probationary period, and the
day of the visual medical tests, the Doctor was taken ill, so the Duty Officer
gave me a First Class Medical Certificate. He didn't bother doing any eye tests,
he just made me carry a hundredweight of sand up and down a ladder." The
Mayor breathed in deeply and counted to five.

"How very quaint. Never mind that now. Puccini was going to make a film
in The Wool Shop. It was all very innocent. You and Lady Crewdley were
auditioning for, 'Women in Love'." "Which part was I playing?" asked the
colour blind Fire Chief.

"Gerald!"

"Gerald who?"

"For goodness sake! Show some initiative! Read up about it! The Court case
is on Friday and it's one part you'd better know the lines for. Good morning!"

The Mayor went back out through the Fire Station where the man was still
cleaning the tender. " Did you find him?" he enquired.

"Unfortunately yes. Make sure you've had a proper eye-test," said The
Mayor, "it's in your interest to know if you're colourblind, you could have an
accident!" The man stared and threw his rag hard into the buckcet of soapy
water as The Mayor walked out to the Forecourt. "Bloody politician! Who
voted for him?", he said under his breath.

"One thousand and forty nine people, thats who. Good Morning! And
make sure you get your eyes tested!", said The Mayor, realizing he had just
addressed one of the many non-voters in Crewdley. He would work on him to
convince him that his job was dependent upon his patronage, which of course,
given the political situation, it certainly was.

He returned to the Civic Rolls Royce, got in and leaned over to the dividing
partition.

"Drive through the Forest for about ten miles, then come back and we'll
have a drink in "The Star and Garter" he said.

"Yes Sir, it's been quite a while since you were there Mr Mayor," replied
Robespierre, pulling away from the Fire Station.

"Mmmm, the things I do for Crewdley in the line of duty Robespierre, is something of which even the Great Crewdley Public is not aware."

The interior of 'The Star and Garter' was virtually the same as it had been on the last occasion that The Mayor had visited it some ten years before. After all, a man of his stature could not be seen mixing with the Proletariat at their own watering hole, at least for as long as he was returned to office with the biggest majority in Crewdley. If that situation were to change at all, for instance if Natasha Hardie ever looked like conducting a serious campaign against him, then perhaps he would rub shoulders with McGurk's clients for the duration. But he still had nearly two and a half years of Office to run and so this visit would almost certainly be a one-off. "Hello Robespierre," someone shouted, "you owe me a drink."

"Who's that?", The Mayor asked, "he looks an unsavoury character." "He works part-time at Bettingers," answered Robespierre.

"Buy him a drink and ask him if he's seen The Flack Sisters or any of the others," said The Mayor, "and I'll have a large Scotch!" The unmistakable voice of McGurk himself boomed out loudliy. "It's on the house Mr Mayor. In fact, oi'll be puttin' a plaque on that very seat if yuh sit there. It's bin so long since yuh were in here for a drink."

The Mayor acknowledged McGurk with a half-wave of the hand.

"Here are the drinks," said Robespierre, "they were on the house."

"Yes, I heard, and so did everyone else in the pub," replied The Mayor, "what did Bettinger's man have to say?"

"Nothing, but he's going to keep his eyes and ears open. If he gets any information on The Flacks or Mr Puccini, he'll let me know. He's frightened of Inspector Bramley, if he sees him, he'll run the other way. He says Bramley is out to get anyone connected with what went on at The Wool Shop.."

"And how does he know that?" asked The Mayor.

Robespierre hesitated, then reluctantly admitted, "I don't know Your Honour."

"Bring him over to me. I want a few words with him." "Yes Sir," said Robespierre,"'straight away Sir." He returned with the man who seemed to have adopted the same, fearful attitude to The Mayor as he had to Bramley.

"You told Robespierre that Inspector Bramley was going to get everybody who had anything to do with The Wool Shop. Where is he?" "I can't say," said the man.

"You will say," The Mayor insisted, "or else I will personally turn you over to Bramley when I find him and tell him you were the one who told me where he was. Now, are you going to tell me or not?" "He's in room 13 at The Forest Hotel. I went by mistake. I was supposed to repair the T.V in room 3. For God's Sake, please don't tell him it was me who told you. He said he'd hang me up by my thumbs for a week", the man said in obvious distress, "I' m learning to play the piano, please don't tell him."

He hurried away as quickly as he could, leaving his drink and sandwich untouched on the bar.

"Nice to know community policing is alive and well in Crewdley," said The Mayor.

After several more drinks on The Mayor's part and an obligatory tonic water for Robespierre which kept him inside the drink-drive limit, they left the proletarian facilities of 'The Star and Garter' for the refined furnishings of 'The Forest Hotel'.

The Mayor instructed Robespierre to wait in the Foyer, "Only approach room 13 if you hear a God almighty row erupt," he said, "but I think Bramley will behave himself." The sound of light music wafted from behind the door of room 13 as The Mayor approached. He knocked and waited. A hail of bullets did not greet this retort and he wasn't told to lie down on the floor and suck dirt from the shag pile. "He hasn't completely freaked out then," The Mayor said quietly, knocking the door again. "Come on in Mavis," shouted Bramley, "I'm ready for you now!"

"Old habits die hard 'eh Bramley?" said The Mayor.

Bramley jumped off the bed, utterly startled at the sight of his adverary. "You! Who told you I was here?", he demanded.

"No one, I merely followed the sorry trail of ravaged waitresses, and here I am," The Mayor answered.

"You're wasting your time! You'll all be sent down," Bramley replied defiantly, "my officers saw what went on. You're all guilty." The Mayor adopted an extremely relaxed and confident posture, a quite deliberate tactic which he knew would upset the Crewdley Cop.

"I've got a letter here Bramley....... Do you want me to read it?"

He waved the letter under Bramley's nose and smiled.

"Sod off! I don't care if you've got a sick-note from Doctor Scargreaves. It won't make any difference. I'm pursuing this case to the bitter end," answered Bramley.

"That's fine by me. I'll read it to you anyway. It was written and signed by The Director of Public Prosecutions; Let it be known, that having considered the evidence, or more properly the complete lack of evidence regarding the Prosecution of Harold Presbyterian, The Crown finds there is no case to answer and therefore all charges against him in relation to his arrest at the Crewdley Wool Shop, be dropped. Furthermore, he shall be awarded the sum of £1,000 for his wrongful arrest and subsequent loss of liberty, plus costs of £350. It is recommended that the Arresting Officer, one Horace Bramley,

Inspector of Crewdley Police Division, be given a mandatory caution regarding his conduct both during and after the arrest" signed Esmond Tavistock-Nugent, Director of Public Prosecutions, letter ends.

The Mayor smiled again, "I told you to keep a low profile until you retired. It isn't surprizing that The Director of Public Prosecutions sees things extremely clearly when the explanation comes from a sweet, young woman in London who was accomodating almost to the point of embarrassment. It's also not surprising that such a young and beautiful woman could have been obtained at such short notice."

Bramley looked dejected but didn't speak. He seemed bewildered and disorientated by what he had heard, the impact of both the letter and The Mayor's arrival in his room, appeared to strike home for the first time, and culminated in a debilitating and powerful shock to his system. "I'll get all the rest and I'll get you next time you swine!" Even this pathetic little outburst was far below Bramley's normal wrath and seemed sadly devoid of genuine menace and far short of real commitment for revenge.

"If I see Mavis on my way down, I'll tell her you've got a headache," The Mayor baited him as he left the room, "and for goodness sake Bramley, get a shave. You look an absolute disgrace!" "You weren't very long Your Worship," said Robespierre, as The Mayor got into the car.

"It's getting dark," he answered, "I think we'll go to The Town Hall and have a few drinks and an early supper, then this evening, we'll go to the Bonrire and watch the fireworks display." "Yes Sir, that sounds marvellous," Robespierre replied, "I'll prepare a special hip-flask for you to keep out the cold. Napolean Brandy guaranteed to keep your spirits up Sir."

"Thank you Robespierre, you'd better prepare two. I shall be taking Mrs Pippa Monroe for a drive through Crewdley Forest afterwards. In fact, have one yourself and bring the large travelling blanket. And make sure you have the Elgar tapes in the cassette. I'm in a good mood ......this is the winning team, Robespierre, the winning team!"

They attended the Bonfire, staying for about an hour before The Mayor indicated it was time to leave and enjoy Fruits of the Forest with Mrs Pippa Monroe. The Rolls pulled up outside 'Caspian House' and the net curtain moved the tantalizing inch which indicated to The Mayor she would shortly be joining him.

"Put the Elgar tape on Robespierre," he called through the partition, "atmosphere is everything at moments like these."

Pippa Monroe stepped seductively into the car to the sound of, "The Dream of Gerontius".

"Pressy darling, they're playing our tune...... how sweet," she purred.

"To the Forest Robespierre!", he called, "Drive on! Drive on!" Though the night was cold and extremely dark, without moon or stars, the two lovers were in a state of bliss as the Rolls cruised effortlessly through Crewdley Forest and 'Gerontius' cascaded over them.

At a little after midnight, the car pulled up discreetly near to 'Caspian House' and they engaged in one final, long kiss until Robespierre turned off the engine. "Good night darling," she purred, "it's been heaven."

"May it always be so," he answered, "Goodnight Pippa ...... sweet dreams."

He watched her go inside 'Caspian House' and saw the bedroom light go on. She blew a kiss before drawing the curtains.

"Now take me home, before I change my mind and follow her," said The Mayor. Robsepierre pulled away along the Quayside at a gentle pace.

"You're a bloody good chauffer Robespierre," he added. "Thank you Sir, I try to please," he answered, welcoming the compliment, if not for it's absolute sincerity (though at that moment this may have been the case) then certainly for it's rarity. Life was sweet for 'The Boy from The Bastille,' and he repeated what he'd heard but a moment ago - "May it always be so," he said quietly, "May it always be so."

The Mayor had left word that Beard should report to The Council Chamber at 10am on Wednesday 6th November and at 9.55am he was extremely nervous. His small office seemed as forbidding as a prison cell for the condemned. There was no mistaking the heavy footsteps of The Mayor followed by the lighter ones of Robespierre, as they came down the old, wooden staircase. The hour of reckoning was at hand. Would he be sacked for his conduct as well as fined at Court? Perhaps a prison sentence was staring him in the face?

The 'Pox Doctors Clerk' had had plenty of time to contemplate the error of his ways as he went into The Council Chamber at 10am precisely. The Mayor had decided intimidation was to be the order of the day, and he was sitting in his normal and elevated position in the Mayoral Chair, several feet above the floor of The Chamber. Robespierre stood impassively at his side.

"Come in Beard!" The Mayor said loudly, "and listen to me carefully." "Yes Sir," he answered, "where shall I sit Your Worship?"

"You'll stand right there," The Mayor answered, pointing directly to the floor below, "for the time being at least, although perhaps later, I might want you to kneel." Robespierre was already enjoying himself at Beard's expence and allowed a grin to spread over his face, almost daring Beard to rebuke him and knowing the wretched man could do no such thing.

"Friday's Court case Beard. How are you going to plead?", asked The Mayor. Beard shifted from one foot to the other, scratched his head and mumbled.

"Speak up man. I can't hear you!" "I don't know Your Worship," replied Beard, "I've never been to Court before. Does one have a choice ?"

"It's not a bloody quiz Beard, you stupid fool. Will you plead Guilty or Not Guilty?" "Guilty," he answered.

"I see," said The Mayor, "so you really want to lose your job and your pension and spend three years in prison do you?" Beard began to break down and spluttered, "No .... no I don't ! But I am guilty. I went to The Wool Shop, intent on debauchery and bad behaviour..... uhu..... uhhuu," he sniffed, "behaviour unbecoming for a Town Clerk."

"Yes, you did, you disgusting little man. Does your wife know?", The Mayor asked accusingly. "No! I told her I was going out for a walk," Beard answered.

"Very interesting. And what reason did you give her for not returning home until Friday morning?"

Robespierre smirked as Beard hesitated and replied, "I told my wife I had lost my memory. She is an extremely trusting person Your Worship."

"The mind boggles Beard," said The Mayor, "however, what you told your wife is your affair. What you will tell the Court on Friday is another." Beard listened attentively as The Mayor glared down at him from the podium.

"You will plead, Not Guilty," The Mayor insisted. "But ... but how can I plead Not Guilty, Your Worship, when I took part in an......"

"Quiet! You took part in an audition for a film. You were asked to go to The Wool Shop by Mr Puccini. Is that understood?" Beard looked lost.

"Is that understood?" "But I can't act Your Worship."

"You'd better learn your lines by Friday Beard, or else you'll be appearing in the prison pantomine."

"Yes Sir, by Friday," Beard repeated without conviction or understanding as to what exactly was going on. He was out of his depth, and paying heavily for a temporary loss of self-control. "What was the film called Your Worship?"

"You were to audition for the part of a Sewerage Inspector in a re-make of 'The Third Man'." "Thank you Sir," he answered, with a totally blank expression, "Was it anything at all to do with cricket?"

"No you idiot! It was to do with Austria in the late 1940's, or it may have been Switzerland certainly Harry Lime mentioned bloody cuckoo clocks. Part of it is filmed in the sewers, and that's where you come in Beard - got it!"

"Yes Sir...... a Sewerage Inspector in 'The Third Man' thank you Your Worship."

Robespierre seemed delighted with the performance of each actor thus far, and hoped for an encore, as Beard's embarrassment and lack of comprehension seemed to be devouring him at The Mayor's feet.

"I was actually charged with indecent behaviour and conduct likely to cause a Breach of the Peace, Your Worship ......oh.... and also of making lewd and improper suggestions to a young female Police Officer."

"That's no problem," The Mayor assured him. "It's the kind of thing that your sort of Sewage Inspector does all the time.

You were told the Police were in the same film, they were all actors, just like you. Now have you got that Beard? Has it finally sunk into your extremely thick head?"

"Yes Sir," he answered dejectedly.

"Good! That's the first part out of the way. Now we can come on to the issue of your job." Beard started to shake and The Mayor helped the process along by delaying his next contribution for about half a minute before he continued.

"How long have you been employed by Crewdley Council?"

"For nearly forty years Your Worship." The agony was too much and he cracked. "I don't want the sack Your Worship..... I couldn't stand the disgrace. I couldn't walk the streets of Crewdley with everyone knowing that I'd been sacked. I'll do anything......... please don't sack me ....don't sack me."

He rushed up to the podium, fell to the floor, and crawled up to The Mayor, "Oh please let me keep my job," he cried, holding The Mayor's foot as if it was a life-line into a raging-river and he was about to go under.

"Beard! Control yourself man! You're pathetic! Get back to work at once and make sure you give the performance of your life at Court on Friday!" "Oh thank you, thank you!", Beard blubbed, and began to crawl away towards the door.

"Get up you idiot!", The Mayor demanded," you look absolutely pathetic!"

Beard stumbled to his feet to face his mentor and began to walk backwards to the door, bowing his head fervently, but all the time, keeping eye contact with The Mayor until he was able to open the door and let himself out.

"I expect you enjoyed that Robespierre?," The Mayor asked. "Oh yes Sir!" he answered, "I certainly did. Very much indeed!" The Mayor smiled, "And so did I Robespierre, so did I!"

Lunch time found The Mayor once again dining at The Forest Hotel, but this time Robespierre was not allowed to sit outside in the Civic Rolls Royce.

His instructions were to track down The Flack Sisters and Fredric Puccini, but The Mayor did not really expect him to find them. He had lit a cigar and had ordered coffee and brandy as he finished off the remainder of his Black

Forest Gateau. He wondered if Bramley was still sweating it out upstairs in Room 13 (with or without Mavis) or if he had returned to the Police Station to brag about his raid on The Wool Shop and the subsequent arrests. Because The Mayor considered Bramley to be almost completely demented and in a state of extreme anxiety, he opted for the Room 13 scenario. This gave him much pleasure as he considered the prospect of Bramley in a permanent state of mental anguish, not really knowing if, after all his efforts, success would be his. With a bit of luck, by Friday and the Crewdley Court case of the Century, Bramley would be completely up the wall. He finished his brandy, paid the bill and put a fresh cigar on a plate. "Take that to Room 13," he asked the waiter, "he'll know who it's from."

With that, Harold Presbyterian, Mayor and Magistrate of Crewdley, left the Restaurant to enjoy a casual stroll through the town , back to The Town Hall. Robsepierre was waiting in the Hallway outside The Mayors Parlour. "Come in and tell me what you have discovered," The Mayor asked him. "I haven't found them yet Your Worship, but I'm working on it," answered Robespierre, "I just need a little more time."

"Nonsense! We shan't see them until Friday morning, if at all," replied The Mayor, "but I'm seeing Blondel with Romeo and Juliet in a few minutes, so go and set up a Guillotine in the Council Chamber, there's a good fellow." Robespierre looked concerned. "It was a joke," said The Mayor, "but you can prepare the recording equipment. I think a few confessions, captured forever on tape, might be good for their souls and I shall certainly enjoy playing them when I'm bored."

"It's awfully nice of you to see us Harold," said Councillor Barry Blondel, "but isn't it a bit off having Robespierre in here?

After all, it's extremely likely one or two relevations of a rather personal nature might come to the fore."

"If you're concerned about being embarrassed in front of Robespierre, you should have thought about that possibility before you indulged yourself at The Wool Shop," The Mayor replied fiercely. "Oh no! I'm not embarrassed old boy. You know me too well for that Harold," he added, "it's my two colleagues!" A look from The Mayor at Councillors Morton Muggeridge and Mrs Louise Evans-Jenkins, was suffient to confirm Blondel's concern. They were embarrassed about even being summoned together by The Mayor and guilt was written all over them for merely having to acknowledge their 'special relationship,' irrespective of what may have happened at The Wool Shop.

"Be that as it, may, we're one big happy family, aren't we? Robespierre stays exactly where he is," confirmed The Mayor. He gave a slight inclination of his head towards his man, who returned a wink before carefully and without notice, switching on the cassette-recording equipment. "What are we going to do Mr Mayor?", asked Mrs Louise Evans-Jenkins, "It's all that swine Bramley's fault," she cursed, "I hate him, he's an absolute brute."

The hostility towards Bramley was lost on Blondel, "Now then Louise, he was only doing his job. You can't really blame him for that" he suggested. "It's all right for you! You're not married!" Councillor Muggeridge said rather indignantly.

"Enough!" said The Mayor, "it's all your own fault. What concerns me now, is that the good name of Crewedley is not spoilt. I therefore instruct you all, for the good of the town, to plead Not Guilty on Friday. "Oh God, if only we could Mr Mayor," Councillor Mrs Louise Evans-Jenkins regretted, "but I'm afraid we were caught making love in a hammock."

Robespierre immediately looked down to the recording machine to see if it was still working properly. It was. "Never mind about that," insisted The Mayor, "it was all in the script!"

"You've lost me Mr Mayor!" Muggeridge admitted.

"You were all three taking part in an audition for Mr Puccini's film!" "Oh I say, how interesting! That's rather clever actually," Blondel condescended, "what a cracking little idea! Oh yes! I do rather like that Harold, well done!"

"I'm so pleased you approve Blondel - how about you two?", The Mayor asked, looking to Councillors Muggeridge and Mrs Evans-Jenkins. The hammock-swinger turned to his partner and stared deeply into her eyes, "We'll have to go through with it Louise, you do see that, don't you?" "Of course darling," she answered kissing him quickly, "If it keeps us together. I just couldn't stand losing you Morton ..... the thought of you rotting away in some prison for years, knowing that my husband would certainly kill you when you came out ...." "My God!" he said with real emotion, "you really care, don't you Louise?" They began to kiss and embrace as if no one else were present. Robespierre watched the recording-machine operating and regretted not having the whole scene filmed, as he considered it to be an extremely emotional, even tearful little scene, which he would have enjoyed watching on many future occasions.

"That's quite enough of that!" The Mayor chastized them, "just make absolutely certain that you get the story right in Court." "It's all rather exciting isn't it?" she said, breaking away from her lover, "I know ! We could have been auditioning for Anthony and Cleopatra?"

"Mmmm, 'Carry on Bonking', might be nearer the mark, but never mind, I'll leave the details to you," said The Mayor, "the whole point is to insist you were at The Wool Shop at Puccini's request and everything was perfectly legitimate. If everyone sticks to that, Bramley's case falls and you can all sue him for wrongful arrest. Any questions..... no? Good! Then in that case, this interview is at an end."

"O.K old boy," said Councillor Blondel, "it's nice to know that the legal system is on our side, eh? Good Afternoon!"

"Thank you Mr Mayor," added Councillor Muggeridge, "we're extremely grateful."

"Yes, byeee," said Louise Evans-Jenkins, with a wink and a wave, "awfully good of you Mr Mayor, thanks a lot."

The Mayor waited for them to leave The Council Chamber and looked over to the recording-machine, "Switch it off Robespierre and put the tape on my table in The Parlour. I fancy an early tea .....something light..... I'll have a pancake and a mug of drinking chocolate."

"Yes Sir, Your Worship," replied Robespierre with a smile, "and will you be calling at 'Caspian House' this evening?"

The Mayor walked on into The Foyer and stopped at the foot of the old wooden staircase, before turning to his aide de Camp and replying, "How very perceptive of you Robespierre. I'm quite surprised you haven't got your Doctorate in Psychology. Or was it a wild guess?"

The Mayor did indeed visit Mrs Pippa Monroe at 'Caspian House' later that evening, returning to the Civic Rolls Royce and his ever patient chauffer, in the early hours of Thursday morning.

"Take me to The Town Hall," he said quietly, getting into the car, "and don't wake me up too early in the morning. Even The Greatest Mayor in the history of Crewdley has to have his rest. I'm bloody knackered!" Robespierre let The Mayor sleep until just before nine am, when he served breakfast in The Parlour. "Good morning Mr Mayor. It's raining hard and it's cold outside," he said.

"Any news of Puccini or The Flack Sisters?", The Mayor asked, "they haven't appeared on Breakfast T.V or anything like that?" "No Sir, Your Worship."

"Good! And we haven't been contacted by the Tabloid Press?" "No Sir! I would have informed you right away Mr Mayor," said Robespierre, placing his toast firmly into the rack, " and here's your copy of 'The Weekly Weaver.'

The Mayor took the paper and put it on the table as he ate his breakfast. Robespierre was pouring coffee when a loud, "Aargh!" from The Mayor made him spill it on the table cloth.

"That bastard McSnadden! Look what he's done!" he roared, showing the headline to his man. "Oh dear," said Robespierre, looking at the paper properly for the first time, and beginning to read aloud,

" ' VICE DEN COP BUSTS EVIL NEST OF VIPERS IN CREWDLEY RAID'. The sensational story as given to The Editor of 'The Weekly Weaver', Mr

Archibald McSnadden. " "Shall I go on Mr Mayor?" Robespierre continued, "'In another 'Weekly Weaver' exclusive, Inspector Horace Bramley told me exactly how he and 20 officers from neighouring Police Divisions had raided The Crewdley Wool Shop and arrested many of Crewdley's leading citizens from the political, commercial, legal and religious professions, which included even a titled Lady'".

"Swine!" shouted The Mayor. Robespierre read on, "'Bramley claims, 'a den of vipers' exists within the highest levels of Crewdley society, and the raid uncovered lurid scenes of sexual depravity unmatched in Amsterdam, Soho or even Bangkok. 'This is just the tip of the ice-burg, said the tough cop when he gave me an exclusive interview at a secret Hotel hide-away.' "There's more to come. I'm determined to clean up Crewdley if it's the last thing I do. I've had threats made against me. There's a web of fear in Crewdley, but the Ring-Leaders' will be dealt with by the Court on Friday. Inspector Horace Bramley is 54......... continued on page two........... "

"Never mind page two," said The Mayor, "I think I've got the jist of it. It's my own fault that it's even in the wretched paper! I should have spoken to the owner, but I thought it was sufficient to have threatened McSnadden. He obviously spoke to Jelleyman himself and got the go-ahead to print the story. You can't trust anybody nowadays Robespierre." "What will you do now Mr Mayor?", Robespierre asked anxiously.

"I'm going to finish my breakfast, then we'll look for Puccini and The Flack Sisters. I'm sure they're somewhere in Crewdley and I need to have a very serious talk with them, if Bramley hasn't got them already!"

After breakfast, they left The Town Hall in the Rolls. It was very noticable that strangers were in town. On every pavement, on every corner, journalists were springing up like mushrooms. Even the Car Park of 'The Forest Hotel' was filled by cars with strange number plates.

"This is hopeless," said The Mayor through the partition, "they're like a swarm of insects. It wouldn't be safe to even get out of the car. Drive through the Forest, then take the River road for half an hour. I need time to think."

The Forest was in it's Autumn Glory, many of the oaks, horsechestnut, beech and birch trees still wore their golden mantles, though the light wind and rain were even then carrying them to the floor of the Forest in sweeps of turbulent movement.

"The Elgar tape Robespierre," he requested, "but not too loud." The occasional cottage came and went, as did a small country pub or two, even a red deer was sighted by Robespierre who saw it standing in the hedgerow of a field beneath an ancient oak tree. The Mayor was in deep thought, but quite relaxed, in spite of Bramley's relevations in 'The Weekly Weaver' and the Papparatzi plaguing Crewdley. Give or take a day or two after the Court Case, they would disappear back to London, no doubt intent on scooping the next would-be sensational story, irrespective of the issue or it's worthiness. In the meantime, he would have avoid them.

"Drive on Robespierre," he called, "we're going to spend the day deep in the country side, out of harms way and tonight too, so pull in at the next decent pub and ask if they could put us up. Make sure you park the car off the road, I don't want to be disturbed."

Some three miles further on, Robespierre pulled into the car park of a small country pub and parked the Rolls around the back. He went inside to make his enquires and quickly returned. "Yes Sir, they can accomodate us and it's a nice quiet little pub," he said.

Indeed,that proved to be the case as The Mayor checked in at the Reception Desk and then went to look at his room. Robespierre always ensured that at least a small travelling bag was included in the boot of the Rolls for such an emergency, as well as seasonal hampers, hip-flasks, car blankets and very often, swimwear, a shooting-stick, binoculars and of course, permantly implanted beneath a flat-bottomed petrol can, were ten golden half sovereigns.

He laid out his pyjamas on the bed and looked at a quite nice little original water colour landscape hanging near to the window. An unmistakable tapping at the door indicated Robespierre's presence.

"Come in," said The Mayor, "did you book a table for lunch?" "Yes Sir, it seems we shall be dining alone. No one else is resident at the moment," he answered.

"Excellent, give me five minutes Robespierre and I'll see you in the Bar." The Mayor took off his overcoat and put it into the wardrobe with one or two items which Robespierre had brought up from the car. He found Robespierre sitting on a stool in the Bar drinking a pint of beer and eating from the dish of nuts. The barman served him a double whisky and returned to his private quarters.

"Here's to success at Court tomorrow Robespierre," he said, "some of them are in for a big shock when they see who the presiding Magistrate is going to be." Robespierre smiled and took a long drink, "Yes Sir, especially Inspector Bramley. But what about The Sisters Flack and Mr Puccini?" The Mayor looked stern, "Yes, I need to speak with Dorothy and Myrtle. It doesn't matter about Puccini, it's his word against everyone else." He took out a large cigar and lit it as Robespierre ate more nuts from the dish on the bar.

"Where on earth would two half-demented old women hide around here? They must be lying low somewhere." "Maybe they're in Sicily, Your Worship, or down town Chicago?"

"Maybe Robespierre, but somehow I don't think so - where the hell has that barman got to, I want to order lunch?"

As if by magic, he appeared from behind a partition.

"Oh, there you are. Two steaks, both well done, potatoes, peas, carrots, and apple pie to follow," he said impatiently, "You don't seem to have a Menu?" "No Sir," replied the man, "Chef's off sick, but we'll see what we can do eh?"

"Marvellous,"said The Mayor, "shall we say for 12.30 or would you like Robespierre to cook it?" The man scowled and shuffled off to the kitchen area as if the joy of living had temporarily, at best, deserted him.

Lunch was extremely basic and unappetising, yet nevertheless complimented by two rather good bottles of claret. The Mayor rested in his room during the afternoon and Robespierre watched T.V in the lounge. At 5pm, they went for a walk at the edge of the woodland which surrounded the Hotel.

By 8pm, The Mayor was just about ready for dinner, although his expectation for something rather less than Haute Cuisine left him unenthusiastic about even this. He was not disappointed, the Hotel's idea and interpretation of Lancashire Hot Pot, was sadly lacking in all respects.

After two hours of playing cards in the Lounge, The Mayor was ready for bed. He settled the bill, rather than take the chance of the barman, who seemed to be the sole representative of the Hotel's staff, not being available the next morning.

"Wake me at 7am," he said to Robespierre as they ascended the stairs, "and if that idiot isn't around, make the tea yourself and bring it in." "Certainly Mr Mayor, goodnight," answered Robespierre as he went to his room, somewhat the worse for having had too much to drink, yet taking particular note of his employer's instructions, "Seven am Mr Mayor, goodnight Sir."

The impact of Friday 8th November 1991 failed to register with Robespierre at 6.30 am, but after a frenzied attack on his alarm clock, he got out of bed, washed, dressed and went down to the kitchen (which was in total darkness) and made the tea. The Mayor was dressed and waiting by the time Robespierre knocked his door.

"Enter!" he called, "I suppose that nincompoop is nowhere to be seen?" "Good morning - no Sir, he isn't," replied Robespierre, "I would suggest I prepare toast and a cereal."

"Huh! Bacon and eggs you bugger, I'm starving! I'll be down in fifteen minutes," The Mayor admonished him.

Robespierre returned to the kitchen and did as he was told. The barman finally poked his head around the door, but had no desire to intervene. By just after seven thirty, they were on their way from the Hotel to Crewdley.

"Put the Elgar tape on," called The Mayor, "and turn the volume up loud. I want to get completely in the mood for the day's event." The Rolls glided on through the countryside and The Mayor became engrossed in 'Gerontius'. He spotted a sign post which indicated the distance to Crewdley was now but seven miles.

"Enough!" he shouted, "I need time to think." Elgar was cut off in his prime and The Mayor contemplated the coming drama of the Court Room. Would Puccini show up? Would The Flack Sisters pretend to be dear, sweet little old ladies? Would The Vicar plead insanity? Would Elsie Finney offer fish and chips all round and would Lord Crewdley run a dagger through the heart of Smokey Flint the Fire Chief? He didn't know, but was soon to find out.

The spire of St Crueds Church peeped over the horizon before the familiar peripheral buildings of Crewdley drew nearer. The Forest Hotel had a dozen cars on the Forecourt and the Police Station was protected by two Officers who stood either side of the main entrance.

They drove on past 'The Star and Garter,' Bettingers and Finneys Fish Shop before Robespierre turned sharply into Church Street to ease his way around the Church on the 'home run' towards The Town Hall. Several Papparatzi were already littering the area and made a beeline for the Rolls.

"Open the gates Robespierre," said The Mayor," and then you can pour boiling oil over them from The Parlour window." Robespierre stopped the car and opened the Town Hall gates as half a dozen Reporters tried to get a comment from The Mayor who sat impassively throughout, until Robespierre returned and drove into The Foyer.

They proceeded rather quickly upstairs to The Parlour.

"Make the tea," said The Great Man, picking up the telephone and dialling a number he hardly ever had occasion to use.

"Beard! Why aren't you at your desk?" "It's about an hour early Your Worship," Beard replied, "and it's the Court Case today."

"I know that, get round here straight away and make absolutely certain you've learnt your lines or else," The Mayor told him, "you can forget your Pension and your job!" He opened his post, filing half of it into the waste bin. The one that mattered spelled out arrangements for The Court Session. It was stunning information! The Mayor would not be the only Magistrate sitting on the Case of the Century.

He would be joined by two others, a Mr Partridge and a Mrs Denning. For once in his life, Harold Presbyterian had been naive. Of course The Bench would have to consist of three Magistrates - how could he possibly have over-looked such an elemental point? He cursed himself for not finding out earlier, but still had over an hour to come up with something.

He rang the Lord Chancellor's Office, but it was too early for them to reply. "Damn!", he cursed,"Robespierre! Where's the tea?"

At a quarter to ten, The Mayor was joined in his Parlour by Mr Partridge and Mrs Denning. "What a thoroughly disgusting case" she said contemptuously, " The worst I've come across in forty years on the bench." The Mayor had a problem.

"Would you like a drink?" he asked. "Never touch the filthy stuff," she barked," The Devil's Brew, awful habit." "Yes please!" said Partridge, "a small whisky would be nice."

His words were music to The Mayor's ears, but it was soon drowned out by Mrs Denning's continued and sharp barrage. "You're new aren't you?" she said, "I'm the Chairman of the Bench for this Division, expect you know the rules? Majority decisions acceptable unanimous preferred." The Mayor's mind was racing ahead. Nothing on earth would alter this woman's mind...... he would have to bribe Partridge.

From the look of him, he was near retirement anyway..... a nice lump sum, in cash, surely wouldn't go amiss? The Mayor would bide his time, and if necessary, ensure he had private opportunity to strike an agreement. But.... but.....experience had taught Harold Presbyterian never to act in haste ...most things were possible, but some more likely than others. Bramley might have lost all of the papers relating to the Case, but that was most unlikely.

Mrs Denning could suffer a fatal heart attack, (images of Octavia Bland percolated his thoughts). However, he would have to play his cards exactly how they were dealt ,but he certainly would risk all to fix the deck.

"Just a quick run through of the procedure then," announced Mrs Denning, "We shall hear all of the cases ...there are twenty. We shall retire for lunch at one o' clock and reconvene if necessary, then consider the verdicts. Maximum is six months in prison or three thousand pound fine any questions .... No? ... Good ....the Prosecuting Council is Mr George Jeffreys, a very good man with all the right family connections...... he won't stand any nonsense and neither will I. If any of those vile members of The Press or the Public utters so much as a word, out they jolly well go. Everybody clear? Lead on Mr Presbyterian!"

They trooped out of The Parlour, down the old wooden staircase and entered The Counil Chamber, which now was co-opted as The Court.

The Mayor certainly resented the authority which Mrs Denning purveyed and from the look on his face, this view was shared by Mr Partridge.

"She's a right old battle-axe," he whispered to The Mayor, "I'm glad it's not me who's got to go in front of her today."

This was a sentiment certainly echoed by The Mayor himself, and just for a moment, an ice-cold hand touched the back of his neck sending a shudder through his entire body.

Two policemen were standing near to The Mayor's table and two others attempted to check the identity of the Magisterial Party until Mrs Denning took command, "You know very well who I am Constable,"she said, "just get on with your work."

A dapper young man dressed in a three piece suit strutted over to greet them,

"Morning Chairman," he said to Mrs Denning. " Morning Mr Partridge... ah...you must be the new Magistrate?"he asked rather un-enthusiastically.

"And Mayor of this Town," replied the new boy, "and you, I take it, are Mr George Jeffreys?"

"Indeed," he answered sharply, "and what a case you have for us today Mr Presbyterian! I must say, I am amazed at the absolute debauchery that exists in a town such as this."

"Now then Jeffreys, innocent until proven otherwise," replied The Mayor, "we mustn't pre-judge the case, must we?" "Huh!" grunted the hostile Mrs Denning, "that's a matter of opinion."

The apprehensive figure of Anton Robespierre walked hesitantly into The Chamber. "Who's that!" demanded Mrs Denning.

"The Usher!" answered The Mayor. "Huh! It's not usual", she added, pulling a face as sour as curdled yogurt.

"Well it's going to be in this Court," The Mayor announced, staring daggers and determined now to stamp his own authority into the legal quartet, "Come over here Robespierre," he insisted, "stand by for further instructions." The Clerk to the Court entered quietly, bowing his head several times before sitting down and clasping his hands together in a manner more befitting for a Church than a Court. Here was a man who knew his place. "Twenty on the list then, Mrs Denning?", Jeffreys delighted in saying, "it's almost as bad as The Poll Tax." Even this laconic humour was lost on the Chairman of The Bench. "Let's get on with it," she said with relish as the clock moved inexorably towards ten.

The magistrates took their places on The Bench and The Clerk stood up, "The Court is in Session," he called," bring in the first defendant." All eyes were on the Court Entrance, as the doors opened and several people came in. The Public Gallery also began to fill, and members of The Press took their places. "Where's the Defence Lawyer?" asked Mrs Denning, "or haven't they got a defence?" Jeffreys smiled supercilliously, "They're going to try to defend themselves, "it should prove most interesting, even entertaining Madam Chairman," he gloated, as the Kissogram Toy Boy and the older woman with flaming red hair seemed to be at the head of the scrummage of accused, who were by now surging into Court. The Mayor did a quick head count. There were seventeen, which included Mrs Finney, Blondel, Lady Crewdley and the rest, but The Flack Sisters and Puccini were not there. The Accused were led into some of the seating usually reserved for Members of Crewdley Council. "The Court will rise!" said The Clerk, "Mrs Denning presiding, Prosecuting Counsel, Mr George Jeffreys."

Jeffreys responded to the mention of his name by walking across the floor and staring at The Accused, then pacing backwards and forwards in front of The Bench. Superintendent Horace Bramley appeared suddenly and un-announced to take his seat at the front. The Mayor was filled with trepidation as his own Baptism by Fire began. Councillor Blondel winked at them as if to suggest all was well, but it made him even less secure. Mrs Elsie Finney was obviously already enjoying the sense of occasion and The Kissogram Toy Boy seemed spaced-out. "Your Worships!," Jeffreys snapped, "with your permission, I shall set out the Prosecutions case against The Accused. In the early hours of Friday 1st November 1991, Superintendent Horace Bramley of Crewdley Police, raided local premises known as The Crewdley Wool Shop. During the raid, twenty people were arrested."

The whole Court stopped to count The Accused and collectively concluded that the number in The Dock was seventeen. "I think we have all had good opportunity to count heads," said Mrs Denning, "And I have counted seventeen. We seem to be three short, Mr Jeffreys - where are they?" "I have no idea Madam Chairman," he answered abruptly, as if it mattered not a jot. "That's extremely careless of The Prosecution," said Mrs Denning," extremely careless indeed. Please proceed Mr Jeffreys." Prosecuting Counsel looked, just for a brief moment, to have been made extremely uncomfortable by The Chairman's comment, but he was too professional to indicate as much, and he quickly moved on. "It is The Crown's contention that these seventeen people brought shame upon the good name of Crewdley. As Inspector Horace Bramley will testify, the scenes being played out in The Wool Shop were absolutely disgraceful."

"Here here!", said someone from the Public Gallery " Silence!," shouted Mrs Denning. "Sorry, " came the reply, from a voice which sounded very much like the dulcet tones of Lord Crewdley. Mr Jeffreys continued, "At precisely 1.51am, Inspector Bramley led his team of Police into The Wool Shop, under the auspices of a Search Warrant signed by your good self Madam Chairman."

"Quite so!" she concurred, with a face as severe as a Siberian Winter, looking for all the world as if she was suffering extreme discomfort, and just for good measure, to underline her willingness, she added, "Absolutely quite so!" The Mayor looked at Bramley who grinned back at him like an idiot. Jeffreys began to play to the Public Gallery, "Needless to say," he said thoughtfully, "that during the course of their normal duties, the Officers of our good and loyal Police Force have much to contend with that is both difficult, awkward and even dangerous. However, even for these brave young Officers, the raid on Crewdley Wool Shop proved to be an extremely unpleasant and unsavoury ordeal." The Mayor stared back to Bramley, who grinned even wider, in the mode of Oliver Hardy - unconcerned, happy, care-free. He knew of the whereabouts of the three missing defendents all right, but where were they?

Jeffreys paced across the floor of The Court, tugging at his jacket collar and twitching nervously before continuing with his address. "To suggest they were surprised by what they discovered, would be an understatement." He grimmaced and stared at those in The Dock. "The Police discovered and subsequently arrested, many of the most eminent citizens of Crewdley." A quick glance at The Public Gallery indicated much whispering and The Press Corps were busily scratching at their note pads. "It would seem perhaps fair to suggest, that the scene bore more resemblance to an orgy in Nero's Rome, than that which is to be expected in a small English Town!"

This statement seemed to have the desired effect, and was greeted by gasps, groans, ohh's and aahh's from the assembly. "Silence!", Mrs Denning demanded again, "carry on Mr Jeffreys!"

"Thank you Madam Chairman. People were in various stages of undress, some even completly naked!" he said rather loudly. "Ooohhhh!!!" came the response. "Be quiet!", came the reponse to that.

Mr Jeffreys was stirring them up and The Mayor recognized, though reluctantly, here was a fellow-professional at work.

"In short, the Police discovered a Den of Sin.... a Place of Ill Repute and Debauchery, a Disorderly House ....a veritable Brothel, a Place of Prostitution in which an Orgy was in progress .."

"Oooohh!!!!"

"Silence! Silence!", shouted Mrs Denning, "I shall have silence in my Court!"

"There was fornication!", shouted Jeffreys, "there was sin, there was improper and lewd behaviour, corruption of morality and riotous assembly!" "Ooohhh!!" "For the last time be quiet!", Mrs Denning demanded, obviously not wishing to miss any of the Prosecution's detailed description of the alledgedly-sordid case.

"Bring forward Kevin Farquar and Marian Carter!", said Jeffreys with a sweep of his hand to a Police Officer.

The Accused stepped quickly into The Dock and took the Oath. Neither seemed particularly concerned, in fact the young Mr Farquar seemed pleased to be there.

"I also call Superintendent Horace Bramley of Crewdley Police Force," added Jeffreys with some flair. He came forward and swore the Oath, then stood to attention as Jeffreys turned again to The Accused.

"You are Kevin Farquar," he asked, looking now to The Public Gallery, as he waited for an answer. "Yes, " Farquar finally replied.

"And how do you plead?" "Not Guilty," he answered.

"And you are Marian Carter," he said, turning quickly on his heels to face her. "Yes," she answered, "that's right."

"And how do you plead?" "Not Guilty," she said quietly.

"And what is your occupation Mr Farquar?"

"I work for an Entertainment Agency," Farquar replied.

"Indeed, and what exactly is your job title?"

"I'm a Kissogram Toy Boy," he announced to some laughter around The Court. Mrs Denning was in need of explanation and clarification.,

"You are a what?" she asked, leaning forward, so as not to miss his reply.

"A Kissogram Toy Boy........I'm invited to parties............"

"What sort of parties?", Mrs Denning enquired, by-passing the formality of allowing Jeffreys to ask it for himself.

"All sorts of parties, birthday mostly, but also office parties, surprise parties I even do retirement parties," he replied looking straight at The Elderly Chairman of the Magistrates.

The point was well taken. "Please get on with it Mr Jeffreys," she said, "we haven't got all day."

"And what exactly do you have to do at these parties?", Jeffreys enquired.

"Well, I ring the bell, someone lets me in and takes me to the person they're having the party for........."

There was an expectant hush, as Farquar casually looked at his watch and then at Ms Carter. "Well, then I kiss them. There's nothing wrong with it," he said defiantly, "I only kiss the women!"

There were a few chortles of laughter at this, but they were soon quelled by the evil eye of the Chairman. "And you Ms Carter," said Jeffreys, "what exactly were you doing at The Wool Shop?"

"I went to buy some wool," she said.

"At two in the morning!"

"No, I went at five o' clock and Mrs Flack invited me to stay. They were crochet knitting a shawl and I'm very interested in crochet-knitting. Anyway, a lot of people arrived later and I asked if it was O.K to have a shower, so I did. I'd just got out when the Police arrived. Mind you, I did have some of the old ladies' Elderberry wine, so it's all a bit hazy," she said with a smile. Jeffreys looked perplexed, "Do you really expect the Court to believe that nonsense!"

She bent down to retrieve something from a bag. "Here you are - look!" she said, holding up a beautiful crochet-knitted shawl, "Isn't it nice?" Jeffreys was wrong-footed at this rather natural performance by Ms Carter and reacted by creating a distraction of his own. "Superintendent Bramley!" Will you step forward into the Witness Box please?"

Bramley walked to the appointed area and looked grim. "Superintendent Bramley.......how long have you served in the Police Force?"

"Over twenty-five years Sir," he answered. "And for how many of those years have you been an superintendent in Crewdley?"

"For ten years Sir." "Thank you .... I would like you to tell The Court exactly what happened during the early hours of Friday 1st November 1991?"

"Yes Sir," said The Great Oink, "at 1.51am precisely, I led my team of Police Officers into The Crewdley Wool Shop. There were 14 male Officers and 6 female Sir, plus 9 vans with drivers outside."

"Indeed! Quite a force to be reckoned with for a nice, quiet little town like Crewdley eh?"

"Yes Sir." "Superintendent Bramley, please tell The Court, exactly why you felt it was necessary to actually go into The Wool Shop in the first place?"

"Well, I had put The Wool Shop under surveillance for quite some time before then. I had reason to believe the Proprietors were keeping a disorderly house. In fact, I'd nicked them, sorry..... I'd warned them recently about selling liquor to minors from Unlicensed Premises."

"Indeed," said Jeffreys, "please go on."

"I'd noticed a lot of coming and going of people into The Wool Shop, people who didn't buy wool. My suspicions were roused and so, on Thursday 31st October, I got a Search Warrant signed by Mrs Denning."

"Excellent. Would you now please explain what you found when you went inside The Wool Shop."

"Right!" said Bramley, warming to his task, "first of all, I had a young Constable shoulder-charge the door, then we proceeded into the shop and up the stairs." He hesitated.

"The next bit is not very nice," he said with false modesty, looking to The Public Gallery. "But The Court has to know," prompted Jeffreys.

"Sorry Sir.......Well...... as I said, it wasn't very nice I've never seen so many people in such a confined space...... they were having an orgy Sir."

"Ooohh!!" the audience responded.

"An orgy? You're quite sure it wasn't a party Superintendent?"

"Oh no Sir! Some of them were naked, including Ms Carter, a lot of them were either engaged in sexual activities or were trying to become engaged in sexual activities or had just finished sexual activities. It was disgusting Sir, at one stage, I had to cover the eyes of one of my young female Constables.

We began to arrest people Sir, as quickly as we could. It was very chaotic, the music was very loud and everybody was running about shouting. Some were naked, others were getting dressed and some seemed drunk and disorderly. One or two particularly were very rowdy and resented being placed under arrest." He looked directly at The Mayor then quickly to Jeffreys. "And are the accused in The Court?" Jeffreys asked.

"Oh yes Sir," replied Bramley, "they're certainly present in The Court." "Thank you," said Jeffreys, "now will you please tell The Court the circumstances under which you and your Constables arrested Mr Farquar and Ms Carter?"

"She was naked and he was kissing her," said Bramley accusingly. "Right!" Jeffreys shouted, "she was naked and he was kissing her!" "I'd been in the shower!", Ms Carter cried loudly.

"And I thought it was her birthday!", concurred Kevin Farquar.

Jeffreys strutted around like a peacock and smirked, "Please return to your places with the others," he told them. The Kissogram Toy Boy and the woman with the flaming-red hair, left The Dock and returned to their seats with rest of The Accused.

"Would Ms Annette Page please step forward and take the Oath?", asked Jeffreys. All eyes turned to the young woman as she went into The Dock. "Your full name please," said Jeffreys rather severely.

"Annette Margaret Page," she answered. "How do you plead?" asked Jeffreys.

"Not Guilty," she replied.

'And what is your occupation Ms Page?"

Her eyes filled with tears, "I'm unemployed, ... I was the Librarian in Crewdley."

"I presume that your employment ceased after the Police Raid at The Wool Shop?"

"Yes," she replied.

"Ms Page..... please tell The Court exactly why you were at The Wool Shop at that time."

She sniffed and dabbed her eyes with a handkerchief. "I went to the party," she said.

"Oh, you went to the party did you?" Jeffreys asked harshly, "and who exactly invited you to the party?"

"I can't remember," she sobbed, "I've tried, but I can't remember. My life has been ruined..... it was just a party."

Jeffreys now turned to Bramley.

"Superintendent Bramley, can you recall the occasion of Ms Page's arrest?"

"I certainly can Sir," he told him, "she was frolicking with one of the men."

"I was dancing!" she shouted.

"She was engaged in what I would call activities unbefitting a lady."

"I was dancing you fool!", the defendent yelled. "And you deny taking part in an orgy, I suppose?" said the smarmy Prosecuting Council.

"Yes!", she said.

"Then why in that case did you resign from your post?", he asked.

"Because I was so ashamed at being arrested," she cried.

"Yes, well I think that The Court will decide on that. Thank you Ms Page, you may step down."

"Rotten sod," The Mayor said under his breath, reflecting on the fact that Ms Page must by now, have been one of the very few Accused who was not in on the Big Lie for the Defence. He watched her return to her seat and wondered again, what the hell had happened to Puccini and The Flacks. Jeffreys seemed most pleased with his performance thus far, and looked down at the list of names on the list.

"I call Mr Bernard Beard!", he said.

Beard walked cautiously into The Dock and took The Oath. "You are Bernard Beard?", asked Jeffreys.

"Yes," Beard answered. "And you are The Town Clerk to Crewdley Council?"

"Yes Sir."

"And how do you plead?"

"Not Guilty!" Beard replied. It was eyes down for the Hacks in the Press Gallery as they scribbled away furiously, and one or two fingers were pointed at Beard from members of the public. "Huh!" grunted Mrs Denning, "Get on with it!" "Thank you Madam Chairman," Jeffreys said curtly, "now Mr Beard, you were arrested with the others at The Wool Shop, is that correct?

"Yes," Beard answered quietly. "Speak up, I can't hear you!," said Jeffreys.

"Yes!", he shouted back.

"And why exactly was it, that you, the Town Clerk of Crewdley Town Council, a man of previous good behaviour, came to be in The Wool Shop that night?"

Beard looked blank, and Jeffreys continued, "It was because you wished to participate in the Orgy, wasn't it?" Beard retained his blank expression. "You went to indulge yourself in pleasures of the flesh! You were caught in an act of a sexual nature - you were wanton in your depravities and gave vent to the full expression of your carnal and disgusting lust!" The silence now became deafening, as the world waited for an answer, a reponse, a denial,....... an obscenity even, from the little man. But nothing came.

"Mr Beard!" Jeffreys taunted him, "Have you nothing to say? Will you not deny the charges or even admit them?"

Beard stood rooted to the spot, nervously looking at those who looked at him. "Mr Beard!" said Mrs Denning, "you must answer!" The Mayor crossed his fingers and bit his lip. "Get it right you stupid idiot," he whispered.

"I...I....", Beard stammered, before coming to acomplete stop.

"Beard!!!," The Mayor roared, "answer the questions!!!"

"Thank you Mr Presbyterian. Come along Mr Beard, we are all waiting," said Jefferys impatiently.

Beard breathed in deeply, it was now or never.

"I was being auditioned for a part in a film," he declared brazenly, to the delight of those assembled.

"What!" Jeffreys shouted above the noise.

"Quiet!" yelled Mrs Denning, "Silence in Court! Mr Beard! Did I hear you say you were being auditioned for a film?"

"Yes," replied Beard without emotion, "I was asked to turn up for an audition."

"This is preposterous!", declared Jeffreys, "how can you possibly say that? May I remind you that you are under Oath?"

"Yes I know, but it's true. Mr Puccini asked me to try for the part of a Sewerage Inspector in 'The Third Man'...... I agreed to have a go .... but I didn't think I was up to Harry Lime."

"Oh, but I suggest you are most definately good enough for that part," said Jefferys with annoyance, "In fact, I consider your present role to be worthy of an Oscar!!"

"Here! Here!" shouted someone from the Public Gallery.

"Oh no Sir, it's perfectly true!" said Beard, "That's why I went! The Film Crew had been in Crewdley for quite a long time......... Mr Puccini asked me to go. My lines were supposed to be 'Hey! You can't come down here! who are you? This is City Property. Wait ....I've seen you before, you're Harry Lime aren't you?'......."

Beard gave a silly little grin, "That's all actually Sir...... he just said, be at The Wool Shop on Thursday night to audition for a small part in 'The Third Man'"

Beard's performance was embarrassing and so awkward, that it must have been perfectly obvious to all present, that he was either, the world's worst liar or a complete idiot.

"Lying idiot," grumbled The Mayor under his breath, as The Crewdley 'Olivier' stood ready to take a bow. He had, perhaps for the first time during The Case, actually sowed the seeds of doubt. The Mayor looked at Jeffreys and then Mrs Denning. Yes, they were unsure, particularly Jefferys, who no doubt knew very well, that his star prosecution witnesses wouldn't be turning up. Hence, no questions from Jefferys about the Flack Sisters or Puccini. Now something else crossed The Mayor's mind. The gruesome Chairman of the Magistrates was equally quiet as to their whereabouts, she certainly wasn't a shrinking-violet, relunct ant to ask for fear of intimidating the defendants or the Police.

"That's it!" he thought, "they're in it together!"

" Mr Beard," said Jeffreys, "are you 'Guilty' or 'Not Guilty'?"

"Not Guilty!" he insisted.

Jeffreys looked perplexed. "Thank you Mr Beard, you may step down," he said reluctantly. "I call John Doolittle and Sharon Hayes."

The odd couple came forward to The Dock and took The Oath. Doolittle was confident and gave the impression of being someone unconcerned by his situation. He was quite tall, extremely well dressed and seemed old enough to be the father of the thoroughly modern Ms Hayes, who was naturally a little over-awed by the surroundings.

Jeffreys turned first to Ms Hayes. "Please tell The Court your name," he asked.

"Sharon Hayes," she answered.

"And how do you plead to the charges?"

"Not Guilty," she answered firmly, "definately Not Guilty." "Thank you Ms Hayes. You are a waitress at 'The Star and Garter' Public House, here in Crewdley, is that correct?"

"Yes," she said.

"And you were arrested during the Police raid at The Wool Shop?"

"Yes."

He hesitated, having surely by now worked out the game plan of The Accused. "And I suppose you are going to tell us you were there to audition for a part in a film?"

"Yes. I'm a part-time model and Mr Puccini said he wanted some photographs and he would let me say a few lines in rehersal," she replied with a rather convincing innocence.

The Mayor glanced at Robespierre. Sure enough, he was lusting again, but little wonder, he thought, when the object of his lust was so charming and attractive (in a proletarian kind of way). Jefferys hesitated again, mentally squaring up to the challenge of pitting his wits and reputation against a fellow Solicitor. "You are Mr John Doolittle, a Solicitor in this town?"

"Yes that's correct Mr Jefferys," Doolittle answered confidently, warmly even, recognizing only too well, the plight of The Prosecuting Counsel. "How do you plead to the charges brought against you?"Jeffreys asked.

"Not Guilty Sir!", Doolittle affirmed positively. Jeffreys resumed his pacing of The Court. "Mr Doolittle - are you being blackmailed?"

"Oohh!," the Public Gallery groaned.

"Certainly not!" the Accused replied indignantly. "Then why are you so willing to tell a pack of lies to The Court?"

"The charges are untrue," said Doolittle.

"You were caught with this young woman in a position which could only be described as one of a compromising sexual nature. Superintendent Bramley says so in his written evidence. Is that not so Superintendent?"

"Yes Sir," confirmed the Policeman," They were both undressed and on the floor behind a settee."

"We were knocked over by your brutal police!" Doolittle countered." Ms Hayes and I were rehearsing."

"Rehearsing what?" demanded Jeffreys.

"The Importance of Being Ernest!", they replied together, "We were in the middle of a costume-change when I was thrown to the floor," Doolittle insisted. "I almost lost my shawl", Ms Hayes protested vigorously. The Mayor was amazed by their polished performance - "Indeed," he thought, "if Crewdley didn't have an'Amateur Dramatic Society' before The Court Case, it certainly should after it." Again, the absence of Puccini and The Flack Sisters spoke volumes, as Jeffreys searched desperately for inspiration. It did not materialize. "Oscar Wilde certainly did not envisage 'The Importance of Being Ernest,' being played by nearly-nude actors, but thank you both, you may step down. I'm sure The Court will draw its own conclusions about your performance here today."

They took their seats, Jeffreys shuffled his pile of papers and The Mayor looked forward to the next act which promised to be extremely entertaining. "I now call Mr Henry Dash, Mr Roland Jones and Mrs Elsie Finney," Jeffreys announced loudly and with perhaps a degree of exasperation.

Dash led the trio from the safety of the stalls into The Dock. They each in turn swore The Oath and it crossed The Mayor's mind, that Mrs Finney was probably fantasising that it was a Mormon Wedding Ceremony and she was marrying both of them.

Jeffreys changed his method of attack and chose to go for Mrs Finney first, his logic having led him to the conclusion, that she would be the weak-link. "You are Elsie Finney, a fishmonger of Crewdley," he said.

"No I'm not! I'm Elsie Finney, the joint owner of Finneys Fish and Chip Shop, "she corrected him, "so let's get that right before we start!"

Jeffreys eyed her suspiciously. "I beg your pardon," he replied sarcastically.

Quite what the man thought of Mrs Finney was anybody's guess. There she stood, resplendent in purple, with a small pill-box hat, complete with feather and black-net mask which partly covered her face. In spite of this ludicrous apparel, the scarlet red of her lipstick shone out like a baboon's behind. Mutton dressed as lamb was a phrase that came easily to mind.

"You are charged with obscene behaviour, disorderly conduct and making improper suggestions to a Police Constable after being placed under arrest. How do you plead?"

"Not Guilty lovee," she replied.

It was going to be difficult for Prosecuting Counsel, but he pressed on.

"Mrs Finney, you were seen by Superintendent Horace Bramley, fondling Mr Jones, kissing Mr Dash and displaying your breasts to a Constable in the van on the way to the Police Station."

"I don't remember lovee. I'd had a drop to drink," she said. "Superintendent Bramley, is the statement concerning Mrs Finney correct?"asked Jeffreys.

"Yes Sir, it was a disgusting sight," he confirmed.

"Hey!.... do you mind?", the Fish Wife protested.

"Do you deny taking part in an orgy at The Wool Shop!", Jefferys asked hopefully.

"Yes!" she said quickly, "I didn't have that much to drink lovee. I think I would have remembered that part, wouldn't I?"

" What exactly were you doing at The Wool Shop Mrs Finney?"

"Delivering fish and chips," she explained, "someone rang up and ordered fish and chips for twenty people, so I took them up myself."

"You weren't in a film then?" Jeffreys tempted her.

"What me? No lovee, I went round with the fish and chips and somebody asked me to stay for a drink. That's all I remember lovee, honestly."

"Thank you Mrs Finney. That will be all for the moment," Jeffreys said, as he turned now to the two men. "Mr Roland Jones, how do you plead to the charges against you?"

"Not Guilty", he replied. "And Mr Henry Dash, are you Guilty or Not Guilty of charges against you?"

"Not Guilty", answered Dash.

Jeffreys took a walk and tugged at his jacket collar.

"Words fail me gentlemen......... you were both caught committing an indecent act with Mrs Finney. You, Mr Jones, were naked at the time of your arrest and Mr Dash had lost his trousers."

"I had just changed out of my costume as Algernon Moncrieff," replied Mr Jones.

"And I was Merriman the Butler," said Dash rather quickly. "Oh indeed!" Jeffreys declared with mock astonishment," and Mrs Finney was your Lady Bracknell, I suppose?"

It was a cheap-shot, unworthy of the Prosecuting Counsel, but he was desperate.

"Not me lovee!" she declared, "I only took the fish and chips!" Jeffreys realized his mistake, as Mrs Finney grinned widely beneath the netting of her pill-box hat and responded graciously to one or two words of approval from The Public Gallery. He looked annoyed at having had a point scored against him by Mae West.

"Well gentlemen, I am amazed that you are prepared to persist with this cock and bull story. Mr Dash, you are a Solicitor with an enviable reputation in this town and Mr Jones, your position as The Bank Manager is surely one which demands the utmost integrity? I realize, of course, that this whole thing may have got out of hand. Perhaps what began as a harmless bit of fun at a slightly rowdy party, developed into the orgy which it became, and each of you is too ashamed to admit his mistake?"

He looked to The Accused, but they didn't bat an eye-lid. "Please now tell The Court of your parts in this wretched case. Perhaps you were each seduced by Mrs Finney - drugged even for all I know? Tell me now and absolve yourselves from the lie you are living - confess your guilt and be at peace with your conscience!"

"Not Guilty," Dash reiterated.

"Not Guilty,'" added Jones.

Jeffreys shook his head vigorously, "In that case, please step down!" he said angrily. His temper had clearly got the better of him, and it had not helped his case at all.

"Muggeridge and Evans-Jenkins!", he snapped, increasing his speed on the carpet as Mrs Finney made her way back to her place with her cohorts, waving to The Gallery as she went.

The Accused couple nervously took The Oath and waited with apprehension for Jeffreys to begin his inquisition.

"Ah! The two Crewdley Councillors!" he said with sarcasm. " Mr Morton Muggeridge, how do you plead to the charges against you?" Jeffreys said harshly. "Not Guilty," he answered. "And you?", asked Jeffreys.

"Not Guilty," she replied quietly.

"Speak up!" he shouted.

His words were too fierce and the occasion too much for her and she broke down.

"You swine!" shouted Muggeridge, "can't you see she's upset?" "Mr Muggeridge how dare you!" The Chairman bellowed, "I've a good mind to fine you on the spot for contempt of Court." "No, please ma'am," said Jeffreys, "don't do that. I can see that the lady is upset. Please Mrs Evans-Jenkins, tell the Court again how you plead."

"Not Guilty," she blubbed, wiping her eyes with a handkerchief thoughtfully provided by Muggeridge.

"I'm so sorry to have distressed you," said Jeffreys, "but perhaps it was the inevitable consequence of your being caught making love together in a hammock!"

"Ooohhh!!" The Gallery expressed itself collectively, loudly and with feeling, before emitting similiar, but quieter sound of approbation, a few seconds later. The members of The Press scribbled and turned pages as all eyes fell upon the Accused couple.

"We weren't!" shouted Muggeridge.

"I see! And so Superintendent Bramley is a liar!"

"Yes!" she yelled defiantly, "a rotten liar!"

The tension rose and conversations broke out all over The Court.

"Silence!" Mrs Denning shouted, banging The Gavel hard onto the table, "Silence! Mr Jeffreys, please continue." He paced the floor, giving everyone, himself included, the opportunity to calm down.

Before he could resume, Mrs Evans-Jenkins had got in first.

"We were going to be in a film by Mr Puccini."

"Swiss Family Robinson actually," added Muggeridge. "Nonsense!" said Jeffreys, "you are having an affair and Superintendent Bramley caught you making love in a hammock!".

"No, it's not true!" she protested, "ask Mr Puccini!" Mrs Evans-Jenkins had once again raised the spectre of the Pimpernel Director, a challenge which Jeffreys ignored.

Her words rang around The Court Room, unchallenged and extremely clear. "Please return to your seats," Jeffreys said coldly, "The Prosecution now calls Mr Barry Blondel and Ms Fiona Lumley."

Blondel, as ever the gentleman, took the arm of the attractive Ms Lumley and escorted her into The Dock, to the general approval of The Gallery. Blondel acknowledged The Press and straightened his bow-tie with a smile, before they each took The Oath. "Ms Lumley," said Jeffreys, "I understand you are a hostess?"

"Yes," she answered, "I was on duty at The Wool Shop actually."

She smiled seductively at him and everyone who happened to be looking. "You are employed by Cheer Girls Hooray! Ltd," he asked rather cautiously, "What exactly is the nature of your work?"

"Well, sometimes I escort men out to dinner or a club perhaps, and I am invited to various parties to entertain the guests, the men of course, particularly at birthday parties. It's all perfectly innocent," she said sweetly, "I pay my taxes just like everyone else."

"Indeed," Jeffreys conceded, "And being discovered in bed with this gentleman is par for the course, I suppose?"

"We were auditioning for Mr Puccini's film," she answered in all innocence. "And which one was that Ms Lumley, 'The Merry Wives of Windsor', or 'No Sex Please We're British'? A few chortles of laughter were soon crushed by Mrs Denning's ferocious banging of The Gavel.

"Doctor Zhivago actually old boy, I was playing the part of Yuri and Ms Lumley was auditioning for Lara!" chirped her partner.

"Ah yes! Mr Blondel or may I call you Councillor?" Jeffreys responded sharply.

"Either will do, but it's Barry actually," he grinned.

"And of course, you wish to plead 'Not Guilty' to the charges against you?"

"Yes, Not Guilty," replied Blondel. "And you Ms Lumley?"

"Not Guilty," she confirmed.

Jeffreys was getting nowhere fast. He was almost reluctant to let them go, but common sense told him that Blondel wouldn't crack and after his rather chastened experiences at the hands of the other female defendants, he had no choice.

"Thank you. Please return to your seats. The Prosecution calls Wifred Wooly and Ms Caroline Cresswell."

"Oh God! And it's all been going so well," The Mayor thought to himself, as Wooly and the young woman made their way into The Dock and took The Oath.

"Please state your full name," Jeffreys demanded, looking directly at the man.

"Wilfred Wooly," he answered.

"Your occupation."

"I am The Vicar of Crewdley."

"And are you 'Guilty' or 'Not Guilty' of the charges?" Jeffreys asked.

"Not Guilty, so help me God!" Wooly replied with emotion. Jeffreys stared at the young woman, who seemed to be aged around eighteen.

"Please give The Court your name," he said.

"Caroline Angela Cresswell," she said confidently.

"Occupation?"

"I am a student at the Crewdley Academy of Music, it's a Private School," she explained courteously.

"How do you plead to the charges brought against you?"

"Not Guilty Sir," she declared.

"Mr Wooly!" Jeffreys said loudly.

"Yes!" he replied.

"Mr Wooly........ do you wish to explain to The Court the circumstances of your arrest?"

"Oh yes please," he said gratefully, "It was all a dreadful mistake."

He turned to face The Bench, working hard to feign an expression of complete innocence, as befitted his position.

"I had been invited by Dorothy and Myrtle Flack to attend a small prayer meeting in their house on Thursday evening. These little services at the homes of my parishioners are quite popular and I must say that it's something that I've tried to encourage, particularly since my visit to St. Vincent .... it happens a lot over there you know .... Religous Worship takes many forms ....prayer meetings in the home are extremely common-place.

However, I fear that on the occasion in question, the dear sweet ladies must surely have overlooked a prior engagement in their diaries.

What began as a small and private prayer meeting, quickly evolved into a gathering of some consequence and I understood Dorothy to have said that auditions were taking place for parts in various films, under the direction of Mr Fredric Puccini. She invited me to stay, and so I did."

Jeffreys was not convinced.

"Ms Cresswell," he said accusingly, "what exactly were you doing with Mr Wooly when you were arrested?"

"I was teaching him to play the harp," she answered quietly." The Academy of Music is situated on the top floor of The Wool Shop. We were practising when Ms Myrtle Flack introduced The Vicar. The harp is an extremely difficult instrument Your Worships, and the player usually sits on a small stool. The Vicar said he would like to try to play my harp, so I sat him onto the stool and tried my best to show him how to play."

"Oh really?" said Jeffreys, "and how plausible it all sounds Ms Cresswell. And you completely deny any improper behaviour between yourself and The Vicar?"

"I deny it most strongly," she replied.

Jeffreys seemed rather perplexed. The two defendants did indeed seem plausible. The Vicar was obviously eccentric and Ms Cresswell looked a paragon of virtue. "You may both step down," he said solemnly.

Ms Cresswell walked sedately to her seat, displaying a dignity unmatched by The Vicar, who stumbled against a litter-bin as he eased himself into his chair.

"He definately needs locking up," The Mayor thought, as Wooly sat awkwardly between Ms Cresswell and Councillor Barry Blondel.

In spite of The Vicar's appalling record of late, The Mayor was grateful that his Court performance, at least, was worthy of congratulation and certainly his choice of female companion was exemplary. The Mayor himself had often considered the harp to be a most beautiful instrument, and perhaps, afterwards, he would ask Ms Cresswell to give him a lesson?

"The Prosecution calls Lady Gillian, Deirdre Crewdley and Mr Michael Flint!" said Jeffreys, as various members of The Press and The Public strained their necks to gain a closer view of The Aristocrat and The Fireman on their way to The Dock. They took The Oath and seemed more nervous than any of the previous Accused.

Lady Crewdley was wearing a turquoise suit and matching hat, looking every inch an aristocrat, though The Mayor sincerely hoped her nervousness had no historical parralel with her French cousins when presented with the prospect of The Guillotine. Flint, as befitted his position, wore his Fire Service uniform and stood rigidly to attention.

Jeffreys sensed a half-chance. They were extremely ill at ease.

"Lady Crewdley - how do you plead?"

"Not Guilty," she answered.

"And Mr Flint?" Jeffreys asked, almost casually.

"Oh Not Guilty Sir," Flint answered nervously. Jeffreys smiled and went nearer to his intended victims. "No doubt, you are going to tell The Court all about your little dramatic roles at The Wool Shop?"

Neither responded to this loaded and biased suggestion and after a few moments, Jeffreys continued.

"Lady Crewdley - how long have you been interested in dramatic art?"

"For quite some time," she replied.

"And Mr Flint" he asked, turning to the Fire Chief.

"Err, well actually, not very long at all Sir, in fact, I only went for a bit of a laugh."

"Thank you Mr Flint. And apart from having a bit of a laugh, you wouldn't consider it part of your normal duty as the Fire Chief to have sex with Lady Crewdley?"

"Oohh!...... Arrgh....... Ooohhh!," the audience reacted loudly to this accusation.

"You insolent little monkey! How dare you say such a thing about my wife! I'll bloody well horse-whip you, you bugger!!"

Jeffreys had obviously touched a nerve-end with Lord Crewdley.

"Silence!" shouted Mrs Denning, "Lord Crewdley, I must ask you to remain silent or you will have to leave The Court!"

"I'm not having that little rat speak about my wife like that. Apologize you toad or I'll take you outside and flog you!!!" he roared, to the approval of everyone in the building, with the possible exception of four people and the more he looked at Mr Partridge, the less The Mayor considered him to be at odds with The Mob.

"Apologize you bastard!" Lord Crewdley demanded.

Mrs Denning used The Gavel like a sledge-hammer, banging it furiously onto the table, with an expression on her face which resembled the gruesome pose of an out of control tobogganist whose jowels and whole face was being squeezed by a severe attack of dense air-pressure. She was not enjoying having to silence The Lord of Crewdley Manor in such a way, as she certainly considered him to be her social equal. It went against the grain and her face contorted into a grotesque mask of severe displeasure.

"Apologize !!" he roared again to the delight of The Mob. "Madam Chairman. I must protest!" Jeffreys shouted, "That question is central to the Prosecution's case."

"I demand that he withdraws his foul accusation," said Lord Crewdley.

"Sit down!" insisted Mrs Denning, trying her best to impose her full authority as Chairman of the Magistrates onto all concerned. Lord Crewdley stood defiant, "Is he going to withdraw it, or do I have to come up there and punch his head?"

"Right, that's enough!" said Mrs Denning getting to her feet rather unsteadily, "Constables - take him out of The Court Room at once!"

Two Officers quickly approached Lord Crewdley, took an arm each and began to escort him towards the door, but he suddenly dug his heels in and broke free, "Fascists!!" he yelled, as the Police jumped on top of him and bundled him outside. The effect of all this on the assembly was startling. Many had stood up to get a better view and the noise of their protests and laughter was now quite deafening. Mrs Denning banged the hammer down for all she was worth. "Silence ....," she demanded, "be quiet or I'll clear The Court!!"

The Mayor leaned across behind her to Mr Partridge, " it's all going remarkably well," he said sarcastically, "do you think we shall have to come back after lunch?"

The assembly began to settle down as Mrs Denning took copious amounts of water and Jeffreys looked extremely relieved with the absence of Lord Crewdley. Flint had maintained his erect posture throughout but Lord Crewley's display of bad behaviour had not exactly had a calming effect on his wife, who no doubt, even at this critical time, had good cause to consider her husband's threat of divorce, if she were to be proven Guilty. Robespierre had serious doubts regarding the benefit of Lord Crewdley's outburst, but The Mayor was quite sure, that as long as Flint and Lady Crewdley held their nerve, his actions may even have helped establish their absolute ' innocence. '

Quite what effect it had all had on the Prosecuting Counsel remained to be seen, but it seemed rather certain he wouldn 't be receiving an invitation to the next Garden Party at Crewdley Manor .

"You may continue Mr Jeffreys!", Mrs Denning called severely, as the man composed himself for the final onslaught.

"Superintendent Bramley", he said, "were these two people caught in the act of love making or not? "

"I 'm sorry to say they were Sir," he answered.

"Thank you Superintendent. Now Mr Flint, " he said, turning to the Fire Chief, "I fully realise the difficulty of your position. Here you are, in the prime of life, a respected member of the community now threatened by a castastrophic end to your career." Flint was impassive and gave the impression of being extremely steady under fire as Jeffreys continued to bait him.

"Let me suggest a reason for your being at The Wool Shop. It was solely to have your way with Lady Crewdley ..... a women of aristocratic bearing, someone far above your own social class, whom you considered an irresistible challenge, once you had discovered the real nature of activities at The Wool Shop."

"My God! He's close .... no he's red-hot!" The Mayor thought, hoping for all he was worth, that Flint wouldn't agree and delight in telling The Court, what pleasure it gave him to have seduced Crewdley's Leading Lady.

He didn't bite!

"No Sir! That's not true. I was asked to take the part of Gerald for 'Women in Love', by D.H Lawrence," he said in a rather matter of fact tone, "so I thought I'd have a go. Mr Puccini, the man in charge of the Film Company, it was him who asked me Sir. He was actually filming the scene when the Police started to arrest everybody. A bit of an over-reaction it was, if you ask me Sir. It was just Mr Puccini doing his best to give one or two of us the chance to try for a part in his film."

"Oh really!" Jeffreys said with annoyance, "you'll be telling The Court next I suppose, that you've been offered a contract by MGM?"

"No Sir, unfortunately not. It's back to the old Fire Station for me, first thing on Monday morning."

"Lady Crewdley!", Jeffreys said sharply, "I assume your attraction for this man equates with the fascination held by some aristocratic women for those men of the lower social classes who prove themselves, almost by that fact alone, to be sexually attractive - a bit of rough, I believe it's called in the trade?"

"You are a throughly disgusting little reptile!" she replied.

"Please answer the question, Lady Crewdley, " said Mrs Denning, "I would be loath to bind you over for contempt of Court."

"I am not sexually attracted to Mr Flint," she insisted, "nothing improper occured between us, one was merely Gudren, to Mr Flint's Gerald!"

With magnanimous approbation, those assembled sent out a sigh of exalted relief.

"In that case Madam, you may step down!" Jeffreys ranted furiously, "and take the Fireman with you!"

Mrs Denning had heard enough, "The Court stands adjourned until 1.30pm!" she barked, immediately getting up to retire.

Robespierre led her through into Beard's small office, an entirely inappropriate room for a Magistrates recess, but he knew The Mayor would not permit her now to use The Parlour.

The Mayor and Mr Partridge quickly joined her and the expression on her face told a thousand words.

"I suggest we retire for lunch to The Forest Hotel," The Mayor said calmly,

"Robespierre - bring the Rolls into The Foyer."

After the bedlam of the Court Room, the Restaurant of The Forest Hotel proved a quiet sanctuary for the three Magistrates. Lunch was taken early, after which The Mayor instructed Robespierre to take The Chairman and Mr Partridge back to The Court, whilst he delayed his return on the pretext of taking the opportunity to make booking-arrangements with the manager to provide accomodation for his guests at a future Civic Event.

He watched the car pull away from the Hotel then began the short walk to the Police Station, where, with the absence of Superintendent Bramley, he would once again exercise his full authority as The Mayor and Magistrate over the Police who remained there on duty.

"You'll take me down to the cells!" he said to a young Police woman, "it's about time this situation was satisfactorily concluded for the benefit of everyone."

"Yes Sir," she answered subserviently, "please come this way. Mind your head down the stairs Sir, it's a very low ceiling."

At 1.30pm precisely Mrs Denning brought down the hammer on the table, "The Court is now in session," she said sternly, "Mr Jeffreys, you no doubt wish to sum up?"

"Indeed Madam Chairman, I most certainly do," he replied, looking around quickly for a moment and noticing the absence of Robespierre, before he continued to address The Court.

"This Case is surely remarkable, not merely because of the nature of the charges brought against The Accused, but remarkable also because Crewdley has been covered with a Cloak of Deceipt by many of those very people to whom its citizens must surely look as standard-bearers of truth and high moral behaviour.

We have heard a litany of lies Your Worships, a deluge of duplicity from those who seek to denegrate the Legal System and the Officers who uphold it! It is the Prosecution's contention, that all of The Accused are Guilty and we ask that the full force of The Law be used against them as a warning to others of the implicit and dire consequences, guaranteed to befall those who seek to lie and systematically deceive, when such illegal and disgusting practices are uncovered. These wretched and sordid people have dragged the name of Crewdley into the mud! Not one of them has had the decency to confess their guilt or to aplogise to this Court!", Jeffreys said angrily and with utter contempt for the motley crew in The Dock. "Were it not for the vigilance and incorruptible nature of our local Police and their intrepid Superintendent Bramley, then this Case would indeed not be before you today. A dustbin of sin would have been permitted to fester in the very body of Crewdley society. Corruption would...... have become common-place, indecency would ....."

189

He stopped abruptly, as all eyes turned to the door and Robespierre walked into The Court with two dear little old ladies. They were greeted by gasps of astonishment and disbelief, from all corners of The Courtroom.

"My God! You have to be Myrtle and Dorothy Flack!" grunted Mrs Denning, as the trio came into the very bowels of the arena.

"Yes that's right," said Dorothy, "sorry we're rather late." It was an understatement, put into its proper perspective by Myrtle who had to speak up loudly, to be heard over the noise.

"We've been kept in a prison cell against our will. Mr Puccini managed to escape, but we couldn't."

"Shame, shame!!" chanted The Gallery, "Disgraceful!" said The Gutter Press.

"Silence!! Silence!!!" yelled the awful Mrs Denning. Dorothy shouted back, "We just wanted to tell everyone how sorry we are that the Police raided our Wool Shop, just because Mr Puccini was trying to make a little film! It's a pity really, because all of the money was going to go to St Crueds Church Fund to repair the Clock Tower!"

"Silence in Court!" Mrs Denning shouted over the noise, "you have made a most serious accusation! You must go into the Witness Box at once!"

Robespierre led them impassively forward to swear The Oath as The Mayor reflected on the cool, deep waters of The Caspian Sea and the radiant beauty of his mistress, into whose arms, he wished soon to be in.

Jeffreys looked distraught and filled with trepidation as The Chairman of The Magistrates took things into her own hands. "You claim to have been held against your will?" she enquired.

"That's right, we've been locked up for days," replied Dorothy.

"Outrageous! ....Poor old things!" the people complained.

"And who exactly do you accuse of locking you up against your will?" asked The Chairman.

There was a beautiful, pregnant moment of absolute silence before The Flack Sisters pointed their fingers and cried out,"Superintendent Bramley!"

The Assembly turned as one to the wretched Policeman.

"Aargh!" he called. "Aargh!!" he repeated ominously, before standing up and uttering a terrifying, blood-curdling "Aaaarrrrgggg!!" Bramley was electrocuted with shock, "Aargh! Aargh!" he yelled, now beginning to trot around The Courtroom to the disbelief and fear of everyone present, even the Police, who seemed more dismayed than even poor Mrs Denning who already held her head in her hands, "Case Dismissed!!!" she groaned, "Case Dismissed!!"

"Aarghhhhhh!!!!!" yelled Bramley, circling The Court like a demented bird of prey, his arms outstretched and with his mackintosh flapping over them like broken wings.

The Assembly stood as one, as Bramley did a lap of dis-honour before crashing through the doors and out into The Foyer. "Get him!" someone shouted and The Mob burst outside into Church Street in pursuit of The Crewley Condor.

"There he is!", they screamed, already gaining on the large and bulky figure of Bramley as he headed for Crewdley Bridge, out of breath and out of his mind.

"Come on! He's slowing down! He can't get away!" Bramley dodged the traffic in the road and reached the brow of the bridge as The Mob closed in. The terrified man scrambled onto the parapet and stood upright with his mack flapping in the breeze.

This unnerving feat had an immediate effect and the scrummage of people now stood still as Bramley stared down into the distant, cold and fast-flowing waters of the River Crewd.

The Mayor pushed to the front of the crowd. Bramley swayed dangerously and looked at his mentor for the last time, then with one final and manic effort, he threw himself into the River. Where, just a moment before, an extremely large figure had stood, there now remained only the ancient yellow sand-stone of the parapet. The Mayor saw Bramley crash into the water and immediately go under. The crowd lent over the wall of the bridge to look for the disgraced Policeman. Suddenly, he re-emerged about twenty yards from his point of entry. The Mayor watched as the struggling figure thrashed about in the water, all the time, being carried rapidly away from the confines of the town, deep into the wide and deadly waters of the River.

Only his head was visible, as he bobbed like a cork. A pathetic arm reached skywards to no avail as the River Crewd took Bramley down, and then, as if from nowhere, the small figure of a young boy appeared on the River bank and threw a life-ring into the water. Bramley reached out for it, and thrashed around in the murky depths, going further and further away from the bridge.

"I hope he drowns!" said a voice from The Mob, throwing Bramley's hat into the water after him. He was now being carried around the bend of the River and was quickly out of sight.

"Do yuh think the bugger got the life-ring?" someone asked impatiently. The Mayor turned away and walked back towards The Town Hall. A large gathering of people were talking excitedly about The Case and The Press was having a field day. He saw Partridge, Jeffreys and Mrs Denning get into a car and drive off, then Robespierre appeared at his side, smiling and obviously pleased that the ordeal seemed to be over.

"And how was it for you Robespierre?" he asked as they walked along together.

"Oh not so bad thank you Mr Mayor," he answered, "The Sisters Flack asked me to mention you will have their full support at Election time."

"Oh how interesting," he replied with his usual indifference, "the day that I have to rely on a couple of demented old bats like The Flacks, Robespierre, will be the day I join Bramley in the River."

The rest of November naturally and thankfully, proved to be a complete anti-climax. Crewdley Town Council held a Meeting on the 25th, during which Olivia Bland slept undisturbed. The two lovers Morton Muggeridge and Mrs Louise Evans-Jenkins decided to sit away from each other, at least until after the Christmas Recess when it was anticipated normal activities might be continued. Lady Crewdley settled safely back into The Manor, but all works by D.H Lawrence were forbidden. The Vicar had begun to prepare for Christmas, thoroughly intent now to behave, but still waking up in the middle of the night to call after his teacher of the harp, Ms Christine Cresswell who did manage to find her way, at The Mayor's request, into the grandeur of The Parlour on several occasions to give lessons on the Harp.

However, he quickly tired of the young woman and spent the last two nights of the month, happily in-situ with his favourite teacher, Mrs Pippa Monroe whose husband had recently been granted a further five year contract for oil in Algeria.

It was quite noticable, that Robespierre was spending much more time in 'The Star and Garter' and McGurk's waitress actually began to take an interest in The Boy from The Bastille. The Mayor would of course, watch that little relationship most carefully, and if necessary, put an end to it. Robespierre could not be loyal to two people. But for the time being, he would let his man enjoy himself. Mrs Elsie Finney reverted back to her normal, boisterous self extremely quickly after The Court Case. Her husband Eric attempted to exert his authority over Crewdley's own Mae West, but on one occasion at least, she was seen going to visit the Bank Manager. Doolittle and Dash re-employed Susie Goodthigh from the Temps Agency and seemed intent on getting into serious, domestic trouble.

And then there was Beard...... Bernard Beard, the wretched Town Clerk. The Mayor was making him pay dearly for his indiscretions, working unpaid overtime and having to make mid-morning coffee and afternoon tea for the Town Hall staff.

Unfortunately, Bramley had managed to grab the life-ring. He was dismissed in absolute disgrace from the Police Force and had already emigrated to his family in Australia.

December 5th was Harold Presbyterian's birthday, and he spent most of it in the back of the Civic Rolls Royce with Pippa Monroe on his way to and from Newquay in Wales, where they had a meal at The Black Lion and read the poetry of Dylan Thomas. At just after one a.m, Robespierre parked the car on The Quay near 'Caspian House.'

"Goodnight Pressy darling," she purred, kissing The Mayor as if there was no tomorrow, "I really enjoyed today. Are you sure you won't come in?"

"Better not," he said, "people might start to talk." He watched her walk into the house, then waited as the bedroom lights went on and for the lace-net curtains to move that enticing little bit, which told him all was well.

"Take me home Anton," he called softly. "Yes Sir," he answered, "Did you say Anton, Your Worship?"

"Yes you idiot. And just you be careful with Sharon Hayes. Women like her can give a man a hard time.... a very hard time indeed."

Their eyes met in the rear-view mirror. It was late, Robespierre was tired, but the bond which existed between himself and The Mayor at that very moment, could never have been broken by a mere waitress at a Public House. However, given his pleasing acquaintance with the woman so far, it would be perhaps less than gallant of him were he not to discover further the joys and pleasure of one so young and attractive as her?

And then there was Ms Cresswell....... Robespierre longed for a lesson on the harp...... and Pippa Monroe herself....... he had lately developed a slight passion for the daring Head Mistress.

He parked the Rolls in the Foyer of The Town Hall and watched The Mayor climb the old, wooden staircase to The Parlour.

All was well with Crewdley and the world.

For 'Those in Favour', tomorrow promised everything that democracy and the good life could offer. For the others, there was always the day after that.

THE END